Conten

Well, the moral of the story
The moral of this song,
Is simply that one should never be
Where one does not belong.
So when you see your neighbor carryin' somethin'
Help him with his load
And don't go mistaking Paradise
For that home across the road

—Bob Dylan, "The Ballad of Frankie Lee and Judas Priest"

For Edel and Joel, my favourite people.

Chapter One
The Article, February 2019

Frog DNA (prologue, sort of)

It all started when Jeff Simmons wrote an article about Jonestown in the local paper. It came as a surprise to everyone that a renowned, award-winning investigative journalist, intrepid world-traveled adventurer, Mr. *New Yorker*, *Boston Globe*, etc., would bother to write a few paragraphs for a local rag. The article, depending on your point of view, was either a tongue-in-cheek view of life in Jonestown or something more philosophical and considered and though most people enjoyed the thoughtful approach, not everyone appreciated Simmons' angle. What's the expression, some of the people some of the time? It wasn't long before it kicked off, but I'll get to that a bit later.

Jonestown, in case you're wondering, isn't anything to do with what happened in Guyana in 1978, though, if you pay attention, you'll see that there's Kool-Aid aplenty being drunk here. Jonestown is the name some people give to our gated community on account that everyone's trying to outdo one another, though I don't really see it as indicative and besides, it's almost entirely outsiders who call it Jonestown. I think Old Jack and a few of the people in The Family Zone like the name. Me, I couldn't care less about keeping up with the neighbors or having a cool car or the latest whatever or a perfect lawn, though Mr. Zimmerman, the chairman of the Residential Community Association or RCA to you and me, does. He's big on rules and regulations and takes great pride in the fact that Jonestown is the top-rated gated community in the state. In fact, he's so proud that during every meeting he makes a point of admonishing the previous head for letting Jonestown go down the tubes. Not that it did, of course. I've lived here for the best part of twenty years and I can tell you with certainty Mr. Tillman, the previous chairman, wasn't remiss in his duties. I think, along with more than a few others, that he was better than Zimmerman for the simple fact that he didn't go around thinking he was lord and master of the place and because he managed to stop Zimmerman from becoming RCA head for years. Zimmerman had coveted the job from the first day he moved in, but kudos to Tillman, he held him off until he just got too old to fight.

Zimmerman, as you may have gathered, is a complete horse's ass, well, I think so anyway. Let me give you an example; as soon as he got elected (to great fanfare — he had bunting and other colorful pointless crap put up around The Hall) Zimmerman brought back the term 'chairman' saying that 'chairperson' was kowtowing to the left and besides, as a man, he felt entitled to the term. It was, as he put it, 'traditional and representative of traditional values.' I pointed out that in Communist China, they use the term 'chairman'. He waved away my comment with the dismissive contempt of a person used to getting their own way. On the matter of returning to the non-PC term, there were a few objections but because Zimmerman had canvassed diligently and had spent years building his base, he had solid support, and the roughly two-thirds majority of 'yays' silenced the 'nays'. I didn't vote for him, that's for sure. In Jonestown when it comes to voting on issues of importance each resident over eighteen has a vote, but the casting vote or votes often belong to the Three Rivers Board of Selectmen. Zimmerman must have cozied up to them like a tick on a hound because it was their influence that got him over the line.

Anyway, he got in and things began to change. There were more rules for starters, the rest you'll find out as we go along. It was typical of Zimmerman to take all the praise for the community's prosperity, especially the long list of people looking to acquire property there. What he failed to acknowledge was that when Tillman was 'chairperson', Jonestown was one of the top-rated gated communities in the state. As I said before, the yays were louder than the nays, and it became normal for Zimmerman to talk out his ass while everyone nodded enthusiastically, but that's hardly a surprise given the donkey ride to hell the world is taking right now.

Since the article and the subsequent events, I knew I had to tell this story, but I wasn't sure how to do it because, for one thing, I don't know all the details and since some of what's written here is a bit weird, I was afraid I'd come across as a complete bullshitter, though, looking back now I was naive to be bothered by that. Who gives a fuck what people think, and who cares if the story is a bit sketchy in places? You can see that I'm not especially concerned with the integrity of the story and as you'll probably agree, the saying never let the truth get in the way of a good story, is nearly always good advice. Anyway, I gathered what I could from what I knew and had witnessed myself. The rest comes from the people whose stories you'll read about in due course. What remains is from a patchwork of sources, not all of which I can vouch for with any certainty. It's like in that movie Jurassic Park when they used frog DNA to fill in the gaps of the dinosaur DNA. In the end, they got their dinosaur. So, here's my dinosaur. For amusement, see if you can spot the frog DNA as you go along.

Vermont Liberty

OK, a little background first. Riverside Falls to give Jonestown its proper name is a gated community of twenty-one houses and some fifty or so residents sitting on twenty acres of prime New Hampshire land. In the development stage, it was named Riverside Rise, but someone must have preferred the sound of falls to rise. Rise makes a lot more sense as the community is built on upland and there are no falls nearby. Merrimack Grove was also considered. This name made the most sense, seeing as the Merrimack River flows nearby. I guess there's no accounting for the decisions some people take.

The community is shamrock-shaped, with three cul-de-sacs off a central road that Zimmerman insists on calling the thoroughfare, he even drafted a proposal to name it after himself, but someone must have talked sense into him as the idea sank almost as soon as it surfaced.

It's said that the shamrock shape of the community is because there were so many Irish involved in the building it just ended up being shamrock-shaped, but that's a stupid joke if you ask me, and besides, it was mostly Abenaki and Penacook who built the place, probably on one of their burial grounds too. It was built in the early '90s, but has a kind of 50s charm about it. I know the original intention was to build a haven away from the rest of the world, but since Three Rivers is like something out of a Garrison Keillor story, I'm not sure what the developers had in mind, apart from making a shitload of money. It was opened officially on May 1st, 1994 by Three Rivers mayor Elias Ramirez. He's no longer in office, he ran off to Guatemala with his secretary and about a million in council money, or so they say, it might have been less. Whatever the truth is, he made off with a lot of cash. He's not been seen since and if he's in Guatemala he's not coming back, that's for sure. One thing about Three Rivers is it has a not-so-proud history of philandering mayors. I guess every utopia has its dark underbelly.

The homes in Jonestown are pretty much identical with some variations in size and layout, but they all conform to a basic style of wood and brick frame with nice porches, four or five-bedroom, spacious (mostly), large but manageable gardens, and so on. If you imagine something modern but with a strong dash of New England colonial thrown in, you get the picture. All houses are painted the same white or off-white. According to the rule book, variations on anything related to exterior appearances are discouraged with a very strictly enforced list of colors allowed for detailing fences, porches, and so on. My color of choice is Vermont Liberty. I find the irony amusing.

While everyone complies with this aspect of the rules with little trouble, there have been a few notable incidents of rule breaches. A few years ago, someone wanted to install a basketball hoop over their garage (not allowed on account of aesthetic incompatibility). Others sought to add tacky water features of cherubs pissing into a pond and other such things. About four years ago, the Petersons were forced out on account of their garden gnomes. Mr. Tillman was in charge then and despite being a nice guy about it, he did point out the subsection in the rule book pertaining to garden ornaments. It was no big deal really. However, the Petersons were stubborn and fought hard, arguing that a 'degree of flexibility should be allowed. Then one night soon after their gnomes disappeared, and the whole place developed a collective 'I didn't see nuthin'. Maybe no one did see a thing, but the Petersons got whatever message was being sent straight away. There was some finger-pointing and a few sideways looks for a couple of weeks. Eventually, it blew up into a big showdown on the street, with Zimmerman striding in like Wyatt Earp to diffuse the whole ruckus. This event effectively marked the end of Tillman's time as head of the RCA, as I said he was getting too old to fight and Zimmerman had used the incident to his advantage. Still, something must have left a bad taste because The Petersons sold up a month later and the Andersons moved in. I sometimes wonder what might have been had Mr. Tillman not been so by-the-book, or had he managed to hold off Zimmerman a little longer. Maybe the Petersons would have stayed. It's a moot point anyway, Zimmerman was on the charge, and it was only a matter of time before he nudged Tillman out of the light. We never did find out who stole the gnomes, but I'd bet my life it wasn't Tillman.

The gates that protect Riverside Falls from the real world are like something out of *The Lord of The Rings*. The original gates weren't so imposing, but one of the first things Zimmerman did when elected was to replace them (at considerable expense, too, I might add). They are bespoke iron with leaf clusters and gold casting and other pretentious bullshit. Zimmerman's RCA campaign was all about more security, bigger gates, etc. and people had bought it. Not the locals though, I've seen them walk by and turn their eyes to heaven.

To gain entrance, you drive up to the gate (hardly anyone walks) beep your special access code and once the gate opens you drive a little further to the security cabin (lodge) and there you meet Barney. He's the chief security guard. You'll find him there from early morning until late at night most days of the week. I like him, he's funny and doesn't care for most of the crap that he sees and hears. He's also the only African American you'll find in Jonestown. There were two African American families up until Zimmerman came to power, but they've moved on. I can't say why they left exactly, maybe it's a coincidence, but no smoke without fire as they say. Put it this way, if I saw Zimmerman dressed in a bedsheet wearing a pointy hat it wouldn't surprise me, not that I've ever seen him act in an overtly racist way, but I've heard stories and anyway, most rich white guys prefer to keep the company of other rich white guys. But let's get back to Barney. He doesn't let any of the Jonestown shit bother him. He's been around the world and seen lots of weirder stuff than the quiet desperation of rich white people. I like to stop and chat with him about his travels. Occasionally I see him in town, and we have a coffee or a beer. He knows almost all there is to know about Jonestown, which is surprising as he's only been there about two years, the last guy was an old dude named Buck. Last I heard, Buck was shucking oysters on Cape Cod. It was a surprise when Barney got the job, but I think there was pressure from The Board of Selectmen to appoint someone 'ethnically diverse'. Barney's appointment was seen as some sort of compromise. I know Zimmerman wasn't too pleased, but he had to hold his tongue.

Most of what I know about the politics of Jonestown comes from Barney. He likes me because I don't treat him differently from anyone else. He hates Zimmerman, not because he thinks Zimmerman is a racist, but just a dick. As Barney told me one time, being racist is usually society or your parents' fault, but you can learn to be a dick all by yourself. Over a beer in Wally's last week, he said.

Motherfucker [Zimmerman] looks at me like I'm offending his eyes or something, like he needs to put in drops afterward. Never says hello except when he has company, and then he makes a big deal about being nice. Thank you, Barney, how are you Barney, you have a good day Barney. It's all bullshit. You can tell his game right off; prick don't give a shit about anything but optics. Perception is reality, so they say, and most folks here look at Zimmerman like he's the king of the fucking castle, so I guess he is.

I agree, I've seen Zimmerman do his thing. He's got his act down, and I must admit, grudgingly, that it's pretty good. He knows how to work a room or a group or a one-on-one with the confident ease of a southern preacher. I can take or leave most people, but Zimmerman is a different animal altogether. Barney has more than a few stories about him.

One time I'm sitting in the cabin, it's late on a Saturday, and I'm looking to lock up for the night, but Zimmerman is out, and he calls me to ask if it's OK I wait a while and let him in. I said it was. So, I wait until after midnight, which according to the rulebook I shouldn't. At twelve-thirty, Zimmerman arrives with a couple of girls from town and Joe Miller, the mayor. The girls were maybe twenty, I dunno, it was dark, and I'm kinda glad it was too. Zimmerman strolls up to the cabin and smiles and reaches out his hand towards me. I don't know why, but I do the same. He places a roll of green in my hand and winks. He tells me it's our secret, and before I know it, he's gone up the driveway and to his house. For days after, I can't get the smile out of my head. I can't describe it, but I can tell you it freaked me out some like I had no control. Thinking about it, it seemed that the others were under some kind of spell too. Zimmerman might just be the devil, so I ain't gonna fuck with him.

Zimmerman might just be the devil; I'll guess you'll find out in due course.

Once you leave Barney you go up the central road and there you can take a left, right, or go straight ahead around a large circular island that's locally known as The Park. The Park is about three acres and is itself surrounded by an ornate wrought-iron fence about two meters high. Each household has a key to The Park. Inside there's a bandstand, several benches, and places to sit. A path that runs around the perimeter with spokes leading into the center where you'll find 'The Hall'. The Hall is where RCA meetings are held. Anyway, enough of that for now.

Twilight Zones

I may as well start with the left fork in the road, as it's arguably the least interesting. This cul-de-sac is called The Family Zone, and it's designated that way. Families only, no singles, couples, or communes. There are seven houses and seven families. As per the rules, there are no more than three children in each family. You'd be surprised how compliant people become when faced with rules and besides, there's a waiting list so if someone kicks up a fuss, well, you know what happens, they steal your gnomes, or worse. This family only part of Jonestown keeps to itself, and I'd be struggling to name all the families. I know there are Watsons and McDonnells and a family named Brantley. They're all nice. I think Jim Watson is an executive somewhere. He and his wife, Trish, I think, though it could be Trudy or Tasha, I don't know, but they have three kids who are all blonde and blue-eyed and just as nice as you like. I've seen Zimmerman chatting with them. I think he likes Jim's wife. She's always laughing vacuously and touching Zimmerman's arm, and you can see her mouthing 'you're so funny'. I honestly think she means well, and I hear she's a good mother, so that's fine by me. The McDonnells are quiet. I don't know their first names. They run an online business of some kind. The Brantley's are florists with some high-class clients, so I hear, like flowers to The White House clients. And that's it, I'd be guessing to name any others in The Family Zone.

Continuing the sequence, you get to the top of the shamrock. There are also seven houses here and right up top in a big white house, you find Zimmerman but seeing as you know about him already, and you'll be hearing a lot more about him, I won't bother you with any further details. Three of the houses are occupied by solitary elderly people. Mr. Tillman who you've already heard about lives in the first house on the left, the bottom of the horseshoe as it were. He's about eighty or so now. He was RCA head from 2005-15, and now he busies himself by taking a walk into town every morning. He spends much of his afternoons pottering around his house. I drop in from time to time, and we chat about old times, not that I'm old, but rather I listen to him reminisce. He was good friends with my father, and sometimes he likes to share stories about him.

Beside Tillman is Old Jack. Jack went to 'Nam as a young man and got skewered on a punji stick. When he got patched up, he figured the water was safer, so he became a submariner. He rose to captain, I think. He watches TV and drinks a lot. He's been married two or maybe three times. Given that he's drunk a lot, his house is not the tidiest place. He often talks of downsizing and going somewhere south, but he hasn't yet, and I doubt he will. He tells me about how his family has abandoned him and about how many women he screwed in his day, 'one in every port'. I don't mind listening to him, as I think his heart is in the right place, and he's a bit lonely and can't do anything about it.

Next door to Jack is Mrs. Osman, and beside her is Zimmerman. Zimmerman, to his credit, takes good care of Jack and Mrs. Osman. I know I've portrayed him as a jerk, but he makes sure Jack and Mrs. Osman are comfortable, that they have food and are kept warm, and so on, especially in the cold winters. I know he calls Jack's eldest son every week. Jack, mostly owing to stubbornness and the rest to booze, feels that the world has slighted him and is estranged from his family. There's more to it than that, but I don't have the whole picture and since Jack drinks, it's hard to know what's real and what's drunk talk. Anyway, Zimmerman makes sure that Jack's family knows he is alive and about as well as can be expected.

Mrs. Osman has no kids. Like Tillman and Old Jack, she and her late husband Randall were among the first people to move into Jonestown. Randall was a retired postmaster and the first head of the RCA from 1994-2005. He died three years ago. He was a really nice guy, big and loud but gentle and kind too. He didn't have time for nonsense and when Zimmerman and Tillman were contesting the leadership of the RCA, he was the main voice opposed to Zimmerman. Typical of the man, he was the first to congratulate Zimmerman when he won.

For all their decency, there's a really sad fact about Randall and Lily Osman's marriage that proves that being a good person doesn't always guarantee life will treat you fairly. In the early '70s their only daughter, Marianne, disappeared. She had just finished high school and had gone to California with some friends who were going to University there in the fall. Marianne was going to UCAL in Riverside to study education and after checking it out she went waitressing to make some money before school started. One afternoon she left the apartment she was sharing near Newport Beach to walk the two hundred yards to where she worked and was never seen again. Some people said it was Bundy as he was in the area at the time, she was certainly his type. In Mrs. Osman's house, there are pictures of her. She was tall with long brown hair and deep brown eyes, kind of like Jaclyn Smith, but then again kind of like a lot of girls at that time. I remember when they gave Bundy the chair in 1989. I followed as much coverage on the tube as I could. I asked my dad what it would be like to die in the chair. He told me if it was done right the person being executed would pass out pretty much straight away, but if it went wrong — which it sometimes did, he added- it was like being cooked from the inside out. I think it must have been done right in Bundy's case. I'll never forget seeing the picture of him in the paper, the one after his execution. He looked at peace, there was even a hint of a smile as if he knew things no one else did, which is true, I guess. Anyway, who knows what happened to Marianne? I can tell you one thing though; Randall Osman didn't stop trying to find out what happened to her right up until the day he died.

The other side of Zimmerman's house is unoccupied. Rumor is that Zimmerman bought it for privacy. The previous occupants were an elderly couple named Bill and Marge Harrison, but they moved into assisted living about six months ago. It was sudden if I recall. They don't have any children and apparently, there's a lot of red tape holding up the sale of the house. I would expect the sale would go towards Bill and Marge's upkeep, but so far, no FOR SALE sign. Mr. Tillman tried to requisition the relevant information about the house from the RCA, but it was refused. He tried again with the Board of Selectmen, but the red tape kept tying him up, so he stopped. Despite the rumors and uncertainty, I'm pretty sure Zimmerman owns the house and has left it deliberately vacant, and wanting privacy seems reasonable, but these houses are expensive, and the tax alone is a killer, so I can't see any financial sense in Zimmerman's actions, but then again, money and sense don't often go together, and besides, Zimmerman is loaded. Still, I can't help but wonder if he's got himself written into Mrs. Osman's will, so he can, in time, live in a kind of splendid isolation. I can't see Mrs. Osman hanging around too long as she's in her mid-eighties and the cheese is starting to slide off her cracker if you know what I mean. I hope she goes peacefully when she does, she's a nice lady, and she's had some tough times in her life. As I see it, the least she deserves is an easy ride to the finish.

Continuing around the horseshoe, you have Al and Ethel Waterman, a real love-hate couple. She likes to drink, and he likes to do nothing. There's not much else to say about them.

Gretchen Sweetman lives in the last house in the zone. She's fierce and wonderful. A redhead in her late forties or early fifties. She looks great whatever age she is, real glamour. She's had two marriages, the last of which resulted in her getting the house in Jonestown. Her most recent ex-husband Pete Henriksen was about twenty years older. He was involved with the real-estate firm that handled the buying and selling of properties in our community. He used to live here in the early days, but moved to New York after becoming very well-to-do. It was there he met Gretchen, and they had a good life for a few years, but as Gretchen put it 'there was more pop than crackle' and it went south pretty quickly. Henriksen had retained the house as part of his property portfolio, and Gretchen liked it. It was a pity in one sense, as the people who lived there before she moved in were nice folk. She moved in about eight years ago and is the one person in Jonestown, other than perhaps me, who is not true-blue Jonestown material, you know, doesn't fit the terms and conditions as it were. At least that's how others see it, and certainly, as Zimmerman sees it. She's disagreeable and cannot be placated in any way. I've seen her and Zimmerman lock horns a couple of times at RCA meetings and talk about an unstoppable force meets an immovable object. She's rarely home and spends most of her time traveling. She's a perfumer by trade and often goes to France where she consults for Dior. We've shared more than a few bottles of wine in our time, and I very much enjoy her company. I take care of her place when she's not there, feed the fish, and so on. Anyway, I've always found it a little strange how minimalist her house is, even for someone who travels as much as she does. If you didn't know and were to guess, you'd say that a monk lived there and not a woman at the cutting edge of fashion. After I'd got to know her a little, I asked her about it, and she said that I should see her Paris apartment since that was where all her opulence was. I guess that's the point, the person sometimes doesn't go with the place. Anyway, she says it's easier to care for if there's only the bare minimum and as I'm the one that does it, I have to agree.

And now to the final piece of the jigsaw that is Jonestown, the place where it all went off and where the story begins. Jonestown Proper, you might call it. I know I said earlier that the name comes from the fact that everyone is trying to keep up with one another and so far, I've shown that's not really the case. No one in The Family Zone is interested in petty social climbing, or if they are, they keep it to themselves, which makes no sense. And in Zimmerman's Zone (for want of a better term) there's a bunch of old people and Gretchen Sweetman, none of who are setting the world alight with one-upmanship, except Zimmerman, but I'm not sure you'd call his activities social climbing as much as some type of empire building.

So, where is the beating heart of our gated community, I hear you ask? Jonestown Proper is another horseshoe. You won't be surprised to learn that my house is at the intersection of Zimmerman's Zone and Jonestown Proper, meaning, of course, it shares a boundary with Gretchen Sweetman's property- hence the bottles of wine and so on, but before I get to my immediate neighbors, let's work our way back to the other end of the horseshoe.

As you enter Jonestown Proper, the first house is owned by the Johnsons. They're flag-waving, rooting-tooting, 4th of July

Old Navy people, and one of two families not in The Family Zone. They got a special dispensation when they moved in on account of a mix-up by the RCA. They were supposed to move into The Family Zone, but something got garbled in the process. Tillman was in charge then, and he took responsibility for the 'misunderstanding'. The committee amended the rule book afterward. I guess the Johnsons were the kind of people the |RCA wanted.

Karl Johnson owns several car dealerships and sits on the board of the local private school, he is also active in the local church, but he's one of those nice Christians, you know, quiet about it, never mentions it in polite company and if it does get brought into the conversation, he takes it and throws it gently out the window like some bug that's wandered into the air-space. He looks like Kevin Costner in *Field of Dreams*. His wife Jenna looks like Grace Kelly and is a producer for a local radio station that promotes good living and yoga and veganism and all that woke crap. Their two kids (a son and a daughter obviously) have perfect teeth and perfect smiles and play tennis and get straight As but lack the sense of entitlement that usually leads one to have one's head up one's ass, in other words, they were raised right. The Johnsons are the kind of family who take cycling trips at the weekend and actually enjoy it. I have never ever, ever, seen them anything but happy and full of the joys of life, which makes me wonder what in the fuck is wrong with them.

Next door to the Johnsons is the second family not in The Family Zone, the Mitchells. They are relatively recent additions, being here four years. I don't know what dispensation they got from the RCA, but I'm sure it had nothing to do with a misunderstanding on the part of Mr. Tillman. Brian and Marie Mitchell are both academics. Brian teaches literature, he prefers the term 'lectures', but he's a teacher, just because he teaches young adults at a university doesn't make him any better than the poor deluded idiots who spend their time trying to impart knowledge to apathetic teens no matter how much he wants it to be true. Marie teaches gender studies or something like that (whatever that is). I don't mean to disrespect people who are gender fluid, non-binary, gender-free or genderqueer, or any other available option, but it confuses the crap out of me. Live and let live, for sure, but do we need to complicate it by making it an academic course? Though, as life would have it, and as I've said before, you can't make this stuff up — ironically, or not, (I don't know if it's ironic or coincidental), the Mitchells have a daughter, and she's gender fluid or identifies as a boy or something. I know Zimmerman mentioned it one time in private that he finds the whole thing weird and strange, but since The Mitchells are discreet and play by the rules, he's willing to let it go so long as Kris (whose real name is Elizabeth) doesn't start flying brightly colored flags or bringing any undesirables to Jonestown. Kids today have it tough and people like Zimmerman don't help.

The Johnsons and The Mitchells have a reasonably mild passive-aggressiveness going on, or more accurately The Mitchells have a mild passive-aggression towards the Johnsons. The Mitchells think they're better because they're academics, and they know everything about life, liberty, and all that, to which Jenna Johnson counters that she and her family are not better, but they do live a more wholesome life. I think they're all idiots because they care about what people think, but people are people. If nothing else, their feud is fun from time to time, especially at RCA meetings. More of that anon.

Next door to The Mitchells is Mr. Stolly or as some people (mostly me) call him, Mr. Snout owing to his big nose and even bigger propensity to stick it where it doesn't belong. Snout must know everything. He's in his late forties and is an economic analyst for one of the big banks. He's the most recent addition to our community, being here just over two years. He looks exactly like what you'd imagine him to. He's almost all ego, not that there aren't a few like that around here, but this guy takes the biscuit, the cake, the whole bakery. He drives a sleek black Chrysler 300, wears expensive suits, is superficially charming, but has absolutely no depth. People seem to enjoy his charm but behind the scenes, plenty of folks think he's weird. The Andersons seem to like him, and sometimes I hear them talking in the backyard when he visits them. He likes to offer opinions on things he has no right to comment on. I've listened to a lot of his bullshit. After a few drinks, he talks a lot about Milton Friedman and The Chicago School. Friedman's ideas led to trickle-down economics, which screwed everything for the poor and middle classes. Fuck Milton Friedman.

Snout divides life into winners and losers and thinks he's a winner because he has the possessions that mark him out as a winner. He gets bored easily, so if you're talking to him about something he's interested in, he finds it difficult to keep up. He's also a little like a bad copy of Zimmerman. I'm sure he wishes he were Zimmerman, but he's way off, miles I'd say. He reminds me a bit of that senator from South Carolina, I forget his name, Lindwood or something like that, you know, a dyed-in-the-wool yes-man. I have to say, Zimmerman for all his faults has class, and even though he's not exactly George Bailey he can pass for a human. Snout is like a reptile.

So, we come to the middle house which is, you guessed it, unoccupied. New owners were supposed to move in, but given what went on here in the last while, it looks like they're holding off for now. Frankly, I don't blame them, though I hope they move in eventually, they seem like the right kind of people for the place. One thing the realtor doesn't tell would-be buyers is that almost everyone in Jonestown is not what they appear, except me, I call it like it is. I've nothing to hide. That leaves us with my immediate neighbors and their neighbor, the source of all the recent commotion. The Andersons are a young couple, mid to late-thirties or so. They moved in from San Diego. Derek was in the Navy there. I think he's from Alabama, he's got a southern lilt when he speaks, which isn't often. He usually wears a MAGA hat and drives a petrol-guzzling 4x4. He sports a wispy beard and has a look and manner that might incline you to be wary of him. That said, he's a reasonably decent guy. He's handy and helps people with odd jobs. He's done work for Old Jack and Mrs. Osman and put solar panels on Zimmerman's roof. He patrols the community every evening with his dog Razor. Razor is a sinewy pit-bull, but is as gentle and affable as a bunny rabbit. I like Razor, and he likes me; I tell him he's a good boy, and he wags his tail and licks my hand and has only really barked at me one, but that was my fault. I asked Derek about Razor's good nature one time, and he told me to try and break into his house and see how nice Razor was then. Needless to say, it's what's left unsaid that's more intimidating than anything else.

Derek doesn't do anything workwise per se, and he's not exactly forthcoming either. I asked him what he did for a living, he told me very basic things about his career in the Navy, and that was it. You know the trick about getting people to divulge information, you ask them a question, and when they answer you just keep quiet, and to avoid the awkward silence that follows they'll babble on. Derek isn't like that, at all. He speaks as if words cost money. Talking to him makes me think he's been on one too many missions and is suffering from some kind of PTSD. He can be jittery and defensive when you ask him questions, and projects an open hostility that shields him from small talk. Maybe he got a big payoff and a nice pension from the Navy that affords him the life he leads? I can't tell if he likes or trusts Zimmerman. Sure, I've seen them talking, but I get the sense that their relationship is more complicated than it appears to be.

Derek's wife Donna is a piece of work and the type of woman your mom might have warned you about. Outwardly she's a ray of sunshine, all smiles, and fake friendliness. She's beautiful to look at from a certain perspective, but I can't shake the feeling there's a bat-faced fat girl in there trying to get out. Sometimes I think she could expand like that kid in *Charlie and the Chocolate Factory* at any minute. You know by looking at her that she has the self-control of a Zen monk. Every fiber in her being screams control and as that repressed energy has to go somewhere it's worth noting that she is surrounded by a whole lot of perfect possessions. Her house is the most picture-perfect of any in Jonestown, seriously, there's not a fleck of paint or blade of grass out of place. Every day, I can see Derek doing something home-improvement related, whether it's oiling a hinge before it gets too squeaky or power washing the driveway.

Every weekend Derek must get time off for good behavior as she has a team of cleaners in to do the place up, not one or two of them, a team. They arrive at 9 am and work until noon. I asked one of them about the house one time, and he told me it's got the best of everything, although at first, he was reluctant to speak to me. I swear I saw fear in his eyes. After a few weeks and more casual questioning, he told me she had a room full of shoes and enough perfume to float The USS Midway. He also said he didn't understand why he was needed, as there was nothing to clean in the first place.

We go in, and it is already *muy Bonita*, but we say nothing, the lady pays us, so we make it look like we are cleaning.

The cleaners have nicknamed the place *Casa Immaculada*.

Donna works at the university. She's a career adviser and hates The Mitchells. As with most hatreds, the source is petty.

When she began working in the university, she was given a car space close to the building she worked in, but there was a mix-up and the parking space rightfully belonged to Marie Mitchell. The upshot was that Donna Anderson had to walk an extra fifty yards or so. As all the houses are detached, it's not often you hear anything from inside, but I remember the day of the car space debacle as if it were yesterday. Donna roared into the cul-de-sac, stopped outside The Mitchell's house, and revved the engine of her little black speedster (it's a BMW convertible with red trim, looks amazing too) before screeching the short distance to her own house. I was in the front yard reading. I looked up and waved. She saw me but walked stony-faced into her house and slammed the door. About an hour later I was in the backyard trying to catch the end of the sun when I heard the following.

How dare that stupid bitch do this to me.

There's silence and then;

Derek, are you even listening to me?

More silence.

I'll get her, her, and her smug bastard of a husband. You should see them, walking around like they own the place.

Derek, did you hear what I said?

I heard you.

This went on for a while and just as twilight descended like a comfortable blanket, I heard Derek Anderson making a whole lot of noise in his garage, he could have been smashing her brains out, and frankly, I expected to hear police sirens, but things settled down. The Andersons have at least one noisy period a week, and Derek Anderson looks more and more scraggly each time I see him. Love is blind, I guess, and dumb.

This brings us to the matter at hand.

The Article Proper

The occupier of the final house, Jeff Simmons, as I said at the beginning, renowned journalist, etc. wrote an expose of Jonestown for the local paper. The paper is called The Three Rivers Telegraph (TRT hereafter) and covers the district and has a small circulation of maybe a thousand or so. It's a bi-monthly publication and is run by a guy called Ernie Waters and exists mostly on goodwill and small advertising by local businesses. It used to have a much bigger readership, but with the rise of online news and all that, papers are going the way of the dodo. So, on a chance meeting with Simmons in town, Waters asked him if he'd write a piece about something local. Waters wanted something to boost readership and Simmons, who'd never thought about doing a freelance piece for TRT, agreed. Waters was delighted and ran an ad in the edition before Simmons' piece saying that local resident and Pulitzer Prize-winning journalist Jeff Simmons would be writing an article in the next issue. Simmons didn't mind the attention and for a while leading up to the publication of the article, there was a sense of excitement. People wondered what he'd write about, especially given that Jeff Simmons was not truly local and had only lived there about eight years. Simmons' work for The New Yorker and The Atlantic and The Boston Globe usually focused on aspects of culture and politics. His article on the future of the Catholic Church in the wake of The Globe's Spotlight investigation in 2002 launched his name and from there he became, for a while, one of the world's best and most sought-after freelance writers. After spending time in Afghanistan and Iran (for which he won his Pulitzer) he withdrew from the frontline and settled in Jonestown where he began work on a memoir. He still contributed to the big publications on a semi-regular basis, but at the time of the TRT article he was heading for proper retirement, and so I doubt his head was really in any of the words he wrote. He was looking forward to being done with it all and occasionally spoke about all the places he wanted to visit and all the things he wanted to do.

The day the article was published, I met him on the street, and he said wryly that he expected he'd have to move on. I asked him why. He told me to read the article.

'It's not meant to be taken seriously,' he said, 'at least not in an obvious way. If people can't tell the difference between satire and facts, that's their problem.'

I don't want to commentate on it just yet, or maybe at all, so here it is verbatim. You can decide for yourself if it's offensive.

NOT QUITE SO PLEASANTVILLE

By Jeff Simmons

When I was working for The New York Times in 1998 I was asked to do a stint of movie reviewing. I didn't care much for it, but as I wasn't in a position to argue, I agreed to it. There were more than a few movies that passed me by in the eight months or so I spent doing it, and I struggle to even think of their names now, but two movies stood out for me that year, and oddly as it seems they were the first and last movies I reviewed. The first was Joel and Ethan Coen's superb absurdist noir 'The Big Lebowski'. To this day, I can't go to a bowling alley without hoping that John Turturro will be there in his magnificent purple attire dancing to Hotel California. Apologies Dude, I know you hate the Eagles.

The second movie was Gary Ross's much underrated and charmingly quaint 'Pleasantville'. The basic premise of which, if you recall, is how a town from a black and white TV show emerges into a world of color. I can't find my review of it any-where at the moment, but I just read the late Roger Ebert's re-view and I now quote 'Pleasantville is the kind of parable that encourages us to re-evaluate the good old days and take a fresh look at the new world we so easily dismiss as decadent.' It's that new world with its decadence or at least self-indul-gence that I want to address.

I live just north of town in Riverside Falls, you know the place. I see you drive by with envious looks, though you really shouldn't. I moved here from NYC eight years ago to get away from it all. I'd been married and divorced, my kids were out of college and starting their own lives and frankly, I was sick of the politics and pace of life in New York. I made a few inquiries about suitable places to live, and Riverside Falls came up time and again. Once Mr. Art Tillman, the then head of the RCA, learned of my interest he invited me to visit, and I thought to myself this might be the place. There was plenty of interest from other parties, but I guess I was the lucky one to be approved by the RCA. I don't know what Art Tillman and his committee saw in me, was it something to do with an award I won? Anyway, I moved in a few weeks later. At first, it was bliss. Everyone was so welcoming. I didn't have to make dinner for a week. The ad-justment was everything I hoped for. It reminded me a lot of my childhood in small-town Pennsylvania and in retrospect, I real-ized that was what I was longing to recreate. I wanted to return to a place where everyone knew everyone else but respected privacy, a place where being neighborly was natural and not enforced by proximity.

I hear that some people call Riverside Falls 'Jonestown'- mocking the keeping up with the Joneses culture that is per-ceived to exist there. I can assure you there are no Joneses in Jonestown, there are plenty of other names I could use to de-scribe them, but Jones isn't one.

In his poem 'Mending Wall', Robert Frost wrote, 'Before I built a wall I'd ask to know/What I was walling in or walling out/And to whom I was like to give offense.'

Gated communities like Jonestown have their origin in the Medieval idea of big gates keeping out unwanted persons. I wonder, does the fact that Jonestown with its big medieval-style gates give offense to anyone. After all, it's arguable that gated communities promote isolation and are a rich person's idea of discrimination veiled by a notion of safety. Our district is not dangerous. I've looked up crime stats for the past ten years, and we've nothing to worry about apart from the occasional parking violation or speeding ticket, so I would invite you to consider, why does Jonestown exist? Is it self-indulgent to live in such a place, or is it a fair privilege earned by hard-working people who just want a bit of privacy?

Perhaps one could see Jonestown as symbolic of a wider worldview. A safe place, but at a price. I must admit it's not quite the Pleasantville I wanted, but it's not NYC either. And why do I think this?

Community life is not easy. Keeping up with the Joneses is not easy and in today's world where you can never be sure who's who, people seem to be drifting away from the traditional values that used to keep society together. Maybe I'm just being sentimental and should embrace progress as there's a lot of good things about moving forward, but I can't shake the nagging doubt if it really is such a good thing? I guess you can ponder that one yourself. The essence of 'Mending Wall' can be summed up in one line; 'Good fences make good neighbors'.

And considering the neighbors I have, I'm glad I have good fences.

I liked the article, I thought it was interesting and asked some interesting questions. I couldn't for the life of me see how it would offend anyone, even if it suggested that the residents of Jonestown affected an air of superiority. It was true. All the residents were well-off, higher by far than the national average. All were white and all had come from a privileged background. Now, at the time, I didn't think there was anyone who lived in Jonestown that was so thin-skinned as to find Jeff's article anything but thought-provoking and perhaps a little poignant. I remember Zimmerman saying he liked it, he used the word 'philosophical' and felt the wider point was well-made. I read it to Old Jack and in a rare moment of lucidity, he said the whole damn world is putting up walls and keeping one another out, look at all the immigrants who want to get away from their country because of war and stuff, and what do we do? We build walls and flip them the bird.

No, it seemed all was well. The article boosted sales of the TRT, and Jeff said he'd write another one soon. I guess he was considering it until the morning he was in town having a coffee in Arlene's when some guy came up to him and served him with papers.

Jeff took the papers and opened them. They were from The Andersons, who were suing him for libel. He finished his coffee and on his return to Jonestown, he dropped into The Andersons to ask them what the fucking shit is this?

Donna Anderson wouldn't open the door, saying that his language was foul and abusive. Jeff stood there for a short timing waiting for his neighbors to at least look him in the eye and when it became apparent that they wouldn't, he went into his own house and I guess he called his attorney.

Chapter Two
Simmons v Anderson (preliminary hearing), March 2019

Donna Anderson's Christian view of 'love thy neighbor' did not extend to accepting their sense of humor (I think she's Evangelical, certainly behaves like one anyway, you know, claims to love Jesus but hates his message of tolerance and kindness). A court hearing was set for two weeks after Jeff Simmons had been served, and boy that was a frosty fortnight. Simmons was utterly bemused by the whole thing, but sensible enough not to stir the hornet's nest. I spent a lot of time watching and listening, and regularly saw Donna Anderson peeking out of an upstairs window or from behind curtains to see if the coast was clear. When she knew it was, she'd emerge in all her finery and shoot off somewhere in her black speedster. During the whole ordeal, she'd taken time off work to cope with the stress. She'd managed to convince some quack that Simmons' article had damaged her mental health, though I really couldn't imagine how it could be made any worse.

I saw Zimmerman about a week before the court date and asked him what he thought. He was typically reticent and said he hoped natural justice would prevail. I asked him directly if he thought it was a load of hooey, and he smiled and said good fences make good neighbors, let's just leave it at that. I said it was a good article and that if Donna Anderson was awarded a red cent, then the idea of natural justice was just about as real as elves. Simmons has plenty of money, he can afford the best, I bet it'll get thrown out, said Zimmerman admiring a rose bush. We'd best keep out of it. I told him I'd no intention of getting involved.

To establish that libel has taken place, a person must prove that:

· The statement is false
· It caused harm
· It is made without proper research into the validity of the statement

According to the papers, the defamatory/libelous statement was *considering the neighbors I have, I'm glad I have good fences*. Donna Anderson claimed that Simmons must have been referring to her and her husband, as there were no neighbors on the other side of Simmons' house. She also felt that the entire article had ridiculed the community and lessened the value of fellowship between the residents. I have to admit I nearly fell off my chair when I read that. Anyway, the whole thing went to the preliminary hearing. It was quite an event too. That morning, Jeff Simmons left his house about 8:30. The hearing was scheduled for 9:15 and as Jeff said to me this isn't my first rodeo, best to be there early. He was dressed in jacket and trousers but nothing overly formal, as he said he'd been there before. The Andersons, who I can only assume were making their debut as plaintiffs, left their house about five minutes after Simmons and with all pomp and ceremony of a state funeral. Donna wore black and despite there being little or no sunshine, she wore sunglasses, probably Versace or Tom Ford. Derek didn't wear sunglasses, and I was sure there was a passive acceptance in his eyes as if to say it had nothing to do with him, and hopefully, it would be over soon. He wore a very sharp suit and had shaven, or been shaved, for the event. He certainly didn't look his usual self.

The hearing was held *in camera,* so no one really knows exactly what was said. Jeff never said anything and neither did The Andersons, and I couldn't get any details from the court reporter or bailiff. But Judge Reinhold who presided over the hearing gave me a loose version of events after I'd gotten a few bourbons into him. Rather than describe the events, I've written it as a short play.

The Anderson Courtastrophe — a play in one act

It is early in the morning of March 12th. Assembled are Donna and Derek Anderson, their attorney, Jeff Simmons and his attorney, a bailiff, and a court typist.

ENTER JUDGE REINHOLD
BAILIFF: All rise for the honorable Judge Reinhold.
JUDGE R: (*Gruffly*) Sit down, let's get this done. I'm golfing later this morning.
Donna Anderson mumbles something.
JUDGE R: What did you say (*looking at the document*) Ms. Anderson?
Donna Anderson sits impassively.
JUDGE R: You watch what you say in my court, young lady.
ANDERSON ATTORNEY: She said her father is a keen golfer too.
Judge Reinhold smiles wryly, his face then reverts to a cantankerous scowl. Apparently, he's gained a stroke on his golf handicap and is mighty sore about it.

JUDGE R: OK, as I understand it this whole fuss is that you (*pointing to The Andersons*) claim that this man (*pointing to Jeff Simmons*), you doing alright Jeff?

Simmons nods. Reinhold smiles. Donna Anderson looks aghast.

JUDGE R: You claim that Mr. Simmons in writing the article that appeared in The Three Rivers Telegraph dated February 26th, 2019, defamed you and your husband, and you're looking for reparations to the extent of two million dollars. You add that the article has led to you being unable to work and has created a deep divide between the residents of Riverside Falls and the wider community of Three Rivers so that the wellbeing of the community in general and the wellbeing of you and your husband has been irreparably damaged.

Judge Reinhold furrows his brow and lets out a long whistle.

JUDGE R: (impatiently) Well, cat got your tongue?

ANDERSON ATTORNEY: Yes, your Honour.

Judge Reinhold rubs his jaw and then beckons both counsels to the bench. He leans forward across the bench as they lean in.

JUDGE R: (*to The Anderson attorney*) Billy, what are you doing? Why did you take this case?

ANDERSON ATTORNEY: Someone had to and also, I was afraid if I refused, she'd rip my face off.

Judge Reinhold peers over his glasses at Donna Anderson.

JUDGE R: I see what you mean. Now, you know this is total baloney. Your client has no grounds for libel and frankly has wasted my time. I suggest you ask them to drop the charges, so I can get to the golf course.

ANDERSON ATTORNEY: Why did it go to prelim then?

Judge Reinhold's eyes narrow.

JUDGE R(*whispering*): I didn't read it closely until this morning, most of what I deal with is people parking in front of

Arlene's and causing nuisance or Maggie Wilkes going off about something the school board has done. I haven't done a libel case in, damn, twenty years, but, if you want to argue this one, let's do it.

ANDERSON ATTORNEY: Sorry your honor, but I have to try.

Both councils return to their benches.

At this point, I imagine there was a bit of back and forth between the councils, so I'll fast forward to the Johnnie Cochran moment.

SIMMONS ATTORNEY: It is simply absurd to think that a respected and award-winning journalist of the highest integrity intended malice in this case. I think we have shown that the Plaintiff has no case for libel and the First Amendment while not a license for inflammatory speech is a basic right and allows informed, intelligent, and insightful citizens to make observations about their community without being subject to petty grievances because someone didn't like Robert Frost's poetry.

Judge Reinhold nods sagely. He gestures for the prosecuting attorney to make his closing arguments.

ANDERSON ATTORNEY: There's no question about the excellence of Robert Frost's poetry and to quote the very poem the defendant used in his libelous article.

SIMMONS ATTORNEY: Objection.

JUDGE R: Be careful, Billy, my patience isn't without limits.

ANDERSON ATTORNEY: Withdrawn. The poem also says, 'He is all pine and I am apple orchard.' And, towards the end of the poem, it reads, 'I see him there/Bringing a stone grasped firmly by the top/In each hand, like an old-stone savage armed.' Mr. Simmons does not refer to these lines in which Frost so eloquently describes the difference between himself and his neighbor, but I would like to suggest that Mr. Simmons has implied that my clients are all pine and old-stone savages, which in layman's terms might equate to them being backward or at the very least not his kind of people, and that is libelous.

JUDGE R: That it, you done?

The Anderson attorney nods.

JUDGE R: OK, stand up, come on, now, stand up. We've been here for over an hour and I've just about had enough of all this. (*Pointing at The Andersons*) I accept your right to be offended and to make a case for reparations, but I have to scratch my head wondering how in hot damn you thought you were going to win, and even if you did win how you were going to get two million bucks for your trouble.

Donna Anderson's eyes are little black dots. Derek Anderson's eyes have gone beyond embarrassment and now have the far-away gaze of a stoner.

JUDGE R: Regardless of Mr. Simmons' impeccable and, I must say, courageous, career as a journalist of the highest esteem, even if he were a local hack, his article was insightful and entertaining and sure gave me and my buddies at the Elks a chuckle. (*Addressing Simmons*) That work you did on real-estate fraud in New York in the late 80s was terrific. I know it was the war stuff that got you the Pulitzer, but the way you helped show those developers for the snakes they were was such a powerful community gesture. I must say I've admired your work ever since.

JEFF SIMMONS: Thank you, your honor, it's nice to be appreciated.

Judge Reinhold pauses for a moment to gather his thoughts.

JUDGE R: (*looking at the Andersons*) I'm going to dismiss this out of hand and suggest you two stay the hell out of my courtroom unless you have a real issue. It might be worthwhile for Ms. Anderson to invest in a sense of humor. The man's article wasn't an attack on you or your husband or your dog or anything to do with you. It was a fair consideration of how our society works.

DONNA ANDERSON: I think you're being unfair. I think your friendship with Mr. Simmons has clouded your ability to be impartial.

JUDGE R: (*wide-eyed*) Billy, you want to do something about this?

The Anderson attorney speaks to Donna Anderson in an attempt to calm her down. She turns and says loudly, 'IT'S TRUE!'

JUDGE R: Ms. Anderson, unless you want to spend the night in a cell, you'd better listen to me and listen good. In my courtroom there is no bias, there are facts and there is my judgment based on those facts. While you may feel you have been wronged you have not proven that Mr. Simmons intended to cause harm, nor have you shown that the implication of his statement is false, on the contrary, the outspoken and aggressive manner that I have witnessed this morning inclines me to agree with Mr. Simmons and to make you pay reparations to him for treating him this way. It is certainly within my power to do so. Now, any further outburst from you and I'll find you in contempt. Do I make myself clear?

Donna Anderson says nothing.

JUDGE R: Cat got your tongue, be like that if you want, but you'd better not lose the run of yourself in my court again missy, you want to say anything, Jeff?

JEFF SIMMONS: No, your honor, I'm just glad to have it done with and to get back to normal.

JUDGE R: Jeff, you're free to go. To close, I'd like to quote the words of the British writer G.K. Chesterton: 'We make our friends; we make our enemies, but God makes our next-door neighbor.' I hope you all can once again be neighborly. Good fences may indeed make good neighbors, but by-gones should be bygones. You all can reflect on that a while.

Reinhold stands up and with a swish of his robes leaves with the sprightliness of a much younger man.

*

OK, so it probably didn't go exactly like that, but Reinhold is old-school and wouldn't have had any time for the Anderson bullshit. I know him well and he's clear on one thing, he thinks people are too soft these days and that they find offense in everything. He says China is going to eat us up and that what we need to do is go back to basics, give kids more discipline and less love. A kid craves discipline and rules, he needs to know his place in the world. This snowflake stuff is beyond me. I was in 'Nam and I saw things that today's kids couldn't even comprehend. I had an uncle that ran up Gold Beach in '44 with nothing but the blind will to survive and when Obama was elected, he said to me he'd seen it all and was dead within a week, not that he had anything against Obama, it was more that he'd seen such a change in the world he was glad to leave knowing it was a better place, how many of us can say that?

It's difficult to stop him once he goes off on one. He always brings D-Day into it. It's his yardstick for comparing the men of today with those of yesteryear. If he's had a few beers, he likes to talk about Thurman Munson and how Munson's death changed the shape of baseball forever. I'm inclined to agree with him on that one. Munson had grit, the kind of grit that built this country. He was from a different era, he played hard and fair.

Hard and fair summed up Reinhold too, the kind of hard and fair that Donna Anderson found completely unfair.

34

In the end, normal life went on for a little while. Donna Anderson returned to work and I was surprised, but she seemed to grow for having learned her lesson. She was good-natured and agreeable and when the prospective new occupiers of the vacant house beside Jeff Simmons came to view the property, she formed part of the welcoming committee. She even went as far as to say hi to Jeff and share a joke with him — for the benefit of the viewers no doubt, but you have to start somewhere. At that point, I had high hopes that the whole thing could be put behind them and that they may even become neighborly.

Derek Anderson, on the other hand, kept a low profile and during that time I saw very little of him. He usually stayed indoors, coming out at dusk to walk Razor. Barney told me he saw him with Zimmerman a couple of times after dark. It looked like they were having a serious discussion about something.

I emailed Gretchen about it, letting her know what had been going on. She was tickled pink by the whole thing and said she was sad to have missed it.

About a week after the court case, Jeff Simmons came out of his house to find a large turd on his lawn. It was one of those spring mornings when the sun has heat in it and radiates light in such a way as to make one feel good to be alive. However, the sight of shit on your neatly manicured lawn does tend to diminish any feelings of goodwill towards existence. If anything, it symbolizes exactly what life is.

Jeff Simmons looked at the turd for a short while before walking calmly and resolutely to his neighbor's house, where after several loud knocks Derek Anderson answered the door. They spoke momentarily and then Anderson followed Simmons to the lawn where Simmons proceeded to show Anderson the offending article. There were words and then Anderson laughed and went back to his own house. Simmons was left standing there like he'd been stood up. Later that day, Simmons opened all the windows in his house and played Wagner's *Parsifal* -all five or six hours of it- at full volume.

For two days, this tit-for-tat stuff went on. It reached its crescendo when half a dozen different pizza companies delivered to the Andersons at the same time. Barney was in on it. Simmons called the pizza companies and afterward called Barney. Barney had agreed to let them all in at the same time. There were rules about deliveries, and the appearance of six pizza vans outside the Anderson home was a bit too much for Zimmerman's sense of propriety. An RCA meeting was called immediately.

*

TO: gretchen@sweetman.net
SUBJECT: The curious incident of the dog crap in the night-time.

Hey,

Are you in Paris or Milan? I never seem to remember. I know I just emailed you about Jeff and the Andersons going to court and how things settled down eventually, well, it's gone a bit nuclear since. A couple of days ago, the Anderson's dog Razor took a huge crap on Simmons's lawn. Jeff and Derek had a bit of a tête-à-tête about it. I can't be sure what they said, but I'm pretty sure Derek Anderson called Jeff a 'dumb fuck'. Jeff got him back royally, though. He had every pizza place in the district deliver simultaneously to the Andersons. It was a hoot. Given the size of the commotion, you'd swear someone had grown an arm out of their ass.

Zimmerman didn't like what he called an 'ugly situation' and used the little red rule book to call a meeting, as both the Andersons and Jeff were in violation of about a dozen sections and about another dozen subsections. I bet Zimmerman gets on to the Alderman about amending it.

The meeting was such fun and had the biggest attendance since the trick-or-treat fiasco last fall. Zimmerman tried his best to keep order and did more gavel banging than Nancy Pelosi, but whatever had been festering in Donna Anderson since the court hearing came to the surface. She accused Jeff of deliberately provoking them by planting the dog crap. Jeff in contrast was reasonable and never lost his cool. He stated that as the Andersons were the only people with a large dog in the immediate neighborhood, the logical conclusion was it was their responsibility. I get the distinct impression that logic doesn't have much of a place in Donna Anderson's thinking. Is she an evangelical?

It ended with a shouting match — well, Donna Anderson shouting at just about everyone. Marcie Mitchell waded in, saying that Razor should never have been allowed into Riverside Falls in the first place as he was a 'violent breed known for their aggression' — that estimation could have easily been applied to Razor's owner too. Zimmerman defended Razor's admittance to the community and cited the (amended) rule. Marcie accused Zimmerman of favoring the Andersons, as her pet request had been denied.

The Andersons already had a large dog when they joined the community,' said Zimmerman, 'you are perfectly entitled to get a dog, Marcie, but no larger than fifteen pounds.' I reckon Razor weighs about five times that.

It got so heated that Jenna Johnson and Marcie united against Donna Anderson. Zimmerman was shot down trying to maintain order and then Tillman lit the touch paper when he said, 'this kind of thing never happened in my day'. I was sure the vein on Zimmerman's head was going to burst.

'When you were the chairman, nothing got done,' said Zimmerman.

Tillman nodded and replied, 'the important stuff did.'

For a moment, the shouting stopped as Zimmerman and Tillman went at it. Zimmerman told Tillman he was out of order. Tillman told Zimmerman he couldn't organize a two-car parade. Eventually, Tillman got up, declaring the whole thing a waste of time and saying, 'you can't have a community without unity, and it seems to me and most of us here that Mr. Zimmerman has no understanding of the word. He's nothing more than an uncouth bully.'

Zimmerman kept his thoughts to himself and allowed Tillman to leave, but had Doris note in the minutes that Mr. Tillman had been 'forthright, rude and insubordinate' and proposed a vote banning Mr. Tillman from further meetings should there be a repeat of his actions. Zimmerman bemoaned that loyalty was a quality lack-

ing in some people. I'm pretty sure I heard Tillman say 'asshole' as he left.

All the while I sat with Old Jack and Karl Johnson. We had a good laugh wondering who'd be the first to throw a punch, I got to say it was a little disappointing that no one did but for a while, I really thought Donna and Marcie were going to gouge each other's eyes out. In the end, the whole thing kind of fizzled out without anything being done. Zimmerman ordered another meeting in the next week or so and summarily dismissed everyone.

You need to get back here soon as I have a feeling something big is about to happen.

Talk soon.

M

*

Something big did happen, sort of, a few days later.

Chapter Three
The strange disappearance of
Gene Hackman, April 2019

Gene Simmons

Jeff moved in during the spring of 2011 and within a couple of hours, he knocked on my door. It wasn't to borrow a cup of sugar or anything like that, instead, he'd wanted to tell me that he'd known my father. When we'd met briefly while he was viewing the house, he remarked on my surname. I didn't think anything of it at the time, but the day he knocked on my door he told me that he'd noted my surname as it rang a bell in his memory and that after a bit of searching through his grey matter, he'd finally made the connection. Turns out that Jeff had covered a case Dad had worked on just before he retired.

Dad was a medical examiner. He'd spent most of his career in or around Northern California, did some big cases too, The Night Stalker, Richard Trenton Chase, he also did some work on The Zodiac. About four years before he retired, an opportunity came up near Clearwater in Florida. He and Mom were happy to see out their final working years there. Mom was only doing a bit of sub work then, more for something to do than for money. But despite their joy, I wasn't the least bit happy about it, as I was in high school and had some good friends. It wasn't the first time I had to give up friends, but I remember hoping at the time it would be the last. I'm pretty sure Dad took the job in Clearwater to give us all a fresh start, especially my sister. California might be good for the complexion, but for people like my dad, there was only so much of it he could take.

Now, let me say this, Clearwater is a heck of a place, but back then I felt like we'd moved to a retirement village. My older sister, Beverley (Bev), was a newly qualified teacher and had just taken a job in Wisconsin for some reason I still don't understand, I mean she had the whole country to choose from and she went to the land of cheese and Norwegians. She's now the principal of an elementary school in some dot on the map called Lacrosse. She married the local undertaker. That's actually a lie, I couldn't resist. She never got married as far as I know. I don't have much to do with her these days. She flew the nest and flew hard. Mom had hoped Bev would take a job in or around Clearwater or even Tampa, but Bev had no intention of that and couldn't get away from us quick enough. In truth, she couldn't get away from me quick enough.

So, finishing high school in Clearwater was about as exciting as a church picnic. Days would drift and merge into a watery-sunny blur and after about a year I was immune to the tedium, in fact, I kind of liked it. I had some new friends, not as good as the ones I had in California, but they were OK.

As you can guess, not a lot went on in Clearwater. It's kind of small and perfectly middle-class. I saw the attraction it held for my dad soon enough. He played a lot of golf and didn't have a lot of head-scratchers at work. He only worked mornings and when I asked him about it from time to time, he'd say coronary or cancer or stroke, old people's diseases, and so forth. He liked being away from cops and courtrooms and all that went with his life in California. He was always a fairly chilled-out guy and Florida was making him almost supine, so when the phone rang one night, and I was pulled from sleep to hear Dad cursing and muttering to himself, I knew something had gone down.

'I was freelancing then, mostly doing investigatory stuff, white-collar fraud and misappropriation, that sort of thing. I spent a lot of time away from home. My wife didn't care for it, but it paid the bills. We lived in New York and she was pushing me to take a full-time position at *The Times*, the editor liked my work and wanted me to join the team, but I was still relatively young and liked the travel and the intrigue. I wasn't ready for a full-time desk job just then,' said Jeff Simmons.

I indicated if he'd like a beer and he nodded. I went to the fridge and grabbed two Sierra Nevada IPAs (I could never stand domestic beer, give me a craft beer any day).

'In the end, it was this case that compelled me to stay in New York. It didn't seem right to be away from the kids.'

I didn't reply and in the growing silence, he continued.

'*The Miami Herald* had me on retainer and they asked me to cover what had happened up in Clearwater.'

'Where you met Dad,' I added.

'Yep, not exactly a nice way to meet someone, though.'

I'd read the details in *The Tampa Bay Times,* but as Jeff explained that day, there was a lot more to it.

'They'd pulled something out of the bay at Sunset Point Rd. The papers reported it was a child but didn't say that the child who was probably about nine months old had been butchered and neatly put into a cooler box and that they never found the head.'

'I remember, it troubled him,' I said.

'It wasn't the gruesome nature of the event that bothered me, but rather the pointlessness,' said Jeff, 'I think that's what got to your father too. I mean, he told me he'd seen some pretty horrific stuff over the years, and I had covered some pretty horrific stuff too, but this child was never identified, and no one ever brought to book. I guess we both saw the world differently afterward.'

He swallowed a mouthful of beer.

Of course, I knew the real reason why it had bothered Dad so much, but I never said anything to Jeff.

'I met with your father a couple of times to get some facts about COD and stuff like that. One night we had a few beers. We were both a bit beat up about the incident. He told me about you and your sister and how he was looking forward to retiring.'

'He retired a few years later,' I said.

'He called me Gene,' said Jeff.

My brow must have arched. He went on to explain.

'After Gene Simmons of Kiss. I think it was his way of taking the heaviness out of the situation. He wanted both of us to associate something else with our time on the case.'

'I wonder if it is still an open investigation.' I asked.

Jeff shook his head and straightened up in his chair.

'It's been over twenty years,' he said, 'it's cold. I've covered quite a few cold cases in my time. A guy I know at The Herald keeps me updated.'

'I guess someone knows what happened,' I said, sipping my beer.

'Someone does, but I doubt there'll be justice. Some things get buried so deep they never surface.'

'My dad used to say things like that. He said his job was trying to read the secret history of a person's final moments.'

'I'm sorry I didn't get to see him before he passed.'

Dad had died a few months before Jeff had moved in. As it turned out, Jeff had begun looking at Jonestown the same day Dad went in the ground.

'Probably best you remember him the way you do,' I said.

44

Jeff nodded and took a swig of his beer.

We talked for a while longer and I told Jeff about life in Riverside Falls. It was different back then, for one there were no Andersons, and two, Zimmerman was only beginning to flex his muscles. Jeff left my house just before sundown, and we've been good neighbors ever since. I prefer the term neighbors to friends, as they're not the same thing. A good neighbor doesn't get too close or stay too distant. They stay in a place where they mind their own business and yet you can have a beer, coffee, etc. with them and shoot the breeze. There's no ego. I think that's the problem with most relationships. Once the ego is involved, the potential for conflict arises.

About two years ago Jeff's older daughter Carrie dropped by unannounced. The visit was so unexpected that Jeff was out of town and Carrie, who by this time knew me well enough to ask me a favor, asked if I could do her a favor. She seemed a little flustered and without really thinking I agreed. I assumed it was passing on some information or something like that.

'Of course,' I said, smiling, inviting her to come in. I was always a sucker for a pretty lady who needed help.

Carrie is one of those people that are always busy and near the edge of a nervous breakdown. She declined my invitation to come in and without a word ran back to her car. She returned carrying a rectangular box with a handle on it.

'I could wait or come back tomorrow, but I'm busy and if you'd take this it'd be such a godsend.'

She actually said godsend.

'What is it?' I asked.

She flashed her pretty smile and placed the box on my porch. Carrie's about forty and wears her years well despite the frantic nature of her mind. I returned her smile and looked at the box. A kind of low humming began to emanate from it, like someone using a pneumatic drill off in the distance. My first thought was that it was a box of bees.

'It's Gene Hackman,' she said, pronouncing each syllable the way a children's entertainer might.

'Is Gene Hackman a dog?' I said.

'Try again,' said Carrie.

Now, I don't know about you, but I fucking hate cats, or did back then. A wave of uncomfortable realization that it was a cat swept over me and all my muscles began to tense up. I must have given off a vibe because Carrie sealed the deal quickly and was gone lickety-split.

I stood on my porch with a humming box of malevolent fur and claws, a litter box, and a tray of cat food wondering what the fuck had just happened. I lifted everything inside and sat down and called Jeff.

'It's a cat,' I said, 'called Gene Hackman.'

'What?'

'Carrie left it just now.'

Jeff was tight-lipped for a few seconds before saying, 'goddammit.'

'What is it?' I asked.

'She's been talking about getting me a dog for a while now and I've refused as I don't want to deal with Zimmerman and the RCA bullshit. I can only suspect this is her idea of a compromise.'

'But dogs are allowed,' I said.

'Not the kind of dog I want,' said Jeff.

I examined the box. Between the slats, two green-gold eyes gleamed, followed by a yawning mouth with needle-sharp fangs.

'I don't really like cats,' I said.

'Sorry,' said Jeff, 'but I'd be obliged if you could hold onto it until I got back. Should be about noon tomorrow.'

The clock on my mantelpiece said it was just after three. I did the math, twenty-one hours with a cat didn't appeal to me at all.

'OK, Jeff, no problem,' I said.

'Do you know how to take care of a cat?' he asked.

'Yes,' I said, 'we had a cat when I was growing up.'

'That's great, shouldn't be a problem,' said Jeff before adding a very awkward 'thanks.'

'Jeff,' I said just before he hung up, 'why is the cat named Gene Hackman?'

'I don't know, you'd have to ask Carrie. She probably likes him.'

'The actor,' I said.

'Yes, the actor, what did you think I meant?'

'Nothing,' I said, 'I'll take care of things here, don't be late picking him up.'

'I'll be there at noon. Thanks again, I'll see you tomorrow.'

Jeff hung up and I looked at the box. The two green eyes were glaring back at me. I began to think about the family cat from my childhood. His name was Billybird. He was Mom's idea. Her grandparents had a farm in Kentucky which her parents had taken over and while the farm didn't hold so many good memories during her adult years, she held onto all the good ones from her childhood like a lifeline. She always shared them with us. She insisted on focusing only on good things and would sometimes become almost hysterically forthright. She repressed a lot, and frankly, I don't blame her.

So, this incarnation of Mom's good intentions, Billybird, came into our lives when I was six and my sister was ten. Dad didn't care much for him, but it didn't bother him either, he had more troubling things to think about at the time, we all did. Billybird, or to give him his proper name, Billybird III (as there had been two previous holders of that name on the Kentucky farm) joined the family and pretty soon had left his mark. Literally.

'The farm was such a wonderful place growing up,' said Mom as we drove home after collecting Billybird III from the cat shelter.

Even then, at six years of age, I was acutely aware of how strange Mom's behavior was given what had happened on the farm shortly before we got Billybird III.

'I sure loved the farm when I was a kid, you would have too.'

'I know, I've only been there about a million times,' said Bev sarcastically.

'Oh, it was so different back then,' said Mom, ignoring Bev.

'It was about fifty acres and there were animals everywhere, horses, cattle, dogs, cats, you name it. It was like something out of a Steinbeck story.'

'Like the one about the guy who shot the retard in the back of the head?' said Bev.

I laughed, retard was a funny word, and along with dork was the insult of choice among my peers.

'That's not nice,' said Mom, 'don't say that.'

'But it's true, he was retarded, and anyway, he'd killed that girl, so he deserved it.'

'Beverley, please don't say that word.'

'But.'

'I don't think John Steinbeck would appreciate you condensing one of his greatest stories into the guy who shot the simple man in the back of the head.'

My sister folded her arms. She hated it when adults contradicted her. Mom was good at instilling those kinds of feelings in us, it often deflected from her sense of guilt about the real reason for Billybird III being in our lives. I think she swallowed so much guilt over the years, it ate her alive from the inside out.

'Were there wolves and coyotes and snakes?' I said, hoping to stir the pot. I'd heard the same story with the same enthusiasm more times than I cared to mention.

'No, there were only nice animals,' said Mom with the same enthusiasm as if I'd asked the question for the first time.

'Cats are evil,' said my sister, 'witches had cats and they used them to kill kids.'

And so, from pastoral reflection to witches, a squabble broke out between Bev and Mom I was on the side-line and tried to stay there. All the time, Billybird III was curled up quietly in a box on the passenger seat. I swear to god, but I remember feeling the furry bastard was enjoying the ruckus.

When we got home, the cat's first action was to occupy the couch. He was only a kitten then, but I already knew he was not to be messed with. Later that day, as I leaned in to get a closer look at him, he opened one eye, sat up, and swiped his sharp claw at me. I didn't even know he'd got me until my sister saw the blood and shrieked. It was then that a terrible stinging began just below my right eye. He'd scratched a perfectly straight line about two inches below my eye. I still have a scar there. Dad called it a *memento mori*.

I debated that if I let Gene Hackman out, would he give a similar problem. Much and all as I didn't want a cat roaming about my house, I thought it was probably cruel to leave him in his container until Jeff came back. I prepared accordingly by putting Gene Hackman and his stuff in the laundry room, just off the kitchen. I opened the cage and half expected the cat to come bounding out like something from *Gremlins,* but instead, he just stayed there and stared at me. I decided to leave him. I reckoned I could use the opportunity as a learning experience and a chance to fix some of the damage Billybird III had done.

That night was OK, though I made a couple of big mistakes. Firstly, I let the cat into the garden just before dusk and he ate some grass and chased some bugs. I was beginning to enjoy his company. Then, rather than keep him in the laundry room, I let him into the living room while I watched TV. The consequence of this was that when Jeff arrived to collect him the next morning, Gene Hackman had no intention of leaving and hid under the sofa while Jeff and I tried to entice him out with ham. In the end, Jeff reached in, grabbed him, receiving a few scratches along the way, and threw him in his container. About an hour later I found him in my laundry room curled up on a pile of shirts. I brought him back to Jeff and suggested that Jeff close his windows.

Carrie called over a few days later and when she was leaving, I could see Jeff smiling through gritted teeth. Over the past two years, Gene Hackman has come to visit my house and only my house about a dozen times a month. He stays for anything from an hour or two to a few days. Jeff doesn't mind, and it suits him when he's out of town for me to look after his cat. I'm sure that somewhere Billybird III is laughing his ass off.

Gene Hackman meets Razor Anderson

Gene Hackman is a Maine Coon; Barney likes to joke that the cat is the only coon allowed in Jonestown, and once said so in a brilliantly deadpan way at an RCA meeting. A lot of awkward silence followed. Old Jack and I laughed. Zimmerman wasn't impressed. Barney attends RCA meetings sometimes to give us updates on security and stuff like that. He doesn't get to vote. No surprise there.

When Gene Hackman moved in, it wasn't long until he met Razor. Razor, you'll recall, is the Anderson's pit bull, the one who took a crap on Jeff Simmons' lawn, the one I've led you to believe is a good dog. He is, but he's a dog and when he first saw the cat, it was from the street while out for a walk. The cat was dozing serenely on the window ledge, and as Razor walked by something must have gone off in the cat's primal center as it suddenly sat upright and stiff and stared at the dog. Razor with a deep guttural growl pulled at his lead so hard that Derek Anderson had to get physiotherapy on his elbow afterward. It was with considerable effort that he managed to drag the dog away from Jeff's house. All the time Gene Hackman sat unmoving and unblinking as if saying to Razor 'come at me bro.'

I think that may have been when things started to get frosty between the Andersons and Jeff. Derek called over to Jeff a day or two later, politely suggesting that Jeff might have informed him about the cat.

'I got to wear this sling now on account of your dumbass cat,' said Derek.

'I'm sorry Derek,' said Jeff, a thin smile forming at the edge of his mouth,' it was a gift from my daughter. I hope your elbow gets better soon. Razor's a helluva strong dog.'

Anderson didn't smile.

It's more of a testament to Gene Hackman's stealth than Jeff's good care of him that he managed to avoid Razor, but it was inevitable that the two would come into close contact. As I recall, the cat was in my front room asleep on the window ledge. It was getting near sundown, and I had things to do the next day, so I picked him up and was going to throw him out the front door when I saw Derek and Razor beginning their evening patrol. I decided then to deliver Gene Hackman directly to Jeff and was turning into Jeff's driveway when Razor, mad with bloodlust or horniness or something, broke free from Derek's grasp and made a beeline for me and the cat. Jeff had just opened his front door and I dropped Gene Hackman, who ran into the house like wildfire spreading through a forest. As

Jeff went to close the door, Razor slammed into it and burst it open. Jeff was thrown back and Razor proceeded to barrel through the house looking for the cat. In the end, it took ten minutes for Derek, Jeff, and I to subdue Razor and get him out. As Derek pulled Razor's lead so that the dog could only let out a hoarse yelp, I got a powerful sense we were being watched and instinctively looked up at one of the bedroom windows of Jeff's house. Gene Hackman was perched majestically on the window ledge, nonchalantly licking his paw and rubbing the back of his head. He paused and rolled his back before stretching full length and bringing his paws together and settling into a Sphinx-like pose. His eyes closed slowly, as if he were permitting us to go about our business once more. I noticed that Derek Anderson was now looking at the cat. He was glaring and turned his eyes on me when he saw me looking at him. He grimaced and rubbed his elbow.

'Fucking cats,' he said before grabbing Razor's collar and dragging the dog home.

Derek's elbow flared up once more and though I can't be sure I bet it was he and Donna who went to Zimmerman about Gene Hackman because a few days later there was an amendment to the rules stating that cats must be kept indoors at all times and that failure to comply would result in the animal's destruction. When Jeff saw the change, he said nothing, but brought it to my attention. I said if Razor couldn't catch him, there was no chance of sixty-five-year-old Zimmerman catching him. Jeff wondered if the local animal catcher would be called. I told him I'd handle it. The local animal catcher is a friend of mine and would be more than happy to refuse Zimmerman's invitation.

You can probably see why Jeff wrote the article now.

But before he did, and for about a year, everything died down, though it was more by accident than design. Jeff kept

Gene Hackman in as best he could, and the cat seemed content to be kept in. Winter was on the way and like a lot of communities in winter, Jonestown got sleepy and quiet. All through November and December, Derek and Razor did their evening patrol and Gene Hackman sat either in my window or Jeff's watching the world turn white and powdery. It was much the same this year too, except that the cat spent more time in my house on account of the woodstove I installed last October. He would curl up on the floor about six feet away from it and apart from the occasional yawn or flick of his ear you'd think he was dead.

We had an unexpected flurry in January and, Karl Johnson and Derek and I cleared all of the driveways and porches in Jonestown Proper and The Zimmerman Zone. I spent a few afternoons chatting with Old Jack. He was full of bluster, saying that this year The Eagles would finally win The Super Bowl. We debated the various merits of the playoff teams and it was a lot of fun. About mid-January, I was leaving Old Jack's when I saw Mrs. Osman standing at her door. It was cold and she wasn't properly dressed for the weather. She was just standing there, looking at something off in the distance. The whole time I watched her closely. As I approached, she didn't move a muscle, but her mouth was moving furiously as if she were trying to empty her breath of every word she knew. As I neared, she lifted her hand and pointed. I turned around to see what she was pointing at. It was the unoccupied house beside Zimmerman's.

She was cold to the touch when I got to her, and I tried to usher her back inside.

'In there,' she said.

'In where?' I asked.

She pointed to the unoccupied house.

'Bill and Marge are in there,' she said.

I smiled.

'No Mrs. Osman, they left before Christmas, remember? They went to a new home where people would look after them.'

She ignored my comment and kept pointing at the house.

'Do you want to go in there?'

'No, if I do, I won't come back out.'

She didn't say anything further, and I helped her back inside. She smiled at me and I got the distinct impression her grip on reality was slipping with every minute.

'Can I help with anything?'

She smiled again and then with sudden vivacity said, 'some tea.'

She got up and moved surprisingly quickly to the kitchen, emerging a short while later with a pot of tea and some cups on a tray. The tea was lukewarm, but I drank it, well some of it. We sat a while longer and I asked her if she needed anything. She smiled benignly and told me that Mr. Zimmerman had everything under control.

As I got up to leave, she grabbed my arm, harder than I expected for such an old and frail lady.

'I haven't seen Marianne in a while. Randall went to find her, but he hasn't come back yet.'

We all knew it, but it was the first time I had that immediate and powerful understanding that she needed care. As I was leaving for the door, I was a little relieved but also saddened when I saw some literature from a residential care facility near Concord on a small bureau. I picked up the leaflet and flicked through it. It was standard fare, comfortable but banal. I read the name Juniper Hills, thinking at least it wasn't Sunnyville or Happy Valley or something like that.

'Who gave this to you?' I asked.

'Mr. Tillman,' she said.

I was pleased it wasn't Zimmerman. Even though Zimmerman was helping her with day-to-day stuff, I didn't like the idea of him running her life.

'Mr. Tillman from down the street?' I asked just to be sure.

'Yes, he said it's a good place.'

'I'm sure it is, but make sure you tell me or Karl or somebody if you want to go there.'

'Mr. Tillman says they are coming to visit me in the spring.'

I nodded and she held my hand and squeezed it.

'I think Marianne will be back soon,' she said in a bright voice.

There was a flicker of something in her eyes, I didn't know what exactly.

As I walked down her driveway and onto the road, I glanced towards Zimmerman's house. He was standing on the porch smoking a cigarette. I gave him a wave and he lifted his hand to acknowledge me. Before I put my head down against the cold, I looked at the unoccupied house and remembered with a fright that Mrs. Osman had been pointing at it earlier. I admonished myself for being spooked and hurried home.

But enough of that, getting back to the present, it seems that Gene Hackman has disappeared. Now, I know what you're thinking, cats go missing all the time for days, weeks, even months and just trot back as if nothing had happened. Billybird III disappeared for about a month when he was one. When he returned all tattered and scrawny, Mom fed him and let him rest and then brought him to be spayed. When Jeff first got the cat, I suggested he get him neutered, and Jeff agreed. 'It'll stop him pissing all over the furniture for one thing.'

So, why do I think the cat has disappeared? Well for one, neither Jeff nor I have seen him and what's more, Barney hasn't seen him either. Not much gets past Barney, literally, and he says he hasn't seen the cat in about a week. Normally his routine is like clockwork. He gets up from whichever house he finds himself in, goes out, does his business and finds a cozy spot in whichever house he decides he prefers at that moment and stays there to repeat the pattern, and, as I told you, he only moves between my house and Jeff's house.

Four days ago, Jeff asked me if I'd seen him and when I said I hadn't, he told me it'd been almost a week since he'd seen him.

'When did you see him last?' I asked.

He looked at his phone.

'Today is the 9th, I think it was Sunday the 1st, the evening of Sunday the 1st.'

'April Fool's Day,' I said.

He frowned, 'what?' he said.

'Nothing, eh, I think I saw him about then too,' I said before adding 'he'll be back, he's just wandered off somewhere.'

'What did you mean about April Fools?' he pressed.

I stood back. There's something about a missing pet that can bring out primal emotions in a person. A rising sense of panic and helplessness was evident in Jeff's normally sanguine exterior.

'Nothing Jeff, I just noticed it, that's all.'

'OK, sorry,' he said, 'I'm just a little anxious.'

A small smile like a wrinkle broke on his face.

'I like the little guy; I'd hate it if he didn't come back.'

I nodded in the direction of the Anderson's house.

'You could ask Derek, or more precisely Razor to help, he might be able to sniff him out?'

Jeff's expression softened and he shook his head involuntarily as if he were checking his head was still attached to his neck.

'Maybe, I'll think about it,' he said and then without another word turned and left.

I watched him go and thought, poor guy. He reminded me a little of Mom when Billybird III finally bit the dust. He was about eight and hadn't really been himself for a couple of weeks. Normally he'd be vivacious and more than a little temperamental, but he'd been quiet and then one afternoon he went under the house and stayed there three days and on the third he died. Mom spent hours on end on her knees or crouched down trying to coax him out, but all he'd do was let out a meek miaow and stay still.

'What's wrong with Billybird III,' I asked.

'He's dying,' said Mom flatly, though there was a tiny tremble in her voice.

When he closed his eyes on the third day, she knew it was for the final time. She just lay there on her side looking at him. I thought it was weird, but knew even then that grief works differently on different people and that the death of a pet is as keen as the death of any family member. After about an hour, Mom asked me to crawl in and get him. I reluctantly agreed, and somewhere in the layers of my teenage indifference felt a measure of pity for her. I had never really taken to Billybird III (by mutual consent) and I felt at times Mom took it personally as if her idea of family happiness had a crack in it and no matter how much she tried to bring me and the cat together we resisted like oil and water. As I shuffled on my wrists and reached for Billybird III in the cramped space I half expected him to take a lunge at me, but he didn't, and looking at his face I got the impression he was happy enough to be done with life. There was an eerie contentment in the way his mouth had settled. I patted his head and for a second his eyes opened. He looked at me with bright eyes that flashed as if startled and then, seeing it was me, closed them again and lay still.

The vet said that sometimes cats die relatively young, just like humans. She reckoned that Billybird III had cardiomyopathy and reminded my sister who pointed out that 'he was only eight' that eight was middle-aged for cats and that an active outdoor cat like Billybird III might develop cardiomyopathy sooner than an indoor cat. This explanation didn't give my sister any solace, and she moped around the house for a few days afterward. Mom went quiet all of a sudden and at times and had to check herself when she began to ask 'where's…?' or, 'I can hear…'

Bev got over it quickly, but it lingered in Mom's mind for a long time, it was another loss, another failure. I can't say why exactly, other than perhaps Billybird III's death was like a little piece of her childhood dying. I saw it in Jeff's eyes, as if Gene Hackman's disappearance had taken something truly meaningful from him.

The next day, on every second tree and along the fence of The Park were notices that read:

MISSING CAT
Gene Hackman is a two-year-old Maine Coon. Some of
you may have seen him around the place. It's not like
him to be gone this long, and I'd appreciate your help
in getting him back.

Under MISSING CAT was a picture of Gene Hackman sitting on a chair looking happy and content. At the bottom of the notice were Jeff's cell number and email.

Nothing happened for a day or two, except that Zimmerman moaned about how the notices made the place lose its aesthetic value. Still, Zimmerman and the Andersons aside, everyone liked Jeff and were very concerned about his cat. Search parties formed. We gathered in The Park and scoured the place for signs of the cat, but nothing showed up. Then about lunchtime four days later and with no sign of Gene Hackman, there was a knock on my door.

Chapter Four
A Blonde to make a bishop kick a hole in a stained-glass window, April 2019

When I opened the door, a sudden and disorienting beam of sunlight hit me. I instinctively shielded my eyes and had to squint before I could make out who was standing in front of me. I rubbed my eyes and took a step back to where the light wasn't burning into my face.

'Sorry for disturbing you, were you asleep?' said a smooth, assured voice.

'No,' I said, 'it's the light, it's bouncing off your car.'

A sleek cherry red car sat on the pavement outside my house. I looked over the person's shoulder to take it in. I recognized the model straight away.

'Is that a Firebird?' I asked.

'Sure is, you like cars?'

I nodded.

'Sort of,' I said, 'that's a cool car, you don't see too many of them around here.'

It was at that moment that I saw clearly who I was talking to. She was about thirty, maybe a little older, and stood with the poise of an athlete. I could tell straight away that she took care of herself. She was dressed in jeans and a jacket, smart but casual at the same time. Her clothes fit perfectly around her perfectly proportionate curves. Her face was angular with sharp green eyes and her top lip was slightly fuller than her bottom one. Her nose was dusted with a light sprinkling of freckles which made her look vaguely girlish and surrounding her beautiful face was layered blonde hair that reflected microlights of copper and gold and bronze. I stood back to take in her full length and must have zoned out because I did not hear say my name.

'What?' I said.

'Are you Matt Lowell?'

'Yes,' I said slowly, 'how may I help you?'

She put her hand out and I shook it. Her skin was soft and her grip was firm.

'My name is Beth Becker, I'm a private detective.'

I looked up and down the street, expecting to see a film crew for one of those TV shows where people get pranked.

'Sorry?'

'I'm a private detective, Mr. Lowell,' she repeated, 'Jeff Simmons hired me to find out what happened to his cat.'

'No way' I said emphatically and then added; 'really, Jeff did that?'

She reached into her jacket pocket and took out an ID badge. There it was BETH BECKER PI, fully bonded licensed with the state of New Hampshire, etc.

I was dumbfounded. Not only was there a stunningly attractive woman standing at my door, but Jeff had hired her to find Gene Hackman.

'May I ask you a few questions?'

'Yep, fire away.'

'Not here,' she said, 'may I come in?'

I let out a chuckle and stood aside with a sweeping arm movement.

'This way, please.'

She smiled a little awkwardly but walked confidently into my home. I led her into the kitchen, where she sat at the breakfast bar. I popped a pod into my coffee maker and asked her if she'd like a coffee. She nodded and sat and waited until I was done.

'You have a nice home, Mr. Lowell,' she said as I handed her a tall glass with a handle.

'Nicest one in Jonestown,' I said.

Her brow wrinkled and she looked confused. I felt heat rise in my face.

'The houses are all the same, more or less,' I said, 'it was a joke, never mind.'

'On the outside,' she said.

'I suppose,' I said, feeling less stupid for my attempt at humor.

'Most of an iceberg is below the surface,' she said cryptically.

Now it was my turn to be confused, but after thinking about it for a second, I realized what she meant. She smiled and sipped her latte. A thin milk mustache formed on her upper lip. She licked it away instinctively as if she knew I had noticed. Her eyes moved around the room, taking in its dimensions and probably the nearest exit.

'Do you cook?' she said.

Her eyes had landed on the array of cooking utensils that hung from a rack over the range.

'I can cook,' I said by way of clarification.

'Got a signature dish?'

'Not really, I just use what's in season. It's only me here, and it's not often I have guests.'

She was looking at me the way Mom used to look at me when she was trying to figure out if I had told a lie.

'I paid my taxes, all of them,' I said, holding my hands up, 'every last cent.'

'I'm not interested in your financial affairs, Mr. Lowell.'

After that, there was a pause in the conversation. I didn't feel entirely comfortable in her presence and began to think about the various skeletons in my closet, well, one in particular.

'You seem a little nervous,' she said, 'there's no need, I'm not here to investigate you.'

I smiled, hoping it would convey I believed her, but couldn't completely shake my doubt.

'So, Jeff hired you?' I said.

'Yes,' she said, but before she continued, I interrupted her.

'He sure loves that cat, but a private detective isn't that a bit over the top?'

'Not to Mr. Simmons,' she said and then asked, 'what do you do Mr. Lowell?' dismissing my observation in one fell swoop. I took a deep breath.

'Please call me Matt, Mr. Lowell was my father.'

As soon as I heard myself speak, the more rational part of my brain became embarrassed for both of us. It began to wrestle my libido for control of my mouth. I hadn't been this giddy in years, and I was afraid if I put my foot in my mouth one more time, I'd fall over.

'What do you do, Matt?'

I thought for a moment before responding.

'This and that,' I said.

'OK,' said Becker,'care to elaborate?'

'I work from home,' I said, 'why?'

'No reason, just being polite. I don't care what you do. It's more of an icebreaker, really.'

The connotations of her statement made me shift slightly in my seat.

'I write, or at least try to.'

'You must be good,' she said, 'to afford a home like this.'

'Have you any suspects?' I asked, choosing to steer the conversation to where it was less about me.

She opened her body a little more and drew her left arm up to her face where she pushed her hair behind her ear.

'You're the first person I've spoken to, other than Jeff, of course. And why would there be any suspects?'

'I don't know,' I said, 'isn't that how this usually goes?'

I must have been staring because her expression went from friendly and business-like to stern in a split second, the kind of stern a law enforcement official went if you made an ill-judged joke or couldn't produce your ID.

'What?' she said louder than normal, a hint of exasperation in her voice, 'what do you want to say?'

I decided to just come out with it rather than feign ignorance.

'Aren't you a bit young and pretty to be a private detective?'

She grinned, but not in a friendly way, more in the way my comment deserved, all face, no eyes. She pushed back from the breakfast bar and looked firmly at me.

'OK grandpa, you want to give me a lecture on morals or something, maybe I should have worn a petticoat, or had a chaperone with me?'

I held my hands up, she was right, I was being rude.

'Sorry, I didn't mean it like that, it's just that in the movies private detectives are fat old guys in grey coats chewing on a cigar, fighting alcoholism and well ...'

Her eyes softened, even if her face didn't follow immediately.

'You're not what I expected,' I said.

'Neither are you. I didn't think there were too many liberally educated guys in their mid-forties that had a conservative rod so far up their ass that it went into their brain.'

I liked her more after that, it certainly broke the ice. She was sharp as a tack and obviously well-used to giving better than she got.

'I think we've got off on the wrong foot, may we start again? I'm Matt Lowell.'

'Beth Becker.'

'How may I help you, Miss Becker?'

'Beth,' she said.

I knew it'd be OK after that.

'Sorry if I made you nervous,' she said.

'Sorry for being an ass,' I said.

It was warm in the room as the sun began to fill the windows, trapping the heat. I stood up and went to the AC and turned it on. There was a rattle as it started up, and soon a cool breeze blew through the room.

'How do you know I got a liberal education?' I asked, returning to my seat.

'I've done some research on you.'

I pushed at my coffee cup. It made a hollow scraping sound.

'Am I a suspect?' I said, looking her in the eye.

'You're fixated on suspects, aren't you?'

'Well, am I?' I said.

'Perhaps,' she said, 'I'm going to try and find out.'

She had a notebook, one of those moleskin things Hemingway used to write in. I remarked on it and told her about Hemingway's house in Key West. Hemingway was a serious ailurophile and kept lots of cats, many of which had extra toes.

'Have you been?' she asked.

I shook my head.

'Maybe the cat has gone there,' she said offhandedly.

She seemed lost in thought and a sort of vulnerability appeared on her face. Very soon after she reverted to her matter-of-fact detective persona which reminded me a lot of Olivia Benson in *Law and Order*, you know, pleasant but immune to charm, professional.

'I spoke with Jeff earlier today and he told me that his cat would regularly come to your house and stay for a while, so with that in mind I thought I'd start here.'

'Makes sense,' I said.

I described the cat's typical behavior to her and she scribbled a few notes.

'Is this your first missing cat case?' I asked.

She nodded as she wrote.

'Must be a bit strange?'

She looked up and put down her pen.

'Missing cat, missing person, it's the same to me. All I can tell you is that Mr. Simmons desperately wants his cat returned and as long as I'm here I'm going to do my best to find him.'

'I still think it's a little over the top, not you, but it's a missing cat and anyway, he might have just wandered off as cats do, it seems a little weird that there'd be foul play involved' I said.

'As you said, he may have just wandered off. My job is to check all possibilities.'

'I guess Jeff has his reasons,' I said while taking a sip of coffee.

'You'll have to ask him yourself,' she said.

'Is much of your work looking for missing persons?'

'This and that,' she said.

I smiled, *touché.*

'Some of it,' she said after a short pause, 'mostly I try to catch cheating husbands or ones that won't pay alimony and child support. There are advantages to being a female PI.'

'So surveillance?'

'Occasionally, but most of the bad husband stuff is hands-on if you get me.'

'Isn't that entrapment?'

She raised her eyebrow and said nothing.

'How did you get into it?' I asked.

'I thought I was the one asking the questions.'

After a moment she relented.

'I did a degree in psychology wanting to be a therapist but ended up in advertising. After a few years, I realized I didn't want to work in an office, or for a boss to be honest, and I kind of fell into this.'

Her tone told me she'd be asked this many times before, and I was getting the standard potted summary.

'What about you? How did you fall into this and that?' she asked.

'I'm sure you know already,' I said.

She flicked through her notebook to the relevant details.

'Matt Lowell, born in 1974 in Sacramento, CA to Thomas and Helen. Thomas, a medical examiner who spent most of his working life in Northern California before moving to Clearwater, FL where he became county coroner before finally retiring in May of 1994. Thereafter moving to Riverside Falls in June of the same year where he lived until passing away in December of 2010 from complications associated with Alzheimer's disease. Helen, a schoolteacher, also retired in 1994 and took up residence in Riverside Falls. She passed away in May of 2000. Two years after her death, you moved into the house to take care of your father. You have one older sister, Beverley, 49, principal of James A. Garfield Elementary School in Lacrosse, Wisconsin. Other details pending.'

'Other details pending?' I said.

'I'll find out what I need to know about you as I go along.'

I scratched the back of my head.

'You don't look like your picture,' she said.

My nose twitched and wrinkled.

'What picture?'

'Your high school yearbook.'

'My high school yearbook,' I said with a murmuring giggle under my words.

'That was almost thirty years ago, of course, I look different. I bet you don't look anything like your yearbook picture.'

'I guess not,' she said.

I began to wonder where she got her information from.

'Google sure is useful,' I said flippantly.

She took the bait.

'I have access to much better search engines than Google.'

Her voice was playful, there was no sense of a threatening subtext to the remark and besides, I had an intuitive sense that she didn't know that much about me or my family. Her quiet manner afterward confirmed it, or almost did. The problem with intuition is that even if you trust it, sometimes you must pretend you don't.

'Teaching runs in your family,' she said, changing the direction of the conversation.

I was happier with this.

'You have no idea,' I said.

'Your sister got any kids?' she asked.

'I don't even know if she's married.'

'So, you don't keep in touch?'

I ignored the question and asked her if she'd like another coffee.

'No thanks,' she said.

I expected her to leave after that the way some people might use the natural break in the conversation as an excuse to go, but much to my pleasure for I was now enjoying her company, she

stayed. She was intent on asking me more questions and satis-
fying whatever she needed to know.

'Can you tell me about the neighborhood?'

'What would you like to know?' I said.

'Anything that might help.'

'What has Jeff told you?'

'That he's not on good terms with his neighbors, that their
dog messed up his lawn, and that the head of the RCA recently
enforced a rule about pets being outdoors.'

'Cats,' I said, 'the rule only applies to cats. Quite a few people in The Family Zone have dogs.'

'The Family Zone?' she said.

'When you came in you went right to get here, if you'd gone
left, you'd have driven to The Family Zone. It's a part of the
community that's designated for families and only families. It's
one of the RCA's rules.'

'Are there a lot of rules?'

'Too many,' I said, 'eternal vigilance is the price of liberty.
Zimmerman, the RCA head, is a bit of an authoritarian, or
would like to be. He's bigger on the rules than his predecessor,
but it's not a big deal, it's not like there are any serious consequences if you break them.'

'You should tell that to my landlord,' she said.

'Landlords are either super nice or complete dicks,' I said.

'You said it, mine is like a prison warden.'

'You're not local, are you?'

'I'm living in Concord right now.'

'Not too far,' I said.

Concord was about a ninety-minute drive away.

'What I meant is you're not from New Hampshire,' I said.

I was good with accents and knew exactly where she was
from.

'California,' she said, 'just like you.'

'I thought so, whereabouts?'

'Bay area,' she said, 'Napa.'

'Wow,' I said, 'I hear it's nice there, are you trying to catch Zodiac in your spare time?'

'I think that case is cold,' she said wryly, 'and I don't have a lot of spare time.'

'My dad worked with Dave Toschi in the late 70s. I even met him, but I don't have much of a recollection of it, being a kid and all. Toschi was the lead detective on the case.'

'I know, he was a bit of a celebrity when I was growing up,' she said.

She wasn't particularly impressed. The enthusiasm went from my face like air from a balloon. I decided to persist, I wanted to discover if she knew her stuff.

'He also did some work with Robert Ressler. Dad, not Toschi, that is.'

'Robert Ressler, who's he?' she said.

'You never heard of Robert Ressler,' I said incredulously, 'he was the guy who invented behavioral science.'

She stuck out her lower lip and pulled her hair behind her ear.

'There was a documentary about his work on TV last week, did you see it?'

'I told you I don't have much free time and when I do, I'm more an outdoors kind of girl than sitting at home watching TV,' she said, folding her arms.

'I don't watch much TV either, but I watched this show because it all happened when I was a kid, and I was curious to see if they'd modeled a character after Dad.'

'Did they?' she asked.

'No,' I said.

The anti-climax was intentional, I'd found out what I wanted.

'Tell me about Mr. Simmons' neighbors, the Andersons?' she said.

I told her what I knew, much, if not all of it, concurred with what Jeff had told her.

'I read the article,' she said, 'I really can't believe it went to a hearing.'

'Some people are prickly,' I said, 'and stupid.'

She unfolded her arms and tapped her lower lip with her pen, and then wrote another note.

'Is Zimmerman prickly?' she asked, 'seems to me he might be given all the rules you mentioned.'

'I don't know much about Zimmerman,' I said, 'no one does.'

It occurred to me how little any of us knew about anyone, but the thought rolled down my mind like a droplet of rain on glass, and I continued telling her what I knew about Zimmerman.

'He arrived here in early 2005. I remember the day he moved in because Dad and I went along to welcome him as part of the general community welcome. Randall Osman was head of the RCA at the time, in fact, he was almost done with it, but he was the sort of guy who made a big deal about welcoming new people to the place. Anyway, it was icy cold but there was no snow, it was one of the few years we didn't get buried, we usually do around here.'

'I've noticed,' she said, 'it's not easy moving from California to here.'

I wanted to ask her how long she'd been in Concord, but decided not to.

'So, Zimmerman arrives in a cab and when he steps out, you'd have sworn he was the reincarnation of JFK. He was wearing a tailored suit that must have cost a small fortune and these 20s-style wingtips. He's got a plush red tie and a match-

72

ing pocket square. He looks like a CEO or a governor or something like that. He sure enjoyed the attention and went around shaking everyone's hand as if it was a political rally. When I shook his hand, I remember feeling that he looked at me as if I was the only one there.'

'He sounds like quite a guy.'

'Remember what you said about icebergs?'

'It's all surface?' she said.

'Let's just say first impressions fade and cracks appeared after a while.'

'You don't like him?'

'Not much, no. I reckon he's a bit of a schemer, but if you talk to people around here, you'll get mixed opinions, like very mixed opinions. He helps with a few of the older folk, he's decent to them, so I guess he can't be all bad, although my dad didn't like him off the bat. When he first met him, he told me it was like shaking hands with a snake-oil salesman.'

'I can't wait to meet him.'

'That's if he'll talk to you,' I said, 'he's extremely private.'

'I'm sure I'll find a way,' she said.

I imagined her dressed up at a bar talking to some guy who was thinking he'd hit the jackpot. I reckoned she could ooze sex appeal if she wanted and if her bread and butter were bringing bad husbands to book, I figured she'd have no problem with Zimmerman. I recalled some of the things Barney told me about Zimmerman's conquests. If there's one thing about powerful men, they find it hard to keep it in their pants.

'It's not exactly easy to become a resident here,' she said, pinching me out of my daydream, 'you need money and references and things like that. Zimmerman obviously has money, do you know anything about how he got accepted?'

I shook my head, 'not really. I know he was friendly with Randall Osman at first, but later Osman opposed Zimmerman's proposal to become chair of the RCA. Why, is it important?'

'No, probably not,' she said.

'Just getting a feel for things?' I said.

'Exactly.'

She wrote a note and stretched her arms out in front of her, tucking her chin into her chest.

'Do you want to sit on the couch?' I said, 'it might be more comfortable.'

'Thanks,' she said, 'but no, I've got a few things to do.'

She stood up and placed her notebook in her jacket pocket.

'What next?' I said.

'I'm not sure. I'll have to talk with Jeff.'

'Well, I hope you find him.'

She looked momentarily as if she'd no idea what I meant, but I might have imagined it.

'Gene Hackman,' I mean.

She laughed.

'Who calls their cat Gene Hackman?'

I shrugged, 'a movie fan, I guess.'

We shared a chuckle.

'You've been really helpful, Matt.'

'Anytime,' I said.

She smiled and held out her hand. I shook it and led her out of the room and into the hallway. I opened the door; the sun had changed position in the time we'd be talking, and the glare from her car was not as pronounced.

'That's a sweet car,' I said, 'is it yours or a rental?'

'It's mine,' she said.

'You drove it all the way from California?'

'Yep,' she said, 'nothing like a road trip for purifying the soul.'

'I'll bet,' I said.

'Do you ever go back to California?' she said.

I hadn't been outside New Hampshire in about a year, and not to California for even longer.

'No, that was a whole other life,' I said, 'I kind of lost my way back over the years. There's nothing there for me.'

'There's always something in California,' she said with a wink, 'you should go back sometime, you never know what might happen.'

'Maybe one day,' I said noncommittally.

I began to stare at her car again. She noticed.

'It's not a typical chick's car' she said.

'I wasn't thinking that,' I said.

'In case you're wondering about it, my father and brothers are in the car business and I grew up around it. I spent most of my teens smeared with axle grease and engine oil. I've always liked muscle cars.'

She stepped off the porch and as she walked to her car, she stopped at my Hyundai Sonata sitting there in all its generic ordinariness. She tapped the hood.

'You get good mileage?' she said.

'I guess so, though I hardly go anywhere.'

'Oh, I almost forgot,' she said, reaching into her jacket and taking out her wallet. She handed me a business card.

'If you think of anything.'

'I'll call you,' I said.

She nodded and took one more look at my Sonata and said 'nice car' before waving cursorily and turning her back to me. She got in her car, put on sunglasses, and started the engine. The car revved and purred. It was perfectly tuned.

I stood there watching her. She reversed the car and, in a smooth sweeping maneuver, turned the other way and drove off. Her car moved on the road with ease and authority. I looked at my Sonata and felt totally inadequate, I was sure by 'nice' she meant sensible or something equally derogatory. I laughed; my car was exactly that. Soon after, another thought crossed my mind and made itself at home. There was no way in hell she was here to find Gene Hackman, so the question was, what was she looking for? I read her business card.

BETH BECKER
Private Investigator
(415) 537-3262
beckerb85@bluerock.net

I also have ways of finding out things Beth Becker, I thought as the sun sent lines of light through the birches, *better than Google, better than you. I'm the son of a coroner, finding out things is in my DNA.*

Chapter Five
The Lowell Exodus, Sacramento
to Clearwater 1987-91

Part One
A tale of three schools

Beth Becker's visit prompted me to think about a lot of things, mostly from my past. We all have secrets and things we're not proud of, and I am no exception. By the time I was fourteen, I'd been asked to leave two schools. I didn't think I was a particularly bad kid, but each time I sat with my parents in whichever principal's office it was, I was compelled to admit that I'd done something wrong. The first was St. Francis of Assisi middle school, and I was twelve. It was a dreadful school, rigorously academic but talk about strict. Mom had thought it would be good for my moral education to send me to a Catholic school. We were Catholics, but the occasional kind. Dad, whose focus lay in the details of death, said he'd seen more evidence for the absence of God than the alternative. 'The evil that people are capable of,' he told me one time, 'inclines me to think that there is no such thing as natural or spiritual justice. There are only things, good things and bad things.' My mom who had come from a more devout background tried her best to bring a religious dimension to our lives. When we were young, she made sure we said grace at meals and prayers before bed. She brought me to Fr. Daniels to train me as an altar boy, but I didn't take to it and Fr. Daniels realized before long that I wasn't what he was looking for. I suppose in a last-ditch attempt to protect me from the inevitable moral degeneration of my teenage years, she sent me to St. Francis of Assisi. My sister was in an all-girls Catholic school where Mom worked part-time. Bev was delighted when I was sent to St. Francis of Assisi and laughed her ass off the first time Mom paraded me in full uniform to the family.

I hated the uniform; it was stiff and uncomfortable. The whole school was like that. We sat at rigid desks, attended uninspiring lessons, and ate bland food. Sports were non-contact and extracurricular activities were limited to wholesome things like board games and music and ballroom dancing. If there's one thing for which I'm actually grateful about my time there is that I learned ballroom dancing, but that's about it. I endured just over two years there, but gradually my patience eroded. I found myself getting into trouble, or what the school faculty deemed trouble, personally I think it was a normal reaction to being cooped up with the entire cast of *Father Knows Best*. Eventually, it came to a head like an angry boil. My parents were invited to visit the school. A date was arranged, and Dad sat me down and explained why my schooling mattered to Mom. After he'd done his fatherly duty, no doubt at the behest of my mom, he gave me a wink and said, 'I never let my schooling interfere with my education'. I had no idea what he meant. 'Think about what I just said, son,' he said, rubbing my head. He always rubbed my head to let me know he wasn't angry.

On the day of my parent's visit (a euphemism for disciplinary-meeting) I remember sitting on a hard chair in front of the principal, a witch-faced old hag named Ms. Cassidy. She sat on a high back leather chair behind an enormous desk full of angles and points and fear. When she leaned forward, her chair would squeak and creak and groan. To her left, the school chaplain sat like a patient hound. His eyes were big and glassy, like a basset's. His gaze never moved from me the whole time, and it really gave me the creeps.

Ms. Cassidy spoke in the standard platitudes to my parents about how I seemed restless and that I might benefit from what she euphemistically called a 'new challenge' and they nodded and said nothing. The reason I was sitting in front of Ms. Cassidy and her dog was because I had become too easily distracted and that my teachers had found me difficult. I felt totally victimized as I had not done anything wrong like break a window or be cheeky or draw dicks on my books like some of the other boys. I think the faculty, much like Fr. Daniels, realised that I was never going to fit into their neat little godly microcosm and Cassidy had gotten fed up with their moaning and like Pilate had decided to wash her hands of me.

'Do you like it here, Matthew?' she asked, leaning forward.

Her manner reminded me of a predatory bird. I kept my head down and said nothing.

'Answer the principal son,' said Dad, his tone respectful of the situation but also gentle for my benefit.

I think everyone anticipated that I'd say something like 'I guess' or simply 'yes' but Dad's subtle tone liberated me and when I replied saying it was 'really boring' that was that. I was immediately asked to leave the room. The chaplain accompanied me and once we got outside, he told me to sit on another hard chair and then went off somewhere. I didn't see him again. About five minutes later, my parents left Ms. Cassidy's office and I stood up and we walked out of the school.

It was just before Christmas and the weather was cool but not cold. As I sat in the car, I was expecting a lecture on how disappointed my parents were and how Beverley never got in trouble, but it never came. Instead, Dad brought us to Leatherby's Family Creamery on Arden Way, where I had a banana split and Dad smoked Pall Malls. Mom looked at him and then at me like she was watching a tennis match.

'Thomas, aren't you going to say anything?' she demanded.

'Nothing to say,' said Dad, 'that school wasn't right for him.'

'Where's he going to go now?'

'It's almost Christmas vacation, we can find another school over the holiday,' said Dad.

Mom scrunched a napkin, and Dad gently placed his hand on hers to make her stop.

'I don't think getting worked up about it is going to do any of us any good, do you, Helen?'

He only ever used my mom's name when she was becoming agitated, otherwise he called her mother. She always called him Thomas, even when friends would come over and everyone else was calling him Tom.

Mom calmed down a day or two later and we had a wonderful Christmas. My uncle J.W. and his wife and kids came to visit from Texas. J.W. was Dad's older brother and was the football coach of the Texas Longhorns at the University of Texas in Austin. He was very pleased to hear that I was changing schools. He had three daughters, so I was the nearest thing he had to a son, and he had always hoped I'd play football.

'So, you going to come play for me in a few years,' he said to me discreetly at the dinner table one evening. My mom and aunt were yapping about something or other, but I still looked at her just to be sure she wasn't listening.

'Maybe, if there's football in my new school.'

'At a boy,' said my uncle, 'you just tell the coach you're my nephew and he'll draft you in right away.'

There was some pedigree in my family. My dad had been a decent tackle in his day, and J.W. played state. He just didn't make the grade for the NFL, but over the years many of the kids he coached went on to play in the NFL.

My uncle and his family stayed for five days and in that time, he showed me how to throw and catch and tackle. Dad just let us at it. I don't want to give the impression that Dad had no interest in my sporting development; it's just that he knew J.W. was better at it, besides I had never really shown any interest in football until that winter.

The following January, I found myself in Rosehill Middle School, where I lasted six months. Rosehill was much nicer than St. Francis of Assisi. For one, there was no uniform and a lot more diversity. Football season was over, but I tried out for baseball and did OK. I told the football coach who my uncle was. He said that I should try out in the fall semester for the under 14 team. I was beginning to really like my time there. The teachers were a lot more fun, and I settled down to my studies. I also made some good friends and for a while, it was like one of those idyllic school times you read about in a Stephen King book. But like a Stephen King book, pretty soon shit got weird.

In my group of friends, there was a Puerto Rican kid named Santiago Garcia. We were ordinary kids, not nerdy or geeky or preppy or anything like that. We just liked one another and hung out. There was a kind of cordiality among us. None of us were cool, and Santi was arguably the least cool of any of us. He was the son of an engineer and had four older sisters and a loud, wobbly mother who only spoke Spanish and only in the manner of someone reporting at the scene of a hurricane. She mothered him constantly, wiping his face, checking his hair and all that kind of stuff that was so embarrassing at that age. We didn't feel sorry for him though; he lived in a big house with a swimming pool and had the latest clothes and games. As summer got nearer and the weather became warmer, we would often go to his place to swim in the pool and if it was only the boys going, we would go to get a good look at his eldest sister Maria. Maria was eighteen and was lithe and graceful and would lounge by the pool sunning herself. After a while and when she knew all of us were looking at her, she'd stand up and stretch the full length of her body, accentuating her bust and butt before making an audible moan of satisfaction that made one of the guys almost have an accident when he heard it for the first time. Then she would slowly walk to the edge of the pool and dip her toe in before standing back and diving with the smooth curve of a seabird into the glistening water and disappearing under, only to reappear at the other end some moments later. She would then get out, tousle her ebony hair with a towel, and walk by us to return to her lounger. I can't tell you how many times I played that over in my mind as a teenager.

Santi knew what was going on, but he didn't seem to mind. You know how some guys get really ratty about their friends looking at their older sisters in that way, well, Santi was not one of those guys. I think he even preferred when it was just the guys over at his house, probably made him feel normal. He was a hard guy to know. He didn't say a lot and when he did, it was rarely anything revealing. He'd ask us about ourselves occasionally, but in a way as if he were gathering information rather than trying to form a relationship. At the time none of us thought anything of it, so when on a bright morning in early June of that year, just before the holidays, he arrived at school with one of his dad's handguns and shot up the place we were as surprised as anyone.

Once everything was over there were six injured students, three injured teachers and Santi dead of a self-inflicted wound to the head. I remember thinking that the days which followed were like a movie. School finished early for the summer and the day after the event I was taken down to the local police station and questioned about Santi's behavior. I went in the back entrance to avoid the assembled reporters out front. I told the cops what I knew and once they realized that I was no use to them, they sent me home where Mom had upped her Valium to two, maybe three pills a day. My dad was a rock and spoke a lot of sense about life going on and how sometimes kids take a notion and that while it wasn't a reason to scrap the 2nd Amendment, it was a reason for the politicians to take a look at it again. Mom kept saying that maybe it was time to find a new school. I think Mom screwed up that day because her wish was granted. I can't shake the feeling that she could have wished for anything that day, a million dollars, anything, but instead, I found myself yet again in front of a school principal.

Mr. Bryant was a nice guy, the exact opposite of Ms. Cassidy. He was fat and cheerful and wore a jacket he must have got at Goodwill, even though the school was well-off and I'm sure he earned a good salary. He smelled of cheap aftershave too, you know the type that comes in a bottle in the shape of a ship and smells like Glade. I had no idea what to expect when my mom got a call to bring me into the school as a matter of urgency. Dad was away in Boston at a conference, and she seemed so unsure of what to do. I thin in fact, I know, she was a little high. Anyway, we drove to the school and there I bumped into Davey Dillon, one of my and Santi's mutual friends.

'What?' I said as he passed me. He kept his head down. His parents flanked him as if he was a prisoner going to the chair. He looked up, and his eyes told me that something big had gone down. His father pulled him away before he could say anything and glared at me as if I were some sort of deviant.

We went straight into Mr. Bryant's office, where six months before I'd sat with all the hopeful optimism of the Dutch sailors who first saw Manhattan Island. It was different now. The air was pine fresh and subdued. I don't want to bore you with details, so I'll get to the point. Santi had left a note and in it, he talked about how he felt his friends, all of whom he named individually, had failed to hear his cry for help. The school counselor, a gaunt stick of a man, talked about the vulnerability of the teenage years and how I should have been more aware of Santi's mental state. I tried to call bullshit on this and pleaded that I knew nothing and had nothing to do with it. The counselor said something like for evil to prosper all that needs to happen is for good men to do nothing. It's a pity Dad wasn't there, as I think he'd have gone through the counsellor for a shortcut. It was a setup, plain and simple.

Mr. Bryant leaned across the desk and linked his fat fingers in front of his fat face.

'I know you're a good kid, Matt, but this is a serious issue and I'm sorry, but there will be consequences.'

'What kind of consequences?' asked Mom.

Mr. Bryant pushed back slightly and settled himself more comfortably in his chair. He looked up at the counselor and nodded towards the door. The counselor left and the room, for some strange reason, expanded as if it could breathe once more.

'I am reluctant to expel a student unless they have committed some serious transgression,' began Mr. Bryant.

'Expel' said Mom loudly.

Mr. Bryant put his hands up in an open gesture indicating that he had more to say and asked if he may continue. Mom nodded.

'I am not going to expel Matt, but the board and Santiago's parents want some sort of justice.'

He paused for a moment to gather his thoughts.

'As two of Santiago's sisters are still in this school, we have a duty to assist them in their return to something like normal life, and to do that we are asking the parents of those students named in Santiago's eh, note, to find alternative arrangements regarding their schooling. '

'Why can't the girls leave?' said Mom forcefully, 'why would they want to stay here after what's happened?'

Mr. Bryant flushed a little and puffed out his lips. He wouldn't look her in the eye.

'It's complex, and it's the board's decision and it's final. If you'd like to take it up with them, please feel free to do so.'

Mom was seething, but she held her tongue and soon after we got up to leave. Mr. Bryant in an attempt to soften the blow and in a genuine act of what he saw as kindness told me and my mom that there'd be no mention of this on my permanent record but that we would have to sign a non-disclosure agreement barring us from speaking to reporters or TV or radio. I was quite happy about this, especially since there was a permanent camp of reporters and photographers outside our house. Every hour or so, Dad would ask them politely to leave and they would shuffle a few feet back, but no one would go. I didn't mind too much as I spent most of the time in my room listening to music, but my mom and sister hated it. Bev was going into her senior year and found my quasi-celebrity intrusive and distracting. We fought for three days and then on the fourth morning she left the house to go to the library where she was getting a jump on her studies only to come straight back in and tell us the small media circus was gone. There had been a fire in a disused factory where a bunch of homeless people jungled up near Rio Linda, and I guess they'd swapped one tragedy for another. I suppose that's what reporters do; they chase tragedies. Turned out most of the homeless guys who died were veterans.

So, yet again the gnarled hand of fate had intervened, and I spent the summer thinking about uprooting to another school. In mid-July, about five weeks before the first semester commenced, Dad called me into his study. It was relatively rare to be summoned to the study and it always meant business, not necessarily punishment, but more of a heart-to-heart discussion. My parents were never physical with us, and Dad's voice never got louder than a firm baritone. He was a man in perfect control of his actions and his home. Mom wasn't, she was as jittery as a frog on a hotplate, as Grandpa Kentucky used to say. She was chugging Valium like Pez in those days. As I entered the study, I saw Bev sitting on a chair to the left of Dad's desk. I knew immediately she'd received some bad news, and her eyes told me that I was the reason for it. Dad invited me to sit down. He asked me how I was and then he took out his Pall Malls, put one between his lips and lit it. White and blue smoke swirled about his face, and threads of light from the window pushed through it like laser beams.

'I've found you a new school, son,' he said, 'a buddy of mine knows the principal and he's agreed to take you.'

'Where is it?' I asked.

'It's not too far, you should be able to take your bike, or the bus, it doesn't matter.'

I looked at Bev. She was facing away from me.

'Why is Bev here?' I asked.

Bev shifted her feet and sighed.

'Beverley has agreed to switch schools for her senior year to help you adjust to your new school.'

Bev had not so much agreed as been coerced in that gentle but unrelenting manner my dad possessed. He was incredible like that. He could persuade anyone to do anything given enough time, and what's more he did it so amiably. What he really did was blindside you with kindness.

'Now, son, you'll have to be especially thoughtful about the sacrifice your sister has made and to avoid any and all trouble that comes your way.'

I began to protest, not at Bev's 'sacrifice', but instead at the suggestion, even before I'd set foot in the school, that I'd attract trouble. I sometimes overheard my parents talking about me, saying I was born under a bad sign and I was unlucky and so on. I didn't believe it then and I don't believe it now, but my parents did. I think a lot of what happened to me over the years was a self-fulfilling prophecy.

'So, will you be a good boy and make it easy for me and Mom and your sister?' said Dad in his best Atticus Finch voice.

I nodded and he pulled hard on his cigarette and then extinguished it expertly, crushing the stub and folding it into the ashtray.

My remaining years of education at Ulysses S. Grant High School were relatively uneventful, however, Bev's final year was anything but.

.

Chapter Six
The peculiar neighborly gesture of Derek and Razor Anderson, April 2019

The day after Beth Becker's visit, I dropped over to Jeff's to ask him a few things about her. I was still doubtful that she was there purely to find Gene Hackman, and thought with a little casual questioning I might get Jeff to reveal a bit more. I knew Jeff had plenty of money, but private detectives are expensive and while I know he felt a great deal of warmth towards his feline companion, I also doubted that any cat was worth $200 a day plus expenses. When I got to his house, I knocked on the door and waited. I waited a few minutes more, but there was no one there. This surprised me. His car was in the driveway, and Jeff wasn't the type to sleep in or not answer the door unless something was wrong. The car being there meant it was reasonable to assume Jeff was there. I began to think about it, maybe he walked into town. It was a nice morning. Maybe he was pasting more notices around the place. Maybe he'd gone into town to meet Becker. I decided to check around back to see if he was in the garden.

I went around the side of the house and began to scale the gate. Each house has a side entrance into the backyard. It means you don't have to drag lawn and garden shit through the house. One of the first things I had to do when I moved in with Dad was to mow the lawn, front and back. Not because he said so, but because Art Tillman said so.

'You're Tom's boy?' he said by way of introduction.

'Matt,' I said, offering a hand.

'I've not seen you here before.'

'No sir,' I said, 'I've been down south.'

'Ah yes, your father mentioned you were in Florida.'

The truth was, I had not been in Florida, but I didn't want to extend the conversation any further. Tillman looked at the lawn.

'You'd best get on with tidying up the lawn,' he said, in the way a police officer might advise a motorist about a broken taillight. I almost said yes sir and, in my haste, (Dad had mentioned the RCA and the rules and so on and how I'd better not cross them), I didn't think to use the side entrance to bring the petrol mower out front and instead rolled it through the house where it leaked oil on the carpet in the hall. I was trying to get the thing started when Dad came out of the house hollering about the mess. Anyway, I tidied the mess and cut the front lawn and the back lawn. After that, I got rid of the petrol mower and bought an electric one. Nowadays, Jonestown employs a full-time gardener. Zimmerman insisted on hiring one. Obviously, we all contribute to pay his salary, which isn't really that much, but you better believe it created a bit of a fuss. People in The Family Zone were particularly irate at having to pay the levy as many of them had teenagers who would cut the lawn, for free, as part of their chores. This led to a debate about chores and how they shaped a young person's character. Zimmerman's counterpoint to that argument was that the lawns had to all look aesthetically similar and, furthermore, chores were beneath the kind of kids who would go to Harvard and become doctors and lawyers and future leaders of the country. That certainly got Trish Watson turned on, and she gushed and applauded Zimmerman's prescient statement.

'Did you hear that, Jim?' she said, turning to her husband, 'Harvard.'

Jim Watson, who, more by fault than design, had become the *de facto* spokesperson for The Family Zone could do nothing but smile at his wife and look sheepishly at the other husbands whose wives were seduced by Zimmerman's charm. The decision to hire a full-time gardener was voted in by a landslide. Now I get my lawns seen every other week. I like the gardener. As you might expect, he's not local. His name is Diego Jimenez, and he comes from Venezuela. He can speak English perfectly well but pretends he doesn't, that way everyone leaves him alone. I always give him a good tip, and once in a while he brings me a bag of weed for those nights I can't get to sleep. You'll get no negative comments about socialism from me.

The gate I was climbing is attached to the wall dividing Jeff's property from the Andersons. While scaling the gate, I used the dividing wall for support. I suddenly slipped and must have disturbed Razor. He came bounding towards me like the boulder in *Raiders of the Lost Ark* and began to bark like his nuts were caught in a vice. I'm normally quite agile, but my misstep meant I was caught awkwardly between the gate and the wall. My left arm dangled perilously on the Anderson's side. Razor was scrambling frantically trying to climb the wall. I knew if he managed to catch hold of my arm, he'd drag me into his territory and eat me.

'Razor, shut up, it's me.'

Razor jumped, and his jaws snapped so close to my arm a globule of his spittle landed on it. He didn't give a shit whether it was me or Jeff or the fucking President, he was in full-on psycho mode now, and I was doing my best not to overbalance. I tried backing down, but my foot was stuck. Razor, in the best display of his security skills, refused to be impartial. His job was to deter all intruders, whether he knew them or not.

At that moment, Derek Anderson emerged and whistled and ordered Razor to sit. Razor let out a short whine and sat and looked up at me and didn't take his eyes off me. Drool dripped from his mouth and I swear I saw his eyes glow. Derek sauntered towards me. He was wearing a droopy Lynyrd Skynyrd t-shirt that may well have been manufactured when they were at the height of their fame. He stood beside Razor, patted him on the flanks and looked up. He rubbed his chin and pushed his MAGA hat back on his head.

'Morning Matt,' he said, 'looks like you got yourself a situation here.'

'Hi, Derek,' I said.

Derek wasn't a man of many words, and probably fewer thoughts.

'Most folks around here use the front door,' he said.

'I know, I tried it, but Jeff didn't answer.'

'He's not there.'

'OK,' I said and added; 'how do you know?'

'You'd best come down,' he said, 'before someone sees you and calls the authorities.'

There was something in Derek Anderson's eyes that gave the impression he could kill you at any time. His left eye was slightly crooked so that when he looked directly at your face, one eye met your own while the other was somewhere over your shoulder. It was weirdly disconcerting because somehow both eyes followed you. I managed to free my foot and got down straight away, then went over to the Anderson's house. I assumed Derek was going to tell me where Jeff was, but after waiting for a few minutes and no sign of him, I decided to go home.

When I got back, I made some coffee and went upstairs to the guest room. It's at the side of the house and from the window, I could see into the Anderson's backyard. I stood there looking through the slats in the French blinds. They were tilted just enough to offer me some line of sight if I stood at a certain angle. I could see Razor lying on the grass licking his balls. He was really getting in there too. I couldn't see Derek and having had enough of Razor's grooming I drank a mouthful of coffee and went back downstairs.

Ten minutes later, there was a knock at my door. It was Derek Anderson. He came straight to the point.

'I can't rightly stop you from looking into my yard, just as I can't stop Jeff Simmons writing about me and my wife in the local paper. However, I can speak my mind, and, in both cases, I'd prefer if y'all took a more neighborly attitude in future.'

I didn't know what to say. I just stood there. Evidently, he was in the mood to talk. Truth be told, I was impressed by how articulate he was.

'Now, you asked me earlier how I knew Jeff ain't home, and perhaps I should have told you.'

He paused and rubbed his chin. He did that a lot when he was thinking.

'If you must know, earlier this morning, just after sunrise, I was taking my dog for a walk and I saw Jeff leaving with some pretty young thing in some kind of hot rod.'

A hot rod, I thought, *who the fuck calls a car a hot rod these days?*

'Was it a Firebird?' I said.

He stared at me. His wonky eyeball was somewhere over my left shoulder, and I stood back a pace to lessen the weird effect it was having on me.

'You know something about this?' he said accusingly and taking a step forward.

I shook my head; I knew saying no wouldn't do.

'His daughter drives a Firebird,' I said quickly, 'it was probably her.'

'Well, I don't know about that,' said Derek, 'but I can say for sure this woman wasn't his daughter, if you know what I mean.'

'I'm not sure I do, Derek,' I said.

'Well, I reckon you ponder it a while, it'll come to you.'

I nodded and then said; 'I thought you didn't like Jeff.'

He took another step forward, by now he was in my personal space. He's actually smaller than me, I stand at six feet, taller if I wear boots, and Derek is about five-nine, but the combination of his military past, weird eyeball, MAGA hat and the possibility he could go off at any minute made me believe that he was going to kill me.

'That ain't none of your business,' he said, 'the only business that you need to be concerned about right now is that Jeff is not home, and I'm sure he wouldn't appreciate you trying to get into his backyard without him knowin' about it.'

He stood back and flashed me a friendly smile, as if whatever madman had possessed him had suddenly left. I felt my butthole unclench.

'I didn't mean to throw a scare into you, but I'd appreciate it if you or Jeff or anyone did the same for me should you be in a position to prevent an intruder getting into my home.'

'I think Razor would stop anyone,' I said, trying to make light of the event.

'Anyway, no matter,' he said, 'just don't let me catch you doing it again.'

I guess it wasn't Jeff he was protecting as much as the neighborhood. He and Razor were a kind of self-appointed neighborhood watch.

'And before you ask,' he said without any threat or aggression in his voice, 'I don't know anything about that damn cat and neither does my wife, so don't go bothering us none about it no more.'

'I wasn't going to ask,' I said truthfully.

He looked at me closely again, tipped back his hat and said goodbye and left.

When he was gone, I blew out my cheeks and exhaled deeply. I began to think about what Derek had said about Jeff and the pretty young thing. It had to be Beth, she drove a hot rod, and she was pretty and young. I allowed myself a wry smile at the thought of Jeff hooking up with her. Private detective indeed.

I also made a mental note that the next time I need to get into Jeff's yard, I'd enter it via the unoccupied house between him and Mr. Snout.

Chapter Seven
The Lowell Exodus, Sacramento to Clearwater 1987-91

Part Two
Bev Lowell's hard choice

While I meandered into 8th grade with all the resistance of a leaf blown into a fast-moving stream, Bev met Joe Hayes, or more exactly, Joe Hayes focused his attention on Bev. Joe was the youngest of four brothers and lived with his mother and grandmother in a less well-to-do part of town. His older brothers were in blue-collar jobs and had wives and kids, and I think Joe had Bev in mind to join the club. Initially, Bev had no interest, she was devoted to her studies and late in the fall was maintaining the kind of grade point average that pointed to Harvard or Yale. Bev was set on doing social science, and her long-term ambition was to open a clinic where she could help treat drug addicts and lost souls. She wanted to save the world and in the idealism of her youth, she really believed she could. It was a big deal for Mom and Dad. Mom had gotten her education degree in a local college near where she grew up, and Dad had gone to Duke. The thought of having an Ivy-Leaguer in the family was something beyond exciting, it was transformative and sustained Mom through Bev's final year. In fact, when he suggested that Bev switch schools to help me adjust, Mom objected in a way I'd never seen before. Dad had to use all of his persuasion and strength to convince her that Bev's grade point average would not slip and now that things were turning out for the best all was well, but as it often was with my family, it didn't last.

In that first semester, Bev became my very own catcher in the rye. Within the flat-out craziness of her own life, she found time to help me with organizing myself and ensuring I got assignments handed in on or before their deadlines. She protected me as a big sister ought to but when I thanked her one afternoon, she said; 'I'm not doing this for you, I promised Dad I would, so count yourself lucky that I'm someone who keeps their word.'

The result of all this was that I'd begun to resist the pull of the stream and rather than drifting I found a kind of purpose. I met new friends and gained mediocre popularity among a small group of my peers, and once it got around that I had been friends with the Puerto Rican kid who'd shot himself, I developed some serious street cred. Cool people wanted to sit with me and have me recount the story of the shootings. The truth was that I had been late for school that day and was being processed when it all happened, so I didn't see a thing, but that small detail wasn't going to deny me. Truth was a malleable concept and as long as I was consistent and convincing, I could tell it whatever way I liked. The attention was like a drug, and I was riding the crest of a wave with Bev keeping me focused. I had the best of both worlds.

After the Christmas vacation, trouble began to peek over the wall of Bev's life like a meddlesome neighbor. She had initially rebuffed Joe Hayes, and he'd played it cool. I never understood his attraction to her. Bev was ordinary. She was average-looking (and that's without any brotherly bias), a good person, but not the life and soul of a party. She was typically a girl-next-door type, the sort you'd take home to your mother. She wore her hair up most of the time, and she wore glasses too. If you were looking for her, you'd find her in the library rather than at a pep rally. She volunteered at the local Salvation Army shop at the weekend, and she actually enjoyed the company of old people. I wish I could say something remarkable about her, but I can't. There were plenty of really hot girls in school and Joe could have had his pick of them, but I guess what made Bev stand out was her newness and, most importantly, the fact that she was not interested.

As chance would have it, my dull as ditchwater sister went to a party on New Year's. One of her friends threw a small shindig with fruit punch and fireworks and charades and other such wholesome activities. I'm not sure of the details, but Bev went along and when she came home later that evening, she was drunk. It was the first time I'd seen her that way. It was also the first time I saw Dad lose his temper. I mean, really lose his temper. They had a huge fight. Bev wasn't falling all over the place and puking or anything. She'd had a few shots of peach schnapps and the booze had given her a bit of fortification, enough to tell Dad to go to hell and that to stay out of her life. She slammed her door and locked it, and didn't emerge from it in any meaningful way for two days. On the third day, I bumped into her as she was coming back from the bathroom.

'What happened?' I asked.

'Get bent,' she said.

Despite being four years younger, I was much bigger than her. One of the many upsides of my new school was that I'd tried out for the football team and the coach had seen my potential. He had advised me to bulk up, and so three days a week I'd lift weights. I eventually became a starter at Strong Safety. Dad was quite impressed with my discipline, and Mom kept commenting on how big I was getting and how I was eating her out of house and home. Mom was getting better too, she was taking fewer pills but as ever with her, it didn't take much to set her down the wrong road and Dad feared that Bev's indiscretion might start bringing things to the surface again like poisonous bubbles. The truth is, it was my fear too, so when I had the chance, I confronted her.

'Get lost,' she said, trying to push past me.

I put my arm against the wall and held it there. She tried once more to push past me, but she couldn't, and so she gave up trying.

'What do you want?' she said, leaning against the wall and sighing in that desperate way people with loads of stress do.

'What happened the other night?'

'I had a fight with Dad.'

'Duh! I know that,' I said flatly, 'I think the whole neighborhood knows that. Why were you drunk?'

'I wasn't drunk.'

'OK, whatever, you sure as shit weren't sober.'

'I was a bit tipsy, that's all. Why don't you just butt out, it's none of your beeswax anyway?'

I looked her in the eyes. I could tell that she held me responsible for her confrontation with Dad. It disarmed me and, sensing her advantage, she pushed me out of the way and went into her room.

For the remainder of the holidays, it was tense at home, but everyone kept their dignity and distance and Bev's fight with Dad disappeared below the surface of our family life and didn't burst through the thin veneer keeping it there. Everything was stiffly polite at the dinner table, and Mom would make frequent banal comments about the weather or about the neighbors.

'I heard Vern Dickson across the road got a home computer, you should call over and see it, Matthew.'

'I don't know him too well,' I said.

'But you like computers, and it'd be a great way to renew your friendship with him.'

Mom was in a world of her own. For one thing, I did not like computers, at least not in the way she thought and two, Vern Dickson was the most aptly named kid on the street. No one liked him or his family. They were like a cross between *The Waltons* and *One Flew over the Cuckoo's Nest*. Vern Dickson who was about a year younger than me had called over to our house one time after a 4th of July street party. Mom described him as 'a very curious boy' and thought it would be 'cute' if we had a playdate. I found the afternoon a nightmare. He poked around all my stuff and told me all this bullshit about how his uncle had been to Vietnam and killed a bunch of people and saw whole villages burned down and had given him a tooth from a Viet Cong fighter as a gift. Vern Dickson was like a weasel, scurrying around my house looking at things and generally being a colossal pain. Eventually, when he tried to get into Dad's study it got a little bit much for my mom, and she brought him home. The day had been stamped on my memory with a branding iron. It appeared Mom had forgotten about it, or more likely, chosen to forget.

'I'll think about it,' I said to placate her.

And that was how dinner conversations went for the rest of my teenage years, polite but awkward, nobody really wanting to be there but everyone putting on a genteel face.

I sometimes wish I could go back and fix things, but I reckon Mom was too broken and things were about to get a lot worse with Bev.

*

When school resumed in January, Bev barely acknowledged me. In fact, she barely acknowledged anyone. I met up with my friends, and we regaled one another with stories about Christmas vacation. Although my story was nothing more than staying at home and hanging out, my friends appreciated that I was telling it. Most of them had been to Acapulco or The Caribbean. Dad's work, being what it was, meant that vacations were during summertime only, and anyway he was never one for sitting in the sun reading a book or sipping a cocktail with an umbrella in it. When he finished in Clearwater and moved to Jonestown, he said the best thing was the winter air. He would tell me that stepping out into the morning air on a bitter January with snow a foot deep and still rising was the closest thing to a real spiritual experience he ever had. It was his idea to move north. Most folks retire to Florida from the north, Dad did it the other way round, and he dragged poor Mom along too. She always liked the sun, but she preferred to make Dad happy.

At the start of the second week since the Christmas vacation, one of my friends took me aside after a gym session and said he had something really important to tell me. I got up off the bench and followed him into a changing room.

We sat at the back of the room. It was almost evening and most kids had gone home or were in the library.

'I just want you to hear this from me and not from anyone else,' said my friend.

'What?' I said.

He looked at me as if he'd something caught in his throat.

'What is it?' I said.

'Joe Hayes is going around saying he …'

My heart sank, my friend didn't have to complete his sentence, but after a short stammer, he did.

'S-s-screwed your sister.'

I didn't know what to say.

'I'm just telling you because you might have heard it on the corridor or something,' said my friend.

'It's OK,' I said, 'it's no big deal.'

My friend and I locked hands in an arm-wrestle grip and flexed our biceps. It meant that all was well between us and that I knew he'd done the right thing. He got up and left without looking back at me. I sat there for a few moments. A flurry of emotion was pulsing through me. I was envious and angry and confused and embarrassed all in one. Bev was eighteen, and I had a vague idea that she was sexually active, although given her hectic life I wondered where she'd got the time. I had only ever seen a pair of tits, but not touched any, and found the idea of Bev and Joe going at it strangely alluring and disgusting at the same time. Most of all, I was embarrassed and afraid that it would diminish my status if people started to refer to Bev as a slut or anything like that. I didn't want to become Matt Lowell, the brother of that tramp Bev Lowell. And yet within me, there was rising anger directed at Joe Hayes. I mean, how fucking dare he do that to Bev.

Over the next few days, I found out that the alleged event had taken place at the New Year's party and that Joe had spiked Bev's drink to get her in the mood. I began to wonder if my parents knew. Maybe they had some kind of spider-sense that parents have about these things, and that maybe that was why Dad got as close to angry as I ever saw. I mulled over it for about a week. During that time, I kept seeing Joe Hayes around the school. I'd never noticed him before that, but now he was like a bad penny, and it seemed the whole school had turned into him. It got so bad that in History class, Mr. Martin asked me a question about Gettysburg and I said 'Joe Hayes'. The whole class burst out laughing, and even Mr. Martin had a grin.

'I doubt Joe Hayes' achievements will amount to anything near those of General John Reynolds,' he said with a small chuckle.

'Sorry, Mr. Martin,' I said.

'It's quite alright Matt, try to keep up with us, please. It's wonderful to daydream, just do it on your own time.'

I really focused on controlling my thoughts in the wake of my mistake, but the aberration had lost me some of my street cred.

'I heard you got Joe Hayes on the brain,' said some older kids the day after that, 'just like your sister,' added one of them.

'I heard it was on her face,' said another, sniggering like a pig.

I didn't react, instead I made a mental note of who they were and spent that night lying in bed imagining what it would be like to beat them to a pulp. I'd had dark fantasies before and was worried they'd return. In the end, there was some ribbing for a while, but nothing that I couldn't handle. The rumors subsided, and Joe Hayes moved on to someone else and things settled down for a few weeks, in school anyway.

One Saturday morning in February, I woke to hear Bev getting violently sick in the bathroom. I looked at my clock, it was 7:22. I'd never heard anyone be so sick, it sounded like she was trying to bring up her ankle bones. I covered my ears with my pillow to block the sound, but immediately a terrible thought struck me. I jumped out of bed and made my way to the bathroom, where I tapped gently on the door.

'Bev, are you OK?'

There was no sound, but a few moments later she emerged in a cloud of heat that smelled like sour milk. Her hair was clinging to her puffy face like the tentacles of a squid, and her eyes were glazed. I had to move away from the awful smell emanating from the room. Bev moved to one side of the corridor and slumped against the wall.

'Are you pregnant?' I said.

I don't know why I asked it, it just came out. I can't say who was more surprised. The question seemed to jar Bev from her daze. Her head jerked up, but it was clear she was too exhausted from her exertions to answer me. I went over to her and helped her up and brought her to her room, where I made sure she got into bed. Once I knew she was resting, I went into the bathroom and cleaned it up. In her urgency, she'd got puke on the tiles all around the rim of the toilet bowl. Once I'd cleaned up, I sprayed some air freshener and went back to my room where I tried to sleep but found myself staring at the ceiling thinking violent thoughts towards Joe Hayes.

We lived in Arden-Arcade, a perfectly pleasant upper-middle-class part of town. Most of our neighbors were white-collar professionals and the Dicksons aside, everyone was benign and friendly. Hayes lived near Del Paso Heights, though I can't remember the exact address. It wasn't like downtown Detroit, but to a mild-mannered kid like me, it might as well have been. I toyed with the idea of finding out where he lived and defending my sister's honor, but my intention far outreached my power, and I lay there in impotent rage until there was a knock at my door.

'Mom,' I said, 'I'm asleep.'

'It's Bev, can I come in?'

I got up right away and let her in. She sat on my bed and waited until I was sitting beside her before telling me what she wanted to say. She looked and smelled a lot better. She sprinkled some cold water on her face, brushed her teeth, and dabbed some of Mom's perfume on her neck. It smelled of flowers and baby powder. She grabbed my hands and smiled.

'Thanks for tidying up the bathroom, I left a bit of a mess.'

'No problem,' I said.

Bev was never the sort to let anything stop her from speaking her mind, and she got straight to the point.

'I think I'm pregnant, and you can't say a thing to Mom or Dad, OK!?'

It wasn't a question, it was a vow to secrecy, the kind of vow that could never be broken.

'Was it Joe Hayes?'

She nodded. At least the rumors were true.

'Promise me you won't say anything.'

'Did he force himself?'

'No,' she said emphatically, and then her body shrunk into itself as if heavy with doubt.

'I don't remember.'

'What do you remember?' I said.

'Nothing much, the fireworks, a few shots of peach schnapps, and being alone with Joe. It was all a bit of a blur. One of the girls found me passed out, I figured it was the alcohol.'

'He drugged you,' I said.

'What?' she exclaimed, 'no he didn't.'

Bev's voice was becoming a sharp and breathy whisper.

'Seems to me he did,' I said.

'Forget it, Matt, there's nothing you can do.'

'OK,' I said, 'then what are *you* going to do?'

'Get a pregnancy test at Walgreens and if it's positive, I'll get an abortion.'

I remember thinking at the time how much sense she was making. She leaned in and hugged me. I was taken off-guard, but I didn't withdraw from the embrace. It was very short, but while it lasted it was comforting for both of us.

'Not a word to Mom and Dad, seriously, if you say anything I'll never speak to you again.'

'Scouts honor,' I said, holding up three fingers.

'OK,' she said, and went to leave. Before she opened my bedroom door, she turned around and looked at me.

'And stay away from Joe, remember I'm supposed to keep you out of trouble. Just let me sort this out on my own.'

I nodded, and she left my room and went back to her own with the quiet agility of a ballet dancer.

I managed to suppress my desire for vengeance and didn't cross paths with Joe Hayes. It turned out Bev was pregnant and about three weeks after her bout of morning sickness she had an abortion in San Francisco. She told Mom that she was going to an educational conference at City College in Ingleside. Mom believed her and later that evening when she came home looking tired and pale, she went straight to bed saying that she didn't feel well because she'd eaten sushi, and it was probably a bit off. Mom tried to talk to her through her bedroom door, but Bev said she wanted to be left alone to rest. I'm sure my parents knew there was something up, but they played happy families and when Bev came to breakfast the next morning looking a lot better, they were content to continue playing happy families.

Later that day Bev and I went for a walk into town where she told me what happened in San Francisco. She didn't give me the grisly details, but described how she felt like she was a cow at a slaughterhouse. There was no aftercare apart from a tin of soda and a sandwich and then a two- and half-hour bus ride home wearing an adult diaper and hoping it would hold. I had to admire Bev's strength. It was nothing short of superhuman in my eyes.

In the months that followed and leading into Bev's SATs, she gave the outward appearance that all was well, but inside she was crumbling. Her grade point average had dropped and when Dad remarked on it one evening, Bev's excuse was stress and that she'd been overachieving and that her current marks were much more in line with her true ability. Dad didn't buy it, he knew she was clever enough and hardworking enough to get into an Ivy League college and didn't want her to slip. Tensions rose once more between them and Bev, now becoming trenchant in her defense, began to blame our mom, saying that she'd inherited her anxiety and that the upcoming exams were all too much and that if people didn't leave her be she would do something crazy. Dad backed off after that. He was nothing if not pragmatic. It was like a pressure cooker in the house until Bev got her exam results.

She got through the SATs and to everyone's surprise, not least her own, got into Yale. It was definitely the highest point in Lowell family history, still is. No one in the family on either side had got into such a prestigious institution, and every aunt and uncle and cousin and grandparent and well-wisher descended on our house all through that summer and leading into the fall, when Bev would begin studying social and behavioral science.

'You nailed it,' I said, 'going to Connecticut. Talk about boring, though it suits you.'

'Yeah, the first in the family to go to Yale, talk about a big deal.'

'No pressure,' I quipped.

Bev smiled, but she was miles away. During the time leading up to Yale, Dad made frequent phone calls on Bev's behalf in the hope that it would help her assimilate better. Bev found the whole business was overwhelming her, and she became increasingly distant that summer. I tried to ask her what was wrong, but she'd say nothing. One afternoon, she was in the backyard. Mom was in town and Dad was in his study. I asked her straight out if the reason she was being weird had something to do with Joe Hayes. I said it a little too loud, and she gave me a withering glance. She jumped up and got right in my face.

'Shut the fuck up, do you want to tell the whole neighborhood?'

'Sorry, but you've been a bit of an asshole lately.'

'One word,' she said, her eyes were hard like knotted wood, 'just one word and that's it, I'll destroy you.'

I was petrified. True, I could have lifted her above my head and thrown her halfway down the garden, but the venom in her tone of voice cut into me like steel. She held my gaze for much longer than I wanted and then just as I thought a tear was forming in the corner of her eye she cut away and went inside. About two weeks later and about the same amount of time before she was to start in Yale, she backed out and went instead to a community college in Oregon and studied education. My parents put forward a united front and told relatives and friends and neighbors (depending on what lie they wished to promulgate) that Bev had changed her mind because she didn't want to leave her family or friends or simply that she wanted to follow the time-honored family tradition of becoming a teacher. People smiled, saying they understood the situation. They added that Bev was a good girl and that she'd have done very well at Yale, but that family tradition was so sacred, etc. I asked Bev why she had changed her mind, but she wouldn't tell me.

I spent my sophomore year lifting weights and playing football and finally getting a bit of action with girls, nothing to brag about, but let's just say life was much more interesting as a result. Bev would come home for the holidays, but she didn't stay long. She was hitting twenty and I was hitting sixteen. We were at that age where we were naturally drifting apart, and I was so caught up in my life that I didn't really notice. We spoke briefly and only small talk about trivialities, then less and less and eventually, we stopped speaking at all.

The summer before my senior year, Bev completed her degree in education, but still had to do a yearlong placement before she could qualify as a teacher. I was contemplating reading English with the view to becoming a journalist or something like that, but to tell the truth, I had no idea what I wanted to be. J.W. came to watch me play a few games, and although I played well, we both knew that I wasn't going to get a full scholarship. He wasn't disappointed though and told me there was more to life than football.

'You're better off finding out the truth when you're young,' he said, 'I saw guys bust themselves trying to make it and when they didn't make The Draft it was as if the lights got turned out. Some of them never recovered.'

Bev got a placement in Wisconsin in July of that year, and she took it. That was the last time I saw her until just before Mom died. She would speak with Mom on the phone a couple of times a week and whatever rules she laid down for Mom and Dad they didn't interfere, they gave her space. Lots of it.

Around the time Bev fled to Wisconsin, Dad got the job in Clearwater. We left Sacramento and I found myself wrenched from a familiar quiet life into an unfamiliar one. It wasn't until years later, long after Mom died, that Dad confirmed the reason why we left, but I recall vividly locking eyes with him as we were packing up the last boxes and loading them into the truck. *I know, son,* they said, *and now you know I know.* Of course, I might have been imagining things, but something told me I wasn't.

After that, I was glad to be leaving. It was time to escape.

Chapter Eight
The brief star-crossed life of TJ
Lowell, 1980

The night after Derek had caught me trying to sneak into Jeff's house, I had a strange dream. Now, I'd be the first to say that dreams do not predict the future or have any relevance to waking life, and that anyone who believed in that kind of stuff needed their head checked. Dreams were just the nightly activity of the brain as it sorted through the day's shit and to say otherwise was just stupid. I know a lot of people believe in astrology and Tarot Cards and stuff like that, and if you flick through the channels late at night, you'll see commercials for psychic this and psychic that. Call me a cynic, but I think it's a circus act, no more, no less. Sometimes it was done with style like a magician doing a trick but usually, it was done with a forked tongue and a serpentine smile. Mom was plagued by uncertainty throughout her entire life, and sometimes it led her to one of those snakes with a crystal ball. They would tell her she felt vulnerable and unsure, but there was a guiding light on the way in the form of a new friend or that her angel was standing behind her or some other bullshit. I don't recall there ever being any particular light in Mom's life. Not one that lasted anyway.

When I was a kid, there were some bad times. Every family has bad times, and I suppose it's how you deal with them that makes or breaks a family. Some families are strong and can weather even the worst storms, look at The Kennedys for example, they went through the wringer and still managed to do more for the country than anyone since Lincoln. Now, I don't want to get political or anything, but Dad would always lament the deaths of Jack and Bobby Kennedy. Sometimes when J.W. came to visit and Dad could get him off football. They retired to Dad's study and talked about the good old days. As I was the only boy in the house, Bev and J.W. 's daughters didn't want much to do with me, unless it was to torment me, Dad would let me hang out in the study while he and J.W. shot the bull.

'I wonder how this country might have been had Bobby survived,' he'd say.

J.W. who preferred Jack Kennedy would fire the first salvo of the debate, and soon they'd be discussing Vietnam and civil rights and Kentucky State and all sorts of things I didn't really understand but found totally compelling.

'That family was cursed,' J.W. would say.

Dad would nod in agreement.

'It was all Joe's fault. Joe Kennedy sold his family's soul so that Jack could become president. You reap what you sow.'

'And now look at things, the goddamn country is going down the shitter and that peanut farmer ain't going to fix it.'

I'm comforted that Dad died when he did. If he'd lived to see what was going on in The White House these days, he'd have been both outraged and sad. Although his mind was breaking with Alzheimer's by the time of Obama's election, I know he approved. His birth and death seemed to bookend an arc of progress in the history of America. He was born in 1933 in the middle of The Great Depression and died just after we elected our first black president. It seemed fitting that he lived between those events.

'Joe Kennedy got what he deserved,' J.W. would say, 'he buried three of his boys. Now I don't want to wish ill on anyone, but if The Almighty sees it fit that you live to see three of your sons put in the ground, then there must be some reason.'

Dad would nod sagely, but never comment on Joe Kennedy's fate.

The year I turned six and about four months before we got Billybird III, J.W. and Dad stopped talking about politics and fate. In fact, they didn't say much to one another for quite some time.

It was the year my older brother died.

Between Bev and me was our brother Tom, Jnr, or 'TJ', as he was known. In many ways, he was the perfect older brother. There was only a two-year difference, so we shared a lot of the same things and experiences. He acted as a shield against Bev and in my eyes seemed wise beyond his years. I am certain he'd have gone to Harvard had he lived and would probably be a doctor. He was Dad's favorite. There was no doubt about that. In those days before all the mental health awareness and soft liberalism you get today, parents, and especially fathers were often tough and direct. They spoke their minds, and they didn't give a shit who got bent out of shape about it. I don't want for one second to give the impression that Dad was in any way a bad father, he wasn't, he was the best man I ever knew, but while TJ lived, Bev and I played the supporting roles in the Lowell family movie.

TJ's entrance to the world had been difficult. He was a breech birth and had gotten caught up in the cord on the way out. Mom would say given how much trouble it had been getting TJ into the world that it was a miracle I'd been born. I know she meant it as a joke, but something in her voice told me the opposite. Anyway, the rest of TJ's life, until his death, was normal and healthy and filled with love. I know my parents regretted a few things in their later years, but they never second-guessed whether they'd given TJ a good life, short as it was.

When you're a boy and little, and you live in a happy family, your father is, at times, like an older brother. In those times, I felt like I had two older brothers. In the summer when school was out, Dad would take me and TJ to Los Angeles for a week while Mom and Bev went to Kentucky. Bev really got the raw deal and would always ask why she couldn't go. Dad's response was simply 'man stuff' and that was that. Try as she might get out of it, every July Bev found herself in the heartland of Kentucky surrounded by flat green monotony and the smell of manure while Dad, me, and TJ ate ice-creams and hot dogs on Santa Monica Pier or Long Beach.

At the start of July 1980 when we were just about to go on holiday, the body of a 12-year-old girl was found in the Los Angeles foothills. It was Robin Samsoe, and she'd been murdered by Rodney Alcala. Dad was asked to do the medical examination and holiday plans were put on hold until later in the month. That was until Mom decided we should all haul ass to Kentucky. I had only been a couple of times as a very small child, I think TJ might have been a few more times. Dad hated the farm. He hated the sticky humidity, the quiet, but most of all he hated my grandfather's racism. Mom's father was a dyed-in-the-wool conservative who thought nothing of speaking in hugely unflattering terms about blacks and Hispanics and Jews and Irish and anyone he didn't like on account of them being different. He'd never do this in front of us. When he took an interest in us, which wasn't often, he told us stories from the bible. I have a very vague memory of him saying something like, 'Therefore be ye also ready: for in such an hour as ye think not the Son of man cometh.' Bev would tell me years later of her experiences on the farm, and I'm glad Dad had intervened on TJ's and my behalf.

We spent a completely uneventful week with absolutely nothing to do other than play in the rolling wilderness of the farm and environs. There were no other kids, and I couldn't figure out how Bev stood it, except that she read a lot and managed to convince Mom to bring her into town every day.

On the second to last day of our visit, Mom and Bev went to Lexington for a day's shopping. Mom had said it was 'a special gift to Beverley for putting up so graciously with her troublesome little brothers.' In hindsight, I have to agree. TJ and I were a total pain in Bev's butt that week. Since we were boys and bored and restless, we focused our combined forces on tormenting her with such petty annoyances as putting spiders in her bed or frogs in the bathroom. We found a dead grass snake near a woodpile and put it in the toilet just before bed one night. About half an hour later when Bev screamed the house down prompting my grandfather to get his gun and almost have a heart attack, Mom bawled us out so hard that I began to cry. TJ said it was his idea (which it was) and apologized to everyone for the chaos he'd caused. TJ was good like that, even though he was only eight he had a refined sense of justice and would always own up if he'd done something wrong. I think that's what Dad really liked about him, his integrity. I certainly didn't share that quality with my brother. Dad never openly held that against me, but I'm sure in his darker moments he wondered why the universe had selected TJ and not me.

While Mom and Bev were in Lexington, TJ and me went exploring the woods near the farm. Mom had told us not to and had kept a keen eye on us, but with her away and our grandparents dozing in the heat, we decided it was a perfect time to see what lay within the tangled mess of branches.

This was the focus of my dream.

Dark trees, even though there's a bright, pulsing sun overhead. I can see TJ, he's just ahead, but try as I might, I can't make any ground on him.

He turns to call me. He's found something. I try to catch up with him, but the woods stretch into the distance, and then he's gone. I look around and there's no one there, just me and the trees.

I hear his voice as I feel the pull of consciousness.

That's not what happened.

I woke up with a start. I began to wonder why TJ had entered my thoughts after all this time. I hadn't thought about him in a while, and had not experienced that particular dream in years. I had it reasonably regularly for about eighteen months after the event, but it had diminished over time until by the time I'd finished elementary school I was scarcely sure it ever happened. Until it ripped through my sleep every once in a while, as it had just done.

I had read somewhere that dreams are the answer to a question you hadn't learned to ask. That's a bit new age for me, but it set me thinking not about TJ, but about Mom.

In the week after TJ's disappearance, a local woman who was a friend of a friend of Grandma's came to visit the farm. At first, she was there to act as a comfort to my grandma and to help around the house while all of us were caught in a spiral of bewilderment.

'What happened, son?' the Sheriff asked me.

'He was there, and then he wasn't,' I said.

Now tell me everything you remember.

The woman's name was Lottie Baylock and in the short time she spent with us, she and Mom spoke in private a lot. My grandma said Lottie had a gift, that she could see things and that The Lord worked through her. My grandpa's opinion was much more cynical. I guess that's where I inherited mine.

Dad arrived the day after TJ went missing and immediately got to searching the woods and assisting the sheriff's department. I remember the local deputies being a bit put out when the FBI got involved.

'Damn Bureau,' I heard them say, 'think they know it all. They don't know shit.'

A specialist team that dealt with child disappearances and abductions came in from Louisville. As they descended on the farm, most of the local law enforcement hung out and drank coffee and spat on the dry earth and continued to pass comments about the Feds and why they were needed on a simple missing person case. I didn't know at the time, but the FBI was there as a courtesy to my dad.

The day before TJ's body was found, Mom and Lottie Baylock were sitting in the kitchen. Mom had given Lottie one of TJ's shirts, and Lottie was channeling him through it. It was dusk, and I sat with Bev on the porch, staring listlessly at the line of light as it shrank into the emerging night. We didn't say anything. We just sat and held hands.

Dad came back from the woods and when he saw us, he gave us a big hug. We knew what he was going to say. His face was impassive, but his eyes were hollow, as if the light inside him had been extinguished.

'No sign kids,' he sighed, 'sorry.'

Bev tried to smile.

'Maybe tomorrow,' she said.

'I hope so, Bev,' said Dad, and then said; 'where's your mother?'

'Inside with Grandma's friend,' said Bev.

Dad nodded, but you could see instantly that his demeanor had changed from soft and caring and paternal to hard and focused. He didn't say another word until he got into the kitchen and then, in a raised but controlled voice, I heard him ask Lottie Baylock to leave.

'She's here to help,' said Mom loudly.

'Help,' said Dad, 'how is giving you false hope helping?'

We didn't hear the rest as my grandma ushered us away from the scene and brought us to the barn, where we waited until Lottie Baylock left.

When we returned to the house, Dad was sitting calmly in the living room smoking his Pall Malls. My grandpa was chewing on his pipe like a dog with a bone, and Mom sat by the window looking into the dark. No one spoke, in fact, no one said anything until Dad said it was time for us to go to bed.

The next day, they found TJ's body. It was exactly where Lottie Baylock said it would be.

Chapter Nine
Ocean Drive 71597, 2015-present

I called Beth Becker on the afternoon of Friday the 19th. A few more days had passed without sight or sound of either Gene Hackman or Jeff, not that it really mattered. I wasn't concerned about them. The cat was probably dead. If he was alive, wherever that was, he was happy there. There wasn't much point in dwelling on it. As for Jeff, well, I reckoned he was in a motel somewhere drinking Chablis and popping Viagra and having the time of his life with Becker or whoever the young thing Derek Anderson had seen him with. The upshot of my fervent imagination was that when I made the call, there was a dash of jealousy in there. I was hoping to at least interrupt them. The phone rang for about twenty seconds before she picked up.

'Beth Becker.'

'Hi Beth, it's Matt, Matt Lowell from Jones ... from Riverside Falls. Jeff's neighbor.'

'Hi Matt, I was just thinking about you.'

Liar, I thought. *What would she be thinking about me for?* I suddenly began to think of those skeletons from my past. I took a swift breath through my nose. I was being stupid, she didn't know anything, and if she did, it was wrong.

'Isn't that a coincidence,' I said, 'all good I hope.'

'What's on your mind, Matt?' she said in that professional no bullshit, let's get to business voice.

I have to admit, she was difficult to read. It was obvious to me that looking for Gene Hackman was a cover, but for what, to carry on with Jeff, surely not? Why would she need a cover to jump Jeff's bones? I dismissed the thought. OK, if it was something else, it had to do with me or Jonestown. I decided to focus on the latter. There was no point in doing anything about the former unless I had to, and I had managed to avoid suspicion up to now, so why not indefinitely? I heard somewhere that your sin eventually finds you, that may be true, but isn't there an exception to every possibility?

'I had a thought about Zimmerman,' I said.

'What is it?'

I waited a fraction longer than normal to answer. In my experience, the extra second allows for some interesting thoughts to germinate. It allowed me time to work out where I was going with this.

'Have you spoken to him yet?'

'No, I've been busy with other things.'

'Any news on Gene Hackman?'

'No,' she said trying to suppress a giggle, 'such a silly name,' she added.

'I haven't seen Jeff in a few days, he normally lets me know if he's leaving for anything longer than a day.'

She said nothing.

'So I know to feed the cat,' I continued, 'but I guess since the cat's gone, Jeff has no reason to let me know if he's going anywhere.'

'Is there a point to this?' she asked.

I could hear a hint of agitation in her voice. It was time to see if she was willing to play. I got to the point.

'The annual RCA dinner is coming up. It's usually the Saturday before or after May 1st, that's the date the community was officially opened in 1994.'

There was no sound from the other end.

'Anyway, it's at Zimmerman's house on the 27th and I thought we could go together. It'd give you a chance to get a feel for Zimmerman and the rest of the residents. If nothing else, it's a good night out. He gets excellent caterers and champagne and all that.'

'Are you asking me on a date, Matt?'

The edge had gone out of her voice, and in its place was a barely concealed layer of incredulity, as if I'd sideswiped her.

'Not exactly,' I said, 'more of an undercover thing, you know surveillance and all that.'

'Some intrigue, you mean?'

'If you like,' I said, 'but if you're uncomfortable with us going as a couple, you could always say we're cousins. I suspect you're pretty good at pretending.'

She laughed.

'Cousins, that's good, but wouldn't that be more of a southern thing?'

'I thought it wasn't a date.'

She laughed again.

'It's not,' she said, 'it's not anything, Matt.'

'Well, I thought it was a good idea. But if you'd prefer to just roll up to Zimmerman's door and ask him a bunch of questions you can, though I don't think you'll get very far.'

'You don't think that would work?'

'He's very private,' I said, 'and besides I've seen more than a few pretty women leaving his place.'

That's not true. I'd seen nothing, how could I? I live in a different part of the neighborhood. Barney had seen a few things, and I was employing a bit of creative license based on what he had told me.

It seemed to raise her hackles.

'What's that got to do with anything?' she asked.

121

'Nothing really,' I said, 'just that if you had planned on getting all flirty with him, you might be left disappointed.'

I imagined her saying *well fuck you!* In her mind.

'Flirty,' she said as if it tasted bad.

'I'm not sure exactly what techniques you use when you're catching cheating husbands, but I assume there's a certain amount of flirting involved.'

'I have no problems finding out what I need to know from men, young or old, and Zimmerman will be no different.'

I bet you don't.

'Well, as I said, the offer is there. I just thought it might be a different approach, sorry if it's not my place to suggest these things.'

My final comment was added to convey a sense of naivety. It worked.

'I guess your heart is in the right place,' she said, before adding; 'I'll consider it.'

'Could be fun,' I said.

'Thanks for the call, Matt.'

'My pleasure,' I said and hung up.

There was no point in continuing the conversation.

I decided to get back to my blog and wait for her to call back. I was sure she would. One of my guilty secrets is that I write a blog. It's tips, advice, anecdotes, and such about the good life and how to live it. I'm a bit of a fraud as I don't actively live the good life, but I know people who do. I pick their brains and put it on the web. The rest I make up. I know it's not the career in journalism I'd considered in my high school years, but it pays the bills and probably has a wider readership than I might have had if I'd been a journalist for a local paper. I doubt I'd have had the determination to work my way up and write for the big papers.

The blog was Jeff's idea. About six months after he'd moved to Jonestown, he dropped by for a beer. It was summer and the air had a lazy feel like a slow-moving riverboat. I was telling Jeff about how I'd considered becoming a journalist and that part of me regretted not following through on it. He told me that it was probably for the best and that I had avoided a testing fate.

'It was hard in my day, but now it's almost impossible and besides print is dead or dying at least. Everything is online and everyone's got an opinion and what's more, they think it's just as good as the next guy. Also, Obama's government has put gags on investigative stuff. Protect the corporations at all costs.'

'No way?'

Jeff nodded, 'they're all in cahoots with the corporations, democrats, republicans, it's all the same. Anyway, that's no big deal, the real problem is social media.'

'That's the thing about the internet,' I said, 'it gives everyone a voice.'

'Maybe, but the question is, should it? I mean I can write a little, OK, better than a little, but I worked with guys who were real wordsmiths, most of them sportswriters. They could bring a game to life in ways that even Norman Mailer and Joe Heller would struggle to match. You could smell the leather of the ball just by reading their words.'

Jeff had drunk about four or five beers at this point and his voice grew sentimental, he had managed to dampen a potential anti-government rant and turn it towards better times.

'These guys would write ten-thousand-word articles for *Sports Illustrated* or *Inside Sports* before it went bust, and their words would take you on to the field or in the locker room or the boardroom. It didn't matter which sport; they could write about it in a way that made it come alive.'

'I should read some of those articles,' I said.

'If you have time,' said Jeff, 'but don't go in half-hearted, you have to commit to them. That's the problem today, most people don't have the time to read a long piece of writing. They want bite-sized chunks of information, not the whole picture, just enough to see if they want more.'

'People are busy,' I said.

'The hell they are, they just think they're busy. Did you ever play baseball?' he asked.

'Football,' I said, 'in high school.'

'Pity,' he said, 'baseball is America's true sport. Football is good, but it doesn't have the finesse of baseball. Baseball is art.'

I told him who my uncle was, as I wasn't really in the mood for a long-winded appreciation of baseball, even if he was right.

'J.W. Lowell, Cowboys defense coach?' he said.

J.W.'s success with the Longhorns had brought him to the attention of the Cowboys, who hired him as a defensive coach. He helped them win three Super Bowls in four years in the 90s, and then he retired. I suppose once you've won it all, what else is there to do?

'He might have gone on to become head coach,' I said, 'but he was about 65 or so by the time they beat Pittsburgh in '96, and I think he was worn out.'

'I have an archive in my house,' said Jeff, 'clippings of every article, by-line, sentence, every single word I ever wrote, and I must see if I ever wrote about the Longhorns or the Cowboys during your uncle's time. I can't recall if I did, but maybe I have something.'

He never found anything about my uncle. He did, as it turned out, find something much more interesting, but that's for later. Before he left that evening, he suggested that I write something and see where it took me. I asked him what I should write about. He said anything I wanted, it didn't matter, just write and write regularly.

'Why not try one of those blogs,' he said, 'my younger daughter has a yoga blog, she even makes money from it.'

I didn't exactly need money. Dad had provided generously in his will, but I felt I had been plundering that for a little too long and that if I earned my own money, it would give me a sense of accomplishment.

I was excited by the challenge and took to it with enthusiasm. I had no idea what to write, and what came out naturally was my life story. As it developed into a memoir, I realized there were plenty of people I'd met over the years who had interesting views on life and my memoir became a blog that ruminated on life, the universe and everything else. I added some yoga and fitness too because people often look for that stuff. It wasn't really me though, but once a few dollars began rolling in, I was happy to pretend and that's how it was for a few years.

About six years ago, Gretchen Sweetman became the final piece in my blog jigsaw. She developed my writing from patchy remembrances of things past with health advice into something much more sophisticated and profitable. As you might recall, Gretchen is a consultant with Dior. She comes from money and perfumery and cosmetics is a hobby. The rest of her life is typical of someone from that background. She was a socialite, married young, got out of that quickly, lived the life and then decided to do something more meaningful with her time, got into beauty, made a name for herself, married another old guy, got herself a house in Jonestown.

When she moved in, we hit it off right away. There was no sexual attraction, though she's seriously sexy. As I recall, no one took any real interest when she moved in, so I decided I'd be her welcoming committee. I brought a bottle of red and a bottle of white. Both French and both expensive.

When she opened the door, it was clear she'd already begun her own welcome party. She greeted me effusively in French. I thought it was wonderful to hear such provocative sounds coming from such an elegant woman. I introduced myself, and she invited me in, and we sat and drank wine and talked for hours. She told me about herself and her travels and I told her about my life, not that it had the glamour or range of hers, but she found it charming. When she asked me what I did for a living, I told her I wrote a blog.

'How modern,' she said, 'you must show me.'

We had a look at it, and she liked it.

Over the next month, we met frequently, usually at her house, and it was then she advised me to write about the kind of life people wanted, not the one they had. My blog with its mix of homespun wisdom and amusing anecdotes was good for a laugh and had an appeal to my readers, but to really grab people, Gretchen said you had to get them to reach for something. Not just thinking, but wishful thinking, she said.

She used her contacts in the beauty industry, and soon my blog went from discussing the merits and demerits of meditation or getting a good night's sleep to reviewing and promoting the latest Tom Ford fragrance. I began to acquire all kinds of nice things, from the clothes in my wardrobe to the fancy cooking utensils Beth Becker had commented on.

My original blog had been called *Mens sana (in corpore sano)* — healthy mind, healthy body. I know, a little uninspired. I thought the Latin element was hip, but it was just stupid in retrospect. Gretchen and I started thinking of names for my new blog and after a few bottles of wine, I decided to name it 'I would only have shot Versace in the leg.' I explained to Gretchen that I'd been in Miami when Gianni Versace was murdered. I was enjoying my own joke when I noticed that Gretchen wasn't joining in. I could tell by her expression that she found it in bad taste, and the mood of the moment changed instantly.

'Bad joke,' I said.

'It was so sad,' she said, 'such a waste, you know I met him.'

'Versace?'

'Yes, at an after-show in Milan. He was such a doll. He made sure everyone was having a good time. He couldn't have been more accommodating.'

Gretchen called everyone she liked a doll.

'That boy who shot him was so troubled, it was so tragic, all of it.'

I never met Versace or Cunanan, but I knew a guy who'd had a few drinks with Cunanan about a month before the murder. He told me that Cunanan had told him he was going to be famous and that the whole world would soon know his name. I guess he was right, for a while.

'He shot himself about a week later,' said Gretchen.

I knew the timeline in detail, but didn't want to interrupt. It was rare to see Gretchen somber, but this had touched a nerve. Typically, she didn't stay down too long, and we opened another bottle of wine. She wasn't convinced about the name; she said the title must be subtle and if anything must honor Versace rather than poke fun at him. We went back and forth suggesting names until eventually, we settled on 'Ocean Drive 71597', referring to the place and date of Versace's murder. It fit perfectly.

*

While I waited for Beth Becker to call, I finished my piece on the ongoing debate as to what fragrance JFK wore. There's no need to include the whole post, so here's the relevant information.

...There's a romantic story that on a trip to the French Riviera in the summer of 1937 by chance he got talking to a Parisian perfumer named Albert Fouquet and became instantly captivated by the Frenchman's scent. JFK managed to persuade Fouquet to leave a sample of the cologne at his hotel. It arrived the next morning with a short note that read; 'in this jar, you will find the dash of French glamour that your American personality lacks.' Upon his return to Paris, Fouquet received a letter from JFK thanking him again and telling him of how popular the fragrance was with his friends. He asked Fouquet to send eight more samples and one for 'Bob'- JFK's younger brother Bobby- Fouquet labelled the shipment EIGHT & BOB and within a short time, he was receiving requests from Cary Grant and Jimmy Stewart who'd discovered the fragrance through Joe Kennedy. Sadly, Fouquet died in a car accident, but his faithful butler Philippe ensured that the fragrance and its formulation survived the war.

The other, less interesting story is that JFK wore Creed Vetiver, not the modern one in the green bottle, but a more refined version formulated in 1948. As I write, I have EIGHT & BOB on one wrist and Creed Vetiver on the other. Both are elegant and refined, and it's easy to imagine the 35th president wearing either of them, but if you want my two cents, I'll just say this; I prefer the EIGHT & BOB story but if I was going to a wedding or even dinner with friends, I'd wear Creed Vetiver every time.

I posted the piece and within an hour received an email from Gretchen telling me she'd enjoyed reading it and to update me on any Jonestown news.

TO: gretchen@sweetman.net
SUBJECT: Le chat perdu

Hi,

Jeff's cat, you know, the big bushy tailed one, went missing about three weeks ago. OK, so cats go wandering, sure, but this is unusual, so unusual in fact, that Jeff has hired a private detective. Now, if you have some idea of Peter Falk chewing a cigar and saying 'just one more thing' I can tell you this is unequivocally not the case. First of all, the PI is a woman and a knockout at that. She questioned me earlier in the week and I have to say it was quite pleasant, although she's got a bit of a no-bullshit air about her. She also drives a Firebird. I have absolutely no doubt at all that whatever she is, she's no PI. Derek Anderson (weird guy, MAGA hat, looks like his parents were brother and sister) said he saw Jeff getting into a hot rod with some pretty young thing on Tuesday morning, AND to add intrigue to intrigue I haven't seen Jeff since. Can you imagine Jeff in some motel somewhere? Anyway, if he is banging her, he's one lucky guy. The old dog.

Other than that, there's nothing else to report. Oh, the PI lady's name is Beth Becker. I can't find out anything about her online. I might ask Rohit to do a bit of digging. I've asked her to Zimmerman's RCA dinner on the 28th. I've suggested it's the only way she'll get to talk to Zimmerman in person. She seems a little reluctant, but I know she's thinking about it, and I'm hoping she'll agree. I'll let you know how it goes.

Are you coming home soon?

Best,

M

PS: Thanks for the kind words on the JFK post. It's already taken off. Make sure your Creed contact reads it.

Rohit's an Indian guy who follows my blog. He is absolutely nuts for colognes and perfumes. He sometimes sends me pictures of his collection. He's got about five hundred bottles. He works in IT and has helped me with the design of my blog and other software things, but his real usefulness is that he does a side-line on the dark web. Before you get all judgmental, he doesn't traffic women or kids or any of that fucked up shit, instead, he finds out things for a fee. I decided to email him straight away. It normally takes him a while to sift through the swamp, so I wanted to give him some time to dig.

TO: RohitIshant@lotus.net
SUBJECT: Research

Hi Rohit,

I just got a sample of Tom Ford's latest fragrance; it's not going to hit the shops until July, but it's all yours if you want it. In return, could you do some research for me?

Matt

He replied instantly.

TO: lowellm74@usa.net
SUBJECT: Research

Hi Matt,

Sounds good. Could you mail the sample to my work address? Please use usual channels to submit research queries.

Rohit

I had a separate and (according to Rohit) unhackable email account for research queries. Still do.

Chapter Ten
Faith v Reason, 1980- present

Mom said that Neptune in Aquarius in the 8th house indicated death by drowning. Lottie Baylock had drawn TJ's chart and found he had exactly that combination. She told the search teams to look for water, particularly shallow water. I remember Dad saying that a person could drown in two inches of water. This fact made him ever vigilant during trips to the beach. Dad taught us how to recognize riptides and what to do if we got caught in one. As a result, we all became good swimmers, particularly TJ.

I'm sure the irony wasn't lost on Dad when they found TJ in a creek bed about a mile from the farm.

'Can you tell me once more, son, what happened when you went into the woods with your brother?' said the lead investigator.

I noticed that he called me son the same way Dad would. He was short and stocky and had a thick mustache. A sheen of sweat glistened on his forehead. He wore a blue suit and on his lapel was a badge that read FBI. I knew the letters, but I thought it was a word, and I didn't know how to pronounce FBI. In my mind, I sounded it out as fuh-buy.

Mom and Dad were with TJ at the hospital. Bev was with Grandma on the porch. I was sitting in the kitchen on a chair that was too big for me. My legs were dangling from the hard oak and hot golden light streamed in through the window. The FBI man went over to the fridge and took out a coke, which he opened and offered to me. I took the bottle from him, and its coldness jarred me. I slurped a sparkling mouthful right away. The bubbles stung my throat.

'You see, we need to know exactly what happened, son, just to be sure it was an accident.'

'It was an accident,' I said emphatically.

'OK,' said the FBI man, 'it's OK son, don't worry about it.'

He was resting on his hunkers just in front of me. I didn't mind that because his face was kind, and he was speaking calmly the way Dad would. I gulped down some coke, and it made me belch involuntarily. The FBI man and his colleague who was also in the room laughed. It cut through the tension I felt building in my body.

'Now, you said you and your brother were in the woods when he started chasing a critter of some kind.'

I nodded without breaking eye contact with the FBI man.

'A squirrel,' I said.

'Are you sure, maybe it was a chipmunk, they sure are hard to tell sometimes?'

'No,' I said firmly, 'it was a squirrel, a big one.'

'I can remember doing the same myself when I was a boy,' said the FBI man, 'sure was a lot of fun. Never could catch them though, they were always so darn fast the way they'd scurry up a tree.'

He did an impression of a squirrel climbing a tree and gnawing on a nut. It made me laugh. After a moment, he returned to the narrative.

'You said you were trying to keep up, but you fell and when you got back up your brother was gone.'

I kept quiet. The FBI man turned to his colleague.

'It's the same story, he hasn't deviated from it all week.'

'Must be the truth.'

'The FBI man got up off his hunkers and tousled my hair.

'You're a good boy, thank you for helping us.'

I got up to leave, but he gently pressed my head back onto the chair.

'Stay and finish your coke, you've earned it.'

I took another swig from the bottle and the two men left the room. My eyes moved over the domestic environment. The room was old and smelled mostly of cooking and the wildflowers my grandma would keep in a growing box on the window ledge. There were marigolds and coltsfoot and dogwood. Their soft bouquet gave the air a hint of talcum-powder sweetness mingled with the dry scent of the earth. As I gazed absently around, my eyes suddenly fixed on the table and the astrology chart that Lottie Baylock had shown Mom the night before. I was fascinated by the lines and symbols and followed them over the page. Lottie had used a pencil for much of the chart, but she had also used a red marker. I only knew that red markers were for bad things. Sometimes my teacher would use a red marker if I got a spelling wrong. Sometimes she would make a big X mark if I got a math problem wrong. I was so engrossed by the chart that I didn't hear my grandma come into the room, and even when she put her hand on my head, it took me a moment to realize she was there.

She was smiling a wrinkled smile. Her face showed tiredness.

'What's this?' I asked, pointing to the chart.

'It's just a picture my friend Lottie drew for your mom.'

'It's pretty,' I said, 'what does that word mean?'

My grandma studied the chart.

'I don't know, honey,' she said.

'It looks like a map?'

'I suppose it does.'

'Why was my daddy angry last night?'

Grandma brought her hand up to her face. She was holding back tears. Outside I heard my grandpa cough and then spit with a resounding splat followed by a curse word. He wasn't particularly concerned with the emotional nature of the situation. He was more inconvenienced by the presence of federal agents on his property. It had made him more ornery than usual.

'Sometimes grownups don't think the same way as one another,' said Grandma, 'and your daddy didn't like the way my friend was trying to help your mom.'

'To find TJ?'

'Yes.'

I pointed once more to the chart.

'Is that a map to where TJ is?'

'My friend thought maybe it was, and your mom thought the same.'

'But not my daddy.'

Grandma shook her head and the wrinkle of her smile quivered.

The autopsy revealed that TJ had fallen from a height of about fifteen feet into the creek and been carried slowly downstream to the creek bed. His body was badly damaged from being bounced off rocks and dragged along the creek bottom. There were signs of predation from fish and small animals too. According to the pathologist who examined TJ's body, TJ was unconscious when he went into the water. The blow to the head he'd received from the fall meant he never regained consciousness. I guess it was a small mercy to my parents.

The fact that Lottie Baylock had accurately predicted where TJ's body would be raised eyebrows among the FBI men. They questioned her and were becoming suspicious, but ultimately, it was Dad who told them to leave her alone. Dad was a man of hard science and had accepted the tragic and accidental nature of his son's death. He had viewed TJ's body (he wouldn't allow my mom to and had her removed from the mortuary when she asked to see it) and seen evidence that concurred with the medical examiner's observations. It was an accident. TJ fell, hit his head, and drowned. Much, much later, when Dad finally opened up about it, he told me that it was more difficult coming to terms with the fact that people like Lottie Baylock had special insights than the fact TJ was dead.

Mom, on the other hand, grew increasingly devout. It seemed paradoxical that someone who'd lost a child would be able to reconcile it to their faith, but she did. Though she never spoke about it to Dad, she would tell me when I'd listen (or pretend to) that God never gives us more than we can handle. I didn't believe that then, and I certainly don't now; but it got Mom through a lot of bad days. I occasionally wonder if she thought Billybird III possessed something of TJ's spirit. I remember when we went to the cat shelter to pick out a cat, she fixated on him right away. There were much prettier and more affectionate cats, but Billybird III had something Mom felt instinctively. She was drawn towards him. She never said so explicitly, but she wanted him and only him.

We never went back to Kentucky as a family after that. Mom went once a year. Alone. While Mom was away, Dad would take me and Bev to San Francisco on day trips. He'd clear his schedule and devote himself to our happiness, usually at his inconvenience. What he never found out and what I never told him was the truth about why Mom went back to Kentucky. She was consulting with Lottie Baylock.

'Your father never understood, he never tried to understand. It was too much for him to acknowledge that there are things his science could not explain,' she said years later.

I only found out by accident myself. In the weeks leading up to Mom's death, I traveled to Riverside Falls to help out. Bev had spent about a month trying to track me down and was resentful of being the one who had to put her life on hold. When I tried to explain that she was only traveling from Wisconsin whereas I was traveling from Oklahoma, she told me to shut the fuck up, quit whining, and accept my responsibilities. I could have refused and stayed put, but I knew if I was ever to reconnect with my sister, I would have to do things I didn't want to.

When I finally arrived disheveled and really in no fit state to nurse a woman in the final stages of pancreatic cancer, Bev simply gave me a roster and a set of instructions and left for a hotel.

'I'll be back on Friday,' she said.

It was Wednesday and my addled brain nearly snapped, but I got through it and did what I could to help. Bev and I did shifts and like shift workers passing in a dark and unfamiliar liminal space, we hardly spoke as we took over from one another, certainly not in any meaningful way.

The Thursday before Mom died (she died on a Sunday) I was caring for her. Dad was with Randall Osman at the Elks. For a man who'd made his career in death, Dad was surprisingly useless with the dying. Mom asked me to go into the garage and get some old photos. As I was rummaging through boxes trying to find the photos, I came across a bundle of letters. I put them to one side, thinking they were love letters between Mom and Dad. I cynically thought that if I showed them to Bev, it might soften her hard exterior, and maybe we could talk properly about why we'd lost touch.

Mom and I poured over the photos for a short while, but then she got too tired to continue and fell asleep. As she dozed, I went back to the garage and got the letters. I flicked through them. There were about thirty or so. Some were from Dad back in the early days of their marriage. I read the opening paragraph from one, and it was like a bad romance novel. I admired many things about Dad, but his writing was not one of them. I put those letters aside in a kind of vaguely amused embarrassment and continued to rummage. I found about a dozen or so letters from my grandma, nothing of any particular importance, humdrum details of life in Kentucky and such. There were lots of questions about us, when are you and Bev coming to visit? Isn't TJ turning into a handsome boy, you know he looks just like Tom? It's a pity Matthew is such a serious child; it would be nice to have a picture of him where he doesn't look like he's chewing a bee. At the base of the pile, there were eight letters from Lottie Baylock, all written within two years of TJ's death. I began to scan them, but soon became engrossed. It was clear that Mom believed Lottie Baylock was some sort of conduit between this world and the next. Her replies to my mom were all about TJ and how his spirit was at peace. In one letter, Baylock talked about the cleansing ceremony they had performed at the creek and of how all TJ's residual pain had vanished into the air like vestiges of autumnal heat. It was gripping stuff, page after page of hidden family history. I was enjoying the gossip until I read the last letter. It was pretty disconcerting. While the first seven letters were addressed to Mom's school, the final one was sent to the family home.

12/20/1982

My Dear Helen,
    I apologize for sending this letter directly to your home, but with school being out for the holiday season, I was not sure it would reach you in time.

If you remember when you came to visit last July I told you I had been unwell. Sadly, my illness has not abated, and I am told I am not long for this world. The doctors say it has spread to my bones and I may last until summer. I hope so, as you know it gets so lovely here in May.

I was told I should get my affairs in order, and I am taking that advice.

Firstly, I am writing to thank you for your wonderful friendship over the years. I can remember when your mother introduced us. It was springtime and you were two years old. I recall touching your golden curls and sensing that you'd have a life with a measure of sadness in it. I didn't tell your mother that, but maybe I should have, maybe if I had, you could have avoided some of the trials in your life. I can only say I'm sorry if my negligence led to any of your misfortunes.

I know you may want to visit to say goodbye, but I beg you not to, leave me to die in peace.

The truth is, some things are too important to go unsaid. This is the second and gravest reason for my letter.

Let me assure you with total faith in the Lord Jesus Christ our Saviour that TJ is with the angels. I can promise you as sure the sun will rise tomorrow that he is in a good place and will be waiting for you when it's your time to pass. I want you to carry that flame for him in your heart the rest of your days. I also ask you to watch out for Matthew. There will be a lot of darkness in his life, and I urge you to keep him in the light of the Lord. There is darkness around him already, please don't let it consume him, though I feel it might be too late.

*I will pray for you and Matthew up until my last
breath, and will give your love to TJ when I see him.
Please put your trust in God and in the works of his
servants here on earth.*

*With love and gratitude,
Lottie.*

Lottie knew. My first thought was how, my second was why
she covered for me?

I began to think about Billybird III being a conduit or vessel
for TJ's spirit. In my mind, I found links that were persuasive
enough to be considered proof. Both had died at eight, both of
them had been named after someone else, and I was the last
person to see them alive. I shook my head; it couldn't be anything more than a coincidence, but as I was thinking something
compelled me to reach up to my right eye and feel the almost
imperceptible crease where Billybird III had scratched me. My
finger dragged along my skin, sensing the tiny variations where
scar tissue had formed. As my finger moved along my face, I
felt a strange intuition possess me. I was sure it was TJ's way
of reminding me of the truth about his death and how it was
different from what I'd told the FBI.

Chapter Eleven
Nice but odd, April 2019

It was four days before the RCA dinner, and I had accepted Zimmerman's invitation (via email). I had said there was a possibility I'd be bringing someone from outside the community, and he replied saying it was OK. He didn't ask who, which was unlike him, he usually wanted to know everything down to the last detail, but hey, there's always an exception. Rohit had not got back to me, but there was nothing strange about that. In most cases, he didn't turn up anything. I had hoped initially he was like Penelope Garcia from *Criminal Minds* but, truth be told, he's more like Andy Garcia from *Pink Panther II*. Still, I must credit him, he's delivered the goods a few times, and I was hoping this would be one of them.

I did some research of my own, linguistic research. Zimmerman, it turns out, is a German name. It means carpenter. Arguably the world's most famous Zimmerman (apart from the one the Romans crucified) is Bob Dylan. Dylan's real name is Robert Zimmerman. I guess Bob Dylan suited his folky image when he started out. It'd be hard to imagine Robert Zimmerman asking, 'How many times can a man turn his head and pretend that he just doesn't see?' Or my personal favorite, 'I try my best to be just like I am, but everybody wants you to be just like them.' That's from *Maggie's Farm*, not his best song, but I like that lyric.

I don't usually take an interest in literary awards, but when good old Bob won the Nobel Prize, that sure-as shit shook up the purists. The debate in the town library that week bordered on psychosis. When you think of the great writers who'd missed out and then this tattered coat upon a stick comes along and wins, no wonder men and women of letters lost their fucking minds. I thought the literary set was a bit more sedate, but boy oh boy did that open a can of worms. I mean there have been more than a few usurpers in recent years, some of them filling big shoes, so Bob Dylan winning the Nobel Prize certainly can't be considered the worst thing to happen, but literary folk sure are opinionated, and angry too.

On Thursday, the 25th, I had begun to give up hope that Beth would call when not only did she call, but she called in person. It was about lunchtime and the day was as bright, if not brighter, than when we'd first met. I opened the door, but there was no lighthouse grade glare. She'd been thoughtful enough to park her car a little down the street. I wanted to say I'd been expecting her, but I said the opposite.

'I would have called,' she said, 'but I've been up to here (pointing to the top of her head) with work.'

'Gene Hackman work?'

'A little,' she said, 'but other stuff, mostly.'

'Cheating husbands?'

'That sort of thing, may I come in?'

I stood aside and she walked in. She was dressed a little more formally than last time. She wore a dark pencil skirt and matching jacket. Business casual. Her hair was done in a different style. It made her look older. I didn't say anything, but I could tell she noticed.

I put on some coffee and this time we sat in the living room. I don't have any artwork on the walls, no photos either, and I think this disconcerted her a little. She seemed to be looking for a point of focus on the wall.

'It's just easier to clean,' I said, 'putting things up and so on means extra dusting.'

I'm not sure what she made of my reason, but once I had acknowledged the unusual nature of the room, she settled.

'Are you still going to the RCA dinner on Saturday?'

'Yes,' I said.

'In that case, let's go together.'

'Got nothing better to do?'

Her eyes narrowed just a touch. There was no intent in my tone, and her face told me she didn't know whether to respond or not.

'Did you speak to anyone else in the community?'

'A few people, the Johnsons, the Mitchells and Mr. Stolly on this street and a lovely family named Brantley on the other side.'

'But not Zimmerman?'

'No,' she said, 'he's a hard man to pin down.'

Told you.

'Did you find out anything?'

'Nothing except that the Johnsons are the perfect family, the Mitchells think they're better than everyone else, and that Stolly gives me the creeps.'

She was right about the Johnsons, but I decided to quiz her about the Mitchells.

'What gave you that impression of the Mitchells?'

'You're such a gossip,' she said.

'Just curious.'

'No, you're not, you know why I got that impression. You just want me to confirm your opinion.'

She was right.

'How long did it take Marie Mitchell to start bitching about Donna Anderson?'

'About three minutes.'

'Wait until you meet Donna.'

'I'm sure she's nice as pie.'

I smirked, the image of Donna Anderson stuffing a pie into her face flashed through my mind.

'Stolly is a bit weird,' she said, 'I couldn't wait to get away from him.'

A while back, I'd asked Rohit to find out what he could about Stolly. It was prompted by a confrontation I stumbled into around the time Jeff's article was creating waves in Jonestown. Stolly, or Snout as I prefer to call him, headed me off as I was returning home from town;

'Mr. Lowell,' he said.

He rarely, if ever, used people's first names and when he did, he'd use their entire name, so I wasn't Matt, I was Matthew and Jeff wasn't Jeff but Jefferson. It was an idiosyncrasy at first, but later it began to smack of disingenuousness. The more I spoke with him, the more I got the impression I was speaking with a man who wasn't just wearing a mask, but a mask on that mask. He would ask me about myself and how things were and how I was enjoying life in Jonestown and so on, but it wasn't friendly small talk, it was like being probed. He was never quite satisfied with the answers you gave him and after a few minutes of interrogation, you'd become agitated and need to leave. He'd always want the final word, and it would usually be some type of friendly advice or something that only he knew or could influence. It was all an act and easy to see through, but even then, he didn't behave differently, and when you'd finally insist that the conversation ended, he'd appear offended.

Mr. Zimmerman is a good friend of mine, he'd say. Sometimes he'd imply that he was in with The Board of Selectmen and that one day he'd be head of the RCA.

You see, I'm an economic analyst, and with my knowledge and insights, I'd be an ideal candidate. In fact, at the next election, I will be running for the position of secretary to Mr. Zimmerman.

He'd lean in and touch your arm.

I can rely on your vote, can't I?

This bullshit didn't work on me, but somehow it worked on others, especially the Andersons. Snout would regularly visit them for a coffee or occasionally a cookout, though it was just the three of them and doesn't really count as a proper cookout in my book. Tell you what, the Andersons sure enjoyed their barbecued meat. From the upstairs window, their voices would sometimes carry if the wind was right, and I could make out their conversations. It invariably involved the lives of those in the community. They essentially gossiped and fed one another's sense of superiority and self-righteousness.

'Mr. Lowell,' Snout repeated as I walked towards my house. I pretended I didn't hear him, but he was not to be put off.

'Matthew,' he said loudly.

'Mr. Stolly,' I said, turning towards him.

Snout operated in one of two ways, either he wanted to tell you something or he wanted something from you. Judging by his manner and insistence, I guessed he wanted something from me.

'Have you read Mr. Simmons' article in The Telegraph?'

'Yes,' I said, 'why?'

'It has very much upset my good friends, the Andersons.'

'Is that right?' I said.

'Yes, very much,' he said, 'I cannot fathom why Mr. Simmons would write such a thing.'

'I don't think Jeff intended to be offensive.'

'That may well be, but the fact is it was offensive.'

'Not to me,' I said, 'and not to anyone else around here.'

I knew this was a prelude to something else. When Snout wanted something, his voice took on the quality of molasses. He adopted a sense of charm that appealed to your sense of self. He knew what to say to interest you.

'What I really want to ask you about is, as you know Mr. Simmons better than any of us …'

He waited until he felt I was paying attention. I was, but only to hurry him up.

'And given that I feel you have the skill to diffuse any potential situation, perhaps you could speak to him about his ethical responsibility to the community?'

It was chilly, and I didn't want to be out on the street talking to this asshole who couldn't or wouldn't leave me be.

'OK,' I said and turned away.

This was not what he wanted me to do. Suddenly, he grabbed me. He had never grabbed me. He had lightly touched my arm a couple of times, but this was a full-on intrusion into my personal space. I reacted instinctively.

'Fuck off,' I said, 'you fucking weirdo.'

His face dropped. He went from a mild superficial charm to something I can only describe as a mix of petulance, injury, and spite.

'H-H-How dare you call me that,' he said.

He expected an apology, but I was in no mood to give one and began to walk up my driveway.

'I wouldn't walk away, Mr. L-L-Lowell, not unless you want me to divulge what I've heard about you to the wider community.'

I'd had enough. I got right in his face.

'Fuck off,' I said slowly and clearly.

He grinned, all lines and high mouth as if someone was pulling fishhooks on either side of his face.

'We'll see, Mr. Lowell.'

I walked away before I hit him. As I went inside my house, I could feel him looking at me. The next morning, there was an envelope on my porch. It was delivered by hand. I opened it. There was a list of my financial details and recent transactions, nothing incriminating or out of the ordinary in itself. It was Snout's way of implying he knew things about me, and an attempt to follow up his threat from the night before. I tore up the envelope and its contents and went inside. I put it in the woodstove and burned it. After I'd had a coffee, I emailed Rohit and asked him to do some research on Stolly.

*

'He gives all of us the creeps,' I said, 'did you drop into his house or did he stop you in the street?'

'I went inside.'

I'd never been in Snout's house. As far as I could tell, only the Andersons had, maybe Zimmerman too. This was not particularly unusual, especially given that Snout had developed a reputation for being as meddlesome as a small-town pastor.

'And?' I said.

'You've never been inside his house?'

'We don't really get along,' I said.

I could tell from her reaction that she knew where I was coming from.

'Anyway, the bit of it I saw is as neat as a new pin,' she said, 'I mean your place is spick and span, but his is like something out of a Sears and Roebuck directory.'

'Tasteful?' I wondered what other clichés might come my way.

'Not really, not at all, actually. It's more functional than anything else. There's a sense of sterility about the place, like an
operating theatre.'

I tapped my lips and stretched out. I'd been a little restless
lately and not sleeping well. My eyes were drawn to her shoes.
They seemed out of place with her suit, more expensive for
sure, and comfortable. I got the impression her suit was a mi-
crometer too tight.

'I think he's got control issues,' she said.

It had occurred to me that Snout's pathology was a bit more
savage than that of a mere busybody. I had some ideas about
him, but until Rohit got back to me, it was only speculation.

'You can tell straight away why he's not married. Men like
him won't relinquish their freedom or their perception of it.'

'I don't see a ring on your finger,' she said, 'aren't you being
a bit hypocritical?'

'Perhaps, but I'm nothing like him.'

'No, you're not,' she said, 'I could tell straight away something wasn't right about him. With you, it was…'

I waited for her to continue, but when the silence extended
slightly too long for me to bear. I tried to complete her thought.

'Different,' I said.

She nodded.

'I thought you were a bit odd. Stolly is weird, creepy weird.'

Thanks,' I said, 'I guess that's a compliment.'

'I mean odd in a nice way.'

There it was again, nice.

'And that big car in his driveway, talk about compensating.'

Most men in Jonestown had big cars, but I guess Snout's was
fairly ostentatious.

'It wouldn't surprise me if he had an overbearing mother,'
she said, 'he's definitely trying to impress someone.'

'I don't know, but it makes you think about the people we share our lives with, doesn't it?'

'It does,' she said.

'So, how is the investigation going, any suspects since we last spoke?'

'None so far. What time is the dinner on Saturday?'

'The invitation said eight sharp.'

'OK, how about we meet here at about 7:45 and go from there?'

'Sounds good to me.'

'I assume it's black tie?'

'Smart casual,' I said, 'it's not overly formal, but make an effort. Zimmerman likes to mingle with his guests, but you have to look the part. He can't stand anyone who looks ordinary.'

'Common?' she said.

'His words exactly, I heard him say it at a meeting one time.'

'I have just the thing,' she said, giving me a wink.

'Have you got some time?' I asked.

She looked at me with curiosity.

'I might, what did you have in mind?'

'Let's go visit someone I think you'll like.'

*

A short time later, we were knocking on Old Jack's door. I had three reasons to visit Old Jack with Beth. The first was to give Old Jack a bit of excitement. As he'd got older, he'd talked about the spirit being willing but the flesh being tired.

Time was when I was in the service, I'd get shore leave for a night, drink ten beers, have fun with five women and be ready for duty the next day without so much as a stray hair on my uniform, he'd say.

I knew he'd enjoy Beth's company. The second reason was to walk by Zimmerman's house and hopefully be seen together. The third reason was to surprise Beth with something I knew she'd like.

Jack opened the door. He was sober, which was a start, but the consequence of his sobriety meant that he was a little ratty too.

'God damn it, I thought you were Zimmerman,' he said.

He didn't notice Beth, who was standing just behind me.

'This is my friend Beth,' I said by way of introduction.

When Jack saw her, he didn't quite have the same reaction I had, but he smiled broadly and gave her a warm welcome.

'A friend of Matt's is a friend of mine. Why don't you come in?'

We went in. I was a little wary. Visiting Jack was a bit of a hit or miss. On a good day, the place was tidy, well, sort of, and didn't reek of booze and what can only be described as old guy smell. On a bad day, you could add a blocked toilet to the other interesting aromas and maybe a little puke on the floor. Thankfully, today was a good day. It was actually the cleanest I'd ever seen it.

'You must have been expecting us,' I said with a chuckle, 'you had the cleaners in.'

Jack laughed, 'darndest thing,' he said, 'but Zimmerman had those Puerto-Ricans here, and they had buckets and mops and lemon fresh zest, and they gave the old place the once over.'

'It's a very nice home you have here Mr…' said Beth looking at me to complete the sentence.

'Captain James K. McDowell, USS Frank Cable, at your service, but everyone here calls me Jack or Old Jack.'

'It's nice to meet you, Jack,' said Beth.

Jack, who often wore a baseball cap, tipped his hat.

'Now,' he said turning to me, 'there's no way you're here on a social visit, much and all as I appreciate it when you come over, but the presence of your friend says to me that you'd like to look in the garage.'

'You got me,' I said.

'You like cars?' said Jack, addressing Beth.

'Yes,' said Beth, 'it's the family business.'

'Whereabouts?'

'California.'

'California's a big place,' said Jack.

'San Francisco,' said Beth.

Jack's face seemed to shine at the mention of the city. He smiled broadly.

'I painted that town red a few times as a young man, though I was mostly in San Diego.'

He paused for a moment, as if he'd forgotten exactly where he was or what he was doing.

'Anyway, let's go see the car.'

We followed him through the hall and into the kitchen. Access to the garage was through the laundry room.

'I don't go in here much,' said Jack, 'so you'll have to forgive me about the mess and the spiders.'

Beth's eyes shifted sideways, and her brow wrinkled.

'Jack had an infestation of house spiders last year, but don't worry, the exterminator got rid of them.'

'They were darn well everywhere, on the floor, up the walls on the ceiling,' said Jack opening the door, 'makes me want to scratch every time I think about it.'

'You don't like spiders?' said Jack.

'Childhood trauma,' said Beth.

Jack chuckled and opened the door and turned on the light. By the expression on Beth's face, she was grateful not to see any spiders.

Seems like I've found your Kryptonite, I thought to myself.

In the middle of the garage, covered in a dust sheet, was Jack's car.

'Want to guess what it is?' he said.

Beth examined the shape, length, and width of the car.

'It's not long enough to be a Cadillac,' she said, 'it could be a Plymouth Fury or a Corvair.'

'Lady knows her cars,' said Jack.

I was both pleased and disappointed. I had thought her enthusiasm for cars was a ruse and part of me hoped she'd flounder if asked, but, if I'm honest, it was impressive to watch someone with expertise put it to the test.

'I'm going to say Corvair, but not with a lot of confidence.'

Jack laughed out loud and slapped his thigh. I couldn't remember what make the car was and going on Jack's reaction, Beth was right.

'You get a silver star for guessing it's a Chevy, but no gold.'

With a flourish, Jack pulled off the dust sheet and stood back, and smiled.

'Now ain't that something,' he said.

Beth didn't say anything at first, but you could see the joy in her face.

'That there is a 1960 Chevy Impala,' said Jack, 'restored to her former glory.'

'The chrome is beautiful. Did you do the work yourself?'

'When I got her, she was rusting and beat up. Bought her from a local farmer. She'd been sitting under a pile of junk in a barn for about twenty years.'

'The detail is amazing,' said Beth as she walked around the car.

When Jack had shown me the car, I had pretended to be interested, but the truth is I know relatively little about cars. The only reason I know about Firebirds is that Jim Rockford drove one, and I'd always thought they were cool. Looking at Jack's car now, more closely, and being in the presence of real motor-enthusiasts gave me a new appreciation of the care Jack had taken while restoring it. The chrome, the contours, mirrors, and alloy wheels had been returned to their former glory. I thought briefly of Dad and pictured him driving something like this when he was a young man. The image didn't fit. Dad was a practical man and didn't like to show off. He'd have enjoyed the car from an aesthetic point of view, but wouldn't have wanted it outside the house.

'Would you consider selling it?' said Beth.

The question seemed to surprise Jack. It certainly surprised me. Jack rubbed his head as if he were considering the request.

'Sorry to disappoint you missy, but I don't think so,' he said, 'much and all as I know you'd take good care of her, I'd like to leave it to my eldest boy when it's time.'

Beth understood. She ran her fingers along a wheel arch.

'My father would love to see this, mind if I take a photo and send it to him?'

'Take as many photos as you like, young lady.'

Beth snapped about a dozen pictures from various angles, and afterward Jack invited her to sit in the cockpit. As the two of them sat in the car laughing and enjoying the mutual excitement, my phone beeped. Before I could look at the message, Jack got out of the car and went to the garage door. He pressed a button on the wall and the door rolled back.

'I wouldn't be much of a host if I didn't let the lady take her for a spin. You coming?'

Beth was a bit giddy and waved her hand, inviting me to get in and go with them. I sat in the back and off we went. Beth was in her element and where someone like me would grind the gears or turn on the wipers looking for the turn signal, she took to the car instinctively as if it were an extension of her person.

We left Jonestown and headed into town. Jack suggested we go to Arlene's for a coffee. We agreed it was a good idea. As we got into town and Beth searched for somewhere to park the car, I remembered my phone. There was an email from Rohit. It was short and to the point.

That is interesting, I thought as I got out of the car, *very interesting.*

Chapter Twelve
Fire and Ice, Sacramento, 1991

About six weeks before we left Sacramento for Clearwater, there was a fire in Del Paso Heights. There were two victims, Joe Hayes' mother and grandmother. Both had been asleep, and both had died of smoke inhalation. Dad performed the autopsies. Two weeks later, he came home and went straight to the fridge and got a beer and sat down at the kitchen table. He said absolutely nothing until he'd finished his drink. This was unusual, in fact, it was unheard of. Now, you can imagine most men grabbing a beer after a day's work and retreating into some kind of masculine shell before returning to the normal rhythm of family life, but with Dad, it was always the other way around. On any typical day where he wasn't working late or was out of town, he'd come home about 6 pm. It wasn't quite clockwork, but when you heard his car pull in, you knew it was close to or just after 6. He would sit in his car listening to the news for about ten minutes before coming into the house and checking the mail. This would take a few minutes, especially if there was something that required his attention. Then he'd greet whoever was there, which was usually just me, since Mom usually did after-school stuff until about 7 pm. We'd have to wait until she came home to eat. Dad could man a barbecue without too much fuss, but almost all other cooking skills were beyond him. So, once his news and mail rituals were done, and he'd said hi to me (this usually involved him checking that I was doing or had done my homework) then and only then would he grab a beer and sit in the living room and allow the thoughts that swirled in his mind to settle like leaves on a path. But this day was different.

He finished his beer at the kitchen table and then got another and went into the living room. I'd been hovering around doing nothing, and he'd noticed me but stayed silent. I figured he was in a mood and didn't want to make things worse. Things had been up and down. In my naivety, I thought the up and down nature of life was normal. I was doing OK in school. I'd managed to avoid any trouble and was optimistic about senior year. Bev had just completed her degree and was considering a placement in Wisconsin. As you know, she had drifted in and out of our lives since finishing high school. Mom and Dad's relationship was functional. He performed his role, and she did hers. Life wasn't perfect, but it was a far cry from some of the things I'd heard from some kids in my school. Most of the kids I hung out with had similar home lives, but a few had it much tougher, so I counted myself lucky that the most intrusive my parents got was to ask me about homework and what I was thinking about doing in college. Our communication was to the point. I guess all our lives were functional. Bev would still call, but it was down to once, sometimes twice a week, and usually not for that long. If I was home at the time of her calls, I'd ask Mom to give me the receiver, but by the time I'd got there, Bev would have hung up or at best say she couldn't talk as she had to be somewhere. I guess she was distancing herself from what had happened in her senior year, but I couldn't understand why she was distancing herself from me. I'd kept her secret and, as far as I knew, had done nothing wrong. I thought about writing to her, but I couldn't work up either the courage or the words. I must have started fifty letters. Dear Bev, Hi, how are you? Dear

Bev, Hi, things are quiet without you … I had no trouble with the opening paragraph, but when it came to the crunch, there was nothing. What was I supposed to say? I was afraid that if I mentioned Joe Hayes, it would be a violation of trust. I thought if I wrote and asked her about it, she'd say I broke our secret and that would put an end to everything.

Dad called me from the living room. I went to him, anxious to know why his behavior was out of its normal pattern. I expected him to tell me that he and Mom were getting divorced or that the school had called (though I couldn't think of a single reason why). Instead, he told me to take a seat and once I was sitting, he took a long drink from his beer and exhaled deeply.

'Everything OK in school, son?'

I nodded. He asked again. He wanted me to speak actively rather than communicate in passive gestures.

'Yes, sir,' I said.

I had never called him sir, it just slipped out. I had no idea why. My mind flashed back to when the FBI man interviewed me after TJ's death.

'You'd tell me or your mother if there was something wrong.'

It wasn't a question. It was a method for him to arrive at where he wanted to be.

'Yes,' I said.

'I know you would,' he said. 'I got to be honest son, since you moved to this school you've been doing well.'

'Thanks.'

School was almost out for the year, and the truth was I had been doing well.

He swirled the remaining beer around in his bottle and finished it in one long gulp. He shook the bottle from side to side and nodded towards the kitchen. I got up and fetched him another.

'Why don't you grab one for yourself if you want,' he said from the living room. I felt a mix of fear and elation well up inside me.

'What if Mom…' I began.

'Let me worry about that,' said Dad.

So, there I was at seventeen years of age sitting with my father having a beer.

'I know this isn't your first beer, but maybe this will be the first one you'll enjoy.'

He was referring to an incident the previous Christmas when I'd been at a party and puked in the trash when I got home. Dad heard all the noise and rather than bawl me out he asked me if I'd eaten something that was off. I don't remember what I said, but he took me inside and got me to drink water and take some aspirin, and then he put me to bed with a bucket beside me. The next morning, when I came downstairs, he said I'd better clean out the trash can before Mom found out. He didn't mention it again. Until now.

'You're finishing on Friday,' Dad said, lighting a Pall Mall.

'Yes.'

'And then it's senior year.'

I think he was trying to signpost the conversation, give it some direction. It was warm in the room and the cold beer was refreshing, even though I was only taking nervous sips and never when Dad was looking at me.

'That was an awful tragedy in Del Paso Heights last month.'

My heart jumped. I knew what was coming next.

'You heard about it?' said Dad, sitting upright and leaning forward slightly.

I nodded and gulped down a mouthful of beer.

'The boys in that family, well, they're grown men now, they all went to your school, did you know that?'

Dad's eyes were tired. He'd taken to wearing glasses in recent years. He was almost sixty, and I suppose all those years working under artificial lights had taken their toll. He wore horn-rimmed glasses typical of the 1960s, and it gave him a retro coolness, but it also gave him a hitherto unseen sternness. This authoritarian quality was all I could see in him now. He reminded me a little of the framed photo of Harry Truman above the doorway of the school library.

'Yes, the Hayes boys. I believe the youngest boy, Joe, was in the same class as your sister.'

At the mention of Bev and Joe Hayes in the same context I almost pissed myself, he must have noticed my reaction, but not enough for him to pursue it. Maybe he didn't see my reaction, but I saw his. Either way, he said nothing. I became increasingly self-conscious and didn't want to draw any further scrutiny. I figured that if I didn't do something, I'd clam up and maybe even freak out, so I decided to go for broke and adopt an overly familiar approach.

'He was a footballer,' I said, 'Coach Ferguson said he had the potential to go all-state. He still gets talked about in practice.'

'What position?'

'Wide receiver.'

'J.W. says anyone can be a decent wide receiver if they have good hands and speed, but he also told me it's one of the most difficult positions to become great in.'

Dad took a slug of beer and exhaled through his nose as if he were pondering his statement. In truth, he knew relatively little about sports.

'Did Coach Ferguson say what happened to him after school? '

'No,' I said, and then added, 'but I heard he got in trouble with the law.'

'That's what I heard, too.'

Like his brothers, Joe Hayes had gone into a blue-collar job straight out of high school. Coach Ferguson had been right about Joe's potential, but Joe was lazy and, like some working-class people, he resented the idea of further education rather than seeing it as an opportunity to better himself. In the end, he gave up football despite the offer of scholarships. I guess he was through with school and couldn't stand the idea of four more years of it. From what I heard about Joe, he was a guy who lived in the moment and had no long-term plans.

'A buddy of mine in the police said the fire was started deliberately.'

'How do they know?'

'There were traces of accelerants found at the scene.'

'Do they know who did it?' I asked.

The beer had begun to work itself on him. He had relaxed and now lounged comfortably in his chair.

'They booked Joe Hayes for it just this afternoon.'

I sipped my beer. It was no longer cold and fresh, but lukewarm and bitter. Despite the taste, I swallowed it.

'Of course, he says he didn't do it,' said Dad, 'but there's a string of evidence, and he was there that night, so he's got no alibi. He's got previous too, not fires, but other things.'

'Makes sense,' I said.

'What makes sense?'

'That he'd be there. At home, I mean.'

Dad shifted in his chair, pushing his weight back. He looked as if he was unsure what to make of my comment and lit another cigarette.

'He says he didn't do it and if he did, it was accidental, said he could have started it by tossing a cigarette away, but that doesn't explain the accelerant.'

I didn't say anything.

'Do you think he did it?' The question caught me off guard. Why would he ask me if I thought Joe Hayes could start a fire?

'I guess.'

'Trouble seems to follow kids like him,' said Dad, 'as if they can't escape it. A kind of sad destiny.'

'Is he in trouble, even if he didn't do it?' I said.

'He's up a creek for sure, and it doesn't matter what he says, the fire Marshall who examined the scene said it was set deliberately so unless they pin someone else for it, Hayes is in a whole pile of trouble.'

'What's going to happen to him?'

Dad paused for a moment before replying. It was as if he was reaching deep within himself for the words. I remember how strange it felt.

'If he's found guilty, then he'll go to prison for a long time. Maybe if they can prove it was deliberate and get him on first-degree murder, they'll sentence him to death, who knows.'

'Death, like the chair?' I exclaimed.

'Not too likely though, there hasn't been an execution in California since 1967, but with Pete Wilson in the Governor's Mansion, there might just be a chance. Republicans sure love state-approved murder.'

Dad had seen the consequences of the very worst of man's inhumanity to man. He'd taught me the Latin term *homo homini lupus est*, man is a wolf to man, and would sometimes say it as he read the paper or watched TV. He'd done autopsies on children who'd been raped and murdered. He'd discovered that a victim was alive when her killer stuck a red-hot needle in her eyes and yet for all the brutality he'd seen, he was vehemently against the death penalty. It rarely came up as a topic, but if he was listening to a radio show or watching a TV show, and it was mentioned, he'd say something about how revenge was never the way to do things. I guess when you spent as much time around death as Dad you went one of two ways, you either became immune to it and therefore didn't have an opinion on it, or you got tired of it and didn't want to see any more than was necessary. I think he was just tired of death.

'Why would he want to murder his family?' I asked.

Dad tilted his head back and closed his eyes.

'You'd better put that beer bottle on the table beside me here. I think your mother will be home soon.'

I stood up and crossed the room to place the bottle on the small table beside Dad's chair. When I got there, his eyes opened, and he sat up and reached for his bottle. His timing startled me, and I dropped the empty bottle. He smiled and sat back.

'You know what motive is, son?'

'Yes,' I said.

'Well, my police buddy said that a potential motive for the killings was financial. Hayes was probably hoping for an insurance pay-out. As you said, he was known to the police and hadn't really made much of himself since high school, so it stands to reason that he saw an opportunity and took it. A guy like Hayes probably doesn't think too hard about things and maybe if he's arrogant enough, he probably thought he'd get away with it.'

The front door opened. The familiar sound of Mom's voice echoed through the house. From her tone, I knew she was in a buoyant mood. Dad's eyes rolled in their sockets. She went into the kitchen first and put down what I assumed were grocery bags.

'I'll get dinner ready now. I bet you boys are hungry.'

I said I was. Dad grunted. She must have heard him because she came into the living room soon after. She looked at me and her eyes narrowed. She then looked at Dad and sighed.

'Thomas, are you drunk?'

'No, Helen, I am not drunk,' said Dad emphatically.

'There are three bottles on the table beside you and one on the kitchen table. Now, unless Matthew had one, it looks like you've had four beers.'

Mom was surprisingly direct. Normally, she wouldn't pass comment on anything Dad did but for some reason, she felt like it now.

'I had a few beers, so what. It was a tough day.'

Dad had way too much self-respect to mention Mom's use of Valium, but I bet he wanted to.

'It's not like you, that's all,' said Mom, backing down.

'I know it's not,' said Dad with a sigh, 'but today was a doozy.'

My mind was racing with the frantic chaos of a kindergarten playground. Nothing made any sense. Did he know about Joe Hayes and Bev? Did he think I had something to do with the fire? If he did, what was coming next?'

'Helen, could you get me another beer, and maybe one for yourself while you're at it.'

Mom was in the process of leaving the room when the second part of Dad's request registered with her. It was like when a ghost tapped on Shaggy and Scooby's shoulders, you know how they'd turn around and wouldn't realize it was a ghost then all of a sudden, they'd get it, and their hair would go all spiky with terror, and they'd run away in a cloud of dust. Well, it wasn't quite the same, but Dad had never suggested that Mom drink a beer, in fact, I don't think I'd ever seen her drink beer. Mom didn't drink much. She might have a small glass of punch at a party or eggnog at Christmas, but that was about it. Her mother had abstained from alcohol and wouldn't allow it in the house. Rumour was that Grandpa Kentucky had a still in the hills near the farm, and that one of his whiskey batches made a guy go crazy and run off into the wilderness for three days. When they finally found the guy, he was up a tree naked claiming he'd been abducted by aliens, but that's not necessarily unusual for Kentucky.

'I don't drink beer, Thomas,' she said, 'you know that.'

'OK, but you might want one after what I tell you.'

She got Dad a beer, but not one for herself. Instead, she held a glass of water, which was shaking ever so slightly. Dad sat up and pushed his glasses up his nose.

'Now, before you get all fidgety, I've been thinking about this for a couple of weeks. It's not something that just jumped into my mind a minute ago.'

Mom said nothing. I shrunk into the background. I felt my part had been played, and now I could relax a little and become an audience member.

'There's a job in Florida, it's low-key, less stressful, shorter hours, and better paid.' Mom looked at me, but my eyes were on Dad. What was being discussed was not up for discussion. Dad was using his head of the household voice and nothing contradicted it.

'Florida,' Mom said unemotionally, as if all her feelings had bottlenecked and blocked one another.

My first thought was hurricanes and then alligators.

'Yes, Clearwater. It's a sleepy little Gulf Coast town, not much crime, nothing like here anyway.'

'But we've been in Sacramento since we got married,' said Mom, 'and what about my school?'

Mom and Dad got married in 1968 and Mom had been at the same school since 1974.

'I did a bit of checking and there are some excellent schools in the area. A teacher of your experience would have no problem getting a job.'

'But I like my job here,' said Mom, her voice becoming slightly strained.

'I do not want to work in Sacramento any longer, Helen. I am sick of what I see every day and I need a change.'

Dad was a man who thrived on routine, so for him to say what he said meant something else was at play.

'What about Matthew?' said Mom, looking at me.

'Hasn't he moved schools enough in the past few years? And he's going into his senior year.'

Dad directed his attention at me.

'You wouldn't have a problem moving to a new school, would you?'

I shrugged and then shook my head.

'I found you a good school, and I've already spoken to the principal, and he's more than happy to take you, especially as you play football, and your grade point average is good.'

'What about TJ?' said Mom. Her voice was direct, unambiguous, and sharp. This was her final attempt to change Dad's mind.

'TJ will always be with us,' said Dad softly. Mom didn't have a follow-up. She must have realized there was no point in escalating things. She sat wearing a defeated and glum expression, and Dad reached forward and kissed her on the forehead.

'If you want, I could make a call, we could bring TJ with us,' said Dad.

I don't know if Mom was confused or shocked by the idea, but I noticed her hands clench violently.

'Thomas, don't,' she said.

Dad realized he'd made a terrible misjudgment and bowed his head. A deep silence followed, the sort of silence you find in an empty church.

'It'll be OK, a fresh start for all of us,' said Dad after what seemed a long time.

'We're too old for a fresh start,' said Mom in a deflated voice.

'That's why we need this,' said Dad, 'we've become old here, old before our time. I've seen the most awful things here, and it's all a bit too crazy for me now. You agree, don't you?'

Mom nodded.

'With the extra money I'd make you could work part-time, maybe do work in the community like you always planned, you could visit Bev too.'

Mom hadn't visited Bev in over a year. Bev had made Wisconsin her home and whenever she would return from visiting, she'd take days to unwind. She never said a lot about the visits except that it was cold and there was nothing to do, although Bev was very happy there. It made no sense to me. I knew Mom was deflecting. The fact remained that whatever had forced Bev to the icy land of cheese up north had not been resolved.

'When would we go?' I asked.

'In a month,' said Dad.

Mom stood up. Dad held on to her hands for as long as he could before she pulled away and left the room. He caught me looking at him.

'Don't worry, she'll be fine, you know all she needs is a day or two to accept what's happening.'

I wasn't particularly worried about Mom, she'd been through a lot worse in her life and besides, I think somewhere she understood that moving away was a good thing. Dad sat back once more and closed his eyes. He looked relaxed and peaceful. Maybe it was the beer, maybe it was something else. I went over to him and removed the empty bottles from the side table, picking them up by sticking the tip of my fingers in them to avoid making any noise. As I was about to leave, Dad spoke.

'Get me another, will you?'

I brought the empties into the kitchen and placed them in the glass refund box. Since TJ's death, it was my responsibility to recycle the cans and bottles in the house. At first, I engaged with the task gleefully as I got half of the proceeds. It was better than doing a paper route like some of the kids I knew. Mom wouldn't let me get a paper route after what happened to Johnny Gosch and those other kids, even though Dad had said I should get one. It was one of the few times Mom won out unequivocally against him. To paraphrase Oscar Wilde, I guess she thought losing one son was a misfortune, but to lose two was careless. I was glad Mom won. The kids I knew who did paper routes hated their jobs and complained about the hours and how Mr. O'Hare would bully them if they threatened to quit. True they got more money than I did but one thing I learned young and learned well is that I'd rather have time than money. As I opened the fridge and took out a beer for Dad, I could hear TJ's voice in my head clear as a bell on a still day.

That's two you've got away with.

I almost dropped the bottle. I reflexively looked around the kitchen. I didn't expect to see TJ standing there or anything, but I was unnerved by what I'd heard or thought I'd heard and left the room and hurried into the living room.

'You look like you've seen a ghost, son,' said Dad, who was sitting up and rubbing his mouth.

'The neighbor's cat jumped on the window ledge and startled me,' I said.

'I don't want that beer anymore, could you put it back.'

I didn't really want to return to the kitchen, but I did as asked and then drifted back into the living room. I knew intuitively that he had something more to say.

He had put on the TV and was flicking through the channels for something to watch. He stopped at The Simpsons.

'Do you ever watch this crap?' he asked, lighting a cigarette.

I didn't watch a lot of TV as a kid, I still don't, but I liked The Simpsons.

'Yeah, it's funny.'

Dad grunted and flicked through the channels again, finally settling on *Night of the Hunter.*

'You should watch this movie,' he said, 'I saw this at a drive-in when I was about twenty-one or maybe twenty-two, and it damn scared the heck out of me.'

'But it's in black and white,' I said, sitting down.

'Just watch,' said Dad.

The movie had just started. We watched quietly for about half an hour. I was trying to figure out what might have frightened Dad back when he saw the movie for the first time, and was at a loss. Despite this, the movie was absorbing and by the time Lillian Gish appeared and the movie's plot got moving, I understood what was unsettling about the story.

'He'll never stop,' said Dad, 'he'll do whatever it takes to get those kids and get that money.'

Even at seventeen, I could appreciate Robert Mitchum's performance. He embodied relentless menace under a cool exterior. He reminded me of Arnold Schwarzenegger in *The Terminator.*

TJ's voice echoed in my mind again, and it made me sit bolt upright, like when you're drifting to sleep, and you feel like you're about to fall.

'I told you it was scary,' said Dad, laughing.

We watched the remainder of the movie in silence. I had to hand it to dad, it was a good movie, and I was glad he'd made me watch it.

'You can't hide from your sins,' said Dad, getting up and stretching.

'What?' I said.

'The movie,' said Dad, 'Powell, couldn't hide his true nature. The kids saw through it, they knew he was sinful, even though he had the adults fooled. His sins finally caught up with him, just like that Hayes kid.'

'It's just a movie, Dad.'

'Nothing is just what it is, there's always something else below the surface, like an iceberg, don't you read poems and literature in school?'

I nodded.

'Well, then you know what a metaphor is, don't you?'

I nodded again.

'Anyway, you might want to think about it for a while.'

He waited until I had acknowledged his suggestion.

'Now,' he said, 'best get an early night and don't worry about moving to Florida, everything will work out fine.'

I smiled and he smiled in return. He stretched once more, this time twisting his entire body in a way that seemed unnatural.

'Good night, son,' he said and left the room.

I sat in the gloomy silence and took a deep breath. My heart was pounding at my ribs like some crazed witch doctor beating a drum. I stood up and felt a sudden wave of dizziness that compelled me to sit back down. Once it passed, I stood up, only this time slowly and used my chair for support. I couldn't stop my imagination from running away from me and left the room quickly and ran up the stairs, filled with the kind of dread a child has when they have to turn out all the lights before retreating to the safety of their room. I shut my bedroom door behind me and lay on my bed. The room was bright and as I stared at the ceiling, focusing on a random spot to control my thoughts, Dad's words rattled in my head like hailstones on a tin roof.

You can't hide from your sins.

I tried to dismiss the words and the realization that during the movie, TJ's voice had said the precisely same thing.

171

Chapter Thirteen
The RCA Dinner, April 2019

Amuse-Bouche

It had not occurred to me until I was waiting for Beth to arrive that Zimmerman probably knew she was a private detective and that any intrigue or undercover aspect to the evening was not going to happen. I had no idea who else (other than Old Jack) would be at the dinner, but I was willing to bet my life that Snout would be there and the Johnsons too. Beth had said she'd spoken to them as part of her investigation and though I could be reasonably sure that the Johnsons weren't the sort to tell tales, I knew Snout was. One of Snout's problems was that he wasn't half as clever as he thought, and his ego tended to give away a lot of information about him and his motives.

He'd said Zimmerman was his 'good friend' and I was sure as night followed day that once Beth had finished speaking to him, he'd have been on the phone to Zimmerman telling him about the woman who was looking for Jeff Simmons' cat. I had hoped Beth and I could have pretended to be a couple and I could have played the straight man to whatever persona she'd chosen to adopt for the dinner. I really wanted to see her work her seductive magic on Zimmerman, not for any kind of gratification, but rather to see if she could. Barney's stories about Zimmerman keeping the company of much younger women had piqued my curiosity. OK, Zimmerman had money, that was the first thing, and despite being sixty-five he looked no more than mid-fifties. He was also charismatic and carried a certain old-world charm and to be honest, my mind was cartwheeling between jealousy and mischievousness. I didn't know how I felt about Beth. It was true that I found her seriously attractive, and I sensed she liked me too, but the information Rohit had given me had complicated my clarity on the matter. I was thinking about this when there was a knock on the door. The evening was warm and there was a cool breeze coming from the southeast. I had decided on a pair of light pants, a shirt, and a sweater. I had toyed with the idea of wearing a jacket and tie but thought it would be too stuffy and besides the evening was supposed to be informal. I had been to most of the annual RCA dinners since I'd arrived in 2002. Back then they were held in Arlene's and were more like a coffee morning than anything else. Once Art Tillman became head of the RCA, he suggested we have them in The Hall and that was the case for a few years until too much drinking one night led to unneighborly words and the evening was suspended for a year. Tillman reinstated the evening in his own home, where it became a much more sedate affair. It was on the brink of being discontinued permanently when Zimmerman got elected head of the RCA and held an open-air party in his garden complete with a marquee and music and servers in uniform waltzing through a seriously impressed crowd with silver platters laden with all kinds of fancy nibbles. That was a great night. I remember Gretchen singing *Non, je ne regrette rien* and the whole sky swirling with stars as I lay with her on the lawn after a few too many glasses of champagne. I didn't expect the same to happen with Beth, though I hoped it would, however unlikely that might be.

I opened the door and much to my surprise saw Old Jack on one knee, dressed in a tuxedo, with a rose between his teeth.

He removed the rose from his mouth and began to sing *Night and Day*. I didn't know exactly what to do, so I joined in. A few seconds later the evening air was filled with the sound of our singing, and soon after that Razor Anderson began howling. The dog's accompaniment to my duet with Jack prompted raucous laughter from the side of my house. It was Beth. She emerged from the half-light of the slowly setting sun, and its beams caught her hair, giving it an amber glow. She had worn it up, and it revealed her slender neck. She looked stunning in a one-shoulder black evening dress.

'Wow,' I said and meant it.

She walked towards us and smiled at Old Jack.

'Sorry, Matt, I thought it would be fun if Jack serenaded you.'

'Sure was,' said Jack, 'though I never serenaded a guy before, and don't go telling any of my old Navy buddies.'

'Don't ask, don't tell,' I said.

We all shared another laugh.

'The look on your face,' said Jack, 'you were like a rabbit in the headlights.'

I exhaled, I'm sure I was.

'You make quite an impression, Jack,' I said.

'Me and Beth had another spin yesterday, and we got it in our minds to play a trick on you.'

'You have to have some fun sometimes,' she said.

'That's for sure,' I said.

We all turned abruptly to the sound of Derek Anderson roaring at Razor to shut the fuck up.

The dog had been barking ever since Jack and I began singing, and once again the slightest thing had inconvenienced the Andersons. Razor growled and then let a whimper and then growled again.

Derek appeared at his front door with the dog on a leash. He was dressed like a homeless person. I reasoned he wasn't going to the RCA dinner. He nodded to us as he walked down his driveway and onto the street where he walked briskly towards The Park with Razor keeping pace.

'That's one serious guy,' said Jack, 'he needs a drink. Hell, I need a drink.'

'He was in the Navy,' I said, 'based in San Diego, I heard.'

'He told me a little about his time there,' said Jack, 'though not that much, to be honest. He was a SEAL. Had to quit on account of his eyesight.'

'But he doesn't wear glasses,' I said.

'Probably contacts,' said Jack.

I felt like going after Anderson and asking him if Beth was who he'd seen with Jeff a short while back. The uncertainty around Jeff's possible tryst with Beth was bothering me more and more.

'Still,' said Jack in the sincere tone men of a certain age often use when giving credit where it's due, 'he's proper handy, fixed up a few of the things in my house that I'm too old to do now. Nice guy, but a bit too quiet for me.'

'I think he's got a few issues.'

'We all do,' said Jack wistfully.

A brief somber moment descended and lingered and then, like an insect resting on the surface, tension rose again and was gone. It was almost eight, and we hurried along in the growing twilight.

'I hope it's not too much,' said Beth, indicating her dress.

'No, it's perfect,' I said, 'Zimmerman will definitely notice you.'

'Let's hope so,' she said, and then checked herself as if she'd said something she shouldn't have.

We were the last to arrive at Zimmerman's house and just made the eight o'clock deadline. Snout was standing at the front door and directed us to the side of the house and into the backyard. He was dressed in a jacket and tie and, as always, was superficially polite and deferential. He recognized Beth straight away.

'Miss Becker, how lovely to see you again.'

Beth smiled. Snout examined me, squinted at my outfit, sneered almost imperceptibly and returned his attention to Beth.

'Your dress is marvelous Miss Becker, I am so pleased to see someone made an effort. I think Mr. Zimmerman will be pleased, too.'

'I hope Zimmerman is giving you a nice big tip for being his doorman,' I said to Snout, 'you seem naturally suited to the role.'

Snout didn't respond, but Beth smirked. Snout noticed it and became embarrassed. His embarrassment flustered him.

'I v-v-volunteered, if you must know. Mr. Zimmerman is entertaining his guests, he hasn't t-t-time to stand here.'

There was a faint aggression in Snout's tone, like an image trying to break through static.

'Well, I'm glad you do,' I said to Snout, 'we'd have been lost without you. You may get that personal secretary gig after all.'

Jack had wandered into the backyard and seeing this I put my hand out and Beth held it. We then followed Jack, leaving Snout twiddling his cufflinks and fiddling with his tie as he tried to regain his composure.

'That was fun,' said Beth.

She gave my hand the slightest squeeze and then let go as we emerged from the side of the house and into a very impressive and brightly lit scene.

There was a marquee about fifteen feet from the back of the house and in the corridor between them there was a broad trellis arch maybe eight feet across adorned with red, white and blue lights. My immediate instinct was to think it garish but when Jack said 'now that's classy', I realized that Zimmerman was putting on a show for his supporters and that my opinion didn't matter a jot.

Snout brushed past us while Beth and Jack enjoyed the scenery. He got very close to me and as I watched him beat a hasty path towards the house, I reckoned he had wanted to hit into me with his shoulder but had chickened out at the last second, that or give the impression of that.

'Let's get a drink,' said Jack.

He did a quick survey of the environment and was off like a bloodhound following a scent.

'This is pretty impressive,' said Beth.

This was very similar to Zimmerman's first hosting of the RCA dinner. The patriotic trellis was a new addition, but I didn't see any servers whizzing around with drinks and hors d'oeuvres which, to my mind, was a poor trade.

'It's a bit ostentatious,' I said.

'Would you like to get a drink?'

I nodded; it was time to put on a face to meet other faces. There was light jazz music coming from the marquee. We followed it on the air and as we got closer the music mingled with the sound of voices, not a clamor but enough for me to know that plenty of people had accepted Zimmerman's invitation.

The marquee was square, and I guessed it was about fifteen by fifteen meters in size. At the center was a long table and on the table place settings for perhaps fifty people. I noticed some of The Family Zone inhabitants, but I didn't really know any of them well enough to do anything other than wave politely or say hi.

Beth and I went to get a drink from a pop-up bar in the back left corner when Karl and Jenna Johnson intercepted us, and we made small talk. They asked about Gene Hackman and then asked us if we'd seen Jeff, to which I shook my head and Beth shrugged her shoulders. After the pleasantries were done, we left them and said we'd chat again later.

After wading through more smiles and enthusiastic but meaningless greetings, we finally got to the bar and there popping up from behind the pop-up bar was Barney. He was dressed in a bow tie and reminded me of Ted Lange in *The Love Boat*.

'I ain't serving you any liquor after what you did last time,' said Barney.

I laughed. Beth looked confused.

'Seriously,' he said, looking at Beth, 'took me two goddamn hours to clean up the mess.'

'You getting overtime for this?' I said.

'You better believe it,' said Barney, 'a whole two hundred bucks cash money.'

His eyes moved from me to Beth. I almost expected him to say, and what have we here? Like when Lando Calrissian first meets Princess Leia in *The Empire Strikes Back* but instead, he just said, 'hi Beth, you know this guy is a total loser?'

It was my turn to look confused. Barney joined the missing dots in my thoughts.

'How else is she gonna get into this place, I don't see her climbing that motherfucking gate, do you?'

'Barney checked my ID before letting me in the first time,' said Beth casually.

'Any sign of the cat?' said Barney.

'Nope,' said Beth, 'he's still on the lam.'

'And now no one has seen Jeff either,' said Barney, taking out two bottles of beer from a tall cooler behind him.

'I spoke to him last week,' said Beth, 'he said …'

I decided to go for it.

'Derek Anderson told me he saw Jeff leaving with some young woman last week.'

Beth gave no sign to suggest she knew anything about it.

'I didn't see anything,' said Barney, 'Anderson said that, did he?'

'Yep, he said that Jeff went off with some pretty young thing in a hot rod.'

I turned to Beth.

'I thought he was talking about you.'

'Me?' said Beth.

'You are pretty,' said Barney, giving her a wink, 'and that car of yours could be described as a hot rod.'

Beth laughed.

'You are very charming Barney, thank you. But before Matt interrupted me, I was going to say that Jeff told me that he was going on a short vacation and that he'd call me when he got back.'

'So, who's the pretty young thing?' I said.

'I don't know,' said Beth in her no-nonsense voice, 'I'm just looking for his cat, I'm not his mother.'

'Seems like you two have got a situation here,' said Barney, chuckling to himself.

I felt my face go red, luckily for me, the lighting hid it. Beth's eyes sparkled in the light the way they sometimes do in the movies, and I couldn't help but dive into them. Beth smiled and tapped my arm subconsciously.

'You thought Jeff and I were a thing?'

'I thought it was a possibility,' I said.

I began to ruminate on what Derek Anderson had actually said. I was sure he said a pretty young thing and hot rod, but was I imagining the rest? Did he really suggest they were being intimate? Could it have been one of Jeff's daughters, and they were merely hugging as any father and daughter would? Could Derek have misinterpreted a hug for something else? I guess it was possible, after all, I jumped to the conclusion that Beth and Jeff were together.

'I like Jeff,' said Beth, 'he's a nice guy, but he's the same age as my father and frankly that's a bit icky.'

'Well, if it isn't the devil himself,' said Barney.

I turned around, half expecting to see Zimmerman's snakish smile but instead saw Old Jack.

'I knew there was a bar here somewhere,' he said cheerfully.

Barney reached over and shook Jack's hand.

'And what does my man want on this very fine evening?'

'Dealer's choice,' said Jack.

'You got it,' said Barney, turning to fix him something.

'Where were you?' I asked Jack, grateful that he'd found us.

'In the house,' said Jack.

As far as I knew, no one had been inside Zimmerman's house. He always conducted RCA business in The Hall and if he had something he wanted to discuss with a resident of Jonestown he'd either visit them at their home or use The Hall. After Dad died, he'd called over to the house to offer his condolences and told me in that friendly but insincere way that if I needed anything, I should drop by his house etc. I never needed anything from him, so I never dropped by. I'd heard from Karl Johnson and Jeff that Zimmerman jealously guarded his privacy. I thought this was reasonable, after all, Jonestown was a place that walled itself away from ordinary society, so why shouldn't its residents wall themselves away from one another?

'I was looking for the bar,' said Jack, laughing.

'Did you find it?' I asked, realizing that he obviously had not.

'No, you dumb cracker, that weird guy was there.'

'Who?' said Beth.

'The guy out front when we got here, what's his name?'

'Snout,' I said.

'What, no, it begins with a d,' said Jack.

'Mr. Stolly,' said Beth.

'Whatever his name is,' said Jack, ignoring her, 'he told me to get out. I said I was looking for a drink and then the john, so he brought me to the garage, there's a john in there. He said that Zimmerman didn't want anyone in the house. I asked him why he was in the house, and he started to stutter like fucking Woody Woodpecker. Anyway, there was no booze inside, so there was no point in being there.'

Barney called Jack's name and presented him with a glass the size of a fishbowl. It was full of a vivid blue liquid and elaborately decorated with umbrellas and slices of citrus fruit. Jack's eyes lit up.

'You remembered,' said Jack, in earnest gratitude.

He took the drink with both hands and puckered his mouth trying to find a straw. Once his lips grabbed onto one, he sucked with gusto and then, satisfied, let out a loud groan of appreciation. Barney laughed and Beth and I looked at one another, wondering what Jack was drinking. Jack put the drink on the bar and reached for Barney. They locked arms around each other's shoulders.

'I told Barney a story about a time I was in Key West,' said Jack, 'I was in Sloppy Joe's with this knockout, and she was drinking a bright blue cocktail called an Aqua Velva.'

'And?' I said.

Jack withdrew his arm from Barney and became suddenly coy.

'Well, the rest of the story isn't really appropriate to tell in polite company.'

Beth smiled, 'don't mind me, Jack, I have older brothers, and I've heard about as much locker room talk as anyone. Did you seal the deal?'

Jack grinned, 'I sure did.'

We all laughed and once the moment had passed, I turned to Beth.

'Want to sneak into the house?'

'Why?' said Beth.

'Well, it's either that or listen to Jack's stories.'

'I like Jack's stories.'

'Yeah, but they're all the same, come on, it might be exciting.'

'Intriguing, you mean,' said Beth, her eyes lighting up.

'Snout's keeping people out. I'd love to know what he's protecting.'

'We'd be trespassing,' said Beth, 'anything we discovered would be inadmissible.'

'In a missing cat case?' I said.

'Curiosity killed the cat,' she said.

At that moment, our eyes met. I think something synchronized there. I don't want to sound all mushy and say that sparks flew and that doves rose into the air, but there was a connection. Something. I knew, given what Rohit had discovered, that any romance with Beth was unlikely, but at that instant I felt that we understood one another, that we shared a wavelength and were happy to surf it as long as it lasted.

'Well?' I said.

'Let's do it,' said Beth.

Chapter Fourteen
The Desk, Sacramento 1987

When I was a kid Dad's study had a sacred aura around it. It was the one place in the house that was uniquely his. Access was strictly forbidden except for special circumstances usually involving serious conversations. Even Mom was forbidden to enter without Dad's permission. Most married men found refuge in their sheds or garages where they could while away weekend afternoons fixing up stuff or just listening to a ball game, but not my dad. He wasn't handy or interested in working on his car like other dads. Sure, he could mow the lawn and unblock a toilet, but he didn't take any particular pleasure in the kind of home improvement projects other dads did. Whenever I'd visit friends at the weekend, I always remember their father being busy banging something with a hammer or using a buzzing machine in the garage. If we had something to do around the house that required expertise Dad paid an expert. I guess we had the money and he, like me, preferred time to pursue more absorbing activities rather than hours under sinks or up in the loft. His father had been dean of admissions at the Dominican University of California in Marin County and living on campus my dad grew up with a respect for books and an appreciation of scholarly seclusion.

I never knew Dad's parents. His mom died when he was about twenty and his dad died when I was a baby. He rarely spoke about them and when he did, it was always respectful and with an air of sentimentality. I think he modeled his own parenting on their approach. He spoke about his father having the calmness of a monk and never losing his temper or engaging in what he termed emotional recklessness. He also said his father was distant and more like a manager than a parent, at least in modern terms. Nowadays, a lot of dads are hands-on and are expected to be. I remember Karl Johnson talking about it at an RCA meeting and my immediate thought was my dad wasn't like that. Karl spoke about how he and Jenna were equal partners and how biology no longer determined roles. It was interesting and affirmed without a doubt that I'd made the right choice in remaining solitary. I couldn't see myself changing diapers and giving night feeds. Karl had gone from talking about a proposed curfew for Jonestown children to child safety before wandering onto the joys of being a modern father. Anyway, Dad like his dad was at times aloof and stern but was almost always calm and kind and instilled a healthy regard for boundaries and rules. My fascination with his study began early, and he sensed or noticed it so, at four years old, he gave me the grand tour. It was like being invited into the cockpit of a plane or backstage at the theatre. The room was paneled oak with inbuilt bookshelves and smelled of dry wood and cigarette smoke. It was meticulously clean. Dad was always neat and well turned out. He'd grown up in a time when young men wore good suits and tailors knew their craft. I still have one of his suits from the sixties. I had it altered to fit me. The quality of the fabric and the fit is amazing, I rarely wear it but when I do, it makes me feel like I'm ten feet tall. It also makes me wonder what Dad was like back then.

Dad's study was dominated by a robust nineteenth-century kidney-shaped mahogany desk with a green leather inlay. It had belonged to his dad and though he never said, so I think it was his most treasured possession. It traveled to Florida and then to New Hampshire where it now sits in my office and on which I'm typing these words. Back when Dad was giving me the tour of his study, he let me sit in his chair at the desk. On the desk was a picture of Mom and me and my brother and sister. There was also a picture of him with his parents on the day of his high school graduation. Other than that, there was a notepad, an ashtray, and a telephone. Dad had a private line direct to his study and sometimes late at night it would ring out, and I'd hear Dad rising to answer it and sometimes after that he'd go out, presumably to the scene of a crime, but it wasn't very often that happened.

When matters of discipline needed attention, Dad would speak to whoever had broken the rules in his study. It was not a frequent thing, but it did happen, usually to me. Being the youngest I got away with a lot, but not always. TJ was very protective of me and Bev was too, but not to the same extent. Being the youngest meant that to impress my older siblings or simply to get attention, I had to cause some kind of trouble. The first occasion Dad really gave me a proper ticking off was when I cut some of our neighbor's prize Damask roses to give to Mom on Mother's Day. I didn't protest the way Bev would have but rather sat there, took my medicine, promised not to do it again and all was forgiven. Our neighbor, a surly man named McConnell must have spent the rest of his life spying on me because any time I got near the boundary between our gardens he'd yell, and I'd run. He died when I was about thirteen and must have spun in his grave when the family who moved into his house dug up the rose beds to build a barbecue pit.

It was around that time that I began to be drawn towards Dad's study with increasing fascination. Up until then, I'd been respectful of his wishes and never sought to pry. I hadn't even peeked through the keyhole, not that there was much to see.

Bev had never shown an interest in discovering the secrets within, I guess she associated the room with getting chewed out, and besides, she didn't have that intense curiosity that boys often do. TJ had died before any sense of curiosity had arisen in him but something in me said had he lived he'd have protected me from myself and discouraged my explorations.

The study was locked when Dad was out of the house and usually when he was home too. Because of this, my teenage mind, coupled with stories of what my friends had found under their parent's mattresses and in their dad's shed and so on, became devoted to discovering what lay within Dad's desk.

In the compartment under my pa's toolbox, there's a titty magazine, want to see it?

Playboy and *Penthouse* and the occasional *Hustler* came our way, and we studied them with academic interest. One time, one of the guys found a naturist magazine. It was filled with fat, hairy middle-aged men and women, and it scared the hell out of us. Each of us longed for a private stash or at least access to one, but finding nothing in the usual places, I was convinced that Dad's desk contained the holy grail of pornographic magazines and that if I could somehow find a way in and show it to the guys my status within the group would go from esteemed to exalted.

I knew that Dad kept a spare key in the house but didn't know where, and anyway the likelihood of finding it was so remote I decided to get into minor trouble in school to facilitate a talk in the study. Sometimes if Dad had to attend to something before giving me a telling off, he'd tell me to wait for him in the study. I was hoping this would be the case and was delighted to have a full five minutes there unsupervised while he spoke with Mom about insurance or some other mundane domestic matter. Up until that moment, I'd never moved a muscle while I was waiting for Dad, but this time I did a quick check of the desk drawers. I didn't find anything except papers and folders with more papers in them, however, in the bottom drawer on the left side of the desk, I found two folders marked SFPD and CONFIDENTIAL. Seeing those words printed in red and thinking that Dad might walk in at any moment got my heart fluttering like a hummingbird. I opened the first folder. It was full of documents and letters in a distinct kind of handwriting. There was another letter that had a load of symbols on it. I remember, at the time, thinking they were like the ones on the chart Lottie Baylock had drawn when TJ went missing. I decided it wasn't that interesting, and I put it back and picked up the second folder. When I opened it, several glossy photos displaying the most depraved violence I'd ever seen screamed back at me like a vision from the deepest part of hell. All I remember was that they were girls, they were around my age, and they were dead. I recoiled from the images in disgust, but composed myself enough to place the folder back where it came from. I had to be certain that Dad wouldn't notice if anything was out of place.

At the time, I had half an idea about Dad's job. I knew he worked with the police and that it involved dead bodies, but until I actually saw those photos, I had no concept of the visceral horror Dad saw day in and day out. I sat back in the chair where I'd been told to wait and closed my eyes for a moment. That was my mistake. Immediately, the image of one of the girls surfaced from the depths of my imagination like some terrible fish. Her neck was sliced so deep that it looked as if her head might fall off. Her eyes were staring and lifeless, like a doll's eyes. Her mouth hung open in a silent scream or perhaps some final words beginning her killer not to take away her life, either way, nothing could be said now, and no one would ever hear it. As the image rose, it expanded into my mind so that I could see the whole thing. Her neck and face, although grotesque, was not too far beyond what I'd seen in some of those movies that come on after midnight. No, the truly disturbing and disgusting image was of her body. She'd been slashed straight up from her genitals to just below her breastbone. She reminded me of the pig carcasses I'd seen in a documentary about the meat industry in school, only she had been a person, someone's daughter, someone's sister. Suddenly and forcefully, an uncomfortable rise of nausea whooshed through me. I felt a searing heat flush my body, and my stomach felt like it would jump out of my mouth. I ran from the room and just about made it to the kitchen sink, where I spewed up the half-chewed hot dog I'd had for dinner in school.

Mom came from the living room and helped me without fussing. I think moms are immune to puke and things like that. She scooped bits of hot dogs out of the sink and put them in the garbage disposal unit. She then ran the tap, asked me if I was OK and when I said I was she rinsed the sink and told me to sit down. I wiped my mouth and Mom then got me a glass of milk. Dad appeared at the door.

'It's those awful school dinners,' said Mom, 'a hot dog is not proper food, no wonder you got sick, it was probably diseased. I don't know why you didn't come home and eat a proper dinner with your father and me.'

It was meatloaf night. I really didn't like Mom's meatloaf and would usually find some pretext to avoid it.

'I had practice,' I said glumly.

'If you're going to do sports your body needs proper nutrition,' said Mom, 'you don't see baseball players on television eating hot dogs.'

Maybe not, but the people who watched them sure as hell ate them. Mom was like one of those spinning plate tricks, whizzing in and out of control at the same time. Her tirade against hot dogs was just her way of keeping the plate going.

'Son,' said Dad, 'we can talk about what you did tomorrow, for now, it looks like the old karma bus has run over you, reversed and run over you again.'

'What's the karma bus?' I asked, thinking it might be a word for food poisoning.

'Karma,' said Dad looking at me the way a lawyer might look at his client, 'is the idea that if you do something wrong the universe gets you back, so you being sick right now is payback for what you did earlier.'

The way Dad phrased it, I couldn't be sure if he meant snooping around in his desk or getting a phone call home from school.

'That's nonsense, Thomas,' said Mom, 'the boy ate something bad. His body did what it was supposed to and got rid of it. There's no such thing as karma, you're being silly putting ideas like that in his head.'

Whether it's real or not, I never forgot the idea of karma, and it has occupied a place in my mind ever since.

Dad wandered off to his study and closed the door. Mom made me drink the milk even though I didn't want to and once I'd managed it, she sent me to bed. I objected on the grounds it was barely eight o'clock and that I had homework to finish.

'I'll write you a note,' said Mom.

'But I feel fine.'

Mom gave me a look that told me I had two choices, bed, or she'd get Dad to deal with me. I figured after what I'd stumbled upon in his study and his words about karma, it'd be a good idea to keep my distance, so I reluctantly made my way to my bedroom. I passed Bev's room, the door was open. I watched her for a moment. She was listening to music while she studied. She sensed I was there and turned towards me.

'Get lost, creep,' she said, getting up and closing her door.

I wanted to say a sassy comeback about how I wasn't a creep and how she was a bitch, but I didn't get the chance. After it occurred to me that I was being a creep, I was staring, and I didn't know what compelled me to. I'd never stood at Bev's door watching her without her knowing. Maybe when I was a little kid, but now that I was older and confused and awash with hormones, I wondered if a more primal force was at work and felt weird. I was relieved by the time I got to my room and lay on my bed. All thoughts of my sister had disappeared into the dark. What replaced them, however, was arguably worse.

I lay staring at the ceiling, waiting for sleep to swallow me. I wasn't tired, and the fright I'd received in Dad's study had pumped so much adrenaline into my system that my mind raced with a fizzing intensity that made me shake. My thoughts wavered from clear and vivid to scattered and incoherent. The central image was that of the murder victim from Dad's study. I kept thinking about how someone could do that to another person, how it felt, how you could get it in your head that you wanted to do something like that. TJ's death wandered in there too. I saw him as he fell, his eyes were as wide as plates. The look on his face was not so much fear as disbelief.

Matty help.

I began to wonder in the shooting neurons of my brain if there was a connection between TJ's death and my growing fascination with the images I'd seen earlier. Something in the eyes of the girl and TJ formed a link in my mind, or more exactly a feeling in my body. At first, I tried to reject it. I didn't want the sense of excitement to rise in me, but eventually, I just gave in and as sleep started to lap up against me like waves on the shore, I imagined I was following the girl from Dad's study through the woods. TJ was nowhere to be seen. The girl was calling to me in a voice that dragged out like an echo. Each time I got close to her, I felt a surge of anticipation, but each time she'd vanish, and I'd have to start again. I must have chased her a dozen times before I caught her. As I grabbed her, a cascade of wild energy rushed through us and took us to the edge of the creek where TJ had met his death. Another surge of energy carried us over the edge. We tumbled headlong into the water. The water was warm. We were naked. Her body was no longer mutilated. Her eyes were shining and alive and full of watery energy and radiating a vivid opalescence. Her hands moved all over my body, making it tingle. As she reached up to my face and began to kiss me, I felt a jolt of electricity flood my body, wrenching me asunder. I awoke with a start and lay there sweating and heaving as with a fever. A few minutes later, I got up to change my pajamas and wipe down the bedclothes.

The next morning, after Mom checked my temperature by placing her hand on my forehead, she rang my school and said I wouldn't be coming in. Dad and Bev had both left already, and Mom told me to rest before kissing me on my warm forehead and leaving for work. I lay on my bed and listened for her car to leave the driveway before getting up and peeking through the blinds and watching it disappear down the street. I got dressed and went into the kitchen. On the way, I checked Dad's study. It was locked. Even if it was open, it had lost its fascination. I now had a more pressing concern. I grabbed a slice of cold toast and sat and ate it. Fifteen minutes had passed since Mom had left, so I knew it was highly unlikely she'd be back. I went out to the shed and grabbed my bike and headed to the library.

It was the definition of irony, a kid who wasn't particularly academic, or at least not inclined that way, having the unexpected bonus of a day off school and using it to cycle for all they were worth to the local library. The library was four blocks away, and it opened at 9. Sometimes Bev would go there to study at weekends or during the holidays. I hadn't been in a few years, not since I grew out of books and got into sports and comics and just hanging out. As I got to the library and went inside, I began to feel nervous. The old librarian Mrs. Peck knew Mom and even if she didn't recognize me, she'd recognize my name from my card, and maybe she'd ask why I wasn't in school, and it'd get back to Mom and then Dad. I hesitated and decided to turn back when I noticed a young woman standing behind the counter. She wore a navy dress with a floral print and wore her auburn hair up. She had a pencil going through it and was busily stamping books. I waited for about a minute to see if Mrs. Peck would appear, and when I was sure she wasn't there, I went in. The woman behind the counter smiled at me and resumed her task. I went to the index box and flicked through the cards trying to find what I was looking for, but my rudimentary understanding of the Dewey Decimal Classification had me going down rabbit holes and dead ends.

'Are you looking for anything in particular?'

I looked up. It was the librarian. She was even prettier close-up. Her eyes were a golden brown, and they shone in the light. I felt a little embarrassed.

'Are you doing a school project?'

I nodded.

'What's it on?'

I realized I'd have to say something, but it couldn't be the first thing that came to mind. I paused before answering her.

'It's on Jack the Ripper,' I said, 'for history class.'

She tilted her head slightly and frowned. The frown wasn't reproachful, but rather conveyed her surprise at my response to her question.

'We have to pick a figure from history. I decided I'd do it on Jack the Ripper. My friends are doing theirs on Abraham Lincoln and Doctor King. I want mine to be different.'

'Wow,' she said, 'that is different.'

She gently moved in beside me and began to flick through the index cards. My eyes were drawn towards her cleavage and as she became aware of what I was doing, she stopped suddenly.

'Shouldn't you be in school?'

Her tone wasn't accusatory, it was more curious than anything.

I said nothing. She giggled to herself.

'I've never heard of a kid playing hooky in a library before.'

I felt a wave of dismay when she referred to me as a kid.

'I didn't want the school librarian to know what I was doing my project on, in case she thought I was weird. She's not like you, she's old and doesn't understand things.'

'I know that type,' said the librarian, 'did you ever meet Mrs. Peck?'

I nodded.

'She retired last year. She spent her final few months showing me the ropes. I felt like quitting almost every day. I was so glad when she left.'

I smiled. I was delighted. Our mutual dislike of Mrs. Peck meant that the librarian would probably help me with no questions asked.

'Here we are,' she said, 'The Encyclopaedia of Murder and Violent Crime.'

She handed me the card.

'The number there, 'she said, pointing to the card, 'is the reference number. If you need any other help, just ask.'

I smiled and thanked her and made my way to the appropriate bookshelf. I had no interest in Jack the Ripper *per se* and scanned the titles on the shelf. They all related to murder and crime. After a few minutes, I had selected three books and found a desk in a secluded part of the room. The books were:

The Stranger Beside Me by Ann Rule, *Zodiac* by Robert Graysmith, and *The Man Who Killed Boys* by Clifford L. Linedecker. Rule's book was about Ted Bundy, Graysmith's book spoke for itself, and Linedecker's book was about John Wayne Gacy. All three killers were names I'd heard Dad discussing. All the books were doorstops, but I wasted no time scanning them for relevant information. Bundy interested me because he'd lived in California and his crimes still resonated in the state. I looked for parts of the book that focused on Bundy's early years. I did the same with the book about Gacy. I wanted to know what drove these men to commit their crimes, and I wanted to know if I was made of the same stuff.

Back then, it was difficult to research serial killers. There were plenty of books dealing with the topic, but very little to do with their psychopathology. Nowadays, everyone who watches TV or has seen *The Silence of the Lambs* is an expert on serial murder. A simple search of the internet will not only give you facts, but photos and all sorts of other grisly morsels to satiate your morbid interest. The embarrassing truth about my dream was that it had frightened me. I had heard Dad speaking about sex crimes. Sometimes he'd leave the door of his study slightly open, and I would listen to his side of whatever conversation he was having. He'd refer to anatomical terms like vaginal and anal trauma, and occasionally say that whoever committed the murder or murders was sexually motivated. I didn't know it at the time, but the original profiler Robert Ressler was working on a book about serial killers, and Dad was one of the many people helping him with research. The book would become *Whoever Fights Monsters,* which for my money is the first and last word on serial killers.

I spent the rest of the day in the library pouring over anything I could find that related to the psychology of serial killing. I didn't find much and got so absorbed in my search that I lost track of time and only made it home about ten minutes before Mom. Before I rushed out of the library the librarian gave me a wink telling me it was our secret. I resolved to come back every chance I got.

One interesting thing I discovered that day occurred while I was looking through the book about Zodiac. Everyone in northern California had heard of Zodiac and even though it had been a while since his crimes, there was an enduring fascination with them because he'd never been caught. He was, in one sense, America's Jack the Ripper. Of course, all of this was new to me at the time. Until I'd looked through Graysmith's book Zodiac was a name I'd heard Dad mention on the phone, and only briefly. In the book, there were pictures of Zodiac's letters to *The San Francisco Chronicle*. I looked at them with proud amazement. They were identical to the ones I'd seen in the folder in Dad's desk. *My dad hunts serial killers, I* thought. Immediately that thought turned to fearful questioning. I wondered if he'd noticed anything in my behavior that reminded him of his work. I decided that knowledge was the key. Curiosity was only a spark to light the fire of my knowledge. I had to learn what type of behavior was common to men like Bundy and Gacy. If I knew the signs, I could learn to disguise them.

Chapter Fifteen
The RCA Dinner, April 2019

Entrée

The back door to Zimmerman's house was shut. I turned the handle and pushed gently, but it remained firm. Beth told me to hide in the shadows and wait while she knocked on the door. About thirty seconds later, Snout appeared. He peered through the glass and unlocked the door. As the door moved, Beth tried to step inside. Her slender leg moved out from the split in her dress and Snout followed it like a heron hunting a fish in a shallow stream.

'I-I'm sorry, Miss Becker, but Mr. Zimmerman doesn't want anyone in the house.'

'Oh, I'm Sorry,' said Beth with a slight slur, 'I'm looking for the little girl's room.'

Snout fidgeted with his cufflinks and looked back into the house.

'It's in the garage, just over there,' he said, nodding towards the far end of the house.

Beth hiccuped and laughed. She pointed in the direction of the garage and swayed on the doorstep.

'Would you be a sweetheart and show me the way. I've had a few glasses of champagne, and it's gone to my head. I'm worried I might fall over and, in this dress, well, I don't have to paint you a picture.'

'I-I really can't,' said Snout trying to close the door, 'it's just over there, you won't fall.'

'But if I did,' said Beth, 'Mr. Zimmerman would be very upset, wouldn't he? I am a guest, after all, it might be embarrassing for him?'

Snout hesitated, patted himself down and stepped out of the house. Beth called him a sweetheart and grabbed clumsily on to his arm.

'Don't go too fast,' said Beth, laughing.

I moved from the shadows and just as I opened the door, Beth affected a timely stumble.

'Ooops,' she said, 'it's not easy in these shoes.'

Snout must have caught her up or whatever because I heard her describing him as a true gentleman.

Zimmerman's house, at first glance, was the same as mine and although it was a little bigger, I was willing to bet the layout was identical. This gave me an advantage as I wouldn't be creeping around unfamiliar surroundings.

The back door led directly to the kitchen adjacent to the laundry room. I hid in the laundry room and waited for Snout to return. A short time later, I heard keys clicking as he locked the back door from the inside, followed by his soft footsteps moving through the kitchen and into the hall. I then heard the living room door close and waited for a couple of minutes before emerging from my hiding place and going to the back door. I opened it slowly and with lithe grace, Beth slid into the room as if she were water.

'Great idea,' I whispered.

'OK, what now?'

'I don't know,' I said, 'I didn't think we'd get this far.'

Beth's private detective instincts took over.

'Where did Snout go?' she asked, taking off her shoes.

'The living room, I think.'

'Is this house the same as yours?'

'From what I've seen, it's pretty much identical.'

'OK, let's go exploring.'

We went through the kitchen and into the hallway. The hallway in these houses is quite long and sweeps around to the bottom of the stairs. Off the hallway are three rooms. To the immediate right, as we looked, there was the living room. Across from it was a mid-sized room of no designated purpose and to the left of the stairs, though we couldn't see it, I knew there was another spacious room like the living room. Beth put her ear to the room on the left. She turned the handle and opened the door without so much as a squeak. She took out her phone and activated the torch. The room was a study of some kind. There was a desk and books on shelves, and nothing much else. Beth went over to the desk and did a quick sweep of the papers on it.

'There's nothing here, it's just his office.'

'What's on the desk?'

'I don't know, bills, that sort of thing.'

'Just bills?'

'Probably, I can't really check,' she said sternly, 'we are trespassing, remember.'

We left the room and moved quietly to the living room door. My heart was beating furiously. As we got to the door, I expected it to open and Snout to emerge. When nothing happened, Beth once again put her ear to the door. She turned to me and shook her head. She then turned the handle. I almost wet myself. It was one thing sneaking around, but entering a room where someone was likely to be, even if it was only Snout, suddenly terrified and excited me.

'What are you doing?'

Beth carefully pushed open the door. She scanned the room with her phone torch and found it was empty. I was immediately struck by the smell. I took out my phone and activated the torch function.

'What is that amazing smell?' said Beth.

'Sandalwood,' I said.

Sandalwood has a distinctly sweet and creamy aroma, and it hung in the air in perfect proportion to the room. It wasn't overpowering or heavy and because of this, I knew it was not imitation or cheap sandalwood, this was expensive, most likely from Mysore in India. I traced the source of the aroma. There was a bowl on a table to the right side of the door, and in it were sandalwood chips. My guess was they were infused with pure sandalwood oil.

'What are you doing?' asked Beth.

I put my nose to the bowl and inhaled the rich sweet woody fragrance. It was definitely Mysore sandalwood. I'd only smelled it once before when a subscriber to my blog sent me a tiny sample as a gift. This stuff wasn't just expensive, this was mega expensive and mega classy too. I pocketed a few chips. Beth gave me a curious look and nodded towards the door. We left the room and headed towards the stair, where we stood for a moment and considered our options.

'If we go upstairs, it'll be impossible to escape if we're caught,' said Beth, 'but that might just add to the fun.'

I enjoyed the suggestiveness of her statement. I decided to push for the hell of it.

'Fun?' I said.

'Not what you're thinking,' she said.

'What was I thinking?'

'What do you want to do next?' she said, indicating game time was over.

'There's a room in there,' I said, pointing behind her. It was what would normally be termed a family room, not quite as large as the living room, but big enough. I use mine as a den. Beth looked in the direction I'd pointed, and straightaway a sliver of light cut through the dark from an open door. We both froze, but when no one appeared, Beth moved towards the light and I followed. The door to the family room was open just enough to see into it and, more importantly, to hear one particular voice from within.

Although I could only see the end of a couch and part of a large bookshelf, I heard Zimmerman's measured voice as clear as a whistle. It was a stroke of luck on our part that wherever he was positioned within the room, his voice carried on the air perfectly.

'How are things moving in Colorado?' he said, his voice rich and resonant.

Someone was on a speakerphone. The voice was female, though I couldn't make out what was being said.

'OK,' said Zimmerman, 'we can make our move here soon. I have her ready to go to Juniper Hills on Wednesday, I'll get her to sign the deeds over before then.'

The voice on the speakerphone said something, but it was indistinct. I thought for a moment the voice sounded familiar, but dismissed the idea.

'About a million in assets,' said Zimmerman.

I looked at Beth, she put her index finger to her lips. I then heard Snout's speaking but like the voice on the speakerphone, it was incoherent.

'They don't know a thing,' said Zimmerman. Snout followed with a comment, which was then followed by Zimmerman saying loudly, 'who?'

This time, Snout's voice was clear. He must have moved into the audible channel. Now he said firmly, 'Beth Becker, I don't trust her.'

'She's harmless,' said Zimmerman, 'she's looking for Jeff Simmons' cat.'

'Do you really believe that?' said Snout, though his voice was softening and less clear than before.

'No, but I don't think she knows anything about what we're doing either. She's just a kid.'

Again, Snout said something inaudible.

'Well good,' said Zimmerman in a rising voice which suggested he wasn't in the mood for conjecture from subordinates, 'I'll get to meet her then.'

Snout mumbled something which clearly displeased Zimmerman.

'What did you say?' said Zimmerman, 'speak to me like that again, and you'll be sorry.'

There was a long pause before Zimmerman added, 'perhaps if I were to expose your little secret.'

Snout protested.

'You don't think I would?' said Zimmerman, 'just try me. You worry about the money and let me do the rest. And don't question me ever again.'

Snout mumbled an apology.

'Loyalty,' said Zimmerman, 'loyalty brings strength.'

Suddenly, a low growl rolled from the room. It was followed by Derek Anderson telling Razor to shut up.

'What's its problem?' said Zimmerman.

'I don't know,' said Anderson, 'I'll check it out, maybe he heard something.'

Beth and I looked at one another and turned on our heels with as much speed as we could muster while trying to stay silent. We had barely made it to the kitchen when Derek and

Razor were in the hall. Razor was barking furiously. My heart jumped. The back door was locked. How could we get out without them knowing someone had been in the house? I grabbed Beth and pulled her into the laundry room. While Derek calmed Razor down, Zimmerman and Snout entered the kitchen. Beth and I hid in the shadows of the laundry room, knowing that if anyone walked in and turned on the light, we were done for. Zimmerman walked to the door, glanced into the semi-darkness, and closed the door. A minute later, Derek and Razor entered the kitchen. Finally, after what seemed an eternity, I heard the sound of the back door opening and then a click as the lock shut. The silence which followed was deep and serene. We waited for a sensible time before moving. With no further sounds emerging and the house returning to its un-occupied state, it was time to get out.

'Was that exciting enough?' said Beth, a little out of breath.

I nodded, and we moved quietly from the laundry room. We went into the kitchen slowly and carefully. For what we knew, Razor Anderson was out there waiting for us. Luckily, he wasn't.

'I think they've gone into the marquee,' said Beth, 'it's al-most nine, it must be time for dinner.'

'OK,' I said, 'how do we get out?

The key to the back door was gone.

'Zimmerman must have taken the key.'

Beth rolled her eyes.

'You're not too good at this, are you?' she said playfully. With that, she grabbed my wrist, and we walked out of the kitchen and to the front door. Before opening it, Beth looked up the stairs.

'It's a pity we didn't go upstairs,' she said, 'I don't suppose there's time now.'

She opened the front door and we walked out. We went around the side of the house and into the backyard. It seemed that everyone was in the marquee and by the sound of it, Zimmerman was making a speech. As we entered the tent, he noticed us.

'I knew there'd be latecomers,' he said, 'they must have got lost on the way.'

Everyone turned to look at us. There was a round of laughter. We were a little out of breath and I could feel blood rise in my face. Jack was smiling broadly and giving me a rousing thumbs-up. I think Beth noticed it too. She flashed me a smile, and we sat at the back of the marquee.

'As I was saying,' said Zimmerman, 'it's so nice to see so many of you here for this wonderful annual event.'

Zimmerman spoke for about fifteen minutes. He discussed initiatives that had come to pass and ones he wanted to implement. He talked about how great Jonestown had become under his leadership and thanked his cadre of helpers including Snout whom he said would be taking over as RCA secretary in the fall. There was a round of applause. Snout looked like he was relishing the prestige. People reached out to shake his hand, and he took them with the enthusiasm of a campaigning politician. Something about Zimmerman's endorsement had empowered him.

'Mr. Stolly will also be incorporating a new and exciting aspect into his secretarial role.'

Zimmerman paused. He knew how to speak to a crowd. He knew making them wait would make them interested.

'As you all know, the finances of our community are managed by the RCA. The fees we all contribute towards maintaining our wonderful gardens and shared spaces and, most importantly,' he said with emphasis, 'keeping our community safe from unwanted intruders will now be put to work in other ways too.'

Zimmerman paused to allow the crowd to take in his words. Once he was satisfied, they understood his message, he continued.

'Mr. Stolly has suggested that our money be invested in his bank, where it will make a tidy profit. This money, Mr. Stolly and his colleagues at First Trust assure me, will be part of a risk-free investment. This will guarantee a dividend for every member of the community by the end of the financial year. This is a one-time offer and only open to residents of our community.'

Most of the audience had taken a few drinks by this time, and the news that their money would make money without any attached risk led to cheers and general noises of approval. Beth was listening intently.

'Sounds like a good deal,' she said.

'That must have been what they were talking about in Zimmerman's house.'

'It's a scam,' said Beth, 'whatever he asks you to do, don't sign up for it.'

'In the coming days,' said Zimmerman, 'Mr. Stolly and one of his colleagues will be visiting each of you in your lovely homes to get some bank details. You do not have to sign up if you don't wish to. You may, of course, pay your fees as you have been, but from what I saw when Mr. Stolly and his colleagues ran figures for me, you'd be missing a truly wonderful opportunity.'

There was another round of applause, and I half expected a chant of 'sign us up' or something similar to begin. Instead, Mr. Zimmerman invited everyone to sit at the table as dinner was about to be served. Beth and I sat with Jack at the end of the table nearest the bar. Opposite us were two unoccupied seats, and they remained unoccupied until, to my utter astonishment, Derek and Donna Anderson sat down. Derek had tidied up and was passably normal, dressed in a crisp white shirt and jacket. He'd trimmed his wispy beard and looked unusual without his MAGA hat. He nodded to us as he sat down. Donna, to be fair to her, was stunning. There was no hint of the frumpiness she tried so hard to conceal. My guess is she'd been in the gym for weeks preparing for this event. Her hair had a wave in it and was draped loosely around her shoulders. She wore two gold earrings with what looked like sapphires in them. Her dress was a rich Prussian blue that drew the eye as easily as a lure drew a fish. She sat with poise and elegance and smiled at Beth and me. Her smile was all lower face, a sure sign it was being forced. I smiled back with the same sincerity and for a moment, a silence hovered and threatened to become awkward. I decided to take the initiative.

'Are you wearing Hypnotic Poison?' I asked.

I could tell straight away she was impressed.

'Wow,' she said, 'you've got quite a nose, Matthew.'

'Call me Matt, please, this is an informal evening, isn't it?'

Donna turned to her husband.

'Matt noticed my perfume. He's got a nose like Razor.'

'Is that right,' said Derek impassively.

'Of course, it's the eau de toilette,' I added, 'the EDT is more refined than the eau de parfum in my opinion. It's an excellent choice for this kind of evening.'

I reckoned that since Donna liked nice things and her husband paid little or no notice to this aspect of her life and knew nothing about perfumes or clothing or anything sophisticated, I could, by being attentive to her, soften the awkwardness of sitting with them.

'How do you know about these things?' said Donna.

She was genuinely interested. So was Beth, whose eyebrow raised as if to suggest I was full of surprises. I mentioned my blog and the fact that Gretchen worked for Dior and had educated me in such matters.

'Gretchen?' said Donna.

After a little more attention to Donna's ensemble, she became my best friend and was hungry for more compliments about her sense of style. I was able to comment on the cut of her dress, the fabric and how her accessories complemented her outfit perfectly. Donna was visibly delighted. I have to admit I was enjoying it too. I rarely spoke about these things in company, and the serendipity of the occasion gave me a great sense of wellbeing. But, like all good things, it was short-lived. Derek stifled the conversation and drew Donna's attention away from me. I don't know if he was jealous or just felt a bit stupid but now, they had turned to one another and were in the process of an important conversation spoken in low quiet register. The catering team, who must have arrived with the food just as Mr. Zimmerman had finished speaking, were busily placing appetizers in front of everyone and taking orders for the main. I ordered a fillet of beef, as did Beth. The appetizer was Alaskan smoked salmon with snow crab. I was reminded of Christmas as a kid. Dad loved smoked salmon and Mom loved crab. I didn't like either. I pushed the plate in front of me.

'You not eating that?' said Jack.

'It's all yours,' I said.

Jack piled the seafood onto his plate and began to eat hungrily.

As the meal progressed plenty of good wine flowed and finally, just as dessert was served, we were all relaxed. Derek remained aloof, but thankfully Jack got hold of him and regaled him with seafaring tales. I think Derek was far happier to listen to them than watch his wife's effort at being the belle of the ball. Donna was being unashamedly flirty, but not with me. Beth was to my left and to my right sat Gary Sanders. Gary lived in The Family Zone and seemed like a nice but uninspiring guy. He was a little older than me and bigger too. He said he played football back in college, and we had been discussing it on and off throughout the meal. Beth and Donna were chatting about something while I was telling Gary about my uncle. Suddenly and a little awkwardly, Donna butted in and began to direct her charm at Gary. Gary didn't seem to mind, but his wife did. She immediately engaged her husband in small talk and away from Donna. Donna was a little tipsy, but certainly not drunk. She turned her focus on the man sitting to her left. Even in her uninhibited state, I'd have expected her to be a little more discreet given that her husband was sitting beside her, but there was no stopping her from doing what she'd clearly decided to. At that moment, I felt a little sorry for Derek Anderson.

Just as dessert finished, Zimmerman came down to our part of the table. I watched him during the meal. He'd sat at the head of the table with his closest supporters. Now, as the meal was coming to an end, he'd been going along the length of the table schmoozing and garnering laughs and admiration. When he got to us, he pulled up a chair and squeezed himself between the Andersons, neither of whom were happy about the intrusion. Zimmerman took a close look at Beth. You could see his eyes moving over her the way a person might if they were appreciating a work of art.

'I don't think we've been properly introduced,' he said, offering his hand.

'I'm Beth.'

Zimmerman smiled. His eyes focused on her to the exclusion of all else.

'Henry Zimmerman,' he said as he held her hand in his. He gave it a small squeeze rather than shaking it.

'I'm sorry we were late,' said Beth, 'we got a little side-tracked.'

She moved in close to me and gave me a warm smile.

'So it would seem,' said Zimmerman, 'but there's no need to apologize.'

'The party is very impressive, thank you for inviting us,' I said.

'My pleasure,' said Zimmerman without taking his eyes off Beth.

'I hear you're searching for Jeff Simmons' cat, is that correct?'

'Yes,' said Beth, 'I'm a private detective.'

'Well,' said Zimmerman, leaning forward slightly, 'I must say you're the most beautiful private detective I've ever met.'

Beth smiled, 'that's easy, most of them are fat old men.'

There was something about Zimmerman's tone of voice that made it difficult to ignore him, even when he was engaged in small talk, it seemed important. His charisma was palpable.

'Indeed,' said Zimmerman looking down the table, 'I don't wish to come across as old-fashioned but, if this were a home-coming ceremony, you'd be wearing a tiara right now.'

Beth blushed and in the same instant, Donna Anderson scowled in a way that would curdle milk. She stood up abruptly and excused herself from the table. Zimmerman eye's shot at her, and she held his glare momentarily before walking off in the direction of the bar.

'She's very uptight,' said Zimmerman softly.

He nodded his head slightly towards Derek and, making sure Derek wouldn't overhear him, he said, 'I think there are marital problems.'

His voice was no more than a whisper and yet, I heard it distinctly.

Derek's face suggested he'd rather be anywhere else. I had wondered why he and Donna had chosen to sit with us, but couldn't come to a satisfactory conclusion. As for marital problems, well, that was obvious.

'It's very unusual for a private detective to be looking for a cat,' said Zimmerman in the calculated but honeyed tone of a chat show host.

'The cat was a gift from Jeff's daughter Carrie. They've since become estranged, and Jeff is very upset about it. He wants to find the cat, as it's the only real link he has to her.'

I began to wonder if that was true or part of Beth's ruse.

'Jeff is a very fine journalist,' said Zimmerman, 'did you read his article about our community?'

'Yes,' said Beth.

Zimmerman nodded and rubbed his mouth.

'So, has Matt been helping you find the cat?'

'You could say that,' said Beth, squeezing my knee gently.

'But sadly, you haven't found it yet?'

Beth frowned playfully and shook her head.

'I'm sure it will turn up sooner or later,' said Zimmerman, 'things have a way of working themselves out don't you find?'

'That's how it usually works,' said Beth.

Whatever Zimmerman was looking for he must have found or given up trying because he flashed us a bright but hollow smile and stood up.

'It was nice to meet you, Beth. I hope you find the cat soon. It's never nice when one of our community is missing, even if it's an animal.'

He wished us goodnight and returned to the top of the table. Shortly after Zimmerman left us, Derek Anderson stood up and without a word moved away to the entrance of the marquee and disappeared into the night.

'That was weird,' said Beth, 'kind of intense.'

I had to agree. As Zimmerman spoke, I got the feeling he was trying to read my thoughts. His whole manner was captivating, even while discussing the most mundane things, there was something magnetic about him. I definitely felt it, and I was sure Beth felt it too. I had to give her credit for resisting his interrogation.

With Derek gone, Jack turned to us.

'I shouldn't have had so much of that crab,' he said.

'Are you OK?' I said.

'Just a bit full,' he said, patting his stomach and groaning, 'I'm going to get out of here and go home.'

'Do you want us to go with you?' asked Beth.

'Nah, you kids stay and have some fun. It's just a few yards to my house.'

'Are you sure you'll be alright?' I insisted.

Jack waved away my question and took Beth's hand and kissed it, and then stood up.

'It's been a pleasure serving with you all, but for now, I must leave the captain's table and retire to my bunk.'

Jack gave us a salute and moved slowly towards the entrance. Beth gave me a look that showed concern.

'He'll be fine, I've seen him a lot worse.'

Beth's nose wrinkled and she scratched it. There was a cool breeze blowing in.

'Do you want to stay?' I asked.

She shook her head. The evening was wrapping up anyway. While the crowd remained, the atmosphere was beginning to lag. We got up and went to the bar to wish Barney a goodnight. We were in the process of doing so when Zimmerman's voice echoed out through the tent.

'Thank you for sharing this evening with me,' he said, 'now, just before we say goodnight, I would like to make a very special announcement.'

I looked at Beth.

'I wonder what this is about?' she said.

Chapter Sixteen
The Macdonald Triad,
Sacramento, 1987-91

My parents were impressed that I was spending some of my free time in the library. Bev was less impressed. She complained, saying that the local library was her place of refuge and that I should be using the school library and that I was only going to the library because I had the hots for the librarian. Dad almost spat out his dinner when he heard this.

'Mrs. Peck?' he said incredulously.

'No,' said Bev laughing, 'she retired. The new librarian's name is Enid, and pervert boy can't take his eyes off her.'

'Liar,' I said, feeling embarrassed.

Dad chuckled.

'That's OK,' he said, 'for a moment I thought we had a problem.'

He gave me a wink.

'It's true,' said Bev.

'Is she pretty?' asked Dad.

'Don't encourage him, Thomas,' said Mom.

I nodded. Dad smiled and squeezed my neck, making my shoulders hunch.

'As long as you're keeping up with your studies son, I don't mind what you go to the library for.'

And that was that. Bev didn't say another word and after a while, she stopped going to the library when she knew I'd be there.

Now that I knew the librarian's name, she became less of a mystery and therefore less alluring. To me, she had been Miss Barnes, but since Bev had filled in the missing first name, Enid Barnes did not sit well with the vision of beauty I saw at least twice a week. I wanted to know why Miss Barnes' parents had been so cruel.

'My sister says your name is Enid,' I said one Tuesday afternoon. I was hoping that she would laugh and say don't be silly, my name is … and then say a name that not only suited her but also completed the dots of her mystique. Miss Barnes cracked an awkward smile. She was surprised by my frankness. I didn't think I was being rude or anything.

'It's true,' she said.

I said nothing, I sensed she wanted to say more.

'My family is from Kansas,' she went on, 'and Enid is a traditional family name. My great-grandmother and grandmother were both named Enid.'

'I think it's a nice name.'

She laughed and then, remembering where she was, stifled it.

'You're sweet to say so, but because I was the eldest, I drew the short straw as far as names are concerned. I have two younger sisters, Maggie and Diane. I guess they did a little better.'

Maggie fit my fantasy far better than Enid. I tried to picture what Maggie Barnes looked like. I got as far as red hair and a short skirt before I had to go and sit down.

In the months leading up to Santi Garcia's shooting spree, I spent my library time reading the American Journal of Psychiatry and specifically articles about deviant behavior. There was plenty of stuff, but it was mostly in dense academic language and referred to other articles in other journals. I did start to find what I was looking for though, albeit painstakingly. The general consensus was that people who grew up to commit murder and other deviant acts mostly had a messed-up childhood. Of course, they used words like traumatic and abuse, but nothing quite cuts through the verbiage like messed up or if you really want to emphasize the damage done, fucked-up. I mean, if you asked one of these guys how his childhood was he wouldn't say it was traumatic or difficult, he'd say it was messed up. And why was it messed up, well, because someone had messed it up, usually the parents.

Now, I appreciate that parenting is challenging to say the least. When I see neighbors or just about anyone in town with their kids, I can't think of anything worse. Kids are loud and demanding and because you can't smack them any more their sass gets amplified. It used to be just smart-ass comments in my day, but now a lot of kids seem to be obnoxious, entitled assholes. But it's none of my business how kids are raised, I don't have any and what I know about them doesn't amount to a sneeze in a tornado. That's not to say there aren't those who have expert opinions based on nothing but their own sense of grandiosity. There are childless people in Jonestown who could tell you all about how to raise a kid. Well, I can't wait until their books hit the stores. A real expert on parenting is Judge Reinhold, remember him, the guy who told the Andersons to stay in their lane and not waste his time in court. Not only has he raised about eight kids and about four thousand grandkids, but he also did a lot of work in juvenile court and still does *pro bono* stuff there from time to time. I remember him telling me that during his tenure presiding over the courts in the Three Rivers area, he'd met so many kids whose behavior could have been prevented if their fathers had taken their belts to them. 'Just once,' he emphasized. 'But today we got all these folk listening to new age crap about wellbeing and mindfulness and understanding. I'm not advocating a return to the old ways, but some of those boys could have been put straight with a good old kick in the butt.' I think he emphasized the one-off use of physical discipline because he'd seen what happened to people who'd been repeatedly abused. According to the articles I was reading, repeated abuse produced a combination of rage and humiliation but paradoxically, and this is where psychology really gets weird, in most cases the person abused by a parent or sickeningly both parents, develops an even greater sense of attachment to them.

There's only one, well, two words for it, *fucked up*.

Dad had hardly ever raised his voice to me, or my siblings, let alone hit us, and Mom was the same. We were always disciplined, but it was by talking and punishment was the removal of privileges, so I couldn't say I had an abusive or traumatic childhood. There were bad things in my childhood, as you know, but my parents were as good to me as any. What I couldn't reconcile or regard as normal was how the pictures of the mutilated girls in Dad's study had somehow got mixed up with the part of my brain that made me horny. As I plowed through more articles, one thing became abundantly clear, serial killers killed to enact sexual fantasies, to make them real. I was at the stage where my bedroom door was permanently closed and usually locked. Mom always knocked. Every time I got turned on, the images of the eviscerated girls got in there somewhere. This scared me, I was certain I would become Ted Bundy or worse.

My anxiety and confusion grew until I read a 1963 article entitled *The Threat to Kill* by John M. Macdonald, M.R.C.P. I hate the way they use letters. Big deal, you're educated. Dad never referred to himself as Thomas Lowell, M.D., or anything like that. Brian and Marie Mitchell do that. When I first met the

Mitchells at some party or other just after they'd moved in, Brian gave me his card. It read Brian Mitchell, Ph.D. M.Litt or some other bullshit. Marie didn't give me a card, but she introduced herself as professor. No wonder their kid changed her identity, abuse isn't only physical.

Macdonald's article outlined what came to be known as The Macdonald Triad. Behavioral scientists love their triads. There's also The Dark Triad which is a combination of psychopathy, narcissism, and Machiavellianism but for now, let's consider the Macdonald Triad. Reading about this gave me a kind of hope because I didn't fit into it at all. The triad consisted of cruelty to animals, starting fires, and persistent bedwetting beyond an appropriate developmental stage, that is to say, five years of age. It was believed at the time that these characteristics or at least two of them were a good early indication of a child's possible escalation into violent behavior. I hadn't wet the bed since I was really little, and then it was because I'd been to a birthday party and consumed about a gallon of pop, so I dismissed that immediately. According to Macdonald, the bedwetting should occur at least twice a week and be accompanied by reproach and humiliation by one or both parents. Cruelty to animals was a little more complex. One afternoon I found a stray cat on the way home from school. It was a small black and white cat, probably a few months old and hungry too. I picked it up, and it began to purr loudly. I figured it had been neglected or abandoned. Whatever had happened to it, it ran into me, and with what was swirling around in my mind it might have been better off if it hadn't. I brought it home and fed it. It ate a tin of tuna and drank some milk, and then became animated and playful. I played around with it for a while. I got a sock and dangled it, and it jumped and caught it. Billybird III sauntered into the backyard where we were playing but paid no attention to us. I carried on playing with the little guy. I resisted giving him a name. I didn't want to see it as a living thing with an identity of its own. After a while, I went to the tool shed and put one of Dad's old scalpels in my pocket. He always kept a couple of used scalpels in the tool shed as pencil sharpeners, I guess he could have used a regular pencil sharpener, but that's practical people for you, waste not want not. I picked up the cat and walked the short distance to a local park. In the park, there was a wooded area that was big enough for me to conduct my experiment. I reasoned that if I could inflict cruelty to the cat, I had one aspect of the triad and therefore had the potential to become a violent person. The cat was more than happy in my company and purred the whole time. I thought of what to do, cut off its ears maybe or slice its eyes, but those acts, while undoubtedly cruel, were not at the level of subhuman cruelty as described in the books and articles I'd read. I decided I'd slice the cat open and see how long it would survive. I lay it down on its back and rubbed its belly. It grabbed my hands with its paws and made gentle bites. It really was helpless and so completely trusting. I removed the scalpel from my jacket and pressed it onto the cat's soft grey belly. I looked into the animal's sky-blue eyes and suddenly let go of the scalpel. I didn't have a moral epiphany or anything like that, instead I heard TJ's voice calmly telling me to let the cat go.

'If you kill the cat, Matty, you'll never find your way back.'

The cat seemed to sense my distraction and purred and rubbed its head against me. I lifted it to my face and looked at it closely. It pressed a tiny paw onto my cheek, just below my eye.

'You deserve a good life,' I said to the cat and gently put him inside my jacket.

On my way home, I visited the local animal hospital and dropped the cat off with them. They were happy to take him and thanked me for my kindness. I decided there and then that if I ever found myself in a position where killing a living creature was a choice, then it had to be for a good reason. *Then again,* I thought to myself, *you killed TJ.* I was somewhat conflicted about the whole thing. It didn't make the neat kind of sense I wanted it to.

Starting fires, however, was a whole other ballgame and made perfect sense.

Since Dad was a smoker, there were always cigarette lighters and matches around the house. I began to take an interest in fire from a young age. In the colder months, Mom would sometimes light a fire and I would sit in front of it, staring into its dark orange heart. The way the flames moved intrigued me. They danced as if they were alive. As I grew older, I'd play a game whereby I'd burn whatever was handy, Dad's cigarette butts, empty boxes, loose papers. I'd pretend that they were spaceships crash landing on a fiery planet and would watch closely to see how long it took them to burn. I imagined there were people in these spaceships and wondered what it would be like to die in a fire. In those early years, there was no intention behind my actions other than a sense of curiosity and interest, but as I approached my teenage years, I began lighting fires and seeing how long I could let them burn before I risked losing control. I would do this in secluded areas and a few times at home when no one was there. I tried to recruit some of my friends into my interest, but none of them found fire as stimulating as me.

I continued to indulge my growing pyromania until around the time Santi shot up the school. Something about the event shook me and made me quit my destructive habit soon after. Not only that, but whatever wires in my brain had linked sex and death seemed to calm down so that by the time I entered Ulysses S. Grant Middle School I was, to all extents and purposes, normal. Part of the fallout from the shooting at Rosehill was that all of us who were friends with Santi underwent mandatory counseling, eight sessions of it. It was the school's way of indemnifying itself for making us leave the school. The counseling sessions were mostly boring, but they did clarify a few things for me. Mom would bring me and wait outside while I sat in a big leather chair and spoke to a man named Dr. Wambaugh. He was tall and skinny with an angular nose. He wore a bow tie and glasses hung from a thin chain around his neck, though I never saw him put them on. He asked me routine questions about how I felt about Santi and his actions, and whether I had bad dreams and so on. While I spoke, he would interlock his hands in front of his face and his index fingers would point just below his nose. This made him look calm, but also intimidating. He would smile at the beginning of each session and then again at the end, but during the hour we'd spend together, his expression was serious and unwavering.

During the third session, we were continuing our discussion about why what Santi did was not my or any of my friend's fault. The school was engaging in a neat Orwellian trick whereby they allowed Santi's parents to blame us while simultaneously counseling us to absolve us of blame and because no one was keeping score, no one was the wiser. In the middle of the session, I asked Dr. Wambaugh why people took pleasure in hurting one another. He asked me if I wanted to hurt anyone, and so began the gradual process that released me from my dark thoughts and troubling behavior. I told him about the pictures I'd discovered in Dad's study and how they'd excited me. I told him about the research I'd done in the library and about the stray cat. I had no problem opening up to him. I felt I could trust him. Over the years Dad had mentioned doctor-patient privilege many times and I knew men like Dad and Dr. Wambaugh took these things seriously. He had also said to

Mom before the first session that anything I said would be held in confidence. I'm sure she interpreted that as anything I said except weird shit would be held in confidence, but I had an idea from Wambaugh's demeanor that I'd have a free run to say anything I wanted. In the first two sessions I sounded him out by saying a few things that he could have said back to Mom, and by session three I was satisfied that he was keeping his end of the confidentiality bargain.

Wambaugh was better than any book in the library and through him, I gained the kind of insights into deviant behavior that I would never have dreamed possible. He told me about case studies and some of the more advanced ideas in clinical psychology. He assured me that my interest in fires was normal and was probably a result of being the youngest and wanting attention. He was impressed that I'd managed to control my impulses and made me swear that if they ever arose again to call him right away. Most reassuring of all, he said it was normal at my age to find any depiction of a naked female exciting, even a dead one. I had trouble believing this, but he convinced me by saying that men like Ted Bundy and John Wayne Gacy who experienced awful childhoods of abuse and neglect were very different to me. When the wires in their brain went wrong, they went permanently wrong. He told me that my crossed wires were now uncrossed and that I shouldn't worry about such things again.

He was right. I wasn't so confused after that. Occasionally, I'd have weird thoughts about things, but they came and went like clouds across a sky. None of my weird thoughts were violent, and I felt fairly confident that I didn't have a predisposition towards violence. I had a good handle on things until Joe Hayes raped Bev. Once I found out about it, the weird thoughts returned. Dr. Wambaugh's work began to unravel, and my mind itched for payback. Bev did her best to hold me to my promise that I wouldn't do anything rash, but it put a strain on our relationship and though we rarely discussed the event after Bev's trip to San Francisco, we didn't look at one another the same way. My feelings about the event rose and fell like a boat on a turbulent sea, but eventually, something had to give. It had taken almost four years, but I decided to do something about Joe Hayes. It was long overdue.

I was seventeen and Hayes was twenty-one. I'd heard he was a tough guy and that he'd just done six months for aggravated assault. Despite this, I wasn't afraid of him or of the consequences should he find out what I intended to do. I mulled it over and figured in a one-on-one he'd kill me, but if I somehow managed to set him up for something, it'd be a fitting revenge. Once I'd come up with what to do, I didn't hesitate to carry it out.

I thought a Friday would be a good day to execute my plan, Friday was day five of the week and Hayes has five letters in it so putting the two together made sense (I'm joking, but that's how an unhinged mind might work- mine was anything but unhinged, it was as clear and focused as great white shark following the taste of blood). I had done practice runs the previous two Fridays. These were to find the quickest route, but mostly they were to observe Hayes. He was on parole and part of his parole was a curfew, so I knew he'd be there. From the darkness across the street, I watched him as he regularly came out to the porch to smoke a cigarette before flicking it into the night.

I waited until just after dusk before cycling to Del Paso Heights. I cycled through back streets and shortcuts through parks and wasteland. I was dressed in dark clothing and felt a rise of excitement pushing through my chest as I swerved around trees and streetlights. When Zodiac shot Paul Stine, the cabbie, at the northeast corner of Washington and Cherry in

Presidio Heights, it was about ten in the evening and three people witnessed it. After shooting Stine, Zodiac calmly wiped down Stine's cab and walked casually north along Cherry before going east on Jackson Street. It was this air of confident power I felt as I arrived just before nine. Hayes had no idea what was coming his way, I mean, how could he? I waited until the house lights went off and Hayes had finished his last smoke of the night. The street was relatively quiet. Cars drove by reasonably frequently, but the street was empty. I had stashed my bike two blocks away and once I was sure the coast was clear I moved from my hiding spot and hurried across the street and waited in the shadows at the edge of Hayes' home. My plan was to start a fire, burn down his house, not to hurt anyone, just destroy the place.

The house itself was a wood frame bungalow with a garage to one side and a porch running the length of the building. I had brought two bottles of paint thinner. I lay on my belly in front of the porch and poured the liquid under it. I then took out a couple of wads of Kleenex and shoved them under the porch too. The dry wood of the frame would catch as soon as I lit it. I didn't expect it to go up quite as quickly as it did. Within a few minutes, the whole front of the house was being consumed by waves of rising orange and yellow flames. The two wooden pillars that held up the roof of the porch soon gave way and with a loud crack and crash, the house really began to burn. Before I left, I saw Hayes appear from the back of the house near the garage. The fire had not spread that far yet. He was screaming and frantically calling for help. The glow from the fire and the noise alerted neighbors, and soon I heard the shrill siren of a fire truck beating its way to the scene. I didn't wait around, and casually and calmly made my way to my bike. Once I'd got about halfway home, I stopped in a secluded area of wasteland where I'd set previous fires. I removed my gloves, hat and jacket and put them into a grocery bag. I used the remainder of the paint thinner to burn everything. Then, satisfied with my night's work, I went home and slept an untroubled sleep.

The next morning, one of my friends called telling me that Joe Hayes' house had been burned down the night before. He said that Hayes' mother and grandmother had been inside, and they hadn't got out until it was too late. For a moment, I felt a jolt of excitement, but almost immediately a flat feeling came over me, as if he'd just told me something entirely banal like the weather or time of day.

'Serves him right,' I said.

The best type of revenge is not the kind where the victim learns what he's done just before croaking it or whatever, because they get closure. For me, the worst thing is not knowing, and I figured that would be the worst thing for Joe Hayes too. While I didn't mean to kill his mother and grandmother, I wasn't sorry either. I was pumped up because now it would become a police case and I thought they might blame Hayes for it. When they did, I was pleased. I'd done my duty as a brother and even if Hayes lived to be a hundred, he'd never figure out it was me.

By the time we had settled in Clearwater, Hayes was in San Quentin. Every year for ten years I'd send him a postcard with 'Speaking in Tongues, side A, track 1' written on it. I know it was a little cryptic, but I hope he got the joke. I never sent it from the same place, and never from a place that could be connected to me. I imagined him sitting in his cell wondering what was going on. I pictured him trying to convince the block captain or even the warden that they were taunts from the real perpetrator. I pictured the block captain or warden laughing at him and telling him he was delusional. Every year for ten years until he killed himself. I guess your sin catches up with you eventually.

Chapter Seventeen
The RCA Dinner, April 2019

Dessert

Zimmerman stood on the podium from which he'd spoken earlier. Snout stood behind him, wraithlike, simultaneously there and not there. The crowd was chaotic and enjoying the reveries. Soon enough, Zimmerman had cooed them into quiet attention with soft words and calming gestures. It was a strange thing to see so many obedient and compliant adults in a casual environment. I immediately recalled the various school assemblies I'd attended during my education, and I never remembered one quite as reverential as this. Zimmerman's words had a hypnotic effect. Once he was happy that the crowd was perfectly attentive, he began to speak.

'There are not many residents of our wonderful community who have been here from the start. Most of us are relative newcomers. We have been drawn to Riverside Falls because we seek privacy and safety and the shared sense of values that only a community like ours can offer. In many ways, our community is like our country. We want what's best for one another, and we want our children and elderly to be safe from unwanted influences. When you honored me by making me the head of the RCA, I promised you that the only thing that would matter is that our community would flourish. Sadly, in life as in nature for things to flourish the old must be replaced with the new. Over the years I've seen many of the original residents depart. I considered many of these people my friends, and I miss them. It is to that end that I would like to share with you a heartfelt appreciation of those people who have been here from the beginning.'

It was completely quiet. Zimmerman's voice was charged with a mesmeric magnetism that had us all corralled like sheep. It was even more compelling than when he'd been speaking about dividends.

'I would like to extend our thanks to Art Tillman. Sadly, Art declined my invitation to come here tonight, but that's hardly surprising, is it?'

A light chuckle trilled through the crowd and then vanished into the air. Zimmerman continued. He was smiling broadly and seemed to glow in the moment.

'Now, you all know, Art and I have squabbled over the years, but only because we both care deeply about the issues that face our community.'

I thought of some of the things they squabbled about and felt the urge to call bullshit on what Zimmerman was saying, but felt that discretion was the better part of valour in this instance. I got the impression that Zimmerman wanted to get the crowd to do his bidding, like a pack of hounds baying for their master.

'I do hope we will see Art during the summer at one of our community events, perhaps the fireworks for the 4th of July.'

Zimmerman paused. The reverential hush remained wrapped around the crowd.

'I am delighted that our good friends The Watermans are here tonight,' said Zimmerman, 'they've been here through thick and thin and I hope they have many more years with us.'

Attention turned to Al and Ethel Waterman, and Zimmerman led a great round of applause.

'And I am thrilled that Jack, our very own raconteur, is here too.'

Zimmerman cast his eyes over the crowd.

'Is Jack still here, I saw him earlier?'

His eyes landed on me.

'He's gone home,' I said, 'he's had a few too many.'

'That sounds like Jack alright,' said Zimmerman, and once again there was a kind of canned laughter. Once it settled down, Zimmerman's grin dropped and his face took on a more measured, even somber look.

'I have a confession to make,' said Zimmerman.

Somebody yelled, 'is Jimmy Hoffa buried in your backyard?' This time there was genuine laughter. Zimmerman laughed. I turned to Beth.

'Maybe Gene Hackman is buried in his backyard?'

I don't think she heard me properly. She held up her hand and frowned to indicate that she was listening to Zimmerman, and I was distracting her.

'I can't say I know anything about that,' said Zimmerman, 'you might have me confused with someone else.'

His expression and tone took on the sincerity of a clergyman at a funeral.

'My confession is that this party actually has an ulterior motive.'

He removed the microphone from its stand and stepped to one side and then the next. He cast his eyes over the crowd.

'If you've been paying attention, and I know you have, you'll have noticed that I have left out our most senior and most respected resident, Lily Osman.'

There was a scattering of murmurs through the crowd, followed by a subdued hush. The gathering turned collectively as Zimmerman gestured towards the entrance of the marquee where Mrs. Osman, accompanied by Derek Anderson, began to approach the podium. I moved forward to be nearer the front. Beth followed me. Mrs. Osman arrived a few moments later, and Zimmerman helped her up to the microphone.

'It is with great sadness that I have to tell you all that Mrs. Osman will be leaving our community next week.'

There were no gasps or sounds of dismay. The truth was that relatively few people really knew Mrs. Osman. Those of us that did know she was struggling to live alone and that she was overdue for admittance to residential care. The only reason why Zimmerman was making a big deal about it was to cynically highlight himself as a caring, kind man who took the time to look out for people like Lily Osman.

'Mrs. Osman will be moving to a new home just a short distance away,' said Zimmerman.

He held Mrs. Osman's hand and wrapped his other hand around it. She smiled and touched his arm. He then let go and invited her to speak into the microphone, which Snout was adjusting to Mrs. Osman's height. She stepped forward and tried to speak, but she was too far away for the microphone to pick up her voice, which was faint in the first place. Rather than making Mrs. Osman take another step, Zimmerman moved forward, took the microphone, and brought it to her. She smiled at him, again in that bemused way. I couldn't tell if she was truly aware of what was going on. I felt like I was watching something from a badly conceived reality TV show.

'Thank you,' said Mrs. Osman.

I think the loudness of her voice startled her. She recoiled a little from the microphone before speaking again.

'Thank you, Mr. Tillman.'

At this, a flutter of chuckles flickered through the crowd. Zimmerman grinned at Mrs. Osman's mistake. He leaned into the microphone.

'I'll thank him on your behalf when I next see him, dear.'

Mrs. Osman looked utterly bewildered now. While there was no sign that she was distressed, it was obvious she thought Zimmerman was Tillman. Zimmerman and Snout began to applaud. It was the humane thing to do, but it also prevented the possibility of Mrs. Osman saying anything further. As the applause rang out, Derek Anderson went on to the podium and took Mrs. Osman by the arm and gently led her out of the marquee. The bizarre pageant finished with Zimmerman wishing us goodnight and beating a hasty path to his house.

'What the fuck?' said Beth in a completely instinctive manner as if it were a reflex.

The whole atmosphere had changed. Where moments before there was almost breathless devotion, there was now a palpable confusion. It was as if something had been introduced to the air that brought everyone to their senses. People began to make their way from the marquee and into the night. Some were shuffling awkwardly like zombies. I couldn't tell if it was caused by alcohol or Zimmerman. Beth and I made our way outside, where I immediately noticed how cold it had become. I gave Beth my jacket, and she pulled it around her shoulders, grateful that it was only a short walk home.

'I take it you're not going back to Concord at this hour?'

'No,' she said, 'I have a key to Jeff's place.'

I thought as much.

The thought that I should check in on Jack crossed my mind, but I was much keener to chat with Beth about the evening's events. We made it back to my house in good time and though we hadn't said much on the way, I knew Beth wanted to talk. We stood on the path and looked at one another.

'Here's your jacket,' she said, handing it back to me.

'You should come in,' I said.

'Why?'

'To talk about what happened tonight.'

'What happened?'

'In Zimmerman's house, all that stuff we overheard.'

'I think they were discussing that old lady,' said Beth.

'And?' I said.

'And what, Matt? She's moving to a retirement home, what's so odd about that?'

I couldn't believe Beth wasn't biting. In my head, most of the dots had been connected. Zimmerman was pulling some kind of scam.

'Zimmerman is up to something.'

'It's late, Matt, I'm a bit tired, can we leave it until tomorrow?'

She yawned and stretched her arms as if to emphasise the point.

I wasn't taking no for an answer, but neither did I want to pull the ace I had up my sleeve, the one thing I knew would get her undivided attention.

'You heard what went on in there. He's moving Mrs. Osman to a care home, and I'll bet she's signed her house over to him.'

I could tell she was trying to resist.

'Come on, you saw it, in fact, you felt it. The control he had over everyone there. Do you think he'd have trouble persuading an old lady with onset dementia to sign over the deeds to her house?'

'Why would he do that?'

I almost laughed out loud.

'What kind of a question is that? Money, why else?'

'Look,' said Beth firmly, 'it's been a nice night, and we've had fun and I like you, and I'd like to do this again some other time, but it *is* late, can we talk about it tomorrow, I'm not really in the mood for conspiracies?'

I had to play my ace now or the momentum would be lost.

'I know you're an FBI agent,' I said.

'What are you talking about?' said Beth.

I had to hand it to her, she was a good actress. She had played the part perfectly since the day we met.

'Jeff Simmons' cat is a ruse, you're undercover, and I want to know what you're investigating.'

Beth laughed.

'I'm going to bed, Matt, goodnight.'

Her acting was so good that I started to have doubts about the authenticity of Rohit's information. He'd been wrong about things before, and I was worried he was wrong again. According to what he'd discovered, her name was Bethany Harper. She was from the Bay Area like she'd said, and she was based, as luck would have it, in Sacramento. It was this detail that really piqued my interest. I couldn't rule out the fact she was looking for me, however remote the possibility. Still, there was one other thing I could use, something that was known only to law enforcement and most likely only those in Northern California. I knew Beth had no choice but to deny what I was saying for fear of blowing her cover, but if what she was investigating was somehow connected to me, I couldn't let her get away. I knew it was a long shot, but I figured since she was based in Sacramento, and she was an FBI agent, there might just be a chance what I was about to say meant something to her.

'He takes their pinkies,' I said clearly, 'I can help you find him.'

Beth stopped in her tracks. She turned and even in the pale streetlight I could see her eyes were wide and alert. I couldn't believe my luck; she knew what I was referring to.

'He uses pinking shears,' I said, 'he takes the pinkie on the left hand. Seems apt, doesn't it?'

'How do you know this?' said Beth, her voice barely a whisper.

'You tell me why you're here, and I'll tell you what I know.'

She looked at me with a mix of curiosity, bewilderment. I could tell she wanted to know not just what I knew about one of America's most elusive serial killers, but how I'd found out she was an undercover FBI agent. I also sensed she'd like to get me in a room without windows and beat me to death with a chair.

'Sorry to spring you like this, but I had to know why you were here,' I said.

'OK,' she said, 'let's go into your house and talk.'

'Curiosity killed the cat,' I said.

She didn't laugh. She turned to me and told me to shut the fuck up about cats.

'I hate cats,' she said.

We went inside and sat in the kitchen. I put on coffee and was about to remark how similar the scenario was to when we first met, but decided against it. Beth was Olivia Benson mode now and though I had the upper hand, humor or attempts at casual conversation were not going to be welcome. This was going to be big talk and only big talk.

'So, who goes first?' I said.

'I guess you should, seeing as you're the one with all the information.'

I was happy to tell her a little about the killer the FBI had nicknamed The Pinkie Killer. It would break the ice on the new development in our relationship, and it would show her that I knew what I was talking about.

'No one's heard from him in a while, have they?'

'I don't know much about the case itself, I'm not on it, but I know a guy who is, and I know he would be very grateful if you could help.'

'Have they hit a dead-end?'

'Big-time,' she said.

It's probably not surprising to know that I keep a casual eye on serial murderer cases in the U.S. I guess it's a hobby, morbid interest, whatever you want to call it. According to those who know these things, there are between 25 and 50 active serial killers in the U.S. at any given time. However, as there are about 330 million people in the U.S. it's not that many. Also, the rough estimate of annual victims is about 100-150, most of whom have lifestyles that are high-risk. I mostly follow news reports and so on, it's not like I'm actively involved but if something crops up in California or Florida, I usually contact a couple of Dad's former colleagues. They think I'm a reporter, and they're only too happy to see what they can find out for me. They're all retired, and it's easy enough to convince them they're helping catch the bad guys by helping me get the inside track. About eight years ago, there was a string of murders that really hooked me. The body of a male hitchhiker had been found along SR 99 near Red Bluff. About a month later, another man's body was discovered near Yuba City. When a third man's body was found in similar circumstances near Modesto, the Sacramento Bureau feared they had a serial killer on their hands. I called Don Drake. He'd been a detective in Sacramento back in the day. He was glad to take my call. It was about a year and a half after Dad's funeral. After the service, Don introduced himself to me. He'd said nice things and told me how he and Dad had worked together, and included an anecdote about calling over to the house to get autopsy notes one night. In the story, it was me who'd answered the door. Like any adult regarding a now grown-up child, he commented on how much I looked like Dad (I don't, by the way) and then asked me what I did for a living. When I said I was a journalist, he told me to call him any time if I needed any information about police work or anything like that.

At the time, the press had very little on what was being called the Route 99 killer. They had the usual, white male 35-45, medium build blah blah blah. It was the standard profile of almost every serial killer the Bureau had ever hunted, a bed wetter, he tortured animals to counteract his feelings of inadequacy. He murders to express his rage at a world that never understood him etc. etc.

The facts were this killer strangled male hitchhikers and sodomized them with a broom handle or something similar, but other than that it was being kept under wraps. I asked Don if he knew anything. He said he'd find out. After about a month with no word from Don, I reckoned he'd forgotten, but one afternoon he called and told me about the pinkie fingers. By now there were four victims. He said that the cops were keeping that detail for themselves to weed out the cranks. He also told me unequivocally that I was not to state that in my article. I told him I was no longer interested in writing an article and my editor had moved me on to something else. I said I was merely curious because it was happening so close to where I grew up. Don believed me and said if there was anything else he'd let me know.

There were a dozen more victims over the next six years, and then in 2017 the killings stopped abruptly, leaving the FBI holding the bag.

The thing was, I knew the guy who was doing it. The fingers were the giveaway, not that it would necessarily help. I'd known him in college, and then only for a short time.

'There has been nothing since 2017,' said Beth.

'Two years,' I said, 'could he have stopped?'

I didn't want Beth to think I knew much about the psychology of serial murder, so I thought asking a naive question would give her that impression.

'They can't stop,' she said flatly, 'they're driven to kill. They have no more control over what they do than any predator does when it hunts. If he stopped, it's because he's dead or in jail.'

I sipped my coffee.

'Did you get training in that sort of thing?'

'I got some basic training, we all do, but if you want the real hard-core experience you go into behavioral science, or more accurately, you get selected to become part of the behavioral science program. Only about one in five become profilers.'

'Wow, it's not like the movies.'

'The movies,' said Beth, 'they've made our job a lot harder. Now everyone is an expert. Every time I work a case, the public uses up a lot of my time with their expertise.'

She gave me a look that conveyed she didn't include me in this. The light flickered and for a moment, it went completely dark. A loud hum grumbled menacingly, and then whatever had caused the power surge stopped and things returned to normal. We both looked up at the light.

'That was weird,' said Beth.

I thought of TJ.

'Why didn't you get selected for behavioural science?' I said.

This seemed to annoy her a little. There was disdain in her eyes.

'I didn't have the skills and besides, it's not my thing.'

This wasn't sour grapes on her part, she didn't have the skills nor the interest. I admired her self-awareness and honesty.

'People who work in violent crime need a mind of steel. It's exhausting, and often you experience things no one should, ever.'

Her voice was growing a little weary. She rubbed her tongue along her bottom teeth, causing her lower lip to bulge.

'Anyway, enough talking shop, what do you know about the guy in California?'

I regarded her closely, holding my coffee cup in front of my face to conceal anything my expression might give away.

'I think I was at college with him in Florida.'

'What's his name?'

'I can't remember just now, but it will come to me.'

I was lying, I knew his name, but I didn't want to tell her just yet. She was looking into my eyes. I'm sure she was trying to work out if I was lying, but I must have done a good job because she didn't push me.

'What college?'

'The University of Florida in Gainesville,' I said, 'I studied journalism there from 1992 to 1995.'

'Did you like it?'

'College or journalism?'

'Both.'

'I enjoyed college, for sure, but journalism was a bit of a drag.'

'Why?'

'I can't say really, it just wasn't for me. I came close to dropping out a couple of times, but Dad insisted I finish.'

'What did your friend study?'

'He wasn't really a friend,' I said, 'but he studied journalism too.'

'At least that narrows it down.'

Beth's eyes were moving across my own, she was searching my face for something. She appeared tired. I'm sure I did too.

'OK, you'll have to speak with my colleague in Sacramento sometime soon. I'll talk to him tomorrow, and we can go from there.'

I nodded. I had no intention of speaking with her colleague, but for now, everything was working itself quite neatly. I could always come up with an excuse later.

'Are you going to tell me why you're here?' I said.

She finished her coffee and got up to grab some more. She put her cup under the machine and put a pod into it. A short time later, the machine kicked into gear and whirred and mashed and produced silky smooth coffee. The rich aroma filled the room.

'I have to say you really are full of surprises,' said Beth.

She was using the coffee to fight her tiredness. I was also tired, but would wait until she told me why she was in Jonestown before going to bed.

'You too,' I said.

'Before I tell you anything, I'd like to know how you found out about me.'

This time, there was no point in lying.

'I know a guy,' I said, 'he finds out stuff for me from time to time.'

'I could arrest you now and seize your computer and phone and get the Bureau's IT people to find him, and then the two of you could go to jail.'

Beth's expression was completely serious.

'I guess you could,' I said.

'I thought I was doing well,' she said, her expression softening a little.

'I'm sorry, but the whole cat thing was a bit over the top,' I said, 'I know Jeff Simmons and while he likes his cat, there's no way he'd pay a private detective to find him.'

'I suppose it was a bit much,' said Beth.

'Was it your idea?'

'The missing cat?'

'What else?' I said.

'It was actually Jeff's idea, but.'

I rubbed my mouth.

'Don't fucking tell me Jeff is FBI too?'

'No,' said Beth in a voice that was light and breathy. She was wavering between her FBI sense of duty and the gregarious person I had come to know. The friendlier side was winning.

'No, the truth is the cat is actually missing. Jeff thought it would be good to take advantage of the situation and for me to pose as a private detective looking for it.'

'Really?'

I hadn't seen Gene Hackman in ages, but once I discovered Beth was working undercover, I assumed he was living the good life somewhere away from Jonestown.

'Yep, Jeff is genuinely worried about him.'

'Is the stuff about his daughter true?' I asked.

Beth noticed the concern in my voice.

'I'm sorry, but it is. He and Carrie had a falling out.'

'About what?'

'He didn't say.'

'Is that where he is now?'

'I don't actually know where he is.'

I sat back in my chair and stretched my legs. I let my weight push down to the floor.

'So other than owning a missing cat, where does Jeff fit into this?' I said.

'It's all to do with Zimmerman, you were right,' said Beth.

'That he's a con man?'

'Yes, one of the most notorious in the country. We've been watching him for two years.'

'We?'

'One of the families in the community has been in deep cover for just over two years.'

Before I could open my mouth, Beth told me not to ask. It was enough that she was telling me all this.

'I'm only telling you this because I think you're the type who could mess up everything if I didn't include you. If you're going to poke your nose into things, I'd rather it was under my supervision.'

I was happy for her to think this.

'We've followed his trail from California, but we've still got some work to do before we can make an arrest.'

'Is that your job, to arrest him when the time comes?'

'No,' she said, 'local law enforcement will do it once we give them the green light. Getting him to trial is the tricky part.'

'Can I help?'

She looked at me and I watched her eyes in the low light. They were even more beautiful than when I'd first seen them. There was something about the fact that her secret was out that softened her features. She no longer had to wear a mask with me.

'I don't want to get in the way,' I said, 'and as you said I might screw things up, so tell me what I can do for you.'

'Can you keep a secret?' she asked.

'I think so, yes.'

'Then keep this a secret, as far as you know I'm Beth Becker, and I'm looking for Jeff's cat. You can bring in the estrangement from his daughter if you like, but nothing else.'

'OK,' I said.

She went on to explain that Zimmerman, whose real name was Dennis Thomson, had been conning old folks out of their homes for years. He had started in New York in the late eighties with attempted fraud, but had been caught and given a reprimand. He then disappeared and changed his approach. Over the next three decades, he'd acquired properties in ten states from California to New Hampshire before settling in Riverside Falls.

'He's been here hiding in plain sight for almost fifteen years,' said Beth, 'you'd be surprised how many criminals do that.'

'So how did you find out about him?'

'Jeff spotted him, thanks to you.'

I furrowed my brow. The story was getting more and more interesting.

'Jeff said that years ago you, and he had a conversation about baseball or something, anyway, wasn't your uncle a baseball player?'

'He was a football coach,' I said.

'OK,' said Beth. She wasn't being rude; she was just trying to get to the point.

'Jeff said he was looking through his articles trying to find if he'd written one about your uncle. Jeff keeps all his articles; he has a copy of every single word he's ever had printed.'

I knew this, I'd seen some of the huge scrapbooks he kept them in. They were an impressive archive in and of themselves.

'He showed them to me a couple of times, mostly to read box scores from famous games he'd covered.'

'That's baseball, isn't it?'

'Yes,' I said, 'you know for someone who's into cars you don't know much about sports.'

She ignored my jibe.

'So, Jeff is trawling through these pages and pages of newspaper cut-outs and whatnot when he stumbles across an article he'd done on white-collar fraud and there's a picture to go with it.'

'Zimmerman,' I said.

'A much younger Zimmerman,' said Beth, 'but Jeff was sure it was him.'

It all clicked together in my mind, but I let Beth explain it.

'Jeff, being the good journalist he is, wondered two things. One, why Zimmerman had changed his name and two, what he was doing in New Hampshire, after all New Hampshire isn't exactly the still point of the turning universe.'

'It's a good place to hide,' I said.

Beth nodded and carried on, 'he didn't jump the gun, though. He did his research and once he'd done enough digging and connected enough dots, he passed on his information to us. We did the rest of the digging and now here we are.'

'It's a good story,' I said, 'if it wasn't for Jeff, I'd say you'd still be looking for him.'

'That's for sure, most breaks in cases come down to either good luck or just dumb luck.'

'We make our own luck,' I said.

'Who knows,' she said, 'now what do you say we go to bed?'

I tilted my head and brought my hand to my mouth.

'That's not what I meant,' said Beth, 'let's go to sleep.'

I got up and Beth followed me out of the room and up the stairs. I showed her into the guest room. She went in. I stood at the door.

'I was thinking something just there,' I said.

Beth flopped down on the bed and lay back.

'What?' she said.

'What Zimmerman is doing isn't technically illegal. I mean it's shitty taking away those people's homes but if they're consenting to it where's the crime?'

'There's more to it than that,' said Beth, 'I'll tell you in the morning.'

I said goodnight and she responded in kind. I closed the door and went slowly to my room. Despite being tired, I lay in bed and drifted into a broken sleep. For the first time in years, I felt a sense of power rise in me. It was the same kind of excitement I'd felt when I'd burned down Joe Hayes' house.

Chapter Eighteen
The Burial of the Dead, Sacramento 1980, and Gainesville 1992-93

The restless echoes of TJ Lowell's ghost

I finished high school in late May of 1992. It had been an uneventful year, but the tension from our move had been unresolved and became a lingering presence in our daily lives. Florida suited Dad, but not Mom. Mom found it too quiet and reserved compared to Sacramento. In the warmer months, she complained it was too humid and the rest of the time she bemoaned the fact that her new job wasn't quite as cozy and familiar as her previous one. The staff in her school were mostly younger and filled with optimistic energy. They had new ideas which Mom found a bit too modern, and it made her feel unappreciated and isolated. Dad, for all his talk about a reduced workload, seemed to be away from home a lot. That's not to say he went on trips or anything like that, but he wasn't in the house much. He'd leave early in the morning and come home late at night. I didn't see much of him. When we did cross paths, he'd ask me superficial questions about school and so on. We didn't have much of a rapport, and I wasn't surprised. Things had changed, and not just between me and Dad. We had grown apart as a family. Now I know that families often grow apart as children get older and things can be especially fractious during the teenage years, but this was different, this was not routine. Leaving Sacramento was not only a physical move but an emotional, even spiritual one, especially for Mom. Our house in Sacramento was the only home TJ had known, and I could tell Mom bore a huge burden of guilt for abandoning him, or more correctly abandoning his memory. You might even say she left his ghost in Sacramento. Though she never mentioned it specifically, I'm certain she had felt his presence around the house in California. Whether this comforted her or not, I can't say. What I can say is for years after his death I felt TJ's presence, and it was more than just a casual occurrence, he haunted me.

When we returned to Sacramento in the weeks and months after TJ's death, we would visit his grave in Saint Joseph's Cemetery every day, then every other day, and then finally it was just Mom who visited. Bev said it made her sad when we visited him. I agreed only in my case, it scared me. Another ritual she kept was the preservation of TJ's room. She wouldn't allow me into the bedroom I'd shared with my brother. She insisted that I sleep on a mattress in her and Dad's room. This went on for a while until Dad got fed up with it. He and Mom had an argument about it, and the next day she cleared everything belonging to TJ out of the room and put it in brown boxes. Dad then repainted the room and things went back to a new kind of normal. Mom asked me if there was anything of my brother's I wanted before giving TJ's clothes and toys to goodwill. I kept some of his *Star Wars* figures and comics, but nothing durable. That was the thing, TJ didn't have any truly permanent possessions. I guess kids don't really get attached to things, except maybe a teddy bear or a doll. There were photos of him, and Mom kept his baby teeth and the blanket they wrapped him in when he was born, but as he'd died so young, there were no journals or keepsakes of any kind, nothing that captured the essence of who he was. I think Dad's argument was that maintaining the room as it was before TJ died, though understandable, was unhealthy and that if we could let go, we could move on. Dad got his way, as he almost always did, not with force but with logic. Mom was full of little yellow pills at the time, and I guess her resistance was probably at its weakest. Anger and guilt and grief had consumed all of her energy, and she had lost the will to fight.

There was a carved wooden sign saying Thomas and Matthew's room on the bedroom door. Grandpa Kentucky had made it. It was beautifully carved out of hickory wood and proved that he was more than just a bigoted drunk. Mom asked me if I wanted to keep it by way of remembrance, and I said I didn't. I said it was my room now and that I agreed with Dad. I think the cold logic of my comment startled her. She removed the sign down and brought it to school with her. Years later, Mom told me that she kept everything important relating to TJ in school because it was where she needed it most. I made the bedroom my own, but was never fully comfortable in it. There was a sense that TJ was around somewhere in the shadowy corners of the room, the places the light doesn't quite reach. It wasn't frightening or threatening, but I could feel it.

One night about six months after his death, I saw TJ in my room as clear as daylight. He was talking, but no sound came from his mouth. I told him I couldn't hear him and when he didn't react, I got out of bed and stood in front of him. I don't know why I wasn't scared, TJ had good reason to want payback and vengeful ghosts were part of the folklore I'd heard during my visits to Kentucky. Grandma would tell stories about Civil War ghosts searching for the souls of those who'd killed them. She also told us about what she called 'watchers' — evil spirits that roamed the countryside at night. The stories were fascinating and a little creepy. Bev hated them and would refuse to listen.

'What do you want?' I asked TJ.

His eyes weren't looking at me, they were looking somewhere else, not in the room but further away. I couldn't tell. I tried to get his attention, but nothing worked. I gave up and went back to bed. I turned my face to the wall and must have fallen asleep. The next morning at breakfast, Mom asked me who I was talking to the night before. Dad's face was tight.

'Answer your mother,' he said firmly.

I dipped my spoon into my cereal and pushed around a Cheerio ring aimlessly.

'I was talking to TJ,' I said.

I guess neither of my parents' reactions was unexpected. Dad frowned and Mom just looked sad, not just in her face, but in her whole body.

'What were you talking about?' said Dad.

'He was saying something, but I couldn't hear him.'

'Think nothing of it, son,' he said.

At this, Mom excused herself from the table, got up and left the room. Bev shot me a withering look as if to say, see what you've done. I heard Mom go upstairs and into the bedroom and close the door behind her. Dad stayed where he was. After a moment, he leaned in close to me and spoke in his usual controlled and collected manner.

'I don't know if what you said is true son, it could be, but you could have dreamed it. It's OK to dream about your brother. Sometimes I do, and I know your mother does too.'

He leaned across and pinched my shoulder gently and then whispered.

'If you dream about your brother again, don't tell your mother, tell me instead.'

After that, I kept all communication about dreams and ghosts to myself.

During the rest of my time in our Sacramento home, I saw TJ about a dozen times. I saw him a few times in the branches of a sycamore while I was cycling along our street. The other times were in my room. The last time I saw him, he was sitting at my desk looking into the distance. No matter what angle I moved along, I could not connect with his eyes. I asked him what he wanted, but as always, he was quiet. By the time I was ten there were no more visitations, and I was only dreaming about him once in a while, and by the time my teenage years rolled around the dreams stopped. Since then, I hear the echoes of his restless ghost from time to time. I guess he has some unfinished business.

A respectable career choice

In the first semester of my senior year, I met with the Career Counselor to discuss my college options. I wasn't too bothered about it, but she was optimistic about my chances and got me to apply to some of the big schools in New England. I thought she was crazy, but I wrote the letters and filled in the personal statements. I told Dad that the CC thought with hard work and some luck I could go to one of the Big Ten. Dad gave me a wry smile when I told him I'd applied for Political Science at Harvard and told me if I got accepted, he'd run down the street naked. Thankfully for all concerned, that didn't happen, the general inconsistency in my grades prevented such an event. It was the same for courses at Yale and Brown.

The CC while well-meaning was a total dreamer. I always thought of her as the cheerleader of the faculty. The teachers, like the students, had cliques. They were jocks and nerds and weirdos and stoners too. The CC's positivity was kind of grating, though, and she convinced my friends to reach for similar far-fetched dreams. All of them fell short. Undeterred, she met with me a few more times until in a moment of revelation she suggested I try journalism. I had suggested it to her at our first meeting, but she had ignored me, stating that my level of English composition, while very good, wasn't good enough. I tried to point out to her that my English teacher was lazy and didn't grade my work accurately. She ignored that too. Before the journalism epiphany, she'd thought my analytical mind was perfectly suited to politics or perhaps something to do with history. I had suggested psychology, but she chuckled, saying I would be bored if I studied it. So, after a lot of bullshit, I applied to the college course I wanted to do rather than one my CC thought I should do. I applied to about a dozen of the better schools and was as surprised as anyone when The University of Florida in Gainesville offered me a place contingent on improved grades and a commitment to play football. I knew I was only mediocre at football, but Coach Ferguson must have put in a good word.

My dad was delighted when I was provisionally accepted to study journalism and encouraged me to put in the hours needed to get the required grades. By then Mom was almost burnt out and while she was pleased, it was in a more subdued way. Bev wasn't talking with any of us except for Mom and even then, their conversations were superficial and banal. Mom was like a worker at the end of a long shift. She was worn out. Bev was essentially absent from her life. She had been uprooted from her home, taken away from her dead son and her surviving son was a poor substitute, or so it seemed. Mom took a back seat and let Dad drive the car that would get me to college. I think she found the thought of an empty house unbearable.

While Dad appreciated books, he was never much talking about them. Literature was flaky in his eyes, but journalism was a respectable career choice and if I worked hard, I could be the next Bob Woodward or Carl Bernstein. I didn't want to tell him that my decision to take journalism as a career had been a vaguely formed thing and was in actual fact a spinoff from my darker interests. By the time I entered my senior year and was considering what to do in college, I was totally immersed in The Zodiac case. I read all I could about it and would sometimes talk to Dad about it too. This wasn't often and usually, he told me he couldn't remember anything. He was lying, he knew plenty. When I pressed him about it, he mentioned the names of people involved in the case, but would not give me any juicy details. He cited the complexity and range of the case, saying it was too broad and anyway, it had gone cold. I told him I was considering the possibility of becoming a crime writer. He warmed up a little after that, but my relentless questions and hunger for detail wore him down. In the end, to get some peace as much as to fire my interest, he called up a colleague and got Paul Avery's number. Avery was a reporter with *The San Francisco Chronicle* during the case, and when I called him, he was very happy to answer my questions. Most of his answers were stultifying mundane and the polar opposite of the sensationalist murder mystery approach Robert Graysmith had taken in his book. Nevertheless, talking to someone who'd actually been there made me think that journalism might just be a good choice of career after all.

'Don't become a journalist,' said Avery towards the end of our call.

'Why not?' I said.

'It'll wreck your life,' he said.

To my surprise I did way better in my SATs than I expected and with a sense of purpose I packed up the car Dad bought for me as a graduation present and headed to Gainesville. I arrived on campus and thought how big the world was and how refreshing it was to be free. This newfound hope was accentuated when my roommate turned out to be normal. I'd heard nightmarish stories about weird roommates and had been a little apprehensive about it. My roommate and I hit it off right away. He was from Wellfleet, Massachusetts and was studying engineering with the view to joining and one day inheriting the family business. He was loud and confident and handsome in that all-American way. I asked him why he'd chosen Florida and in a voice that sounded like JFK, he said he'd chosen *The Unavahsity of Flawida to get away from the gawhdammed snow.* We sat and talked for a while. He told me about his hometown and family. I was more than happy to sit and listen while he told of sailing and sunny beaches and beautiful girls with long hair. He said his father had wanted him to go to *Haahvaadd*, but he didn't want to put in the work. He said his father was a stern and proud man and that he needed to get out of his shadow. While he spoke, he didn't ask me many questions about myself and when he did, I could tell he was only waiting until it was his turn to talk again. I didn't mind this. He was charismatic despite his superficiality.

The first year was a lot of fun. My roommate's larger-than-life personality brought a lot of people into my life. There were parties every weekend and I always got invited. I certainly preferred the social life to the academic one. I found the lectures uninspiring. I had some romantic idea that my tuition would develop me into an intrepid reporter on the front line of the most sensational breaking news. The reality was we learned about style and how to develop a voice and about research and sources. Writing is all about practice, and journalism is all about repetition, one of the professors said on the first day. He looked like he belonged in a different era and spoke mistrustingly of emerging technology like the internet. Most of the faculty were, to my mind, old-fashioned, and I would sit in their lectures and think about almost anything to occupy my mind. I realized while studying for my SATs that I had a facility for improvising and cramming. I knew these attributes would work for me in college, so I didn't worry too much about drifting off in lectures. I knew that once I got assignments in on time and looked for patterns and trends in exam papers, I'd be fine. As it turned out, I did well in my exams and spent the summer on Cape Cod working as a lifeguard. My roommate got me the job. It was easy, all that was needed was to be a strong swimmer and after some basic training, I was good to go. It was a lot better than spending monotonous summer days watching my parents slowly crumble into late middle age. The summer on Cape Cod was about as good as it got for me. Sometimes when the sun is setting and the light catches things in a way that makes them flare out colors of rose and bright orange, I think of Cape Cod and for a moment, I return to the serenity of those days.

My second year was similarly uneventful, at least in the beginning. It was so dull that the only thing that got me through the first semester was the boundless enthusiasm and energy of my tutor, Mr. Hadley. He was in his mid-twenties and had no regard for the stuffy formalities of his senior colleagues. He was from New York and had all the cockiness you'd expect to go with it. There were six of us in his tutorial group, and in our first meeting, he spoke about why grunge music was going to take over the world. Cobain is a fucking genius, he said. I had no idea who Cobain was, but when he played Smells like Teen Spirit, I was hooked. Hadley liked us to call him Dave in an obvious, but not completely hokey, attempt to be down with us kids. In truth, we weren't exactly cool kids. The tutorial group was square and meek. There was a fat Asian guy from Rhode

Island who was constantly eating Three Musketeers bars, a studious girl from Virginia, me and three other nondescript vanilla types. I wondered if Hadley had been sent to inject a bit of life into the group, or given it as a punishment. He was supposed to advise us on assignments and to grade them, but he told us that as long as we didn't betray the group secret, he'd give us all good grades. The group secret was that we didn't have to talk about journalism and other bullshit in our tutorials. The girl from Virginia asked if it would harm her progress. Hadley told her the only thing that would harm her progress was a narrow mind that followed the rules. If you do what they tell you, then you'll end up writing what the corporate machine tells you to write. I liked the sentiment, but wondered how it would work in practice. During my time in school there'd been a few maverick teachers but none of them lasted longer than a year and in a few cases, a semester. Still, apart from Virginia girl's whispered objection, there was a tacit agreement that'd we'd follow Hadley's lead.

And so it came to pass that we sat in the tutorial room once a week for an hour and spoke about life, the universe, and everything else. The Virginia girl even managed to get into the spirit. Life is about more than school, she said to me quietly one afternoon. Of course, I'm exaggerating. Things are never as much fun in retrospect.

Most of our discussions focused on music, books, and film. In the event of a professor or one of the stiffer members of the faculty dropping by, Hadley would seamlessly move into reasons why we shouldn't use semicolons or why the best writing relied on verbs. One time the head of the faculty sat in on a tutorial for almost the entire hour. Hadley was unperturbed and workshopped an article with us. I came out realizing he was a brilliant teacher who really knew his stuff. It made me wonder why he challenged the system. I approached him after the tutorial.

'Come on Matt, think about it, all that stuff is lifeless, it's the rules, it's the game, but it has no soul. Writing shouldn't be constrained by language, it should expand it, push it, make it work for you, not the other way around. You know what I mean?'

I had no idea what he meant. I wasn't sure he knew either, but it sounded impressive and because I wanted to get back to my room I didn't argue.

Emilio

In late October, a new student joined the tutorial group. Virginia girl had grown tired of the lack of structure and had buckled under the weight of potential failure. She said that Hadley's style didn't work for her, but that he was an excellent and enthusiastic teacher and that she had enjoyed his tutelage. I came to understand this is academic-speak for the exact opposite. There was no fallout from her departure for Hadley. I can't say the same for myself.

'I'm Emilio,' said the new student, 'I'm from Modesto, California.'

'You're from California originally aren't you Matt,' said Hadley, 'Matt and Emilio the golden state boys, what about it.'

Everyone in the group laughed.

'You could be great friends,' said Hadley.

'The best,' said the fat Asian kid.

Hadley high-fived him, but I noticed that Emilio wasn't particularly impressed. He was trying to suppress a scowl that said, who are these weirdos? Hadley noticed and told him to take it easy and that it was all a bit of fun.

I was used to Hadley's occasionally inappropriate behavior, but Emilio wasn't convinced by Hadley's words. He looked uncomfortable for the hour we were there.

After the tutorial, which included discussion on why *Aliens* was a better movie than *Alien* and why Predator would win in a fight with Alien, Emilio approached me. He was about my height but had a slighter frame. He was darker than me too, not quite Hispanic, but there was definitely Latino blood in there somewhere. He also gave the impression that he was quiet and reserved. I felt a kind of kinship right away.

'Is he always like that?' he asked.

'Yeah, it's kind of fun,' I said.

'Not really,' he said.

'It's better than trudging through elements of style and composition,' I said.

He looked a little perplexed.

'Didn't he tell you?'

'Tell me what?'

I told Emilio how things were in Hadley's tutorial. He shrugged his shoulders, seemingly satisfied with my explanation.

'Where are you from?' he asked, 'Hadley said you were from California.'

When I said I was from Sacramento, he seemed to warm up. The cold, aloof attitude he'd presented left him. He began to speak enthusiastically about people he knew in Sacramento. I didn't know any of them, but I knew the areas he was talking about, and soon enough our mutual origins led to the revelation of other mutual interests.

As chance would have it, a few weeks after I'd met Emilio, my Massachusetts roommate moved into a frat house. He said he could get me in too, but I declined. I liked the humdrum of a dorm, and the thought of moving into a place with constant noise and where no one slept wasn't my idea of fun. For a while, I really enjoyed having the room to myself. The solitude was refreshing. I was happy knowing that when I closed the door to the room no one was going to drop in unexpectedly as was often the case with my former roommate.

Tutorials had become more interesting with Emilio's arrival. He and Hadley often got into heated arguments about pop culture. Before Emilio's arrival, tutorials were essentially the Mr. Hadley show. It seemed now that his leadership was under threat.

'He's such a prick,' said Emilio after one particularly turbulent tutorial, 'we'd be better off actually learning stuff than listening to his shit.'

'Chill man,' I said mimicking one of Hadley's mannerisms, 'you're just not feeling it.'

Emilio laughed.

'He is full of shit though,' I said, 'but hey what can we do?'

'I guess you're right, as long as he gives us a good grade,' said Emilio.

'You want to grab a coffee or something?' I said.

Emilio was happy to get a coffee. We'd done it a few times before and were becoming friends. By then we were talking about girls and sports and all the usual stuff guys our age spoke about. He was interesting once he opened up and got on topics he knew about. I'd noticed his range of knowledge in tutorials, but he was even more interesting one-on-one. He had read more books than anyone I knew and by that, I mean actually read, not just said he'd read. He was an only child and told me that most of his childhood was spent alone, so books became a surrogate for friends. He wasn't shy telling me about his childhood and life in general and while I thought he could be a little intense, I also thought he was a genuine guy who, like me, was a little lost and looking for some answers. He was telling me about how his parents would often leave him at the weekend while they went skiing when I decided to tell him about the vacant spot in the dorm. I suggested that he might like to move in. The selfish part of my brain was hollering no, but I knew eventually someone would move in, and I figured Emilio would be better than a stranger. He was delighted by my invitation and immediately spoke of serendipity. His roommate was a hypochondriac who studied pharmacology and twitched like a junkie. Emilio was looking for any excuse to move out. Two days later we were roommates.

For the first three weeks, all was well. Emilio was as perfect a fit for me as I could have hoped. He was quiet and didn't have any peculiar habits. He was hygienic and interesting to talk to. We graduated from talk of girls and sports to more enlightened things. Much of our journalism course involved reading about current affairs and crafting articles on contentious subjects, and while our tutor didn't care whether we submitted work or not, we began to complete assignments and pass them on directly to our professors. In this way, Emilio showed me I could actually write. At night, we routinely spoke about the future and politics and philosophy. One night, we spoke about the death penalty, which was a hot topic at the time. I told him about Joe Hayes, though not about what I had done to him, and asked if he thought Hayes should die. He felt that the death penalty should be a last resort and moved the conversation on to methods of execution. He talked about cruel and horrible execution practices throughout the ages. He became animated and vibrant while talking about flaying and boiling people alive and so on. I lay in my bed and listened until I fell asleep. Though the topic interested me, the fact that it was abstract bored me a little, so to bring a little reality into the subject a few nights later I told him about my dad's work and some of the cases he'd consulted on. From the outset, Emilio was intrigued, but it became a bit weird after a while. It was as if he derived energy from talk of death, but talk of actual cases and real people supercharged him. I told him about the autopsy photos I'd seen in Dad's office and some of the conversations I'd overheard. Emilio basked in the details like a lizard in the sun. He didn't ask questions, he simply let me fill the room with descriptions of murder and death and the evil people do to one another. *Homo homini lupus est,* as Dad would say. It excited me to talk about these things, though not in the same way it had when I was younger. I was relieved that I didn't get turned on like before and that the crossed wires in my brain had, as Dr. Wambaugh said they would, uncrossed. I'd never been turned on when I was alone with another guy and while I knew I wasn't gay I was fearful that what I was describing might arouse me in a way I'd never considered and then, in the skewed chambers of my mind, it might lead to something. I'd heard that people often experimented in college. The thought of being a test-subject didn't appeal to me.

One night after speaking about Dad's work for what seemed to be a long time I must have drifted to sleep because when I woke later in the night Emilio was standing over me. He was naked and trying to choke me, I sprang out of bed and pushed him away. I was bigger and stronger, but there was something about him that made me think my strength wouldn't be enough. All of a sudden, he came to as if from a trance and apologized immediately and said he sometimes walked in his sleep and that he was probably acting out something subconscious from our earlier conversation about serial killers. I didn't buy it and got up and left the room and slept in my car.

The next day I returned to the room only after I'd seen Emilio leave the dorm building. I had no idea what to do. Should I go to the authorities or the campus counselor? Dad had taught me to sort out my own problems as best I could and only when there was no alternative, seek arbitration. In the immediate aftermath of Emilio's assault, I did nothing. The next night, I lay in bed thinking about what to do. I hadn't seen Emilio all day and was expecting him to come in at any moment. This made me anxious. I had the worst night of broken sleep in my life. I woke up several times. Each time I found the room empty, but couldn't shake the sense there was something hidden in the darkness.

'TJ,' I said, 'are you there?'

I didn't see Emilio for three days. He wasn't at lectures or the now twice-weekly tutorial, and when I asked others if they'd seen him, they shrugged and said no. On the fourth day after the incident, I was heading back to the dorm when I heard him call my name in the December dark. We were alone and isolated on a shortcut to the dorm. I held my books close to my body and stood there, ready to defend myself if I had to. It was then that he reached into his jacket and pulled out a gun.

'I need your help, Matt,' he said.

The Pinkie Killer

'What are you doing, man?' I said, forcing the words from my mouth.

Emilio looked calm but most disturbingly sounded calm as if this was no big deal.

'I have a slight problem, and you're going to help me.'

I didn't know what to do. The gun was a game-changer. I couldn't run. I could stay and fight, but I didn't have the courage to call his bluff. Something told me that if Emilio had to, he'd shoot me. I decided to talk.

'What kind of problem?' I said.

'Something that needs two people, and a shovel.'

'Why do we need a shovel?'

'I'll show you,' said Emilio, pointing along the path with the gun.

'It's this way.'

I stood still, but when he cocked the hammer, I began to walk. Emilio came up close to me, jabbing the gun into my kidneys. It felt hard and heavy.

'If you run or try anything funny, I'll kill you.'

He directed me to the car park. After a minute, we found my car and got in.

We drove to a hardware store, where he took handcuffs from his backpack and chained me to the steering wheel. He reached across and grabbed the keys.

'I won't be a minute. If you beep or yell, I'll shoot you and everyone else in the store. Do you understand?'

The parking lot of the strip mall was deserted. Emilio had made me park in a dark spot around the corner from the hardware store so beeping or yelling wouldn't attract any attention. He was gone for about five minutes and as I saw him returning with a shovel and something else in a paper bag, I thought this was it, this was payback for TJ and Joe Hayes. This was the karma Dad had told me about. The ironic justice seemed apt. Emilio popped the boot and put the shovel in it. He then walked around to the side of the car and got in. He put the bag between his legs and uncuffed me. He leaned in close and waited there. His face was right up to mine. I thought about head-butting him, but in the confined space it would do no good, and he'd probably kill me. He held his face close for a time and then sat back and laughed.

'What's in the bag?' I said.

'You'll find out when we get there.'

We drove south until we got to the edge of Paynes Prairie Park. Emilio directed me to stop the car near what looked like a ranger's cabin. We got out and once Emilio had retrieved the shovel from the boot, we walked up to the door. The cabin was probably used for storage, there were bags of stuff and rope and things like that stacked around it. There wasn't a sign of life anywhere, and my guess is no one had been here in weeks, maybe months. Once we'd got off the main roads, we'd encountered no one. As far as I was concerned, we were in the middle of nowhere.

'Are you going to feed me to the alligators?' I asked.

'Not unless you make me,' said Emilio, 'I need your help, I told you that.'

'OK,' I said.

Emilio pushed open the door and told me to go in. It was too dark to see anything, but I was immediately hit by a strong metallic smell, like the way your fingers get after handling coins. There was also the sharp tang of urine. I stood in the dark waiting for Emilio to shoot me or hit me with something, but instead, he just flicked a switch in the wall. A single light bulb in the ceiling cast a pale circle of yellow in the center of the room, and a gloomy twilight grew in the shadowy recesses. Once my eyes had adjusted to the situation, I saw Hadley's body. He was the source of the smell of piss and what I now realized was blood.

'Fucking faggot,' spat Emilio.

I thought he was referring to me, but he moved over to Hadley's corpse and kicked it.

'He tried to touch me.'

I didn't speak. I knew instinctively that the less I said, the more likely I was to survive. I couldn't rely on Emilio being predictable and though I was really scared, I took some deep breaths, knowing that staying calm was the key. It was hard to inhale because of the smell and thick humidity trapped within the room. I pushed through my gag reflex and after a few breaths, I felt becoming a little calmer and in control of my thoughts.

'Last week,' said Emilio, 'he came over to the dorm, said he wanted to talk to me about something. I let him in the room. He pushed me against the wall and told me if I didn't suck his dick, he'd flunk me. I told him to get out, or I'd call the cops. He then pushed me onto the bed, but I managed to escape. Once I ran from the room, he left.'

I didn't know what to say. I couldn't even tell if it was true. What was true, however, was that Hadley was dead and Emilio had killed him. The other stuff seemed made up to me. Emilio, as if he sensed my doubt, stepped towards me.

'You know what he's like.' He said, 'you believe me, don't you?'

I nodded. Emilio gave me a small smile and then looked down at Hadley's body. I followed in turn. Blood had pooled around Hadley's head like the halo of a saint. There was no sign of any damage to his skull. The blood was thick like syrup. I couldn't tell how long Hadley had been there, but it was probably at least a few hours. His eyes and mouth were open. He looked like he was trying to speak. He reminded me of the photos I'd seen in Dad's study and the various books about murder I'd read over the years.

'How did you do it?' I asked. I couldn't help it.

'I saw him yesterday and told him I'd do what he wanted if we could go somewhere private. He brought me here this afternoon. He said he brought students here sometimes.'

I was struck by the calmness in Emilio's voice.

'You take his feet.'

I didn't move straight away, but after a brief pause, I went over to Hadley's feet and waited for Emilio to take his head. Before he moved, Emilio opened the paper bag he'd brought from the car. He produced small pinking shears. It had a red handle and a characteristic curved blade. I watched as he held Hadley's left hand and cut off his left pinkie, first with a crunch and then a snap. He took a small plastic bag from his pocket and put the dismembered finger into it. He lifted Hadley under the arms, we then carried him outside in an awkward lumbering shuffle. Once outside, Emilio dropped Hadley's head and told me to drag it around the side of the cabin. Emilio grabbed the shovel he'd propped by the door, and we moved to the side of the cabin where I saw a wheelbarrow. Emilio told me to get Hadley's feet once more, and together we put him in the wheelbarrow. Emilio lay the shovel diagonally across Hadley's body, and then he pointed his gun at me.

'That way,' he said, nodding in the direction he wanted me to go.

I picked up the wheelbarrow. It almost toppled, but I managed to get it steady. It was difficult to maneuver, and the shovel didn't help. Emilio lit a flashlight with a click and walked behind me.

'Just go straight,' he said, 'I'll light the path.'

I have no idea how far we went into the darkness, but it must have been quite far. I was glad we moved along a level path because carrying the wheelbarrow was difficult. It would have been impossible to move through any kind of wilderness. My muscles were beginning to burn. Luckily, not long after aches began to set in, we stopped. Emilio directed the torchlight into a tangle of undergrowth.

'There are no gators, might be a few snakes though,' said Emilio.

I wasn't too bothered by snakes or even gators. I moved the wheelbarrow to the edge of the path. Emilio told me to take the shovel and standing well clear of me he pointed in which direction I had to go. We went about fifty feet, maybe a little more, before the earth became soft. Emilio told me to stop and dig.

It took me thirty minutes to dig the grave and by the time it was finished I was exhausted. Once Emilio was satisfied with things we returned to the path where he made me drag the body to the grave and throw it in. I buried it and once it was done, I fell to my knees. Emilio stood behind me and I heard the gun click as he prepared to fire.

'I could shoot you,' he said.

'I know, but then you'd have to dig a grave,' I said between gasps.

Emilio laughed.

'You're a funny guy,' he said, uncocking the gun.

I got up and trudged back to the path. I picked up the handles of the wheelbarrow, and we made our way back to the cabin. Emilio made me clean up Hadley's blood and wipe down everything we'd touched. He then made me put all the rags and paper towels I'd used into a rubble sack. Once we got back to the car, he opened the sack and took out a rag. He smeared some of Hadley's blood on his seat and the dashboard.

'Just in case you think about going to the cops.'

'I'm not going to say anything,' I said.

'OK, let's get back to the dorm.'

We drove in silence back to Gainesville. Emilio tried to strike up a conversation, but the mood wasn't right, and he knew it. When we got near the campus, Emilio told me to stop and get out. I thought about arguing, but I was too tired.

'I'm going to hold on to your car until I feel you can keep a secret.'

I nodded and got out. Emilio slid over to the driver's side and drove off without another word. I walked back to the dorm in a lethargic haze. Once there I hurried to my room hoping that I wouldn't be seen. My sneakers and clothes were ruined. I stripped and threw them into a laundry bag before wrapping a towel around my waist and walking to the shower. It was after one in the morning, and thankfully I didn't meet anyone on the way there or the way back. Once I felt clean, or at least cleaner, I lay on my bed and closed my eyes. I was asleep before anything dark could occupy my thoughts.

Chapter Nineteen
Revelations, April 2019

I woke early the morning after Zimmerman's party. During the night, Gretchen had sent me an email. I rubbed my eyes and read it.

TO: lowellm74@usa.net
SUBJECT: Update

Hi,

Sorry for not getting back sooner. I've been crazy busy with stuff. I'm in Paris at the moment, but should be home soon. Sounds like there are all kinds of fun things going on. Did you find out anything about PI girl and Jeff's cat? Did she go to the RCA dinner with you? How was Zimmerman's party?

Catch you soon

Love,

G

Gretchen's emails were usually concise. This was about as long as it got. I began to reply when I felt a brief sense of panic. I jumped up and made my way to where Beth slept. I had awoken early in the hope that she'd still be here. The door was closed, and I opened it a sliver and then when I saw Beth sound asleep, I opened it wider. It had been quite a while since I'd had a woman stay the night, and even though nothing had happened, I took some pleasure in seeing her there, vulnerable but peaceful. I retreated from the door and closed it quietly. I went back to my room and replied to Gretchen.

TO: gretchen@sweetman.net
SUBJECT: Update

Hi,

Zimmerman's party was interesting, to say the least. He paraded poor old Lily Osman in front of us and told us she'd be leaving the community and going into a care home. Frankly, I think he's up to something, but will tell you more when you get home. I also discovered that our esteemed leader has an interesting relationship with Snout and the Andersons. As for the PI, she came to the party, and we had fun, but I doubt it'll go anywhere, especially as she's ...

I thought about what to say, I had promised Beth I'd keep things secret. I mulled over it for a minute before carrying on.

... she's involved with someone else (not Jeff in case I gave you that impression), anyway as soon as she finds Gene Hackman she'll be gone.

Feel free to drop by when you're home and be sure to bring a nice bottle of wine.

Best,

M

I had just finished typing my reply when I heard Beth's door open. She made her way to the bathroom. I got up, threw on my robe, and went downstairs. I put on some coffee, thinking we'd both need it. A short time after, Beth appeared, looking disheveled but still good.

'Sleep well?'

She nodded and came over to the breakfast bar, where a cup of coffee awaited her.

'I made you coffee.'

'Thanks,' she said, taking the cup and bringing it to her lips.

I gave her some time to wake up. I was keen to get started on the Zimmerman stuff, but everything was in her court. We engaged in small talk about the party, but eventually, it was time to discuss more serious matters.

'You said there was more on Zimmerman.' I said.

Beth was on her second coffee and had come fully round, not that she was hungover or anything, but her type of work takes its toll whether you're tracking a con man, a serial killer, or doing autopsies. Anything related to crime and criminality was taxing. Dad would sometimes take a while to warm up in the morning.

'OK, let's get one thing straight before we talk about anything else, my career is at stake here. If you breathe a word of this to anyone, I'm in trouble. If that happens, I'll make sure you come with me.'

'I know,' I said softly, 'I'm not even here. You have my word.'

Beth put her hand to her mouth and paused.

'You really got me last night with the stuff about the Pinkie Killer. I should have just walked away.'

'Why didn't you? You were doing a great job.'

She gave me a look suggesting my comment wasn't funny.

I held my hands up.

'I'm sorry,' I said, 'I was also thinking about what I know about The Pinkie Killer, and I'd like to do a trade. You know, quid pro quo.'

'What do you mean?'

The reason I'd awoken before Beth was to speak to her before she'd contacted her colleague in Sacramento.

'You said I'd have to talk to your guy in Sacramento.'

'Yeah, you have information relevant to an ongoing murder case.'

'I don't want to talk.' I said firmly, 'not in person, anyway.'

Beth's eyes were fixed and probing.

'You have to.'

'Listen,' I said. 'I'll call the Sacramento Bureau and tell them everything I know, but I don't want them to know who I am.'

Beth stood up. Her face became hard. I'm sure if she had a gun, she'd have pointed it at me.

'What are you hiding?'

I said nothing. She pressed me and asked again.

'You know, The Pinkie Killer. Was all that stuff about college a lie, then?'

I had to credit her instincts. She'd seen through me. I drank a mouthful of coffee.

'There are a few things in my life I'm not proud of,' I said.

Beth sat back down. She held her coffee mug in both hands. I read it as an invitation to continue.

'I should have been his first victim,' I said.

'What happened?' she asked.

'We were roommates. It was OK at first, but one night he tried to strangle me.'

'Why didn't you report it?'

'I was a kid,' I said, 'and I was ashamed. He was naked, and I thought if I told someone it'd be dismissed as college kids … you know.'

'OK,' she said.

'I managed to get away that night, but a few days later he surprised me on my way back to the dorm. He had a gun, and he brought me to a place outside town and made me do stuff.'

Her face showed distress at my confession.

'Afterwards, he took out the shears and put my little finger in it. He said he'd cut it off if I said anything. That's how I knew it was him killing the men in California.'

'That detail was kept from the public.'

'My dad knew a lot of detectives and when I first heard about the killing near Red Bluff, I called one of them, a retired guy, and he told me about the pinkie fingers. I know I should have come forward, but I was terrified I'd be hounded by the press, and I didn't want that in my life. I just wanted to forget what happened.'

'You could have given any anonymous tip.'

'I didn't think of it, as I said, I wanted to forget.'

'OK,' said Beth, standing up once more and putting her hands on her hips.

'Can you give me a name?'

I nodded.

'Any other details?'

I tried to resist at first, but then I broke down under the weight of the memories.

'He said he was going to kill me and steal my life.'

Beth hesitated for a second, then moved around the breakfast bar and leaned into me. It felt reassuring.

'You mean assume your identity?'

'Yes,' I said, 'he told me he'd kill my family.'

'How long did it go on for?'

I sat up and rubbed my eyes.

'Not long, he left the university a few days after the event and I haven't seen or heard from him since.'

'He just left?'

'Yes, he just left.'

'He was your age at the time, eighteen, nineteen or so?'

'I guess,' I said, 'why?'

'A lot of serial killers take a long time to develop their thing, it might explain why he took so long to start killing in California. Anyway, I'll give you a direct number to call, you can do it from a payphone if you like. Just give them a name, and they'll do the rest.'

I nodded.

'I can do it now if you like? I could call from town.'

'You can do it later,' said Beth, 'it might be best to take a little time in case you remember anything else.'

I was happy that Beth's more natural instincts had overpowered her professional ones during my confession. I decided to add another layer to properly cement our burgeoning confidentiality agreement.

'When we first met, you mentioned some details about my family,' I said.

Beth had moved back across to the other side of the breakfast bar. From an open window, I could hear Derek Anderson's ride-on mower chugging through the morning quiet.

'I wanted to give you the impression that I was a real private detective. You know, surprise you a little.'

'It worked,' I said.

'Not that well,' said Beth.

'Initially, it did.'

'So, what's your question?' said Beth.

'You mentioned my parents and my sister, why not my brother?'

Beth took her time formulating her response.

'I didn't want to bring up the past, it's not exactly a nice thing that happened.'

'I thought as much,' I said.

'And it was so long ago, it just didn't seem relevant to what I was doing.'

'Makes sense,' I said.

She noticed my tone of voice. I was hoping to provoke her into asking more questions.

'Why?' she said.

'Do you know how he died?'

'Not really, I only looked at superficial details.'

'He fell into a creek on my grandparent's farm in Kentucky.'

'I'm sorry,' said Beth, 'that's awful.'

I could tell she didn't want to continue with this line in the conversation. I decided not to risk losing her interest and dropped it.

'Why did you come to me if you were investigating Zimmerman?'

'I had to establish my persona, and like I told you, I needed to get a feel for this place and its residents. Jeff suggested I start with you. Why?'

'No reason really, I'm just curious.'

'I hadn't noticed,' said Beth sarcastically.

We smiled at one another. It was nearing nine and Derek Anderson's mower was in full furious song next door. Other than that, it was quiet.

'Should we check on Jack?' said Beth.

'In a while,' I said, 'he'll surface soon enough, best leave him until at least ten. Last night, you said there was more to Zimmerman than just acquiring property. What's the federal angle?'

Beth pulled the robe I'd supplied her with around her body. I couldn't tell if she was hesitant or just distracted.

'Come on, you said you'd tell me. Considering what I've told you, it's only fair.'

'OK,' said Beth, 'even though I think the less you know the better, but Zimmerman is wanted for fraud and suspicion of murder, although we have no proof of the latter.'

'Murder?'

'Some of the properties he's acquired have coincided with the death of the previous owner. So far, we have no hard evidence that ties him to them, but we're hoping something will come up. Old people die suddenly, but these deaths are not just sudden, they're convenient.'

'Convenient?'

'Elderly women, always alone, no kids or if there are, they're not in the picture. These women would become sick all of a sudden and die in hospital, and the next thing Zimmerman would be the new owner of their property.'

'That is convenient.' I said, 'but coincidental, hard to make stick.'

'In my line of work there's no such thing as a coincidence, anyway, the bottom line is we can accuse him of misappropriation, but that's not going to stop him. His lawyer will argue he's legally entitled to these estates. There's nothing we can really do.'

I suddenly remembered what Mrs. Osman had said about the unoccupied house next to Zimmerman's.

'Have you looked into Bill and Marge Harrison?' I said, 'they lived in the house next to Zimmerman. One day, a while back, they were there and the next, they weren't. Zimmerman said they went to an assisted living facility, but he could be lying.'

'Are you thinking about trespassing again?'

'It might be worthwhile checking out where Bill and Marge are before anything else.'

'We haven't looked into much to do with Riverside Falls, most of the resources have been used to focus on establishing links between Zimmerman and his fraudulent property portfolio.'

'Why don't we visit Bill and Marge Harrison, get their side of the story?' I said, 'and let's keep a close eye on Mrs. Osman as well.'

'What was the name of the place Zimmerman mentioned last night?'

I reached through my memories like someone flicking through a Rolodex, and it came to me.

'Juniper Hills,' I said.

'If that's where he intends to send Mrs. Osman, then we can assume he sent the Harrisons there too,' said Beth.

'OK, I remember seeing a leaflet for Juniper Hills at Mrs. Osman's place. We could drop by and see if she still has it?'

'Good idea. I'm going to jump in the shower if that's OK?'

'Of course, there are towels in the airing cupboard.'

'I meant at Jeff's place; my clothes are there.'

She went upstairs and got into the dress she'd worn the night before. It looked every bit as good on her as it had when I'd first seen it.

'You might get a few looks on the way,' I said, 'you know, nosey neighbors.'

'So what?' she said, 'it's not like I'm moving in, and I know you won't mind them thinking whatever they might think if they see me leaving your place.'

'It's a pity we didn't meet under different circumstances,' I said.

'Circumstances can change, Matt, once this is all over who knows what could happen.'

There was none of the playfulness from the previous night in her voice or body language. I think she was suggesting that something in me would have to change before she'd consider anything between us. I got up to walk her to the door, but she told me it wasn't necessary.

'I'll see you back here in about an hour.'

'OK, we can go into town and I can call your colleague.'

'Great, maybe you could drop in on Mrs. Osman in the meantime, see if she has that assisted living thing?'

'Good idea,' I said, 'I'll check in on Jack while I'm at it.'

'Tell him I said hi,' said Beth, ducking out.

I heard the hall door open and then close again. I sat with my thoughts for a short while before going upstairs and taking a shower. I dressed and made my way to Mrs. Osman's place. When I got there, I saw an ambulance and a small crowd of residents. Zimmerman was among them, and he looked full of concern. He saw me straight away and moved from the crowd, intercepting me just as I got to the ambulance. He reached forward and pressed a hand gently on my chest to block my way, he told me there had been a terrible accident.

'Lily Osman?' I said.

'No,' said Zimmerman, 'it's Jack.'

Chapter Twenty
Psycho Killer, Qu'est-ce que c'est, Gainesville, 1993

A real live wire

In the days after Hadley's death, I tried my best to maintain a sense of order to control my growing paranoia. I was sure Emilio would appear at any minute and shoot me or get me to bury another body, or that the cops would find my car. At the very least, I expected there'd be cops on campus asking questions about Hadley, but there weren't. I attended my tutorials knowing fully well that Hadley wouldn't be there. On the first occasion after Hadley's murder, I arrived late. When I got to the room, I was out of breath from running. I scanned the small space, everyone was there, including Emilio.

'Hey Matt, you made it,' he said before I could feign seeing him and leave.

'I saved you a seat.'

I smiled through my teeth and sat at the seat beside Emilio. I slung my backpack from my shoulders and placed it between us, and then shuffled my chair a few inches further from him. He smiled at me as I did it.

While most of us waited for Hadley to arrive, Emilio kept making remarks about him. I wonder where Dave is. Dave is late, that's not like him, is it? I wonder if he got fired. And so on. He was testing me, seeing if I'd crack and say something incredible. I knew if I did that, he would see to it that the cops would find my car and that would be that. If I protested that Emilio had done it and told the cops the story about the buried body, he could easily deny it. Given his inventiveness, I was sure he could concoct a story that would nail me. Whatever I did, I was screwed.

After about fifteen minutes, the fat Asian kid got restless and packed up his notepad and pens and got up to leave. Just as he was ready to go, one of the professors came into the room. He looked at the fat Asian kid and told him to sit down. He was about Dad's age and wore a bow tie and glasses that made him seem vaguely comical. He looked like he'd rather be anywhere else. He dropped his well-worn but sturdy leather satchel on the table with a loud slap. After a few seconds, spent rummaging through it, he brought out a set of Xeroxed notes and passed them around the group.

'This is your assignment, it's due for next week,' he said matter-of-factly.

I looked at it, it was routine stuff. I could do it in my sleep.

'Where's Dave?' said Emilio. His tone was cool and detached.

The professor peered over his glasses at Emilio.

'If by Dave, you mean Mr. Hadley,' he said with some disdain, 'the simple answer is I don't know.'

'Thanks, prof,' said Emilio, 'it's just that Dave, I mean Mr. Hadley is never late and has never missed a class, as far as I know.'

The professor read down his notes, scanning the names.

'I prefer to be called professor, Mr. Ferrer.'

'Ferreira,' said Emilio.

'I don't know what way Mr. Hadley ran this tutorial, but I'm a bit more traditional. I will call you by your family name, and you will address me as Professor Michaelson. Now, if you'd be so good as to tell me your names, we can begin.'

The tutorial was far less entertaining than any of Hadley's had been, but it was much more purposeful. We worked on language and structure, and then Michaelson briefly went through our assignment and left without a goodbye or any other acknowledgment. When he left, the room began to clear quickly. As I reached to grab my backpack, Emilio tapped my arm.

'Wait,' he said.

Once everyone was gone, Emilio got up and shut the door. He then sat at the top of the table where Michaelson had, pushed his chair back, and put his feet up.

'I like how you've kept quiet, Matt,' said Emilio. There was no menace in his voice, it was unmodulated and relaxed. Outside, through the frosted glass, I could see people moving along the corridor. Emilio noticed me.

'It's been almost a week now, and you haven't said anything to anyone. I think that's good, Matt.'

'I have as much to lose as you do,' I said.

Emilio grinned and leaned back. His chair was balanced precariously, but he was in control. He tapped the whiteboard behind him.

'That's where you're wrong mi amigo, I have nothing to lose, there's nothing on me. It's all on you.'

I knew he was right, there was no point in continuing this game.

'What do you want?'

'I don't want anything Primo.'

'You must want something?'

He leaned forward, bringing his chair down to the floor. Suddenly, he banged the table hard with his palms. The noise startled me.

'Not so easy-going after all,' said Emilio, laughing.

I wanted to tell him that loud unexpected noises gave everyone a fright that it was hard-wired into us, but I knew if I just went along with his game, it'd be over sooner.

'Actually, there is one thing I want,' he said, getting up.

'What?'

He looked at his watch and appeared to be in thought, trying to work something out. After a moment, he arrived at whatever he'd been thinking about.

'I will see you tonight in the dorm room at 9. If you are not there, I will make an anonymous call to the cops telling them where Hadley's body is. There they will find your car. I reckon even they will be able to put the rest together.'

'I'll be there,' I said firmly.

'I know you will,' said Emilio.

He looked at me one more time before leaving the room. There was no emotion in his eyes, nothing to distinguish him as human. I sat back and took a deep breath. Emilio was a pure psychopath and was only now revealing his true nature to me. It had all been an act. He was coy at first, quiet and reserved, then once he knew he'd duped me into trusting him, the rest followed. There was nothing I could do short of killing him, but until I knew where my car and the rags I'd used to mop up Hadley's blood were, I was Emilio's plaything to do with what he wished.

So, rather than spend the time until I was to meet with Emilio worrying about his intentions, I busied myself by completing the assignment Michaelson had given us. By 8:45 I was done and left the library for my room. It was during that walk that the thoughts began to creep in. I kept seeing Hadley's body.

The twisted look on his face, the smell, the indignity of his death and burial. Maybe it was my turn. I was sure if Emilio was what I believed him to be, he'd have no qualms about killing me too. It was enough to think that all he'd wanted was for me to do the donkey work disposing of Hadley's body and now that it was done, he'd kill me and find someone else to torment. I couldn't think of any other reason, but I knew I had to face him. Something in my mind compelled me to not let him win and if that involved me dying then, scared as I was, it was my choice. I opened the door to the dorm building and made my way to my room. As I opened the door and turned on the light, I expected Emilio to be there already, perhaps sitting in my chair like a Bond villain, but the room was empty. It was 8:55 and prompted by my previous thought, I turned off the light and sat in my chair and waited.

Emilio arrived at 9:10. It was part of the game, making me wait, knowing it would first give me hope then take it away from me when he appeared. He opened the door slowly and switched on the light. I had changed the bulb to a lower illumination, so it didn't blind me when he turned it on. I was staring at him, and he looked surprised to see me sitting where I was.

'Waiting in the dark,' he said, coming in and sitting on the bed he used to occupy. I stonewalled him. I wasn't going to let him psyche me out. I knew if I could control myself and had the willpower to hold him off, he'd get bored and either kill me quickly or leave. That's the thing about psychopaths, they get bored easily and if things don't go their way, they become predictable and usually careless.

'You thought I wasn't coming.' he said, taking out his gun and placing it on the bed.

'I knew you were coming, and I knew you'd be late.'

Emilio laughed, 'is that right?'

'That's right,' I said without emotion.

'You think you're smart, do you?'

I didn't answer him.

'Yeah, you think you're smart, but you're not, you're just a scared kid.'

'What do you want?' I said.

Emilio stood up. He picked up the gun from the bed and pointed it at me.

'What date is it?' he asked.

I did my best to remain calm. I doubted he'd shoot me in the dorm, but I couldn't be certain.

'It's the 18th,' I said.

Emilio tapped the gun against his leg.

'And the Christmas break is when?'

'Monday the 23rd,' I said. I had planned to go home for the holidays, that is until Emilio had made me bury my tutor.

'That doesn't give me much time,' said Emilio, 'OK, go to the desk and write this down.'

I didn't move, intuitively I knew what he was planning to do, and he sensed my realization.

'I could kill you now if you'd prefer,' he said.

Inside the room, I had no chance, but if I went along with his plan, I might just be able to get away. I moved over to the desk, opened my notepad, and picked up a pen.

Emilio was smiling from ear to ear. In his narcissistic mind, this was about as pleasurable as things got outside of actually killing.

'My father is in advertising,' he said, 'when I was a kid, I sometimes went into the office with him. Did you ever go to work with your father?'

'My father is a medical examiner, so no,' I said.

'Oh yeah, I forgot, your father finds out what happened to people so the cops can catch the bad guys, how silly of me. Can you believe I forgot that?'

I could, Emilio had probably forgotten everything about me except what he needed to manipulate me.

'Yeah, so my father has a secretary, you know, one of those fat women with big tits. She's ugly but maybe when she was younger, she was OK, you know what I mean?'

I nodded.

'Anyway, my father would sometimes say things, and she'd write them down or type them. He'd say Angela, take a letter, and she'd get ready like it was a game of Boggle or something. I always liked that, the way he controlled her like he could get her to write that everyone who works here is a dick, and she'd write it without batting an eyelid.'

'Did he ever get you to write things?' I said, 'you know, push you around?'

I knew from earlier conversations that Emilio's relationship with his dad was fraught, but he'd never revealed exactly why. The inference of my question had the desired effect. He put the gun hard against my temple.

'You don't get to ask questions,' he said, 'now write this, fucker.'

I held the pen as steady as I could. Emilio withdrew the gun and stood back a little, so he could read what I was writing from over my shoulder. At that moment, there was a knock at the door. Emilio calmly told whoever was outside to come in. It was a guy from across the hall.

'Hi guys, sorry I'm interrupting,' he said, 'I can call back later.'

The gun was in Emilio's right hand and therefore could not be seen.

'We're just working on an assignment,' said Emilio coolly.

The guy nodded, 'I won't bother you, I'll try next door,' he said and ducked back out of the room and closed the door.

Once he was gone, Emilio leaned in. His head was directly beside mine.

'That was close, if he had stayed any longer, I'd have had to kill him too,' he whispered, 'now, let's get your suicide note written shall we?'

Emilio dictated a suicide note that told of how Hadley had molested me and how I'd killed him and buried him, but in a fit of remorse decide to kill myself. It said where his body was buried and nothing else. He made me sign it, and then he put on a pair of gloves, folded it neatly, and put it in an envelope.

'We leave this here, now let's go.'

Run run run run run run run away

Like before, Emilio marched me quietly to the parking lot. I kept reminding myself to play along, that my best chance of getting out of this was by staying calm and giving Emilio the impression that I had bent to his will. When we got to the parking lot, I was pleased in an odd way to see my car. In the suicide note, I'd said I was returning to the place where I'd buried Hadley's body.

'You know the way,' said Emilio.

I got into the car and Emilio handcuffed me to the steering wheel. We drove south. I remembered most of the route.

'I've been watching you since last year,' said Emilio, 'yeah, I saw you on campus one day and decided you were my boy.'

I couldn't tell if this was true or just part of his game.

'I don't even do journalism,' he said, 'but with a bit of know-how, I got myself into the course. You'd be surprised what can be done with computers these days.'

I reasoned that in a university with a student body of some 50,000 it might be relatively easy for someone to manipulate the system if they knew where the cracks were.

'Why me?'

'I really don't know, amigo; I would tell you if I did. You just looked right.'

'Right?'

'Yeah, right, a vibe I got, I dunno, now quit with the questions.'

I didn't speak for a few minutes, allowing him time to cool off. There was no point in getting him worked up until I could take advantage of it. We drove on and once I knew he was relaxed I asked another question.

'Is your name really Emilio Ferreira?'

He smiled, 'didn't I tell you to quit with the questions.'

'I'm going to die, so I'd like to know the name of the guy who's going to kill me.'

'As far as you or anyone else knows it is my name,' he replied, 'I will tell you this though, I am from Modesto, that's the truth.'

'OK,' I said.

'But you know what, I like your name, Matt Lowell, has a nice ring to it. I wonder what it would be like to be Matt Lowell from Clearwater, Florida, eh pendejo?'

As we got nearer to the park, I began to probe Emilio for information, it was almost time to make my move.

'Is the stuff from last week in the car?'

'What stuff?'

'The shovel, the rags I cleaned up Hadley's blood with?'

'They're in the boot, why?'

'I was just seeing if you're thorough, it wouldn't do to forget anything. You know there could be a stray fingerprint of yours on the handle, or maybe they could trace it to the hardware store, maybe they have you on the store camera?'

'I don't think so,' he said.

He reached into the glove compartment and brought out something small and rectangular. It was wrapped in red fabric. He removed the fabric. It was a cigarette box. He opened the box and took out Hadley's pinkie finger.

'I'm going to keep this, though,' he said.

After that, I didn't say another word until we got to the cabin.

'Have you a preference?' said Emilio as we got out.

'What do you mean?'

'I mean, would you prefer to do it in the car or the cabin or outside?'

'I don't care,' I said.

The air was cool and dry, it smelled of the forest and, in the distance, the various sounds of animal and insect life hummed and chirped and buzzed. In the stillness of the night, a gunshot would ring out for miles, though the chances of anyone coming to my aid were about as likely as Emilio letting me go and saying no hard feelings.

'Maybe the cabin is best,' he said, and directed me towards it.

Once we were inside, he produced a smaller gun from his coat pocket and put it on a rickety table in the center of the room.

'You're to use that,' he said.

'OK, but you're going to have to bend over first,' I said.

He began to laugh. In a few seconds, we were both laughing. Once it passed, he trained his gun on me.

'I could shoot you, but the cops would figure that out. I want you to pick up that gun and put it to your head and pull the trigger.'

'What if I don't?' I said. There was no defiance in my words, I just wanted to know his plan.

'I thought about that,' said Emilio, 'it's easy, if you don't, then I tie you up, and I get in the car and I pay a visit to Clearwater and I murder your parents. Then I drive back here and show you their severed heads, and then I kill you. Maybe in the time I'm gone a 'gator will find you, maybe a diamondback, that'd take a lot longer than a bullet to the head. How about that?'

I didn't say anything. I walked over to the table and picked up the gun. It was heavier than I expected. I put it to my head.

'You see, you can be reasonable when motivated,' said Emilio, 'there's no need to be rude.'

He stood watching me. I knew he was waiting for me to pull the trigger. Part of me thought about pulling it, it could be loaded with blanks, it would be the sort of thing a guy like Emilio might do for fun before shooting me himself.

'There's just one thing I want to know before I do this,' I said.

'What do you want to know?'

'Why did you kill Hadley?'

Emilio's otherwise cool expression wrinkled at the edge of his mouth. His eyes moved to the side. A rising smell of wet earth filled my nose.

'I'd like to know,' I said softly, 'I just want to know if you think of me the same way.'

Emilio looked at me searchingly, as if momentarily confused.

'Do you think of me the same way?' I said.

My voice was beginning to quiver. I inhaled noisily through my nose.

'What, no?' said Emilio, 'we're friends Matt, Hadley was a piece of shit. Fucking faggot.'

'Did he really try to rape you?' I said.

I could see it was working. Emilio was becoming agitated. I pressed further.

'It's just that he tried to do the same to me.'

Emilio's grip on his gun tightened.

'Last month,' I said, 'he tried to grab me as I went back to the dorm.'

'What?' said Emilio incredulously.

'It's true,' I said, 'he must have moved on to you when he couldn't get me.'

My words were having the desired effect. Emilio's cool exterior was cracking. Once I saw it strain, I waited and let him twist himself into a tighter knot.

'Fuck,' said Emilio loudly.

'So, you see, he was probably watching you too, the way you were watching me.'

'Shut the fuck up,' said Emilio.

'Which makes you and him the same. You know what I mean?'

I was winning, I knew he would only shoot me as a last resort. His power lay in his control over me and now that it was fading, he began to move like the floor was on fire. He didn't take his eyes off me, though, but I could see he was desperately trying to regain control of himself. He grimaced, opening his mouth as if he was trying to speak. Suddenly, his face became taut. He pointed his gun at me.

'Do it now,' he said, 'shoot yourself.'

His eyes were racing, he was becoming frantic, this was the time to deliver my blow.

'Your father molested you, didn't he? Was it in a place like this, was it on a fishing trip?'

Emilio's hand was shaking. He had completely lost his composure. I knew what he was going to do and dived towards the table. He fired his gun and missed. I fired mine at the lightbulb, hitting it. In the darkness, there were two more shots before Emilio fled from the cabin and ran towards the car. Adrenalin surged through my body and I caught up with him just as he got into the car. I opened the door and pulled him out and began to kick him as he lay on the ground. He dropped his gun and curled into a ball. I picked up the gun and reached down and grabbed him. Even without the great surge of energy coursing through me, I was bigger and stronger than him. He was terrified.

He cowered before me. All his power was gone. I put the gun to his face and pressed it into his cheek.

'Don't kill me,' he said.

I threw him down hard and hit him with the butt of the gun.

'What do you know about my family?' I shouted at him.

'Nothing,' he said, 'only that they live in Clearwater.'

I pushed the gun back into his face.

'I swear, I only know what you told me.'

'What's your name?'

His hands were covering his face.

'Tell me your fucking name, or I'll smash your face and put you in that swamp with Hadley,' I said, raising the gun over my head.

He said a name and then reached into his pocket and took out his wallet. He tossed it to one side.

'You can check my driver's license,' he said as he slumped against the car.

I looked at it. The name and picture checked out, as did the address, Modesto, California. I told him to get up. Then I made him open the boot and take out all the evidence from Hadley's murder. We then went into the cabin and I retrieved the other gun and after a brief search, we found some gasoline. I made Emilio drive this time. We drove a few miles further south, where we stopped and made a little bonfire. During the drive, I managed to find out where Emilio was staying on campus, since he'd left my room. I originally thought he'd gone back to his former dorm room, but he told me the story of his hypochondriac roommate was a cover. I think most of what he told me was untrue. He said that he'd been sleeping in the basement of one of the lecture halls. We drove to campus and I told him to show me where he'd slept. Once we got to his hiding place, I told him to gather his things. We then drove the seventy miles to Jacksonville. I ordered him out of the car and told him if I ever saw him near campus or anything like that, I'd kill him. He fled into the night and I drove back to the campus. About a mile out of town I parked my car on a side road and using the remainder of the gasoline I torched it. I had to be sure there was nothing physical tying me to Hadley's murder. As I walked back to my room, I wondered if I'd made the right decision in letting Emilio go. I was conflicted. I was pretty sure I'd never see him again, and at the time that was what mattered. In retrospect, it was the wrong decision, but it took me a long time to realize it.

Chapter Twenty-One
Juniper Hills, April 2019

I didn't wait for Zimmerman to give me an explanation. Pushing him away, I ran to the ambulance. Inside, I saw Jack on a stretcher. He was still wearing his tuxedo and there was an oxygen mask on his face. I tried to climb in the back of the ambulance, where a startled paramedic told me to get out.

'I'm his friend, what happened?' I asked.

'Sir, you cannot come in here,' said the Paramedic standing up.

From the back of the ambulance, Zimmerman called my name. I turned and he beckoned me with his hand.

'Let him do his work, I'll tell you what happened.'

I looked at Jack. The paramedic's expression suggested I should do as he'd asked. I reluctantly got out of the ambulance. I think I heard the paramedic say idiot, but I might have imagined it. Zimmerman offered his hand as I jumped down. Once I was down, he brought me to one side.

'I dropped by about thirty minutes ago,' he said, his tone was controlled but also kind.

'I have a key to Jack's house, as you know.'

I didn't know, but it didn't matter, nor did the fact that Zimmerman, a guy I knew to be a crook, was talking to me with the same sensitivity as if I were Jack's son.

'When I went into the house, I called for him and when he didn't answer I tried his bedroom and there he was. Luckily, he was still breathing, though I couldn't revive him. The paramedics think he might have fallen or collapsed late last night, though they can't be sure until they get him to hospital.'

I felt a wave of nausea lift from my stomach into my chest.

'Jesus,' I said.

Zimmerman clapped my shoulder in a patronizing but strangely compassionate way. I recoiled. I was angry at myself.

'Don't blame yourself, Matt, how could you have known this would happen?'

'I let him go home by himself,' I said, 'I should have gone with him.'

'You were enjoying yourself, now why don't you go home, there's nothing you can do here.'

'Has anyone called his kids?'

Zimmerman nodded, 'already done, straight after I called for an ambulance. I called his older boy; he's hoping he can get a flight this afternoon.'

I looked at the ambulance again. The door had been closed, and it began to drive off.

'Go home, Matt, I'll take care of things.'

'What hospital are they taking him to?'

'Riverside, they're taking him to Riverside.'

There was a growing impatience in Zimmerman's voice. I immediately understood he didn't want me around. I started to think about the night before. Had Zimmerman said anything to Jack? I couldn't recall. I made a note to ask Beth.

'I actually wanted to speak with Mrs. Osman. That's the reason I came over,' I said, moving away from Zimmerman.

'She's sleeping,' he said.

I pretended not to hear him.

I made my way through the small crowd that had assembled. Snout appeared in the corner of my eye, he seemed to be making his way towards me. I hurried the last few yards and finally got to Mrs. Osman's house. I was about to open her front door when I heard a familiar noise behind me. It was Derek Anderson at one end of a thick chain with Razor on the other.

'She's sleeping,' he said, 'best not disturb her, she's very tired after last night.'

'I won't be a minute,' I said, and before Derek could do anything I went through the door and closed it behind me. I knew what I was looking for, and luckily, it was still there on top of the bureau in the hallway. I picked it up, slipped it into my jacket pocket, and went back outside. Derek Anderson was standing there. He looked at me as if he was a little kid whose nose had just been stolen by their uncle.

'Told you I'd only be a minute,' I said cheerfully, walking past him and back onto the street. Zimmerman and Snout were engaged in an animated discussion about something. As I approached, they both stopped and looked at me. Snout did nothing to hide his sneering contempt, but Zimmerman smiled in his usual way.

'I'll drop into the hospital later to check on Jack,' I said, 'I'm glad you found him. I'm sure he'll be OK. Thanks.'

'He's in good hands, don't worry,' said Zimmerman, waving me off.

I didn't look back again, but I bet if I had, Derek and Razor Anderson would have been within view. Once I got home, I moved into the front room and peeked out the window. I was right, the Anderson boys were doing a slow lap of our zone. It took them a while to get to my house. While they were passing, I stepped out, carrying some old newspapers. I greeted Derek, and he lifted his hand but said nothing. I put the papers in the trash and watched Derek continue his slow walk. Once he was down by Karl Johnson's house, I made my move and scurried the short distance to Jeff's house. I felt like Wile E. Coyote stalking Roadrunner and like Wile. E. Coyote, I was half expecting a huge boulder or rocket to come out of nowhere and get me. I kept my head down and when I got to Jeff's door, I rang the bell and stayed down until Beth answered the door in what seemed like an age later. She looked at me as I was crouched down.

'What took you?' I said.

'What are you doing, Matt?

I scuttled in the door and once inside stood up to my full frame. I ran from the hall and into the front room and peeked out the window. Beth followed slowly. When she got to the front room, she was looking at me as if I'd lost my mind.

'Paranoid much?' she said, 'are you on something?'

'What?'

'What do mean what, surely I'm the one who gets an explanation. You're acting pretty weird?'

Derek had left the zone. I'd got to the window just in time to see him disappear around the corner.

'I went over to Jack's, he's in hospital, he must have fallen sometime last night.'

Beth's eyes widened, and she brought her hand to her mouth.

'He should be OK,' I said, 'they've taken him to hospital.'

'I hope so,' said Beth.

I was about to say something about Jack when I stopped. Beth's eyes narrowed, and she stepped back from me.

'What's up with you?' she said, 'seriously.'

'Zimmerman was there,' I said quietly, 'he tried to stop me from going into Lily Osman's house.'

Beth gave me a quizzical look.

'He must have told Derek to follow me back here, that's why I was doing all that stuff.'

'Come on, that's a bit of a stretch.'

'Seriously, he knows we're on to him.'

'How would he know that?' said Beth, putting her hands on her hips.

'OK, then you explain why Mr. Freaky-Deaky from shitkicker Alabama and his crazy mutt follow me home?'

Beth folded her arms. By now I knew this wasn't a good sign. She was dressed in a thick white bathrobe that was too big for her. It gave her a slightly frumpy appearance. For the briefest of seconds, she reminded me of my mom when she'd give me a talking to. Mom rarely did any disciplining, but when she did, she always folded her arms.

'Can you not do that?' I said.

'Do what?'

'Fold your arms, it's hostile.'

She kept her arms folded, and I sat on the stairs.

'Did it occur to you that Derek is your next-door neighbor and that he regularly patrols the neighborhood with his dog?'

I wouldn't let her have it, it wasn't what I'd experienced, even if it did make sense.

'No way, he was following me.'

'OK, have it your way,' she said, evidently bored or frustrated with my antics.

'I'm going to get dressed and hopefully by the time I'm done you'll have come down from whatever you're on.'

I felt like telling her to get lost, but instead watched her as she walked up the stairs. I focused on her ass as it swayed from side to side.

'Stop watching my butt and make some coffee,' she said as she reached the top of the stairs.

I grinned and went into the kitchen. I was familiar with Jeff's house, not just the layout, but I knew where a lot of things were too. I always enjoyed visiting, whether it was to shoot the bull with Jeff or feed Gene Hackman. One thing I didn't like about Jeff's house was how cluttered it was. Aside from keeping the massive archive of articles he'd written over the years, he kept just about everything else. I'm not suggesting his house was like one of those documentaries about crazy people who'd collected every receipt and bottle top they'd ever used, but it was pretty disorganized. He had a lot of books, and he sometimes stacked them vertically, a sure sign of insanity, but I allowed him some leeway on that one. His tables were covered with papers and notes and cut-outs and pens and whatever else. Jeff's house was more like a classroom where hundreds of kids worked day in day out or like an explosion in a stationery shop. To top it all off, there were dozens of images on the walls, mostly photos of Jeff with friends, family, and famous people he'd met down the years. I stopped in the hall to look at a picture of Jeff with Johnny Cash and Waylon Jennings. It was from some time in the 1980s and was signed by both artists. Jeff's hair was a bit longer then, and he looked like a cool dude for sure. As I was admiring the picture and thinking about what kind of life Jeff had led, Beth came down the stairs and into the hall.

'I like that one,' she said.

'He's had a great life,' I said.

'Why don't you have a whole bunch of photos on the walls of your house?'

'I haven't lived a life like Jeff's,' I said.

'Doesn't matter, you still have family, friends, memories.'

She had forgotten my family history.

'Actually, I don't,' I said, 'not family and friends anyway.'

Beside the picture of Jeff with Cash and Jennings was a wonderful black and white photo of Jeff with his two daughters. The girls were in their teens and the three of them were smiling in that totally uninhibited way. They were standing in front of their New York home, and everything pointed to it being just about the best day of their lives. It was taken just before things started to go bad in Jeff's marriage.

'I hope Jeff and Carrie sort things out,' I said.

'They will,' said Beth, 'fathers and daughters can fight, but it takes a lot for them to become alienated.'

'Maybe,' I said, 'but Jeff's a stubborn guy and Carrie's worse.'

'I think it'll be OK,' said Beth.

'Are you and your father close?'

'Superficially,' she said quietly, 'he's a bit old school, you know, he keeps his distance emotionally.'

'My dad was like that.'

'If you're talking to him about cars or sports or things that don't involve any depth of feeling, he's fine. I think you'd like him; he's nuts for sports, just don't tell him you're into perfumes and stuff like that, he might get the wrong idea.'

'Are you inviting me to meet him?'

'If you're ever in Napa, drop by his place of business and tell him you know me, I'm sure he'd be happy to chat.'

I stood there waiting for her to give me the rest of the information. She looked at me and pointed a finger towards the kitchen.

'Coffee?'

We went into the kitchen and I made a pot of coffee. Now that things had calmed down, I felt a little embarrassed by my earlier behavior. It was a bit paranoid, maybe Lily Osman was sleeping, maybe Zimmerman was being considerate, maybe I'd imagined him staring at me suspiciously and maybe Derek Anderson wasn't following me, but I know what I heard in Zimmerman's house the night before and anyway, the FBI was on his tail.

'Juniper Hills,' I said aloud, giving Beth a fright. She jumped and spilled some of her coffee.

'Will you tell me when you're going to do that,' she said, getting up to find a paper towel, 'what's got into you anyway?'

I reached into my pocket and brought out the leaflet detailing life in Juniper Hills. There were pictures of happy old folk doing aerobics and crafts and enjoying all sorts of wholesome activities.

'I don't want to end up like that,' said Beth plaintively.

'Provide Provide,' I said.

She looked up from the leaflet and tilted her head.

'It's a poem by Robert Frost, in it, he suggests the best way to cope with old age is by having a lot of money and friends, even friends you have to buy.'

'Whatever works for you,' said Beth.

'OK, what do you want to do?'

Beth put the leaflet down.

'That's the first time you've said you instead of we,' she said, 'does that mean I'm in charge?'

'You're the FBI agent, I'm just along for the ride.'

'I'm glad you've got that straight,' she said, tapping my hand.

I laughed; it was nice to have her mocking me in this way.

'Especially given your questionable state of mind,' she added.

I read over the leaflet for Juniper Hills, there was an address. It was north of Concord near Lake Winnipesaukee, about an hour's drive from where we were.

'OK, let's go and see about Mr. and Mrs. Harrison.'

'On the way back, we should check in on Jack,' I said.

'Good idea,' said Beth, finishing her coffee.

Ten minutes later we were on the road. We took my car. Just outside of town, I stopped at a payphone and called in my anonymous tip about The Pinkie Killer. I knew it would create a headache for the Sacramento Bureau and would put Beth in a difficult situation once she found out what I'd said, but for now, I was happy that I'd lived up to my side of the agreement and was glad that Beth and I could focus on Zimmerman and what he was up to in Jonestown.

Why didn't you come into the phone box?' I said, 'for all you know, I could have been calling The Psychic Hotline.'

'For one, it was a little cramped in there and two, I have to trust you.'

'You can always check up anyway.'

Beth's hand trailed on the window like she was doodling.

We got to Concord quickly. It was a quiet morning with little traffic on the highway. As we drove through Concord, I was struck by its mix of small-town charm and old-world class. I hardly ever came into town these days, but made a mental note to visit once things settled down.

'You know Franklin Pierce was from Concord, actually, he was from nearby Hillsborough, but he died in Concord.' I said as we left town.

'Who?' said Beth lazily.

'The 14th President,' I said.

'Sorry, I was miles away.'

'It proves what people have always thought,' I said, 'that Pierce was one of the least memorable presidents.'

'Probably,' said Beth.

'Though not the worst.'

'No,' said Beth, 'I think there's a much better contender for that title.'

Being Californian is not like being American, not in a general sense anyway. Most other Americans regard Californians as different, and not in a good way either. We're like a cousin who doesn't quite fit in, but you must be civil to out of custom. Much of conservative America sees California as the worst example of the excesses of liberalism. And yet, The American

Dream is epitomized by the journey west. Head towards the sun and you'll strike it rich. Nowadays, the only gold in California are the suntanned bodies and all the accessories that go with it. Still, I guess that's the great contradiction of our country, the idea that if you work hard, you can make it overnight. Over the years I knew a lot of people who went to L.A. and San Francisco looking for the meaning of life only to find the primordial expanse of the Pacific laughing at them. Something about being in the car with Beth made me think of the day my family left Sacramento. Something began to pull at me to go back, but I ignored it. New Hampshire was home, for now.

We spent the next while moving between silences and occasional comments, lamenting what was happening to the country. Beth spoke about friends and family fighting along partisan lines and how she'd never seen anything like it before.

'You don't talk with your sister much?'

'No, we had a kind of falling out,' I said, thinking it was time to let my guard down.

'What happened?'

I kept my eyes on the road, I didn't want her detecting anything I couldn't hide.

'Just one of those things,' I said.

'Must have been more than that,' she said.

I gave her a glance. She wasn't looking at me. I think she was genuinely trying to know me.

'She was raped in high school,' I said, 'this guy took advantage of her at a party one night, anyway it all stemmed from that. Things were never the same after.'

We had reached Gilford. Juniper Hills was about two miles away. Though there were a few rises in the earth they weren't exactly hills and though there were lots of trees there were no junipers, plenty of poplars and birches and hawthorns, but no junipers.

'Your family has had a lot of misfortune,' said Beth as we started down the long avenue towards the building.

'Probably no more or less than any other family,' I said.

'Your brother,' said Beth as the imposing edifice of Juniper Hills rose up and swallowed the sky.

I was unsure if I wanted to take the conversation further, and seeing as we'd reached our destination there was little point.

'Ask me later,' I said as I got out of the car.

We made our way to the reception where a short, friendly woman wearing thick glasses greeted us. I asked about Bill and Marge Harrison, and she looked puzzled.

'I don't know anyone of that name here,' she said.

Beth and I looked at one another, we had not anticipated this.

'Sorry,' said Beth, 'are you due to receive a new resident this week?'

'Lily Osman,' I said.

'I'm a little confused,' said the woman, 'who exactly are you looking for?'

Beth asked the woman if she wouldn't mind excusing us for a moment and took me aside.

'Are you sure this is the right place?'

'This is the address on the leaflet.'

I showed her the leaflet. The woman behind the desk was busily typing. I walked back over to her and showed her the leaflet. She flicked through it.

'I've never seen this before,' she said.

'Is this a care facility for the elderly?'

'No, this is a psychiatric hospital.'

Beth grabbed me by the hand and moved to the door while apologizing for the mix-up. The woman at the desk smiled and gave me a look suggesting there was room for me if I wanted it. Once outside, I surveyed the impressive size of the building.

It was red brick and vast, and all the windows were barred. There was no hint of happy retirements or aerobic classes.

'What just happened?' I said.

'I'm not sure,' said Beth, standing with her hands on her hips and looking into the distance.

'Zimmerman is using this as a cover,' I said.

'Looks like it.'

'So where are Bill and Marge Harrison?'

'I don't know,' said Beth, 'but I'm sure if we find them, we can nail Zimmerman.'

'You think he killed them?'

'They're not here, they could be somewhere else, but I wouldn't be surprised if he got impatient and got rid of them. They have no family, no one's been asking about them, have they?'

'Not that I know of,' I said, 'I think Art Tillman might have, but no, I've heard nothing about them since they left.'

'That's the thing about your community,' said Beth, 'there's a lot of talk about being neighborly, but all I've seen is a place where most of you bury your head in the sand. No wonder Zimmerman was allowed to take over.'

'He wasn't allowed,' I said.

'You bet he was, there was no resistance. He walked over all of you, and you didn't care. Everything was about keeping up appearances. Jonestown, they got that name right.'

'Some of us care,' I said.

'I didn't mean you, or Jeff or Jack for that matter, but I can see what attracted Zimmerman to a stuck-up New Hampshire community full of its own self-importance.'

'It wasn't always like that.'

Beth pushed her tongue along her bottom lip, she was agreeing with me.

'I'm sure it wasn't originally, but it's become just another place where everyone pretends to be looking out for one another. Kind of symptomatic of the whole country, really.'

'Derek Anderson looks out for us,' I quipped, 'he's a pillar of the community.'

Beth laughed.

'Can you get your guy to find out about him?'

'Zimmerman?' I said.

'No, Derek Anderson, I'd like to find out what Zimmerman has on him. It's the only way to explain his unflagging loyalty.'

'I can ask.'

'Be discreet,' said Beth using her Olivia Benson voice.

I emailed Rohit. I told him there was something big in it for him. I had no idea what exactly, but I could worry about that later.

'I'd have thought you'd have access to some computer database being the FBI,' I said, emphasizing the I in FBI.

'That's TV,' said Beth, 'this is real life. If I had that kind of information, I'd be back in California, watching the sunset and sipping a beer. Besides, it can take time to dig up dirt, your guy will be quicker.'

I had a compelling image of sipping beer watching a California sunset, it was about as enticing an image as I could think of, provided the Pacific was in a good mood.

'OK, I told my guy it was urgent, he should get back to me within a day or two at the latest.'

'OK,' said Beth, 'I hope he's good.'

'He is,' I said, 'he found out about you.'

Beth gave me a wry smile.

'We need to find the Harrisons,' she said, opening the door and getting into the car, "they're the key to this whole thing.'

Chapter Twenty-Two
Lost years, Gainesville, Baltimore, Florida, Oklahoma, Riverside Falls, 1994-2000

Even six months after I'd chased Emilio away, I lived in constant fear that he'd come back and come back hard. I knew from my own experience that a humiliation like the one I'd inflicted on him would fester in his mind and turn to thoughts of revenge. For some bureaucratic reason, I didn't get a new roommate. I was grateful for this because if Emilio was to return, it would have been difficult, and I didn't want any innocent bystanders. With that in mind, I withdrew from the small circle of acquaintances I'd kept and put my head down and hit the books. I had reported my car as stolen. The insurance assessor didn't have a problem with the idea some kids had taken it and torched it, just like the police said.

Dad had to pick me up for Christmas vacation, and I told him about the car. He was sympathetic and used the opportunity to pass on his wisdom about taking care of things and how best to minimize the chance of your car being a target for 'young punks looking to cause trouble'. I could have argued that I was powerless to prevent such a thing, but I let the old man do his old man thing, and once he felt I'd absorbed his insights he dropped the subject. The insurance money arrived in January. Dad brought me to a friend of his to buy a replacement car. I felt like I was about eight years old as the two middle-aged men spoke about their first cars and then old girlfriends and days spent on Venice Beach and in La Jolla and up as far as Pismo. It got so filled with sunshine and nostalgia, I expected Brian Wilson to turn up and start singing Do it Again. Dad's friend convinced me to buy a teal-colored Volkswagen GTI. I didn't really give a shit about what car I bought, as long as it worked. Dad's friend joked that the car was perfect and so ugly that only a blind person would try to steal it.

There was no word about Hadley until February. It had been thought he'd simply taken off, but when his family hadn't seen or heard from him since before Christmas, there was a brief investigation. One afternoon, a hog-bellied detective spoke to everyone in Hadley's tutorial group. I was the last one he spoke to and answered each question as matter-of-factly as I could. It was all information gathering rather than anything else. I reckon the cops thought Hadley didn't want to be found. Only when the detective mentioned Emilio did I have to make a special effort to make him look in the wrong place.

'The others said there was a guy called Emilio in the group, Emilio Ferreira, is that right?'

'Yes, he wasn't there long, though,' I said.

'He disappeared about the same time as your tutor.'

'I think so.'

'The university doesn't have anyone by that name, do you know anything about it?'

I proceeded to tell the detective about how Emilio and I had become friends and then how all of a sudden, he'd upped and disappeared. I don't know exactly what the detective was thinking, but when there were no further questions, I realized he didn't suspect me of anything. In the months that followed and until the end of the academic year, there was no follow-up. I reckoned that either the Gainesville PD had bigger fish to fry, or they had no ideas. Whatever it was, I was happy with the outcome.

I spent the summer at home. I was fairly certain Emilio was unlikely to appear in Clearwater, but I had to assume he would. I worked as a lifeguard at a municipal pool. It was boring, but coming home each evening and seeing Mom and Dad sitting in the living room or pottering around the house was reassuring. We didn't say much to one another, but gradually the place began to feel like a home for the first time since we'd arrived. A quiet home, a banal place of routine and comfort.

After an uneventful summer, I returned to college to complete my degree. I decided to take the option to finish my degree in three years instead of the usual four. It meant a lot more work in the final year, but given how things had gone, I was happy to remove myself from normal life to concentrate on my studies. Dad thought it was a sign of maturity, and in his own way pressed me about what I hoped to do with a Bachelor of Journalism. I said I wasn't sure. The obvious choice was reporting for a newspaper, but with the rise of the internet and more diverse media, I told him I was keeping my options open.

To ensure my focus was on coursework, I rented a room in a house off-campus. My landlady was an elderly widow named Mrs. Stone. The rent was cheap, but part of the deal was that I helped her out around the house. It was exactly the kind of thing that kept my mind occupied. Her daughter Kim lived in Baltimore, where she worked as a researcher for WBAL. She would visit for a couple of days every month. She was really grateful that I was there to help out. It wasn't just the house stuff; it was the company too. Mrs. Stone's husband had died a few years back and with her children, all grown and scattered to the corners of the country (she had two sons, one in Illinois and another in Oregon, neither of whom she saw much) it was so important that she had someone in the home to give her a sense of security. Kim was in her 30s and unmarried. She was friendly, genuine and fun in a square way. I liked her straight away. She reminded me of the fun side of Bev. She was sarcastic and sharp but a bit goofy too, exactly what you'd expect from someone who worked in radio. She spoke a lot about her work and said she would ask her boss about the chance of an internship once I'd qualified. Radio wasn't really what I had in mind as a career, but I thought it might be just the thing to tell my folks when it was time to leave home and pursue a career. I knew Dad would want an answer and not some wishy-washy I'm going to find myself by traveling around Asia bullshit. He'd want evidence that I was employed with a steady paycheck and that I was putting 10% of it into a pension or savings account every month. I guess I owed him that much for paying most of my college tuition.

I put my head down and graduated cum laude. Not quite as prestigious as Mom and Dad would have liked, but it was good enough so that on graduation day when I had to dress like someone from Harry Potter and feel about as self-conscious as anyone could bear, Mom and Dad felt something close to pride. Once the pageant was done, and we'd all thrown our hats in the air and posed for photographs (I kept that to a minimum, just me and Mom and Dad), Dad took Mom and me and Mrs. Stone to a local restaurant. Mrs. Stone felt like we were fussing over her, but Dad insisted and, to be honest, it was a nice couple of hours. I was happy to leave Gainesville, but especially happy that it was on good terms. As far as I knew the ghost of Emilio had been banished and though I had the death of Dave Hadley to live with, I could handle it, his death wasn't the only death I knew the truth about, and it wasn't as if I'd lost a whole lot of sleep over things like that. During dinner, Dad and Mrs. Stone spoke about Kim and WBAL and the possibility that she could get me a starting position. Mrs. Stone didn't know much about it, but she smiled and listened to Dad rabbit about how I was a good football player and how hard I'd worked for my degree. It was a bit of a blur in the end, and at one point I think Dad was talking about TJ.

I spent part of the summer in Clearwater. Dad was in his final year of work, and I remember him and Mom talking about moving north. Dad had heard through a friend about a gated community that was opening in New Hampshire and had ordered the literature. He became very excited about it, and soon he had the architect's plans, and not long afterward he and Mom took a trip up north to see the place. Mom didn't want to go, but he persuaded her with a trip to New York, where Bev had agreed to meet them for a weekend. When they came back, Dad had paid a deposit on the house in Riverside Falls. Dad kept saying things like, 'this time next year we'll be living among civilized people, our kind of people.' He used phrases like the quiet life and peaceful seclusion, and was as happy as I'd ever seen him. Mom wasn't, but she had her little yellow pills, so it didn't matter how she felt.

In mid-July, Kim called and told me there was a job in the research department of WBAL, but that I'd have to do an interview. I flew to Baltimore and did the interview. The panel consisted of two men and a woman. They were welcoming but all business and were hesitant from the outset about the fact that I had no experience of radio. I speculated about the rise of other media and how it might influence radio. They nodded and bestowed a few friendly smiles, but I left the room feeling like an idiot. Kim took me out for lunch and later that evening I flew back home.

Dad asked me to run what I'd said in the interview by him, wherein he concluded that I'd done better than I'd thought. I was a bit perplexed by this, but I guess he knew what he was talking about because three days later I got a call asking me if I could start the next Monday. I agreed right away. Kim called to congratulate me and told me I could stay with her until I found my own place. A week later I was in Baltimore, and a week after that I was working a job I would come to hate.

Kim's place was terrific. It was modern and close to work. It was just me and her, too, so I didn't have to deal with the potential awkwardness of getting to know a new roommate. Like her mother, Kim said she was glad of the company and while I could stay as long as I wanted, the earlier I began looking for somewhere to live, the more likely I was to get somewhere decent. I had no idea what decent meant, except that it might involve hanging out with other young professionals. I wanted to ask Kim why she wasn't married, but any time the opportunity arose I changed my mind, feeling it would be better not to ask. I appreciated that some things were personal and best left that way. I stayed with Kim for six weeks. She was true to her word and never once complained or dropped hints that I had outstayed my welcome. We did a lot together. We went to art galleries and museums, and one weekend we made a trip to D.C., where we did the usual tourist things. It was during this weekend that I began to question if this was what life was about. I'd always thought about it to some extent. I'd watched my parents work hard and in a general sense live lives that were at best satisfactory. I wondered if that was the best anyone could really hope for, something that was slightly better than satisfactory.

I suppose everyone to some extent experiences a period of existential angst, usually in their twenties and usually not for that long, though that varies a little from person to person. Most people find meaning sooner rather than later and, for most people, that meaning is tied to feelings of love, first for family and friends and then for the person they choose to spend their lives with. It's that willingness to allow another into your life and let them share in your bewilderment at the vast night sky and distant stars that fascinated me back then and still does to an extent. There were lots of young people in WBAL, all of whom had hopes and dreams, and all of whom were actively chasing them. I wondered if it was because I was one of the youngest that I hadn't quite got there, but I stayed in my period of existential angst much longer than I thought I would. I was confused by everything, despite the fact I'd committed manslaughter and buried a murder victim, despite all that, I was as naive about the world as the stray kitten I'd spared when I was a kid. I watched as colleagues dated and then got engaged and finally married. I watched as people got promoted. I listened carefully as my boss told me that I needed to show a bit more drive. I listened again when after nearly two years I was told there was no longer room for me at WBAL and that I'd be better off somewhere else. I remember the glum faces hiding their eyes from me as I made my way through a sea of desks and cube farms and out of the building and on to Hooper Avenue. No one, other than my boss, said goodbye, not one person. I guess they weren't to know, and maybe they didn't want to say goodbye in front of everyone else.

Once I got outside, I sat on the steps for a few minutes and was just ready to leave and wander off into more uncertainty when Kim came out to me. She asked me what happened, so I told her. She'd been so good to me during my time at WBAL, and I felt I'd really let her down.

'I knew your heart wasn't in it,' she said sympathetically.

My heart wasn't in anything. It had been shackled by secrets and lies and a casual acceptance of whatever Dad had told me was the truth about life. I didn't feel guilty about my past, but I felt ashamed about some things in it.

'Radio is not for everyone, Matt, you'll find something that suits you soon enough,' said Kim reassuringly.

'What if I don't?' I said.

I told her that I felt like I was drifting and that I was afraid I'd never find something to anchor my life. She said the standard platitudes about me being young and bright and that if I could focus and trust my instincts, I'd be fine. I knew it was good-natured nothingness, but I mulled over her words for a while and focused on one in particular. Instinct. I'd follow my instinct.

It did no good, though. My drifting turned into a kind of shallow numbness to everything. I stayed in Baltimore for the rest of the summer, but once the leaves began to turn brown, I headed south. Like my sister, I rarely kept in touch with my parents and was quite happy to let them believe I was working my way to the top at WBAL. They were happily ensconced in their New Hampshire hideaway like two squirrels and when I'd call Dad would usually be at the Elks and Mom, probably high as a kite, told me how nice everyone was and how I should come to visit and so on. On the rare occasions I'd speak to Dad, he'd ask me about the price of real estate in Baltimore and if I was thinking about buying there. I was almost twenty-three and alone and with no direction, but I played along and told him I wasn't sure and that if I decided to buy, I'd ask his advice first.

A week before I left Baltimore, I called them for the last time. Dad answered, and I didn't waste any time. I told him that I was leaving WBAL. He asked why, and I said I was moving to Dallas to work there. The truth was, I had no idea where I was going, but I didn't want to get into a one-sided conversation of good old homely advice with my old man. Dad was surprised, but didn't press me about it. I told him I'd get in touch once I was settled. The last thing he said to me was, 'don't start supporting The Cowboys'. It made me laugh, and I promised him I wouldn't. That was January of 1997. I didn't speak to him again for three years.

These were lost years. There's no other way to put it. I wandered south to Savannah and got a job bartending in a hotel. I liked it there. I liked the work too. It was undemanding. The hotel was a renovated antebellum building, rumoured to be haunted though I never saw or heard anything, and had all the charm of the original era. There was a wide range of patrons, but most of mine at the bar were businessmen who were passing through. They'd have a beer or sometimes something stronger and watch the game or shoot the breeze. They tipped well and more often than not told me stories about their youth and how their life hadn't really turned out the way they wanted it to. Some of them would take out their wallets and show me pictures of their kids and say if it wasn't for them, they'd have given up long ago. They were full of wisdom and emptiness and as I served them drinks to numb their pain, I concluded that life was indeed a tale told by an idiot.

I spent six months in Savannah before moving to the Keys. I sent my parents a bi-monthly email. It was total bullshit. I said I was in Lubbock working for a small radio station that played country and western and that I was having a lot of fun. They didn't care much for the email, probably because of its one-sided nature, and so their replies were short. I started in Key Largo and moved my way down to Key West and then back until I found myself in Miami in the summer of 1997. I mostly hung out around South Beach, working in the various bars. It was a lot more hectic and dramatic than Savannah, but the hot sun and the wind from the Atlantic cleansed my soul and for a while, I felt like I was in control of things, not quite purposeful, but my numbness had become a vague sense of vitality. I had friends once more, like the ones I'd had in Sacramento as a kid.

We partied and drank a lot. Most of them did drugs, but having watched Mom slowly dissolve into a self-medicated stupor over the years I refrained. I smoked pot, but didn't do hard drugs. One morning in July while I was napping in the apartment, one of my friends, a beautiful but ultimately vacuous girl named Addie, said someone had been shot on Ocean Drive. I got up and went with her to the scene. I remember the blood on the steps and the sense of shock felt by the entire community. I was a newcomer to South Beach, but the locals and those who'd been there longer loved Versace. He was not just a celebrity, he was royalty. He brought real glamour and sophistication to the superficial surface of the place. He also brought a sense of quiet dignity through interactions with the locals. And now it was gone, torn away in yet another senseless gun murder. When his killer, Andrew Cunanan, shot himself a week later, the utter meaninglessness of both deaths hit people hard. I remember in the days after, as details about Cunanan's murder spree became known, thinking that it could so easily have been me who'd shot Versace, well maybe not Versace, but someone famous. I understood intuitively that Cunanan had murdered Versace and four other men because he needed something to anchor his life with. It scared me, and by the time everything had returned to normal, or as normal as you can get for South Beach, I was gone again.

I spent the rest of the year back in Savannah through to the fall of 1998. Afterward, I did something I said I would after being fired at WBAL. I really did follow my instinct. I had finally understood something about myself, and that was my need to move, to go places. I went to Durant in Southern Oklahoma, where I got my first and only job as a reporter working for The Durant Daily Democrat. I was really happy there too. The quiet, unpretentious way of life suited me, and there were enough interesting people and events to keep me busy chasing stories. I can't say for sure I'd have settled there, but had Mom not gotten sick or Dad not developed Alzheimer's, I know I'd have stayed longer. Once again, something that made me happy had been taken away by something beyond my control.

Bev's email came as a surprise and though I waited for almost two weeks before answering it, I knew I had to leave Durant and head north to New Hampshire. I was wary of how long I'd be there, but my editor, Mr. Letts told me to take as long as I needed. Family is what's important now son, you go be with your momma is what he said. When I got there Bev gave me a frosty welcome, in fact, it wasn't a welcome at all, but you know that. Mom died a short time later. Bev had already made funeral arrangements and though we weren't speaking and haven't spoken since, we played the part of grieving children to a tee. We sat together in the church and thanked those who'd come to pay their respects together. We showed a united front. It wasn't completely cynical, after all, we had Dad to think about. He took it in his stride, death had been his life, and besides, he knew Bev and I weren't on speaking terms. He and Bev were still speaking, but he made it clear he wasn't going to act as a go-between and that we were old enough to sort out our own shit. He sat quietly and implacable in church and looked every bit as dignified and somber as you'd expect. He gave a great eulogy at Mom's graveside. He spoke about their enduring love, their friendship, their early days of adventure, and their later years of contentment. He spoke with dignity of their grief over TJ and how it had shaped their life, forming the backbone of their resilience. Bev sobbed and cried big wet tears. Her whole body shook and though I didn't feel much for my mother, I desperately missed my sister at that moment. A week later Bev was back in Wisconsin, I was back in Durant and Dad was alone in Riverside Falls.

Chapter Twenty-Three
Secrets and lies, April-May 2019

The painted bird

On our return from Juniper Hills, we dropped into Riverside Hospital to check on Jack. He was still unconscious. A round-faced doctor who'd clearly had a bad day said we would not be allowed to see him. He explained that Jack had some swelling on the brain and that they were treating it and was hopeful he'd make a recovery. I asked for more details but as I wasn't next of kin the doctor rebuffed me. Powerless to do anything and somewhat resentful of the doctor's lack of goodwill, we thanked him and left.

As we drove towards Riverside Falls, Beth sideswiped me. She had evidently not forgotten our earlier conversation.

'So, what happened to your brother?' she asked.

I felt my palms suddenly chill, as if the steering wheel had become cold.

'You told me to ask.'

I looked to my left. The land was flat and empty, and the sky was big. I began to think of the day when TJ died and wondered if, over the years, my perception of it had changed. Had it happened as I remembered it, or had it changed in the telling. One thing I did know is that I had lied about it to avoid trouble, and that the last time I'd told the truth about it, there had been terrible consequences. Fighting against my instincts, I told the truth.

'We were chasing a squirrel in the woods near my grandparent's farm. The woods were off-limits. My grandma even told us ghost stories about things in the woods to keep us away, you know how it is. If you go out in those woods, they'll find you, they especially like little boys.'

Beth nodded.

'There were woods near our house when I was growing up,' she said.

Her voice was distant, as if it were coming from the time the memory had been formed.

'Everyone has a story about the woods where they grew up,' I said.

Beth carried on in the same remote voice.

'They weren't that big, but during winter, when it got dark, they'd loom over my walk home from school like some ancient evil. They really scared me.'

'We were told not to go into the woods,' I said, 'we knew it was dangerous, there were wild animals for one thing, but I think the biggest concern was that we'd get lost.'

'Hundreds of people disappear in the wilderness every year,' said Beth, 'I've spent time in search parties. They usually don't end well. Most times they die of exposure.'

'The FBI was called in when TJ went missing. I told them he'd run after a squirrel and that I'd fallen and lost track of him. I said by the time I got up and tried to find him, he was gone. I told them I called out, but there was no reply. I called until I got scared and ran back to my grandparent's place.'

'That's not the truth, though,' said Beth.

'I'm responsible for my brother's death,' I said without any emphasis or any particular emotion.

'What?' said Beth, 'how?'

'The bit about chasing the squirrel is true, though it might have been a raccoon. I didn't fall over, though. I was the one who wanted to catch it. TJ wanted to go back.'

'What happened?'

'Being the considerate older brother he was, TJ let me have my way. We'd lost sight of the squirrel, but since it was the woods, the abundance of wildlife meant another critter popped up soon after. We chased it for about a hundred feet before it scurried up a tree beside the creek.'

'The one your brother was found in?'

'Yes, 'I said, 'though he was found downstream. Anyway, we saw the animal go into a hole about mid-way up the tree and figured it'd be fun to climb up after it. I was nervous about the climb, but TJ with his natural sense of adventure began climbing the tree in seconds flat.'

'Did you follow him?' said Beth.

We were nearing Three Rivers. There was very little traffic.

'I was never a great climber, but I did my best. The tree wasn't that tall, but it was close to the edge of a drop. The limbs TJ climbed were overhanging the creek. He encouraged me, telling me where to put my hands and feet, but once I reached about ten feet high, I got scared and froze like a statue. TJ turned, climbed down and began helping me when I slipped and grabbed onto him. He lost his balance and we fell. TJ fell on the side of the drop and I fell on the hard ground. He was scrambling on to the edge, but couldn't get a proper grip on anything. I was three feet away. He screamed for me to reach out my hand and save him.'

'You didn't,' said Beth.

'No,' I said, 'I was frozen with terror. I thought he'd pull me down with him. I watched as he fell into the creek.'

'Jesus,' said Beth.

'He was calling my name as he fell.'

We drove on for a full minute in a silence that was not only palpable but visceral in its wake. I don't know what Beth was thinking, she was looking out the window. I felt a surge of emotion tighten in my chest and rise in my throat. I wondered if it was guilt or if my memory was attempting to purge itself.

'It wasn't your fault,' said Beth finally, 'you were six and, in all likelihood, he might have pulled you down with him.'

'Maybe, but at the time I was so sure I'd get the blame. I kept it secret for years.'

'Did you tell your parents what happened?'

'No, I couldn't, especially not my mom.'

'Who did you tell?'

'Just my sister,' I said, 'it's the reason we haven't spoken in any meaningful way for almost twenty-five years.'

We drove on without many more words and arrived at Riverside Falls about ten minutes later. When we got out of the car, Beth came round to my side and gave me a comforting hug. We remained that way for a short while. As she held me, I felt a sense of release. The tight feeling in my chest eased.

'You should contact your sister,' said Beth, 'especially as she's all you've got left.'

'Maybe, in time,' I said.

There was more to it than that. On the day of Mom's funeral, Bev and I spoke in private at the church. I was trying to convince her to forgive me for TJ's death, using roughly the same argument as Beth had done. I began to think about the moment when Bev left my life for good.

'It's just you and me and Dad now, one day it'll be just you and me. Then what?'

'Don't try to make me feel guilty, Matt.'

'You're my sister, you're supposed to forgive me.'

'I do forgive you. I forgive you for TJ and I forgive you for every other screwed-up action in your life, but I can't forgive the secrets and lies.'

It was down to that simple fact. There was a side to me that lied and kept secrets. Bev didn't care what my motives were, she simply didn't trust me.

'You told Dad about Joe Hayes.'

'No,' I said resolutely, 'I didn't.'

'Don't bullshit me, Matt, for once in your life tell the truth.'

I hadn't told Dad, but Bev wouldn't be swayed. It wasn't until just before his death that he told me how he knew.

'You've messed up this family, it was because of you, I had to go to that school. It was because of you TJ died; it was because of you that Mom took pills.'

There was no accusation in her voice, she was simply giving me a litany of facts.

'You said you forgave me for that. Stop being a bitch.'

'I'm not just being a bitch, I'm protecting myself.'

'What do you mean?'

'You're cursed, Matt. I don't know how or why, but everything you touch turns to shit. Bad luck follows you. You're like the painted bird.'

In Jerzy Kosinski's book of the same name, a young boy wanders through Eastern Europe after World War Two and suffers various kinds of violence and cruelty at the hands of small-minded villagers. In the incident Bev was referring to, the boy meets a bird catcher who paints one of his captured birds different colors and releases it, only for it to be attacked viciously by its own kind who see it as an intruder.

'I'm sorry Matt, I love you as my brother, but I don't want you in my life, not now, it'll only bring sadness.'

She was right. Lottie Baylock had known it, Dad knew it, and now Bev knew it. I was cursed.

'And what about Dad, are you going to keep in contact with him?'

'He doesn't want to know me, not in any real sense, he never has. It was always Mom who tried to keep us together and now that she's gone Dad will just do his own thing.'

'Can I email you?'

'If you like, don't expect me to reply, though.'

Once I got back to Durant, I emailed Bev a couple of times, but just like the letters I tried to write years before, few words came and the ones that did were hollow and only accentuated the distance between us. After about six months, I stopped and didn't email her again until Dad died.

Beth was waiting for me at the door of my house.

'Lost in thought?' she said.

'Yes,' I said, 'I was thinking about my sister.'

'Call her,' said Beth in a reassuring tone.

'I will, once we've nailed Zimmerman.'

We went inside and sat quietly for some time. Beth must have been feeling a little awkward, or maybe sorry for me, and giving me some space. I didn't need it, but I welcomed the silence. It allowed me to think, not about my family or the past, but about what had happened to Bill and Marge Harrison. While things were swirling around my head, Beth was using her phone to go online. Whatever she was looking at, it completely engrossed her. For the second time that day, I startled her by saying something aloud. This time, instead of spilling coffee, she dropped her phone. It fell on the floor with a thud.

'Jesus H. Christ,' said Beth, 'if you give me another fright today, I'm going to arrest you.'

I apologized and moved over to sit beside her. She looked at me in the same way she'd done when I was skulking around trying to avoid Derek and Razor Anderson.

'I think you need to spend some time in Juniper Hills,' she said.

'The house,' I said.

'What house?'

'The Harrison's house, there has to be something in there.'

'I can't get a warrant right now, if that's what you mean.'

'Guess again,' I said.

'Come on, seriously?' she said with a sigh.

'Yes, who knows what's in there.'

'Anything we find in there will be inadmissible, you know that?'

I hadn't thought about that. I paused for a moment.

'You said that the case against Zimmerman hinges on being able to prove he had a hand in the deaths of those he defrauded, right?'

Beth nodded.

'Well, the Harrisons have to be somewhere.'

'You think they're buried in their own back garden or hidden behind drywall?'

I shrugged my shoulders.

'When do you want to do this?'

We agreed to wait until May 1st, at noon. Zimmerman was giving an annual address commemorating the community's 1994 opening. It took place in The Park and was a brief affair, but most of the community turned out. Beth stayed for dinner. I finally was able to show off my culinary skills, and she was impressed. I made a noodle dish with vegetables and some prawns. I'd learned over the years that the key to good food was simplicity and high-quality ingredients, the rest could be hidden with soy sauce and wine.

After dinner, we had a long conversation about nothing important. Beth wasn't going to broach my family history again, and we were a little weary of the Zimmerman case. We spoke about music and movies, travel and a little politics. Beth told me about her brothers and how being the only girl (her mom aside) in a house full of men had given her resilience and a special insight into masculine behavior. She told me how it had helped with her career. She described the FBI as a 'boys club filled with egos the size of mountains.' After a second glass of wine, she told me that I needed to work on my seduction. She said I was literally tripping over my tongue the first time we had met. I invited her to stay and she agreed. We had a couple more glasses of wine and went to bed, me in my room and Beth in the guest room.

That night, I slept as well as I'd ever slept. Though I'd had a bit to drink, my mind was clear and so was my conscience, or whatever passed for my conscience. I fell asleep thinking of TJ and apologized for not trying to save him. As I was drifting off, I distinctly heard his voice as if he were in the room with me. For all I know, he was.

Your feathers are turning brown, he said.

Gnomes

I slept late and by the time I woke Beth was gone. She left a note thanking me for dinner and how the evening had been the most normal one she'd had in a while. The note also said that she'd call me later to coordinate things regarding our intended investigation of the Harrison's house. I wondered briefly where she'd gone and assumed it was FBI stuff. Maybe she was speaking with local law enforcement, maybe she was talking with her undercover colleagues in The Family Zone. Whatever it was, I didn't care, for the first time in a good while a sense of something on the horizon was looming. I felt purposeful as if

I'd emerged from a fog and though I wasn't entirely sure where I was going, I could see the road again.

I had a quick shower and drove to the hospital to see Jack. When I arrived, Jack was still under. I got to meet his two sons and one of his daughters. They were kind and extremely grateful that I'd taken care of their father. I told them that he was tough and that he'd pull through. I asked the doctors if this was the case, and they said they wouldn't know until the swelling had gone down completely and Jack woke up. Jack's older son took my number and told me he'd call as soon as there was a development. I told him that I'd drop into his father's house when I got back to Jonestown and get slippers and a nightgown and things he might need when he woke up. Before leaving, I asked if Zimmerman had been to visit. I was told he had not, but that he had called that afternoon.

'Don't trust Zimmerman,' I said discretely before I left.

The older son was a little perturbed by this. He said Zimmerman had been nothing but kind to Jack and that there was nothing to support my statement. I realized that my comment was a little vindictive and clumsy. It was another example of the imperfections of my personality that Beth had mentioned. I apologized for implying that Zimmerman was anything other than the pillar of decency they thought he was, and left.

I spent the rest of the day doing some work on my blog, but nothing inspired me and I ended up rehashing old ideas. My sense of purpose did not extend to my writing. To stave off the lingering sense of doubt and deflation that was lurching towards me like some primeval beast, I decided to email Gretchen.

TO: gretchen@sweetman.net
SUBJECT: The Mystery of Jonestown

Hi,

Where are you? I thought you'd be back by now. Anyway, Jack's in hospital. He fell at home after Zimmerman's party, the doctors say it's touch and go, but I'm hoping he'll be OK. I met his kids, they're nice people, they think the world of Zimmerman. I'm not so sure, though, Zimmerman has been acting all weird lately. I can't explain it in an email, you'll have to see it for yourself.

On Sunday, I went to a place north of Concord called Juniper Hills to try and find something out about Bill and Marge Harrison (long story) turns out they're not there — apparently Zimmerman arranged it. Juniper Hills is a psychiatric hospital and never heard of the Harrisons. Do you have any info on this? I know you were on good terms with Bill and Marge. I'm rambling.

Looking forward to seeing you.

M

Through all of this, I missed Gretchen. I knew she'd have been excited by the intrigue and, who knows, might have given Beth some good pointers about Zimmerman's duplicitous nature. I waited for a reply, but nothing came. Beth called in the late evening and told me that all was good and that she'd see me the next morning when we could do our Nancy Drew thing at the Harrison's house. With nothing else to do, I went to bed. I slept soundly, though not as well as the previous night. Just after dawn, I woke to the sound of an almighty ruckus. Razor was barking the place down and Derek was yelling at him. I got out of bed and looked out my window. Derek was straining to hold on to his dog, who'd clearly seen or smelled something and was bursting every muscle to follow it. Derek pulled hard on Razor's chain and the dog yelped. He then looked up at me. I stood back and didn't look out the window again.

Just before eleven, my phone rang. It was Beth.

'I'll meet you at the house just before noon, I'll be on foot.'

'Is your car in the shop?'

'No, I'd just prefer if no-one knew I was here.'

'OK, see you then.'

'Matt,' said Beth just as I was about to hang up.

'Yes.'

'Any news on Jack?'

I told her what I knew and that I was awaiting an update from Jack's son.

We left the conversation at that point, and about ten minutes before noon I left my house and walked the short distance to The Zimmerman Zone. I knew a shortcut that traversed Gretchen's place and was there quicker and less conspicuously than had I taken the usual route. I could hear people in The Park, but once I came out from Gretchen's, the place was like a ghost town. I got to the Harrison house and went around to the side entrance and waited for Beth. She arrived a few minutes later, meeting me at the back door. This time, we didn't need a ruse to gain access. Beth had brought tools to work the lock and after a few attempts, we found ourselves inside.

'Did you learn that in Quantico?' I said as we entered the house.

'My brother taught me,' she said, 'in case I locked my keys inside my car.'

'Sure,' I said with sarcasm, 'cops and robbers are the same kind of people, they just have different ideas about what's right and wrong.'

'Is that right, Mr. Expert?' she said, folding her arms.

'To catch the bad guy, you have to become the bad guy,' I said.

'Is that some Eastern thing?' she said.

'You learn fast, Grasshopper,' I quipped.

'You know I was in Barnes & Noble yesterday,' said Beth enthusiastically, 'but they didn't have your book in stock.'

'It's not out until the fall,' I said flatly.

'Yeah, I can't wait to read it. It was on the cover of *Big Whoop Monthly*. I hear Al Franken wrote the foreword.'

'OK,' I said, 'you win.'

The kitchen was empty and unfurnished. The house looked like a show house except for the fact dust had been allowed to gather. While Beth looked in the cabinets, I made my way to the laundry room. We had no plan or idea of what we were looking for, but agreed we'd know what it was when we found it. I pushed open the laundry room door and there they were. Gnomes, four of them. I called out to Beth and she rushed over.

'What?' she said expectantly.

I pointed to the gnomes.

'Zimmerman,' I said, 'he stole them.'

I told her the story of the gnomes that had belonged to the Petersons and how they'd vanished. It felt good to discover the truth. I bent down and wiped a layer of dust from one of them.

'It's not going to send Zimmerman away, much and all as I wish it would,' said Beth, 'the theft of garden ornaments isn't on a par with obtaining property under false pretenses.'

We left the laundry room and kitchen and moved systematically through the house. There was nothing in any of the rooms except dust.

We made our way to the family room at the front of the house. Even though it was bright outside, there was an eerie twilight to the interior of the house. All the windows were covered by drapes or blinds, and scattered bars of light struggled to throw themselves into the gloom. We entered the room.

'Can you smell that?' I said immediately.

Beth said that all she could smell was the dry, peppery smell of dust.

'It's bleach,' I said.

'I can't smell it, but with your thing for perfumes I'll trust you on this.'

'I bet you'll find something if you use blue light.'

'What?' said Beth.

'The bleach was used to clean up any residual DNA, but they might have missed a spot.'

'More TV,' said Beth, 'if you're thinking blue light will show up blood, you're wrong, LED lights might find something. But you're missing a simple fact.'

'What fact?'

'Whoever cleaned this place might just have been cleaning it, you know, preparing it for showing to prospective buyers or something like that?'

'It's been six months and there's no sign of it going on the market,' I said, 'why keep a house unoccupied all that time?'

'I don't know,' said Beth.

We went upstairs and found much the same. Empty rooms, dust, and slivers of light poking through the drapes.

'This is a waste of time,' said Beth, 'we should leave before that thing in The Park finishes.'

I looked at my watch, it was 12:17. There was still time.

'The attic,' I said.

'OK,' said Beth, 'but I'm not going up there.'

'Spiders?' I said.

Beth's nose wrinkled involuntarily. She nodded.

The attic hatch was beside the bathroom. I reached to the dangling cord attached to the hatch and pulled on it. The hatch opened and I pulled down the ladder.

'I'll be quick,' I said as I began to climb the steps.

Once inside, I reached for the light switch, but the power must have been turned off. I called down to Beth for a flashlight. She stepped gingerly onto the ladder and climbed a couple of steps to hand me the flashlight. It was one of those small, compact ones, but it had a powerful beam. The attic was big and filled with old odds and ends. There were mirrors and paintings covered in sheets and boxes of light fittings and cables and other household junk. I shone the light along the eaves and saw plenty of cobwebs. A spider scurried along a rafter, trying to hide from the light. I moved around the room looking in corners and recesses but found nothing.

Beth was right, it had been a waste of time. I made my way back to the hatch when Beth called up to me.

'Matt, you'd better get down here.'

'Is everything OK?'

'Just come down,' she said.

'Just give me a second, I want to make sure there's nothing up here.'

I backed onto the ladder and climbed down. Beth wasn't there.

'Beth?' I called.

'In the master bedroom,' she said.

A flurry of thoughts flashed through my mind and unable to focus on any of them, I made my way to the bedroom. As I went in, I saw Beth on the far side of the room. She had her hands in the air. My brow immediately furrowed. I took a step further into the room. Derek Anderson stood to my left. He pointed a pump-action shotgun at me and told me to move across to where Beth was. I did as I was told, slowly, never taking my eyes off Anderson.

'What did I tell you about sticking your nose where it don't belong?' said Anderson, addressing me.

I didn't reply.

He chuckled to himself and pulled the pump-action. Two loud clicks echoed through the room and I could feel my heart race. I thought of Emilio and the ranger cabin in Florida. *Not this again*, I thought.

Anderson stepped forward and gave us a wry smile.

'Looks like the two of you are in a bit of a pickle, don't it?'

Chapter Twenty-Four
Unit 262, Modesto, 2017

You're probably wondering why I did nothing about Emilio once I'd discovered what he was up to in California. My initial thought was to make an anonymous call giving his real name, a description along with other details that would nail him, but I reckoned letting sleeping dogs lie was the better choice. It occurred to me that if they got Emilio, and he dropped my name, he'd probably tell them about Dave Hadley and try to pin some of the blame on me as part of a plea bargain. The best I could hope for from that mess would be a whole lot of hassle while the cops poked into my life. The worst and more likely outcome would include the charge of aiding and abetting a murderer. It was too dangerous to stir up, but I had to do something. People were dying and while I wasn't keen on a noble crusade, I found myself thinking about Hamlet. He wasn't keen on his task either, and all throughout the play the burden of responsibility ate him up. My nagging sense of unease wasn't based on moral or ethical righteousness, where I felt compelled to enact justice. It was more akin to a stain on a clean shirt or a scratch on a new car. Emilio's actions were ugly. He'd been given a second chance, but he'd not taken it. I found that offensive. I mean, we all make mistakes, but if we don't learn from them, then what's the point? I had to teach him a lesson.

It took time for my feelings to grow into outrage, six years to be exact. In the beginning, I was content with the quiet life in Jonestown and the thought of going on a manhunt didn't appeal to me, especially as it would involve returning to California. Dad's death had affected me more than I thought it would and while I wasn't depressed or anything, I kept an even lower profile in the first year after his passing. Apart from the house, I'd inherited enough money to keep me going for quite a while, so I made do with a frugal and secluded life. Bev was happy for me to live in Jonestown, even though I'd suggested we sell the house. She said she was good with the portion of the money Dad left and that when or if I sold the house, I could send her a check. I tried once again to make amends, but Bev made it clear that she was happy with her life and didn't want me causing ripples. I think the real reason she let me live in Jonestown was at least then she knew where I was. Her biggest fear was opening her door one day and finding me outside with my bags and nowhere to go.

Each time I got word of another murder along Route 99 I'd spend a couple of days mulling it over and trying to silence the nagging voice in my mind before settling back into the life more ordinary. This ebb and flow went on until 2017 when Emilio crossed the line. Until then, his victims were all young men in their twenties, drifters and hitchhikers moving through California, most likely in the hope of making it rich. Emilio's pathology was borne from a history of abuse, and I think that was what made me feel pity for him the night I'd let him get away. He'd suffered at the hands of his father, and I'd felt at the time that he'd killed Hadley because Hadley had brought it all back, all the pain and humiliation. In my naivety, I thought Emilio might get himself together. I could never have envisaged what happened.

Emilio's final murder was a double murder. He'd picked up and killed another hitchhiker. His MO was to pose as a regular old everyday motorist cruising down the highway on his way home, etc. Once his passenger was comfortable and chatty, he'd offer them a drink containing a roofie and once they'd drifted off, he'd strangle them and violate them. Then he'd dump the body along the highway and move on. He was careful, I have to hand him that.

So, back to the double murder. In the spring of 2017, the body of a man in his twenties was found near Bakersfield. The cops knew it was the same killer. The strangulation, the drugs in the system, the disposal site were all typical of the killer's signature. This time, however, they got something different. While securing the scene, another body was discovered nearby. This person had not been strangled or assaulted, and its proximity to the other body led detectives to assume this person had interrupted Emilio. The second victim was in the wrong place at the wrong time. Tragically, it was a fourteen-year-old boy out on a bike ride.

It was then I decided to pack a bag and headed west.

I flew to L.A. and went to Bakersfield, where I began to hitchhike my way north along Route 99. I knew it was a long shot, but it was the only chance I stood. A week after I'd started my search, I was in Emilio's hometown of Modesto. It was just after two in the afternoon, and I was sitting in a dive bar thinking about going back to Jonestown. I realized that trying to find Emilio by posing as a hitchhiker was as likely as winning the lottery, so, knowing his real name, I called up every person with that name in the phone book. There were no bites. I then remembered that Emilio said his dad was in advertising, and I asked the bar man if he knew anything about it. He said he didn't, but that he knew a guy whose cleaning company had a lot of corporate contracts throughout the city and that maybe he could help. I called him up and gave a bullshit story about being a writer researching for a book on the history of advertising in Northern California. I gave him Emilio's father's name, saying that he was the guy who had come up with the Claymation California raisins in sunglasses.

'No shit, he was the guy! My kids loved that commercial. What a great commercial. He must have made a mint.'

He wrote down my number and said he'd get back to me. Two days later he told me that Emilio's father had died about six months after my dad but that his wife was still alive, and she might be able to help.

'Her name is different now, they got divorced, and she went back to her unmarried name.'

I thanked the guy and was about to start looking through the phone book again when a thought struck me. Emilio's father had died shortly before Emilio had begun killing men along Route 99. It made sense to me that this would happen. Emilio had wanted to kill his father for what he did to him, and when he died, Emilio was forever denied the chance, so he began to kill surrogates. It was standard enough psychological transference. Even though Emilio was in his forties, the cops were looking for an older man, a family man who harbored feelings of intense homophobia. So much for profiling. I knew why Emilio had started to kill. After mulling this over for a while, another thought struck me. Now that his father was dead, did he change his surname too? I looked up all the corresponding names in the phone book. There were three. One was a mechanic; another was an environmental lawyer, and the other had a printing business. My instincts told me it was the printer. Emilio could write and liked words, it would be reasonable for him to make a career out of it, also, owning his own business would give him time to do his thing. I decided to be systematic and went to the mechanic's place of business first. It was evident straight away that it wasn't Emilio. I then went to the lawyer, but that wasn't him either, and so I arrived at the premises of United Graphics wondering how to go about confronting Emilio if he was actually there. I thought about wearing a disguise, but if I did end up face to face with him in his place of business it was unlikely, he'd make a scene. I decided to wear sunglasses. My face had changed since I was nineteen, and I reasoned that Emilio was unlikely to recognize me from a casual glance. The shop was spacious and busy. Several employees were speaking with customers, and a few more manned Xerox machines. They all wore a standard uniform of black pants and red polo shirts. A young woman came up to me and asked if I needed help. I asked for Emilio using his real name, and she told me he was away for the day, but he'd be back the next day. I thought about saying I was an old friend from college and maybe asking for his home address, but the less attention I attracted to myself, the easier it would be to get away with what I planned to do. The employee asked me if I could pass on a message and rather than say no and run the risk of her telling Emilio a strange guy had been looking for him, I told her I was a reporter with the Modesto Bee, and I was doing a feature on local businesses, and I'd call back later in the week. She said she'd pass on the information and I left.

I spent the rest of the day scoping out the area. I waited until the place closed and watched about five of the employees leave and go in the same direction down the street where they turned left. I followed them from a distance and saw they were going to a parking lot. It must have been a private lot as it had a big chain gate and was locked.

This was where I'd wait for Emilio.

The next morning just before dawn I got up and made my way to the parking lot. It was locked and empty. About 07:45 a blue Ford Taurus drove up and stopped at the gate. Emilio stepped out and taking out a key casually opened the padlock and removed the chain from the gate. Though he looked a little older, he had not changed that much. I was in no doubt it was him. He opened the gate and parked his car, and a few moments later headed towards his place of business. I ran over to the lot and wrote down his license plate number. An hour later I called the Modesto DMV saying that a guy had pranged my car and drove off. I told them I got his plate number and could they help me out. Luckily, I got someone with an innate sense of justice, and they gave me an address. I wasted no time in getting to where I needed to. Emilio lived in a quiet neighborhood and I managed to gain access to his home easily enough. Safely inside, I waited.

Thankfully, Emilio lived alone, though I was confident he did. There was no evidence of a wife or partner or kids. His house was a decent size and well maintained and apart from the fact that he'd murdered a bunch of people, Emilio had done alright for himself. Part of me was happy for him to have accomplished so much after his childhood, but it didn't make me reconsider my purpose.

I did a search of the house hoping I'd find a jar full of fingers, but wherever he kept them it was well hidden and most likely not in the house. Around 8 pm, he arrived home, and before he could react, I had a gun in his face. He didn't recognize me at first, thinking I was a burglar. 'Take what you want, but don't hurt me,' he pleaded.

His whiny tone was the same as when I'd overpowered him in Florida all those years before.

I asked him where the fingers were. He suddenly realized who I was. He tried to be friendly, but I didn't want to waste time, so I asked him right out where he kept his other car.

'What other car?' he said.

'Don't mess with me,' I said, 'the car you use when you're picking up the men you kill.'

He tried to protest, but he gave up. He wasn't capable of sustaining a fight when he wasn't in control. He knew I'd figured it all out. He asked me how, and I told him. I asked him if he'd started killing after his father had died, and he said yes. I was pleased with myself for having the insight to guess right about that one, and said so. He called me a prick, and I asked him once more where his murder car was. After a few moments, he told me he had a storage unit where he kept everything. It was about ten miles out of town.

'Looks like we're going for a drive again,' I said.

The storage facility was one of those big places, with hundreds of garage-sized units in long rows. Emilio's unit was at the back, I guess he thought it was more private. The irony pleased me. The place was deserted except for a dozing security guard who didn't even look at the car as we drove in. We got to the unit, number 262 and when we went inside there sat a blue Nissan Altima.

'You have a thing for blue cars,' I said, 'maybe they should've called you the blue car killer.'

He made a noise that was halfway between a laugh and a cry. He began to beg me for his life and told me how it wasn't his fault, but I didn't want to hear it, not this time.

'I got money,' he said.

'So do I,' I replied.

'I need help, come on man, take me to the cops.'

I didn't listen to his words. They were a distraction and meant nothing. I told him to turn his back on me and then, without any emotion, I shot him in the head. The sound of the shot reverberated through the metal walls of the unit, and I could only hope the security guy we'd seen on the way in hadn't heard it. Emilio slumped to the ground and a pool of blood began to form around his head. I went over to him and took a closer look. He was dead, there was no doubt about that. After waiting for a second, I went to the car and pulled the handle on the passenger's side. It was open. As I suspected, in the glovebox there were pinking shears. I looked around the interior, but couldn't find what I was after. I moved to the boot. There were clothes and backpacks and other things that must have belonged to the victims. I rummaged around, but it wasn't until I looked under the spare tire that I found the missing fingers in a mason jar.

I picked it up carefully using a cloth and did a quick count of the fingers. Then without doing anything further, I turned off the light and left. I was tired and glad to be done with Emilio and his crap. The next day, I was on the plane back to Jonestown, happy in the knowledge that Emilio was dead and there would be no more killings on Route 99.

I'd taken a few precautions to minimize the impact of my visit to Modesto. I'd forced Emilio to write an email to the deputy manager of United Graphics saying that he was taking an impromptu vacation to Mexico and that he'd be in touch when he got back. Next, I'd made him access the rental agreement for his storage unit online and using a trick Rohit had taught me I made him pay for five years rental using a hacked account (the price was surprisingly cheap). As I'd suspected, Emilio had used an alias when renting the unit. I wondered how many aliases he'd used over the years. I couldn't be sure, but there were more pinkies in the Mason jar than there were known victims.

Two years later as I stood in a payphone box after dialing the tip line Beth had given me, I thought about what I'd say. After a few rings, my call was answered.

'Sacramento FBI, detective James Marshall speaking.'

'Have you a pen?' I said, 'you're going to need to write this down.'

'OK sir,' said the detective, 'what would you like to tell me?'

'U Lease Storage, about ten miles southwest of Modesto. Unit 262, The Pinkie Killer.'

The detective was trying to keep me on the line, but I wasn't listening. I replaced the receiver and went back to the car, where Beth sat staring vacantly at the New Hampshire land-scape.

Chapter Twenty-Five
Marianne Osman's miraculous intervention, May 2019

'What are you doing?' I said as I put my hands in the air and moved across the room. I don't know why I said it, I knew exactly what he was doing and why.

Derek Anderson said nothing. He just stared and pointed his gun at us. My eyes were drawn to the backpack at his feet. He watched me closely and then with the gun still trained on us, he reached down slowly, picked up the backpack, and threw it over to us.

'Open it,' he said.

Beth reached down and opened the backpack. Inside was a length of orange rope.

'Tie his hands,' said Anderson.

Beth looked at me. I shrugged, what else could we do? She picked up the rope and uncoiled it. I turned around and while she was tying the rope around my wrists, I said a silent prayer, hoping that this wasn't going to be like the gimp scene in *Pulp Fiction*.

'Make sure it's good and tight,' said Anderson.

Beth gave the rope a good tug. It hurt and I let out a yelp.

'Sorry,' she said.

Anderson brought another length of rope from inside his jacket. He told me to move to the other side of the room and then told Beth to lie down on the floor. As he was tying Beth's hands, I thought about running at him but with his military background and questionable mental state, I knew there was little chance of both Beth and I escaping unharmed. It was best just to go along with what he said.

'You can't leave well alone,' said Anderson tying Beth's hands, 'first I catch you trying to climb into Jeff's place and now this.'

'Derek, you're not neighborhood security, no matter what you might think,' I said.

He pulled hard on the rope, and Beth let out a yell as it chafed her wrists.

'Yes, I am,' he said.

With both of us tied up, Anderson frisked Beth. He had no interest in me. He turned out Beth's wallet, keys, and the tool she had used to get into the house. Anderson looked at it and grinned. He then took out Beth's gun and, worst of all, her FBI credentials.

'Well, looky here,' he said admiringly, 'the FBI, ain't that something.'

'Holding a federal agent against their will is a serious crime,' said Beth calmly.

Anderson stepped up close to her. The way Beth's eyes crossed, I could tell she was feeling the full effect of his wonky eyeball.

'So is sticking your nose where it don't belong,' said Derek contemptuously.

'You're making a mistake, Mr. Anderson, you have no right to do this.'

'Don't matter none,' said Anderson, stepping away from her.

Without any further words, he frogmarched us down the stairs and out to the back of the house.

'Where's Razor?' I asked.

'He's around, but don't you worry about that,' said Anderson, pushing both of us out the door and into the garden.

Snout and Donna Anderson stood outside. Snout was grinning from ear to ear.

'Gee thanks, you organized a welcoming committee,' I said.

'I told you they were in there,' said Snout, 'I knew we couldn't trust them.'

Even with my hands behind my back, I made a mock lunge for Snout. He recoiled and let out a tiny shriek.

'Got you,' I said.

Both the Andersons laughed.

Snout patted himself down and stepped towards me.

'You'll be sorry,' he said smugly.

'Is that right?' I said.

Derek Anderson snorted like a pig, grabbed me by the arm, and led me down the garden. Donna took Beth. About fifty feet from the house, there was a gap in the hedge. We pushed through it and into Zimmerman's garden. They took us through the back door into Zimmerman's kitchen. Razor lay dozing on the floor. He lifted his head sleepily to see who it was, and when he saw us began to wag his tail.

'At least someone's happy to see us,' I said to Beth.

I told Razor he was a good boy. He tried to jump on me, but Derek kicked him away.

'Stand against the wall, face forward,' said Derek Anderson in a hard voice, 'you too missy. Go on, move it.'

Beth and I stood facing the wall. We looked at one another. I could tell Beth was calm, she'd been trained for something like this. As Derek approached, she swallowed and inhaled deeply.

Anderson grabbed my wrists roughly and cut the rope, he then moved over to Beth and did the same.

'Both of you through that door,' he said, nodding towards the door that connected the kitchen and the hall. I was expecting him to bring us to the family room at the front of the house where Beth and I had overheard their meeting during the RCA dinner, but instead, he took us into the living room. Once more, the sweet smell of sandalwood filled my nose.

'So glad you could join us,' said Zimmerman.

I looked at him, he was sitting on a plush silver-grey couch. Gretchen was beside him. She wore a flowing black dress that made her look like a witch. She smiled at me.

'Hi, Matt,' she said.

Derek Anderson shoved Beth and me onto a smaller couch facing Zimmerman. A long coffee table lay between us, and on the table were a host of papers.

'Would you like something to drink?' said Zimmerman casually, 'perhaps you could get some refreshments for our guests, Donna?'

Donna Anderson left the room.

'You must have run from The Park,' I said.

'It was a short ceremony,' said Zimmerman, 'and just as well too.'

Derek Anderson perched on the side of the couch Beth and I were sitting on. He casually waved his gun at my head.

'Will you put that thing away Derek,' said Zimmerman, taking out a pair of glasses from his jacket pocket and putting them on, 'I don't think they're going to try anything.'

'All the same,' said Anderson,' I'm going to hold on to it, no point in being careless.'

'As you wish,' said Zimmerman.

Anderson let out a chuckle and stood up and took a seat to our right. He watched us with the unblinking menace of a vulture.

My eyes were on Gretchen the whole time. She was looking at me and Beth in turn.

'You must be the private detective,' she said, 'I'd like to say I've heard so much about you, but Matt doesn't tell me as much as I'd like these days. He was right about you being pretty, though.'

Beth looked confused.

Derek Anderson reached into his pocket and tossed Beth's FBI badge on the table. It slid close to Zimmerman, and he pushed out his long fingers and retrieved it like a spider catching prey.

'This certainly makes things more interesting,' said Zimmerman in a quieter voice than usual.

'Anything happens to me, and you'll...' said Beth.

'What,' said Gretchen mockingly, 'what will happen, look around dear, you don't really have anything to back up your threat with, do you?'

Beth said nothing.

'It's not like we've anything to fear,' continued Gretchen, 'we've dealt with problems like you before.'

'Gretchen,' said Zimmerman, 'there's no need for that, be polite.'

I was trying to read the documents on the table, but couldn't make anything out.

Donna Anderson returned to the room carrying a tray with a pot of coffee on it. She poured two cups and set them in front of me and Beth.

'Thank you, Donna,' said Zimmerman, 'we won't be here too much longer, perhaps you and Mr. Stolly could get things ready for our guests?'

Donna nodded and left the room. I tried, but couldn't quite picture her or Snout digging a grave or lugging a barrel of acid into a garage.

'Please,' said Zimmerman, inviting us to drink.

I picked up the cup and took a polite sip. Beth sat there with her arms folded.

'Is it drugged, or poisoned?' I said.

Zimmerman frowned at the suggestion. I took a longer drink to clear the dryness in my throat.

'Have you made a will?' said Zimmerman as he casually looked at me over the top of his glasses.

'My sister gets everything,' I said.

'Ah yes of course, but is it actually written down, have you spoken to a lawyer about your estate?'

My eyes indicated that I hadn't. Zimmerman sat back and rubbed his chin.

'We can deal with that in due course,' he said in a quiet voice, as if he were talking to himself.

A moment of silence filled the room like a cold wind.

Zimmerman stood up and walked to the chair where Beth sat. He stood behind her. She turned her head, and he smiled at her with avuncular charm.

'How long have you been after me?' he said, 'and don't lie because I'll know.'

Beth said nothing.

'Please cooperate dear,' said Zimmerman, 'I am a peaceful man, but I cannot say the same for Mr. Anderson. I would really prefer if we could conduct this in a civilized way.'

'Go to hell,' said Beth.

'Rest assured,' said Zimmerman, 'if you force me to, I will instruct Mr. Anderson to use whatever methods necessary to get the information I want.'

'I'm not telling you anything,' said Beth defiantly, 'do what you want.'

'I thought as much,' said Zimmerman,' after all you are sworn to uphold the integrity of the fine institution for which you work.'

He nodded to Anderson, and before I knew it, Anderson was on top of me. He pulled the pinkie finger on my left hand back and it snapped. The pain was blinding, fierce, and electric. I roared and told Anderson he was a psycho prick, and then felt sick and almost threw up. Anderson grabbed my other pinkie. Beth jumped up and tried to strike him, but Zimmerman held her back.

'Now,' said Zimmerman, leaning forward and speaking calmly into her ear, 'are you going to cooperate?'

Beth nodded, and Zimmerman let her fall back gently to the couch. While my finger screamed, I did my best to regain my composure and began breathing through my nose like a horse to lessen the pain. Beth told Zimmerman every detail that mattered, except for the undercover agent in The Family Zone. Zimmerman seemed satisfied with her answers and sat back down. The searing pain in my finger had subsided into a throbbing, compressed feeling, and my head began to clear.

'I'm sorry, Matt,' said Gretchen, 'but once we knew you and your girlfriend were snooping around, we had to do something. You really should be more careful with your emails.'

'I trusted you,' I said.

'I know,' said Gretchen softly, 'it's a pity.'

She proceeded to explain how she'd met Zimmerman twelve years before and how they had hatched the idea to use Jonestown as their base. Gretchen, it turned out, was not in Paris consulting for Dior. She was roaming the country looking for old people to embezzle. She said that Dior was another life and while it was glamorous, it didn't pay as well as her current scheme. She then went on to praise my blog.

'I'm going to miss it,' she said, 'but there's no point in becoming all sentimental.'

While this had been going on, Zimmerman was examining the various documents on the table. He noticed my interest.

'The paperwork is a real nuisance, it was so good when Mr. Stolly joined us, he's made it a lot easier.'

'Yeah, he's a real asset to your group,' I said, 'you do know he's a ...'

'Mr. Stolly's proclivities are of no particular concern to me. He serves a valuable function and right now, that's what matters,' said Zimmerman, interrupting me.

I wanted to draw a derogatory comment from him, but I felt it was a waste of time.

'Don't take Lily Osman's house,' I said after a moment, 'do whatever you want to us, but leave Lily out of it.'

Zimmerman removed his glasses and placed them on the table. He sat back and folded his arms across his lap.

'I always thought you were a good guy, Matthew. I even said it to Gretchen when she sounded you out for recruitment. I told her you'd never be interested in our venture.'

'I'll sign the deeds of my house over to you now if you allow Lily to live out her days in her own home.'

'But you see, I've arranged for Lily to move into a retirement home, and anyway she's already signed over her home to me,' said Zimmerman, picking up a piece of paper.

'You mean Juniper Hills?' said Beth as if it tasted bad.

Zimmerman's demeanor remained steadfastly determined.

'Where are Bill and Marge Harrison?' I said.

Derek Anderson laughed, 'they're around, he said.

Zimmerman told him to be quiet, but Anderson persisted, he leaned towards us and winked.

'I only ever feed Razor the best cuts of meat, mixed in with some grain and a raw egg to top it off. He really enjoys it. He's looking forward to getting fed later. I've kept him hungry just for this.'

'Derek,' said Zimmerman loudly, 'do that again and I will take that dog from you.'

Anderson sat back and laughed. He'd had his fun. Zimmerman put back on his glasses.

'It's time,' he said to Anderson and Gretchen.

With that, Anderson stood up and pointed his gun at us. We stood up and he ushered us out of the room. As we were leaving, Gretchen turned to Zimmerman and asked him if he was coming. He said he had some more paperwork to view and would stay, but to let him know when everything was done.

So, that was it, along with the serious discomfort in my finger there was the pain of failure, of letting a man like Zimmerman get the better of me. Derek nudged me into the kitchen. I pushed back and squared up to him.

'Get in, don't make me break more of your fingers,' he said with a hard shove. I stumbled through the door and fell. Razor lifted his head and when he saw me on the floor, he came over to me. He opened his mouth and yawned, displaying his sharp white teeth, and then licked me on the face like I was an ice-cream. Derek Anderson chuckled.

'You can have as much of him as you like later,' he said, bending down to pet the dog. Gretchen went over to the back door and opened it, when with a sudden wailing shriek, a blurry ball of fur shot into the house like a hairy rocket.

'Gene Hackman,' I said as he hurtled by me.

Razor reacted immediately, barking loudly and barging through Derek in pursuit of the cat. Derek was off-balance when Razor hit him, and he spun like a top before falling to the ground. He dropped his gun, which slid across the floor and landed at Beth's feet. She picked it up instantly and Gretchen, rather than stay and fight, ran out the back door. Derek Anderson got up quickly and I tried to tackle him, but he caught me in the face with his foot. He lunged at Beth, and with a calm, professional precision she fired a shot and he hit the ground and didn't move. Beth didn't check to see if he was dead, or I was OK. She ran into the living room and when I had gathered myself together enough to follow her, I stumbled into the room to see her pointing the gun at an astonished Zimmerman.

'That was insane,' I said.

Beth smiled briefly.

'Do you know how to use a gun?'

I nodded and she tossed me the gun. I caught it in both hands. The impact made my finger burn like fire. Beth gave me a sheepish look by way of apology and then took out her phone.

'Shoot him if you have to,' she said.

Zimmerman didn't move. His mouth hung open like a wet paper bag. I'm sure he was trying to form words, but none came.

'If you could see the look on your face, it's quite funny,' I said to him, 'I'd take a picture, but my hand is sore.'

Beth began speaking into her phone.

'I've got Zimmerman and Derek Anderson. Donna Anderson, Stolly, and a redhead in a Stevie Nicks dress are somewhere in the area, OK, I'll see you soon.'

Beth dialed another number and after a brief conversation, she left the room and went into the kitchen. She came back a few seconds later.

'Is he dead?' I said.

Beth nodded. I handed her the gun. She told Zimmerman to get up and took him out of the room and to the hall door. I followed in a kind of glorious disbelief about what had just happened. I was reveling in the movie-like quality of the experience when I heard Razor barking from upstairs, decided to see what the matter was.

Razor was in a back bedroom, his paws on the windowsill, looking out the half-open window at Gene Hackman. The cat, serene as ever, was sitting licking his paw on the roof of the garage. I closed the window.

'Come on boy,' I said to Razor, but he wasn't interested in me, so I decided to leave him and go downstairs.

Ten minutes later, two local police cars arrived. Snout and Donna Anderson had been apprehended at the gate, but Gretchen had managed to escape. Most of the residents had come out to see what the fuss was. I saw The Johnsons and Mitchells wander into the scene, as well as Art Tillman and some of the residents from The Family Zone. I walked over to Beth. She was sharing a laugh with Barney. Barney was wearing a navy jacket with big yellow letters spelling FBI on the back.

'Matt Lowell, I'll be damned,' said Barney, flashing a brilliant smile at me.

'How many of you are there?' I said.

'Just me and Barney,' said Beth.

'But you said …'

'The Family Zone was a misdirection, no one knew about Barney, only me.'

Barney extended his hand, 'Special Agent Billy Conrad.'

I shook his hand.

'You've really helped us out here, Matt,' he said, 'we're very glad you weren't hurt.'

'I was a little,' I said, pointing to my cheek and holding up my left hand.

'Your finger,' said Beth, 'shit I forgot.'

A short time later, an ambulance arrived to remove Derek Anderson's body. A paramedic looked at my finger. It was broken, but it was a clean break and only needed to be set properly. He suggested I ride with them to the hospital, but I asked if he could just put it in a splint there and then. He agreed and after about five intensely painful minutes I was good to go. I thanked him and wandered over to the curb and sat down. I suddenly felt a little deflated. The excitement of the previous hour had given way to an empty feeling. I knew immediately what it was, it was a loss of purpose. Zimmerman and his gang were no more, and the space they had occupied in my life had been replaced by a sort of post-coital vacuum. I stood back and watched things unfold. Donna Anderson and Snout being taken away. Derek Anderson's body being taken away. Zimmerman in handcuffs being taken away. Barney and Beth, their job now complete, leaving. I thought of my empty house and felt a little glum. Suddenly, I felt a vague panic, wondering what I was going to do with the days to come, and the ones after that.

As I sat there scratching in the dust with my foot, I noticed someone approaching from the corner of my eye. It was Mrs. Osman, she was holding Gene Hackman. She sat down beside me and rested the cat in her lap. The cat began to purr loudly. She then patted my hand. I looked at her and she smiled.

'This is Marianne,' she said, rubbing the cat along its long body and to the top of its head, 'I knew she'd come back one day.'

Chapter Twenty-Six:
Californosaurus perrini, Jonestown and other places, 2009-present.

Jonestown redux

Two weeks later, everything was back to a kind of normal. I guess nothing ever really goes back to the way it was, but it was workable, life went on. Art Tillman had temporarily stepped into the breach left by Zimmerman's arrest and had already endorsed Karl Johnson to be the next head of the RCA, should he want the job. Karl agreed, but only if there was a proper election later in the summer to ratify it and that the term be reduced to two years and that a rotation of future heads of the RCA be drawn up. Everyone agreed this was a good idea.

Forensic accountants and real estate lawyers scrambled frantically through papers and deeds and all sorts of stuff to see who owned what and how to go about dealing with the vacant properties left behind by Zimmerman, the Andersons, Snout, and Gretchen. That bit was no fun. I had to make a lot of statements and talk to a lot of humorless people in stiff suits. Worse than that, Beth got into trouble with her superiors for allowing a civilian in on the case. It was only a slap on the wrist, but it annoyed me. I felt it was unfair, she was only doing her job and doing it well. I was questioned about how much I knew, but I managed to talk in circles and in the end, the FBI brass was satisfied that I knew nothing of importance and the book could be closed on Zimmerman and his associates.

Donna Anderson buckled in the face of a lengthy jail sentence and decided to sing her heart out. She said that Zimmerman had compelled both her and her husband into following his orders in return for his silence about Derek's reason for leaving The Navy. She said that around the same time her husband was discharged, Zimmerman approached him saying that he had been looking for someone with a military background to act as security and when necessary, an enforcer. Derek said he wasn't interested, but Zimmerman, it transpired, had bribed an (as yet unidentified) high-ranking officer into divulging a highly classified dossier concerning Anderson's conduct during his time in The Navy. Anderson had been a top-notch SEAL, but after a training accident in which he almost drowned, he began to act out of character. He was removed from his position, promoted to officer, and placed on active maritime duty. Things settled down for a while, but a few months later complaints from fellow officers began to surface. Anderson had a habit of inflicting cruel and unusual punishments on those who were insubordinate. His actions culminated in accusations of sexual assault and rather than discipline him and run the risk of things leaking to the press they discharged him with honors and a good pension provided he kept quiet. It was likely oxygen deprivation had contributed to Derek's change of personality. The exact details of the dossier never came to light, but they were compromising enough for both Derek and Donna Anderson to submit unreservedly to Zimmerman's will (including serving papers against Jeff Simmons as a test of loyalty).

During the follow-up into the goings-on in Jonestown, they found human remains buried in the Anderson's garden. It turned out to be what was left of Bill and Marge Harrison. Had Zimmerman not been stopped I was sure, Beth and Lily Osman, and me would have ended up fertilizing the roses too. I have to admit, I didn't take any pleasure in what happened to the Andersons. They'd done bad things for sure, but they'd been coerced. I guess in a different life, Derek and Donna would have been good neighbors.

My mom always told me I should never take pleasure in the suffering of others, but I was kicking my heels when they got Snout. He's really up a creek. After he was arrested, I suggested to Beth that they do a thorough search of his house. They would have anyway, but Rohit had discovered something about him that needed urgent attention. They found two hard drives. One was in a safe and had details of Zimmerman's finances and the finances of those he'd embezzled. There were passwords to accounts in The Cayman Islands and Jersey in the U.K. and stuff like that. On account of the information in these files, some of Snout's associates in the big corporations will be swapping their Armani suits for orange jumpsuits. That was enough to put Snout away for a long time, but the real doozy was the second hard drive. It was a perfectly normal hard drive with nothing much on it, some personal records, photos that sort of thing but hidden within those files were about ten thousand images of children. Rohit had discovered the hard drive had a kill switch, and one of those clever computer guys in the FBI managed to neutralize it. Beth asked me how I knew. I told her I had intuited something was off about Snout from the beginning. She was impressed by this. Anyway, Snout is about to go to a maximum-security prison, and my guess is he won't last long. My guess is his fellow inmates might get the same vibe from him as I did, or maybe someone will tip them off? I reckon Snout's body will be discovered in the shower, or maybe his cell. It's likely his junk will be in his mouth or stuffed up his ass. I'm not entirely sure what they do to men like him in prison, but I hear it's not good. Anyway, *arrivederci* Snout. He who laughs last and all that.

Anyway, a wonderful upshot from the Jonestown incident is that *The Three Rivers Telegraph* became, for a short time, a national news sensation. Every major newspaper, media outlet, TV station, you name it, descended on the town and based themselves in the TRT offices. The Board of Selectmen estimated about two million has been added to the local economy, though they're probably exaggerating.

So, that's it as far as the bad guys are concerned. Call me biased, but I don't consider Gretchen to be in the same league as the others. She's up and disappeared like dust in the wind, but the feds are on her case, so who knows what will happen. The feds did a search of her house and found nothing. I got in there before them and grabbed her stash of vintage perfumes, which I passed on to Rohit as a big thank you on behalf of everyone in Jonestown. He was delighted. As for Gretchen, even though she betrayed me and the wider community, I like to think she's found her way to Paris. I might send her an email and see what happens. I doubt she'll reply, but you never know.

There's some good and bad news to finish with. The good news is that Lily Osman is perfectly happy at home with Marianne the cat and after assessment from her doctor, it's been decided that she doesn't need residential care. Home help will drop by a few times a week to check on her, but everyone's confident that Lily can live out her days in her own house. Jeff is perfectly happy for Gene Hackman (now Marianne) to live with Lily on a permanent basis.

Jeff arrived back in Jonestown about four days after Zimmerman's arrest. He'd been in Las Vegas living it up, a long story for another time, he told me. He said that just before Beth arrived, she'd advised him to stay out of the way as she wanted to make use of his home for some deep cover work so the FBI, or more precisely the taxpayer, wrote Jeff a big check and told him to go somewhere and have fun. He immediately called his daughters and their families and told them to get to Nevada for the time of their life. He didn't say anything about whether he and Carrie had reconciled, but I'm guessing they have. I did have to ask him about one thing, though.

'Derek Anderson told me he saw you in a hot rod with a special lady friend the morning you left,' I said to him.

Jeff smiled, 'that's Millie, she's an Uber driver. I got to know her over the past year.'

I laughed, 'you keep us all guessing, Jeff.'

One of the innocent bystanders in all of this was Razor Anderson. It was impossible to tell if Derek had fed him human flesh, but someone in the FBI decided that Razor should be destroyed on account of him being a dangerous breed who'd been in the service of convicted felons. I'd been taking care of him in the days after Derek's death and argued that Razor was not guilty of anything and that people actually liked his presence in the community. I managed to raise quite a clamor, and everyone in Jonestown joined the fight to save Razor's life. In the end, the authorities relented when Jeff agreed to take him. They suited one another. I think Razor was the kind of pet Jeff had originally wanted.

The bad news, as you might have guessed, is that Jack did not make it. The swelling on his brain was worse than initially suspected. He died a few days ago. Thankfully, he regained consciousness for a short time and was able to talk to his kids. His son called me last night to tell me that Jack had left me his 1960 Chevy Impala, saying it was 'a damn sight better than the boring piece of crap in my driveway.' I told Jack's son that if he or any of his siblings wanted it, they could have it, but he insisted that we respect his father's wishes. It's in my driveway now. I gave my car to Art Tillman, his own was beginning to give him some trouble. He's quite happy with it. He told me it was nice.

I am not the Zodiac Killer

Jack's death made me reflect on the final years of Dad's life. He was lucky if you want to consider dying lucky, in that he died before things got really bad, but his final two years were tough. He was confused most of the time. He forgot basic things and often thought I was TJ or my uncle or Mom. He got angry and frustrated a lot and was not the calm and collected man I'd known throughout my life. The Jonestown community and his friends at the Elks were a great help. They tried to engage him and even made a book of pictures from his life to help him remember things (that's why I've no photos in my house) and it helped for a while, but ultimately, it was a losing battle. He was fading before my eyes like an image exposed to sunlight. Sometimes he had moments of powerful lucidity. They are what I remember now.

Mostly he'd talk about his childhood and his brother and the good life they'd had. He'd talk about when he and Mom were young and about his working life. It was during one of those moments that he told me why we left Sacramento. We were sitting in the front room, the family room. It was a quiet afternoon in April.

'I knew you'd set that fire,' he said.

For a second, I wasn't sure what he was talking about. His words hit me before I could make any sense of them.

'The Hayes boy didn't do it,' he said, 'you did it.'

I waited for him to continue. I knew from experience he'd let me speak when it was my turn.

'We knew the Hayes boy was innocent, but the police in Sacramento had it up to their eyeballs with him, and they set him up. It happens sometimes.'

It still wasn't time.

'I knew you liked fires, I'd smelled smoke on you a few times, burning smoke not cigarette smoke, and I found things in the garden and the house. You thought you were good at hiding your secret, but you weren't, and neither was your sister.'

'You knew about ...? I said.

'Yeah, I knew, but your mother didn't, and I made damn sure she never found out. I heard you and your sister talking about it one time.'

'She thinks I told you. That's why she doesn't speak to me.'

'She doesn't speak to me either,' said Dad quietly, 'though it wouldn't matter if I told her the truth, what the Hayes boy did ruined her life, just like your brother's death ruined your mother's and mine. We didn't want to lose you as well.'

'Did you suppress evidence?'

'Didn't need to, Hayes was their man, they had a good case, but I would have.'

'Hayes died in prison,' I said.

'He deserved it,' said Dad, 'I don't care what anyone says, he had it coming, bad to the bone that boy.'

We sat in silence for a while. Dad drifted in and out, but he wasn't as coherent again that day, and not for some time after.

About three months before he died, we had our last meaningful conversation. Dad was sitting in his chair. The radio was on and though I had no idea if he was listening to it, he looked as if he was. I went to adjust his pillow and he came round with a sudden and powerful presence.

'That you, Matt?'

'Yes, are you OK, Dad?'

He didn't reply, but I knew he was in one of his lucid moods, and I decided to tell him about the desk.

'I saw files in your desk when I was a kid, photos from autopsies, stuff like that.'

Dad grunted in acknowledgment. I felt a little whimsical, I had a feeling this might be the last time I could ask him anything and be reasonably sure he'd understand.

'They made me think I was different, that I could be like the men you and your colleagues hunted.'

He grunted, 'you're a good boy.'

'Dad, are you the Zodiac Killer?' I asked whimsically.

Dad's eyes opened. He gently reached for me. I leaned in.

'Rick Marshall,' he said faintly.

'I thought it was you,' I said, smiling.

Dad smiled back, 'no, Marshall, Toschi knew but couldn't make a case. I am not the Zodiac Killer,' he said finally.

He closed his eyes. He was done. We didn't share many words after that.

About a month after he died, I arranged for TJ's remains to be exhumed and moved to New Hampshire to be with Mom and Dad. I knew Mom had wanted it, and I figured Dad would forgive me. I hope it gave them the peace they deserved.

The Dinosaur (epilogue, sort of)

In late May, I put my house on the market. It was time to move on and, I figured, if nothing else, I owed Bev the money and hoped, perhaps naively, that if I wrote her a letter it might just make her consider having a long-distance relationship. I don't mind being a boat at sea if there's a lighthouse in view. I know it's a long shot, but it's the best I got. I sent the letter yesterday. I told her about the house and what I was intending to do. I doubt she'll get in touch, but maybe I still have a little good karma left in the bank. Two weeks ago, a lovely African American family put in a bid and I accepted it right away.

I asked Jeff to take Dad's desk, and he was happy to. He's back writing again and now writes a daily column for *The Three Rivers Telegraph*. It's mostly light-hearted and nostalgic stuff, and it keeps the TRT ticking over now that its meteoric stardom has leveled off. Razor gets a mention every so often. Most evenings, Jeff and Razor do a circuit of the community. I think Razor likes the ritual. It's a quieter place now, and I think everyone's happier with that. There's considerable interest in the available houses, and I'm betting that within a year or so it'll once again be the kind of community that people like Randall and Lily Osman, Jack, and Mom and Dad knew when they first moved in. I doubt I'll be back, but who knows.

This morning I loaded my car with what I needed, no more. If there's one thing about doing a clear out, it gives you a sense of new beginnings. The family who bought my house were quite happy to take the contents as well.

I've decided to do what Beth suggested when we first met and take a road trip to California. I'll probably end up in the North Bay area. Before leaving Jonestown, she told me that the place in Napa I should look for is Harper's Motor Services and when I got there, I was to ask for Roy or J.J. They'd be happy to answer any questions I might have. The first question I'm going to ask is what they think of my hot rod and if they'd like to buy it, then I'm going to ask them if they know where I could find Beth. I figure she might want to ask me a few questions about Emilio's storage unit, but maybe not. I haven't heard anything further, and I know they've opened it because it made the front page of The Chronicle and was widely reported across the country. The Sacramento bureau is the toast of law enforcement. Even the President mentioned them on Twitter, and that's saying something.

The first thing I'm going to ask Beth is if she wants to go for a beer. I'm sure she'll agree. I'm also sure we'll go somewhere where the Pacific can show off its majesty.

*

Californosaurus perrini is the name given to the only dinosaur discovered in California. It's an ichthyosaur and resembles a dolphin. It seems fitting. TJ liked dolphins, and I think in some way he has helped guide me through everything in these pages. I hope you think there's more *californosaurus* in my story than frog DNA, but that's it, that's the dinosaur, right or wrong, think what you will.

As I wheeled out of Jonestown on a bright July morning, I found myself in the quiet New Hampshire countryside. Green and yellow fields slipped by like leaves taken on a breeze. My mind was at peace and I recalled an Irish guy I knew while I worked in Baltimore. He was loud and fun and took me under his wing, the way a big brother would. We'd go to bars sometimes and after a few beers he'd give me life advice whether I asked for it or not. Most of this advice was nonsense, but there was one thing he said that has stayed with me. He said do what you want and fuck the begrudgers. I think it's the best advice I ever got. Haters gonna hate. There's no way of changing that. You just got to do your own thing and fuck the begrudgers. Fuck them all.

Acknowledgments

I am unequivocally grateful to everyone who has helped me on this journey.

Thanks to Mark McFaddyn and the whole Sulis team who took a chance on this when others would not.

Thanks to Matthew Hickmott, Darren McCann, Ruth Devane, Gary Quinn, Steve McArdle, Conall Hamill, Fiona Fulton and Jody Toner who read the various stories, drafts and practise novels that got me here. Your insight and support has been invaluable.

Thanks to my family for putting up with me.

Thanks to Edel for believing in the stories I wrote and convincing me they were worth telling. This book is as much yours as it is mine.

Finally, to Flash, I hope wherever you wandered to, you're doing OK.

About the Author

Robert McDermott has published poetry and short stories in various journals and magazines in both print and online. He won the TESEO short story competition in 2019 and 2020. He lives in Dublin where he teaches English and creative writing. *JONE$TOWN* is his first novel.

If you enjoyed this book, please consider leaving an online review. The author would appreciate reading your thoughts.

About the Publisher

Sulis International Press publishes select fiction and nonfiction in a variety of genres under four imprints: Riversong Books, Sulis Academic Press, Sulis Press, and Keledei Publications.

For more, visit the website at
https://sulisinternational.com

Subscribe to the newsletter at
https://sulisinternational.com/subscribe/

Follow on social media
https://www.facebook.com/SulisInternational
https://twitter.com/Sulis_Intl
https://www.pinterest.com/Sulis_Intl/
https://www.instagram.com/sulis_international/

Printed in Great Britain
by Amazon

67978618R00225